Although Lake Forest, Illinois is a real city, the people and places are completely fictional. Any similarities are strictly coincidental.

Divine Disaster

Cover photograph provided by Justine Van Cleve

First Edition

ISBN-13: 978-0692936726

ISBN-10: 0692936726

Dedication

*For those who feel their lives are disastrous—
a story to remind you that something great is
bound to happen.*

Contents

CHAPTER ONE: RIZZ

Do you ever feel like your life is a lie? Like how people see you and how you portray yourself to those said people is a boldface lie? You feel like you want to scream at the top of your lungs on the highest building that 'my life is damn lie!' no? I do.

Cardboard boxes begin to fill the halls of the new house as the movers begin to carry in the belongings from the U-Haul truck. I glance around the living room, and watch as movers set down the suede coach. In the corner of the room I notice that the mini bar has already been set up and used. My brows narrow, as resentment courses through my body. *We haven't been here more than twenty minutes and she has already dived right in.*

My attention shifts to two male movers stumbling through the threshold carrying an oversized family portrait.

"Excuse us, miss," The elder of the two says to me.

I step back out of their way, and watch them as they hang the portrait above the fireplace mantel. I glare at the picture, our *perfect* hair, our *perfect* smiles, our *perfect* family…what a joke. Turning away I pick up a box marked "Rizz" in bold print from the pile of boxes and carry it upstairs.

I place the box on my bare bed, and begin to remove its belongings. I take out Salvador Dali's Persistence of Memory painting, and a painting of the Paris skyline. Following them I take out a picture of me and two other girls standing on either side of me kissing my checks, as I stare impassively at the camera. Taking out another photo of a young girl playing on the monkey bars at a park, I smirk at the memory of the photo and set it on the bed. Reaching into the box again I recover a small hospital wristband. I play with it in my hands, memorizing the feel of the lamination on my fingertips. Closing my eyes, I take in a calming deep breath. Once I am centered I open my eyes and set the bracelet on the bed.

Lake Forest isn't new to me, but it hasn't always been my home either. We lived here before, but after the incident my mother decided to pick up and move. We moved back and forth a lot after that, probably because it kept my mother from leaving us completely, but for some unknown reason she decided to pack everything up and move us permanently back here, where it all started. Who are "us" you may ask? "Us" consists of me, my father, Chip Michael Murphy, and my little sister, Hope

Marie Murphy. Ironic, isn't it, naming your kid Hope? It's almost as if my mother was hoping not to have any more kids, or hoping that she could build up the courage and just leave us already. Aside from my sister being named Hope, my mother gave me the worst name to ever cross someone's mind during childbirth. She must have been so high off of the meds the doctors gave her that she couldn't think anything to name me besides her own godforsaken name. I despise the name. That's why I have everyone call me Rizz. Yes, that's right, Rizz Murphy, plain and simple.

There is a knock at my door. As I turn, I see my father's slim figure in the doorway holding two boxes stacked atop each other. I walk to him, and grab the top box pulling it off of the bottom one. I give my father a small smile before I gesture for him to come in the room.

"I thought you'd be up here unpacking," he says, setting the box on the bed beside the others.

"Yeah, well there is a lot to unpack," I respond opening one of the boxes to find my bed set.

"I'll go grab some more."

"Be careful," I warn as I discard the sheets from the box. "She's began her midday drinking. It won't be long now until she throws a fit."

My father's lips part then close again. I look at him, my eyes widening, "What?"

He shakes his head as he turns on is heels and departs out into the hallway.

My mother was never a loving woman. She was cold and brutal, although she did put on a good show for her co-workers whenever we attended a business function with her. You almost believed that she really did love you; that she really did care, but that all faded away when she was behind closed doors. It was only then that her true colors showed and she'd burst into drunken rampages. Sometimes I just wanted to scream back at her. Maybe someone else raising their voice would startle her and make her trap shut for once. I never did though. I just continued to turn away. It was best just to ignore her. She would tire out and eventually pass out on the living room couch.

My mother likes to fill the house with lavish objects. I suspect to fill some empty void deep, deep inside of her. She would never pass up a chance to spend any of my father's hard earned money. While he was at court fighting to prove someone's innocence or to put criminals away, my mother was dwindling our bank accounts with her expensive tastes. When my grandfather died she didn't have to worry about spending the money my father made, because she inherited everything from her own father. He was a business man, ceo of his own company, and when he died all of his assets went to my mother; his only child. That's how things worked for her. She got everything handed to her without even lifting a finger. She took over his company, and soon became a drunken businesswoman who made a large amount of money, by just waving her hand and ordering those beneath her around.

Then there is my father, Chip. Chip is a very subtle man. He never raised his voice toward my sister and me, but he never kept our mother from doing so. He never even raised his voice to her either. He would just stand there staring at her beat red face waiting for her to stop. I had a feeling this made her angrier, because the screaming never ceased. It's like she wanted to fight with him; like that's how she got her kicks or something. I wish he would just yell back at her for once. I wish he'd stand up for himself and his family, but he never did and I doubt he ever will. Although Chip is a respectable man, he is a coward. I hate that about him. He is the man of the house isn't he? He is supposed to step up and protect us, but instead he lets her scream at us and sometimes even smack us around. That's when I began to see less and less of him. He's always hold up in his home office

working on cases, or avoiding all the brutality—
coward.

I began to lose it when I saw her hit Hope across
the face one evening. All Hope was doing was
coloring in her coloring book on the living room
floor when she accidentally got some pink crayon
on the white rug. I was appalled by my mother's
actions. Who in their right mind would smack a
five-year old across the face for something so
innocent? I could handle my mother smacking me
around; in fact I preferred it to Hope. I was tougher
and stronger than Hope. Getting abused wasn't new
to me. I had been for years now. Scars only visible
under my clothes marked my body. It's not a fate I
wish for Hope, so I began to fight fire with fire.
General Mao didn't seem to like that very much.

My father enters my room with more boxes,
placing them on the bedroom floor near the wooden
oak dresser that sits along the wall closest to the
door.

"She's on her third Martini," he says.

I snort, "At least she's keeping it classy today."

I hear my father snicker as I unload a box of
blue jeans. I pick up a pair and pick at a piece of lint
on the pocket as a memory works its way out of the
depths of my cerebrum.

I remember going to my mother and asking her to take me to the store to buy new clothes. I could remember the way my jeans sagged on my hips, and how I had to cut extra notches in an oversized belt in order to keep my pants from falling around my ankles. My mother immediately dove into a speech of how she provides me with clothes of the latest fashion. "Stop acting so spoiled and be grateful for what you have," she told me, "There are children in Africa with barely a scrap on them." That was the end of it. She walked away. Later that evening I went to my room to find my mother pulling out my oversized jeans from my drawers and throwing them into boxes. I asked her what she was doing, and she simply replied, "I'm giving them away to someone who will be more grateful for them." After that moment I knew I was on my own. So when I turned sixteen, I got a job and never asked her for a cent again.

I pull the rest of my jeans out of the box and turn to place them in the dresser draws.

"Are you excited to see your friends again?" Chip asks, holding up the picture of me and the two girls kissing my cheeks.

"Yeah, I guess."

"Why don't you ever bring them by when we are home?" he asks, setting the picture up on my dresser.

"You know why," I say clipped.

He looks at the pile of items I had set on the bed from the first box, giving up on the small talk. He knew why I didn't invite friends over, or why I didn't let them step foot in the house when my parents were home. I had an image to maintain, and I didn't need the wicked Witch to screw with it. To everyone I was the *perfect girl*. I had them all fooled. The truth is my mother is a drunk and a fake, my father a coward, and my *perfect* persona a lie. A lie, I have worked very hard for years to keep alive. Sometimes the acting gets so intense that I forget it's all a lie, but as my father picks up the small wristband and holds it out in front of him I am pulled back into reality, and how this all started. I'm reminded of the reason we left Lake Forest and the moment my life spiraled out of control and became a sham.

CHAPTER TWO: LANCE

Do you ever feel frozen in time? All you see is the blur of everyone around you. You're put on pause, but life carries on without a care in the world about what happens to you. Then with a flash of light something occurs and you're forced to step back into reality unsure of what to do or where to be. You're lost in time.

I focus on the gleam of the fluorescent lights shining on the back of the guard's bald head. Our footsteps echo in the confined hallway as we follow the guard leading the way. We reach the same metal door with the small eye-window we see every time we visit. The guard shows us in and we take our seats at the metal table. The hairs on my arms come to attention as I sit uncomfortably on the cold metal chair. I look around at the bare walls, and then glance to the empty chair opposite us as we wait for its occupant.

Catching sight of Thom's sorrow stricken face, my body clenches as he stares at me impassively. He's the only person I could ever call a true friend.

I give him a reassuring smile before the door opens, and we both look toward it as the guard leads the familiar five-o-clock shadowed man into the room. Thom flashes him a quick smile, but it fades as the guard removes the handcuffs from the prisoner. I stare ahead at this man, and begin to remember that day. My throat tightens as I remember how my heart sank as I dropped to my knees on the spectating sidewalk that afternoon. How my body burned with hatred as I found out the truth.

"Hey, Dad," Thom whispers, pulling me from my reverie.

"Hi, Son," he responds.

I've told myself repeatedly that what happened was an accident. I remember the feeling of being torn as I tried to calm myself down. I couldn't lash out at this man for what he did unintentionally. He is already paying for it. The accident took its toll on everyone. Thom's mother can't even look at her husband. The man's best friend can't stand to pretend that it's all okay anymore, and every day it eats away at Thom. Thom is the only thing his father has left, and I can't let him go at this alone.

Thom has always been there for me when I needed a shoulder to lean on. He's been my second hand man ever since I was brought to live with my

Pop and his wife. I didn't start out with the best upbringing. I use to live in an orphanage. I never knew my birth parents just that when my birth mom died, my birth father gave me up when I was an infant. The day Pop and his wife Ann walked through those doors changed everything for me. Ann used to tell me stories of how Pop and she were Guardian Angels. She would go on telling me that they saw me struggling from above and came down to Earth to save me. I just wish I could have done the same for her.

After the accident, things began to change. We struggled before my Pop got his new job. He gave up everything for me at one point, even his practice. I suppose he was trying to make up for the accident He wanted to spend all the time with me that he could. It was fun at first, but as we started losing money, and Pop was unable to pay the bills, a lingering darkness followed. That's when we moved. We left, and I had to leave a self-loathing Thom behind. A year later, Pop was offered a job that moved us back to Lake Forest.

Thom and I never lost touch. I tried to be there for him as best as I could when we were thousands of miles away from each other. Thom and I have always been like brothers even through the distance. Even though the accident made us all act different one thing never changed; the bond between Thom and I. Honestly, I think I'm the only thing keeping Thom from falling completely apart. Pop must have noticed this too. When we moved back he purchased the house next to Thom's. With Thom's father in prison and his mom…well his mom spends most of her time at work or at therapy, and when she does come home she heads straight for her bedroom. Like I said, the accident had its effect on all of us.

"Hi, Lance," Thom's father says, shaking me from my thoughts.

"Hi, Mr. Downey."

"How's your Pop?" he asks.

I grow uncomfortable at the thought of small talk. *Why do we force ourselves to make everything seem like it's okay when it's not?*

"He's good," I reply holding back the truth. "He's been working a lot with the new job. The ER has him pretty busy."

"That's the perks of being one of the best surgeons in Chicago," Mr. Downey's lips quirk into a half smile.

"He's been meaning to visit." I add.

"Of course," Mr. Downey nods.

I know he knows that isn't the case. The truth is Pop just can't handle it anymore, and honestly I can't blame him. If it wasn't for Thom, I never would have agreed to come to these weekly visits with him.

I focus on the back of the guard's bald head through the eye-window of the door as mixed feelings begin to stir. *Why do I feel so sick to my stomach?* Feelings of guilt and pain flow through my veins. Mr. Downey is guilty; he's forced to live twenty-five to life in prison for something that was an accident. It doesn't seem right, but at the same time I want him to pay for all the pain he has caused me and my Pop.

"He seemed good today," I tell Thom as we drive along the interstate in my Ford Escape.

"We both know that's a lie," he mutters.

I keep my eyes on the road.

"My mom hates him," Thom says.

"No she doesn't," I insist.

"She won't even visit him, Lance."

"That doesn't mean she hates him."

"Her attorney called the house yesterday," Thom pauses placing his arm on the car door, "her divorce attorney."

My mouth gapes open, and I look at Thom's shattered face, and then back to the road. "I didn't know."

"Apparently, neither do I, "Thom says as he bites his knuckle.

"Thom?" I press.

"This wouldn't have happened if I wasn't there. I caused this all to happen. How can I see my Dad and look into his eyes knowing it's my entire fault." Thom bites his knuckle again and then turns his head to me, "I can't visit him anymore. I can't do it."

"You can't be serious?" I ask as I turn off the interstate exit.

Thom doesn't respond. I glance at his fallen face, "It'll destroy him, Thom."

"I can't do it anymore."

"It's going to destroy you too."

CHAPTER THREE: THOM

The light shines through the tinted car windows as it heads down the city street. People, on a mission, walk along the sidewalks. Some duck into street shops while others continue on their way avoiding bumping into strangers on the street. I watch in awe as the car speeds past all the commotion outside of us. I almost feel safe; in my own bubble in the back seat of the car where no one can harm me.

An ice cream shop catches my eye, and I begin to plead to my father, sitting in the driver seat, to stop and pull over. My father says no, but I am not satisfied with his answer and begin to carry on about getting a scoop of something sweet. My father, watching the street, runs his hands through his hair telling me "no" again. I curse at him under my breath, but he hears me, and turns in his seat to face me. The street light turns yellow, but he doesn't see it. My eyes bold with fear, as he stares at me his mouth twisted and anger rippling through him. All of a sudden there is a loud thud, my father turns and slams his foot down on the breaks, but it's too late. The damage is done. I get out of the car despite what my father orders me to do, and I gaze at her mangled body lying there in the crosswalk. I fall to my knees, as spectators gather around. When I look away I can see my best friend running toward us, and my heart drops. He falls to his knees on the sidewalk, staring ahead. *His face; I can't get his face out of my head. Her body; why can't I stop seeing her body? What did my father do?*

I stir in my bed and jolt awake. I sit up and the sheets gracefully fall around my waist. Beads of sweat slide down my temples. Slowly I try to calm my harsh breathing. The image of her mangled body flashes across my eyes, and I put my head in my hands in horror. *Why can't I just erase this memory?*

Pulling back the sheets I step out of my bed and saunter over to the door. *I need my medication.* Anxiety. That's what the doctors called it. The dreams were caused by anxiety.

I walk into the kitchen and pull a glass from the cupboard. After filling it with water from the pitcher in the fridge, I reach to a cabinet where I keep my pills. They aren't there. Panic washes over me, *where are they?* I grab the edge of the counter tightly and steady myself. *Deep breaths, that's what the doctor said. Just keep taking deep breaths.* I part my lips and exhale as my body begins to physically relax. Picking up my glass I take a long sip of the water, and then discard the glass in the sink.

I head for my mother's room. *She must have taken them.*

I knock on the door, before opening it slightly. My mother never answered anymore, but I always knocked to let her know I am there before entering her room. I stare at my mother's small figure curled up into a ball on the edge of her bed. She looks like she is about to fall off of the edge. I know this is because she is trying to stay far away from my father's side of the bed. I glance at the bedside table and see my opened medication bottle next to a glass half full with water.

"Mom?" I whisper.

She doesn't answer, she never answers anymore. A tear escapes her eye, but she makes no move to wipe it from her face. She just lets it roll down her cheek and to her mouth.

I walk toward her and grab a tissue from the box beside the pill bottle. Sitting beside her, I dab the tissue on her face, drying the tears from her porcelain cheek. Reaching up I rest my hand on her back, "It's okay, Mom," I tell her, rubbing her back. "It's going to be okay."

She tightens the comforter around her; cocooning her.

I crawl into the bed beside her, and rest my hand on her arm, "It's going to be alright."

I stay with my mother late into the night until she falls asleep. When it's nearly time for me to head to school I leave her. She doesn't stir as I drag myself off of the bed, but I know she is awake, "I'll see you tonight, Mom."

CHAPTER FOUR: RIZZ

The public school bathroom stalls are littered with crude sayings written in sharpie: comments about someone being a *whore* and more about girls doing illicit things with guys around the school. I never understood it really. You spend all of ten seconds sitting on the toilet seat and the first thing that comes to mind is to write some nonsense on the stall wall. The toilets themselves look as if the janitors went on strike. For a bunch of girls, they sure are disgusting. Who wants to sit on a toilet seat with crusty dried throw-up from the bulimic girl? *Why didn't Chip send me to a private school?* I stare at the toilet, give up, and leave the restroom. I walk down the hallway and scan the halls for any sign of an authority figure. With no sign of any, I slip into the faculty restroom. *Ah, cleanliness. That's more like it.*

I'm at the sink washing my hands when Mrs. Landon walks into the restroom. *Shit.* She looks startled and then her eyes narrow as she crosses her arms across her chest.

"Miss. Murphy," Her tone clipped.

"Mrs. Landon," I nod at her, as I wipe my hands off on a paper towel and toss it into the trash can. "Have a great day," I chirp heading for the door.

"Not so fast," She beckons. "Students aren't allowed in the faculty bathroom, young lady."

I roll my eyes at her. *I'll show you 'young lady'.*

"Off to the Principal's office you go now. You know the rules."

"I'm petrified," I mutter, following her out the door.

Being sent to the principal's office wasn't new for me. I always told Principal Tucker that every rule was made so one day I could come along and break it. He'd always laugh his boastful laugh and send me on my way. I guess special treatment is what you get when the principal plays golf with your father every Saturday at the Country Club.

"Hello, Rizz. It's a pleasure to see you this afternoon," Principal Tucker says. Motioning to the seat across from him he adds, "Have a seat."

"The pleasure's all mine," I reply, taking a seat.

"What brings you in today?" He asks.

"Oh you know. Just a little rule breaking, nothing out of the ordinary," I say waving my hand in the air.

Principal Tucker chuckles, "What are we going to do with you Miss. Murphy?"

"Principal Tucker. So formal, are we now?" I snicker.

Principal Tucker leans back in his seat, "Rizz, your father won't be pleased to know you had another visit to the principal's office. You really should try to follow the rules."

"I assure you, my father has more things to worry about than my trips to your office."

Principal Tucker gives me a small smile. "How are things going with your college applications?"

My eyebrows arch up.

"You're a Senior, and college is an important step in your academic career. Have you filled out your applications yet?"

"Yes," I reply.

Principal Tucker leans forward in his seat and places his elbows on his desk.

I arch my eyebrow at him.

"Well what schools have piqued your interest Miss. Murphy?"

I lean against the arm rest of the chair, "I've applied to Columbia, Stanford and Princeton."

"I'm glad to hear that. I understand that you haven't let your distractions take away from your grades?"

"I have my eyes set on the goal, Principal Tucker. Surely you know this," I mutter.

The thing was, school was important to me. It was the one thing that ensured that I would get out of this town and away from my mother. Sure I broke the rules, and made inappropriate passes at guys at times, but that never distracted me from getting straight A's in the hopes of receiving a scholarship.

Principal Tucker chuckles, "How are you financially? Have you talked to your parents?"

My body stiffens, but I fight to keep my composure, "No, I haven't."

"You should really talk this over with them. You'll need them to help you. College is a serious step in a young adult's life. It can be life altering."

"That's what I am hoping for." I mutter out loud. *Shit.*

Principal Tucker raises his brows at me, "May I ask why you've chosen those schools?"

To get the hell out of here.

"They are great schools," I reply quietly.

He regards me slowly, "Rizz, I know things have been rough at home ever since—."

I hold up my hand, stopping him from continuing on. "I know you are a friend of my father's and he has enlightened you as to why we left Lake Forest so suddenly, but that has nothing to do with my choosing of schools."

He says nothing, but nods his head.

"Are we done here then?" I stare impassively at him.

"Yes, Miss Murphy. Off to class you go, I've kept you long enough," he gives me a weak smile.

"Thank you," I reply returning the smile.

As I turn out of Principal Tucker's office the bell indicating the ending of class goes off. *Crap, I missed my whole class for that!*

Students begin to flow into the hallways. Some stop at their lockers exchanging books with new ones. Others just lean against lockers and begin to mingle with friends. I walk tall through the sea of my peers, returning waves to those of my admirers. You see at school I'm the popular girl. The girl everyone wants to be friends with, the girl all the guys want a piece of, and the girl everyone wants to know if only for a moment so they can run back and share with their friends. They treat me like I'm some celebrity. *How ridiculous.* It's funny really. How people want to be friends with someone who pretends to be something they are not. Of course they don't know that, but I surely am not going to tell them that. The way I see it, they are all like dogs: loyal to the very end. I just keep them all on a long leash and when I need something I just give one leash a tug and they come running. The more I did it, the easier it became. *Empowerment*, that's what it comes down to. They make me feel empowered.

I don't have a best friend. Of course Nathalie and Charlene would disagree with me on that one. They are my friends, yes, but they don't know me. They only know what I want them to know.

I make my way to my locker where I see Nathalie talking to some guy I don't recognize. *Who is that?* I slow my pace as I continue to walk toward them. Nathalie smiles as she places her hand on his forearm. *She likes him.* With his free arm he reaches up and runs his hand through his shaggy brown hair. He says something, and Nathalie throws her head back in a fit of laughter. *Crap, she really likes him.* As she calms from her laughter she mouths something to him. He nods his head, cups her elbow and squeezes it before walking away.

I watch him as he walks in my direction. His shaggy hair hangs above his jaw line, the ends curled. He's tan, medium height, and his slim figure is carved with the slightest glimpse of muscles. He keeps his eyes peered down, and his jaw tense as he walks past me. *No, I've never seen him before.*

As I near Nathalie, she catches my eye and begins to blush. "Hey, Rizz," she waves, jumping in her spot.

"Nathalie," I reply when I reach her, "Who was that?"

"Oh. Him?" She points in the direction the boy walked off, "Just this guy I invited to my party tonight. You're coming right?"

"Of course, wouldn't miss it," I smile at her.

"Oh goody!"

"So is that kid new?" I ask.

"As new as you are," She says coolly.

Yeah, she likes him.

I roll my eyes at her, "I'm just saying I haven't seen him around before I moved."

"You're not the only person who moves, you know," She says, her brows creasing.

I give her a pointed stare, and she softens a little under my gaze.

"He used to go to private school," she says. "He's going to bring a friend," she adds, her spirits rising a little.

"Is that so?" I ask flatly.

"Maybe—"

"Hey, Rizz," Charlie, a tall bulky football player, shouts cutting off Nathalie.

I glance in his direction. His face splitting grin reaches us in no time. Nathalie leans into the locker undressing Charlie with her eyes. *Geez, could she be any more obvious.*

"Hey," I reply.

He nods at Nathalie, acknowledging her. She squirms, and smiles politely back. He turns his attention back to me and asks, "We still on for tonight?"

A smirk flits across my lips, "that depends."

"On what?" he asks, his interest piqued.

I step toward him so we are almost flesh to flesh, "Do you think you could handle this?"

His eyes light up with amusement, "Yeah, I think I could." His hand reaches up to caress my arm, but I step back. His hand stops, my intention clear.

Then I step toward him again and place my hand on his chest. My eyes wander up his body, and when they meet his gaze I whisper, "You'd be surprised."

His mouth hangs open in shock. *Ha!*

I step away from him and look at Nathalie who is equally as shocked. "Come on," I say to her.

Nathalie leans away from the locker, and follows me into the middle of the hallway.

"What was that all about?" She squeaks.

Oh Nathalie, Nathalie, Nathalie. "You have to keep them on their toes," I reply, gazing forward.

Nathalie says nothing.

"Besides," I glance at her, "I'll see him at your party."

She gives me her *you're brilliant* smile before facing forward.

"It's all part of the game," I smirk.

CHAPTER FIVE: LANCE

My backpack hangs off my shoulder leisurely as I walk through the garage door. Once inside I discard my backpack on one of the hooks hanging along the entry's wall. I work my way out of my polo shirt by tugging at the waist line and lifting it up over my head as I walk down the short hallway toward the kitchen entrance. *I hate wearing that thing. Damn private school.* I tug my white t-shirt that rose up as I discarded the polo from my body and pull it back over my torso. *That's more like it.*

Entering the kitchen, I see my Pop talking into his cell phone. He looks up at me. I give him a small nod of the head and he gives me a grin before continuing with his conversation.

"Yes, okay and how long ago was that? Right, no I didn't know…" My Pop looks up at me, "yes…I'll be sure to mention it to him."

I take a seat at one of the kitchen bar stools on the opposite side of the island than my Pop. He's looking at me with his steal gaze as he wraps up his conversation, "Okay, thank you." He snaps the phone shut. Within a beat he is moving around the kitchen, opening a cupboard, and taking out two water glasses. After filling them, he places one in front of me.

I run my hand flat down along the thigh of my khaki pants, "What is it?"

Pop purses his lips, sighs, and says, "It's Jack."

I stop running my hand down my pant leg as my mind goes four years back to the image of a skinny man standing on the front porch rambling about a bunch of nonsense. He wipes his nose with the back of his hand and then places it on my shoulder, "You're my kid," he tells me. I stand dumbfounded on the threshold. Pop comes storming up behind me yelling all sorts of curses and threats, but I just stand there repeating his words over and over again in my head. *You're my kid...my kid...you're my kid.*

"Is he alright?"

"Yes, he's been in rehab for quite some time now."

"Oh," I mutter.

"Yes, this is news to me too," Pop takes a sip of his water. After placing the glass down he runs his thumb along the side of the glass, "he wants to see you."

I stare at Pop impassively.

"I guess it's part of the program," he waves his hands in the air, "making amends or some crap like that."

I stare at the glass of water that's set in front of me. A bead of water slowly rolls down the side. *Jack wants to see me? My biological father who gave me away wants to see me now.* His words come echoing back, *you're my kid.*

"Lance," Pop says, pulling me back.

I shake my head, "Uh, yeah?"

"Do you want to meet with him?"

The image of the back of his hand wiping across his nose as he sniffs climbs its way back into my head. The image changes and I'm swindled in a baby blue blanket and left at the doorstep of some building. *You're my kid*, his words pounding in my head.

"No," I whisper, "I don't."

Pop looks at me quizzically, "Are you sure?"

I reach up and run my hand through my hair. Leaning forward I rest my elbow on the counter and place my chin in the palm of my hand, "Yes."

Pop's forehead creases as he regards me. "He might have something interesting to share with you, Lance. Maybe you should think about it."

I run my hand through my hair once again as I roll my head on my neck. *Ah!* Standing up from the stool, taking the glass of water with me, I head to the kitchen sink. "Interesting?" I seethe.

"Lance." Pop pushes.

"No!" I throw the glass into the kitchen sink thankful that it doesn't shatter, "Why now? After all this time, why now?"

Pop falls silent.

I tightly grab ahold of the edge of the kitchen sink, "It's too late to make amends. He should have thought about that before leaving me on some stoop."

"Lance," Pop says in a hushed tone.

My face pales. I take a deep steadying breath before turning to face him.

Pop stands, hands at his side, his face ashen, "He could fill in the holes for you."

I open my mouth to say something, but then decide otherwise.

Pop picks up his glass of water, "Just think about it," he insists before exiting the kitchen to the hallway leading to his study.

I walk toward the island and shake my head in exasperation. *You're my kid.* His voice rings in my head over again like a broken record.

Why now?

After a shower, I head back downstairs. Upon reaching the landing of the stairs I hear the garage door slam. Following the slam, Thom's voice carries through the hall, "Lance! Lance where are ya? I've got a good one for tonight. I heard it's going to be the best one yet."

"That's what you say about all of them," I shout back, walking through the hall toward the kitchen.

"Yeah, and I've never been wrong," he grins, leaning against the kitchen island in his khaki shorts and gray V-neck.

Going to parties was Thom's new hobby. I suspect that it distracted him from everything that was going on at home.

"You're in a better mood today," I mutter, walking to the island. I notice a note and some cash lying on the counter.

Got called into work, won't be back until later.

Here's some money, have fun tonight.

-Pop

I glance at Thom's fallen face as he recalls something in his mind. Lifting himself off of the side of the island he grows tense.

"So, this party?" I ask trying to pull him from his reverie.

"Yeah," Thom mutters, still lost in thought. "This girl from school invited me."

"Oh?"

A gleam flits across Thom's eyes as he looks at me, and I know he's back.

Since the accident, Thom had to leave the private school we both attended together, and start going to a public school. He must be putting on a pretty good show there, because everyone seems to like him. I don't think we missed a party yet.

"This hot red head is hosting the party. Invited me personally," Thom boasts.

"And I'm guessing you're going to give her the famous Thom Downey thank-you?" I chuckle.

"That's the plan," Thom smirks.

Thom did anything to distract himself from what was happening. He drank to excess and even got himself into some pretty tough situations where I'm stuck getting him out of. Depending on what was going through his head he'd start running his mouth to girls and guys, and then never back it up. There wasn't a situation where I wasn't able to talk my way out of Thom's mess. I'm not afraid of a challenge. In fact, I thrive for them. But as the messes grew sloppier, I began to tell him to take it down a notch. I'm not going to always be able to sweet talk his way out of any trouble. Aside from growing hot tempered with guys twice his size, he turned to girls. Each one distracted him just long enough, but because he never was looking for anything serious each one was out the door as quickly as they entered it.

"I heard Kayla was going to be there," Thom winks at me.

I roll my eyes, "Great, something to look forward to."

"Man I don't know why you don't give her another chance. She's hot as hell, and she throws herself at you. Do you know how easy that would be?"

"Easy girls aren't my style," I smirk at Thom.

"You're the one who dated her," Thom mutters.

"Yeah, and I dumped her ass too," I pick up the cash from the counter and pocket it in my jeans.

"Pop working late again?" Thom asks.

"Yeah."

"I don't see why you don't throw a rager here one night."

"Pop and I worked too hard for this place just to let some sloppy drunks come in and trash the place for a night."

"Yeah, yeah, poor Lance. I know the story. I'm living it too," Thom snaps, turning his back to me.

"Thom—"

"We better get going before the booze is all gone and the girls are too wasted," he says flatly as he begins to walk to the garage door.

"Is sex and beer all you think about?" I say trying to recover his good mood as I follow him.

"Nah, you forgot about sports," Thom jokes.

CHAPTER SIX: RIZZ

I bring a forkful of mashed potatoes to my mouth as I sit alone at the party sized dining room table. I hear the shuffle of footsteps above me, no doubt my mother stumbling through her closet while drinking a cocktail. I grunt and take a long sip of my water.

"Rizz?" I hear Hope call for me.

"In here," I answer.

Hope appears in the dining room entrance, "Can you help me get ready? Mommy and Daddy are taking me out," she smiles.

I frown inwardly, setting my fork on my plate.

Taking Hope out meant taking her to some elaborate sports bar where Chip can watch the Cubs play ball, and where my mother can down all the alcohol she can afford. It was their routine on Friday nights, and each night ended the same. Chip would carry my mother's motionless body into the house, and Hope would spend the night crying because right before my mother passed out she smacked Hope across the face for wanting to go home.

I smile softly at Hope trying to ease the memories of when it was me who would return home in tears when I was her age.

"Hope," I reply softly, "How would you like to hang out with me tonight?"

Hope's eyes light up, "Yeah?"

"We could get a pizza, and stay up all night. Like big girls," I bribe her.

"Okay," she beams, "Let me go tell Mommy." Hope jumps in her spot and turns around.

"Wait Hope," I call to her as I push my seat away from the table and head after her, "you better let me tell her."

Hope stops by the heart shaped foyer that opens to a double staircase and looks up at me with large eyes.

"I'll be fine, Hope," I assure her, "I'm just going to talk to her."

I head up the staircase on the left hand side of the foyer to my mother's room. Once reaching the closed door, I take a deep breath and knock.

The door swings open to my mother's flushed face, "What do you want?" she snaps, turning back into the room.

"Hi to you too," I mutter leaning on the door frame and crossing my arms over my chest.

"I'm a little busy," she says taking a sip of her cocktail, "so whatever it is make it quick." She waves her hands in the air ushering me to hurry up.

"I just wanted to know if it was okay if Hope stayed home—"

"No," her voice comes down sharply.

I glare at her, "I just thought Chip and you would like some privacy."

"No," she shouts again as she rummages through a bunch of pill bottles in her bedside draw. She finds the bottle she is looking for, opens it, pops a small pill in her mouth, and washes it down with a sip of her cocktail. "Why do you have to ruin everything?" she scowls at me.

"What are you talking about?" I snap, standing up straight.

"You're always trying to take her from me," She sneers, pointing a finger at me as she walks toward me. "Well you can't have her."

My fists begin to ball at my sides as I grow tense listening to her snide comments.

"She doesn't need a screw up like you in her life. You're no good, can't you see that?"

I stare icily at her as she walks closer.

"I bet you're halfway gone," I lash out at her. "You better be careful what you drink tonight. You might go home with the wrong guy. Not that that hasn't happened before. I wonder what Chip really thinks of you. I mean being a shitty mother is one thing, but a trashy wife on top of it? You'll get the gold star for that one."

Before I can register what is happening my face is greeted with my mother's hard cold hand. My head flies to the side, and I cup my cheek with my hand. I gape at my mother and say, "this is what Hope is going through every day of her life with you, and she'll hate you for it."

"Go to hell."

"I'm already there." I say and storm out of the room and down the stairs. As I walk pass Hope her head falls.

"You're going with her."

After attending to my face with a cloth full of ice I headed to my room, where I am now sitting at my vanity. Luckily the hand print from my mother's slap across the face is fading away. *Good, that would have been hard trying to cover that one up from Charlene and Nathalie.* I open up my cover up and begin to brush the nude colored grains onto my cheek, covering what is left of the mark. *There, that's better.*

My phone begins to vibrate on my bed, and I jump from my seat to answer it, "Hello?"

"Hey girl," Charlene chimes.

"Hey," I reply, detaching the phone from the dangling charger and head back to my seat at the vanity.

"I'm about to come over now to pick you up, okay?" She asks as I apply my mascara.

The one thing I hated more than Charlene and Nathalie's babbling about boys and clothes was when they came over unannounced. I had an image to maintain even with them. I didn't want them to know my parents or what my home life was like. Not in the fear they wouldn't want to be friends anymore, but in the fear that they would pity me. How underpowered would I feel then?

I stand from the vanity and walk to my bedroom door opening it slightly, "I'm not ready yet."

"Come on, Rizz. I'm headed out my door now. I'll just help you put the finishing touches on your outfit when I get there."

Downstairs I can hear the opening and then slamming of the front door, "Okay," I say, "I'll see you in ten."

"Okay, ciao!" her voice rings over the phone.

Closing my door, I press the "end call" button and throw my phone back on my bed. I head over to my night stand and pull it away from the wall revealing a small vent. Unscrewing the bolts of the metal door I swing it down and reach in taking out a baggie, a pack of thin white papers, and a lighter. On the floor I quickly get to business breaking apart the plant with my fingers and placing the pieces on one of the white papers. Once finished I roll the paper up and bring it to my mouth sealing it with my saliva. After putting back the baggie and extra papers and do up the bolts on the metal panel, I stand up and walk to my bedroom window and crack it open. There, I stick the joint in my mouth and bring the lighter to the end. I click the lighter and the flame shoots up, and I breathe in a steady hit. *Yes, this is what I needed.*

Taking another hit, I walk over to the full length mirror hanging on the back of my door and comb my fingers through my hair. *What to do with this mess.* I place the joint between my lips and hold it there as I throw my head forward and bend over. I run both hands through my hair using my fingers as the comb and pull it together. Reaching for the hair tie on my right wrist, I pull it over my hand and throw my hair into a messy bun. Standing straight up I look into the mirror and take the hit from the joint. *Mm, that's better.* Walking over to my dresser I kneel on the cream colored carpet and pull out an ashtray from underneath, and put out the joint. I push the ashtray back under my dresser with the end bit of the joint, and rise from the ground as the doorbell rings. *Just in time.*

I head down the double staircase to the front foyer and answer the door.

"Hey girl," Charlene chirps, as she flings a piece of her straight ash-blonde hair behind her shoulder.

"Hi," I respond, opening the door wider for her to walk through.

She steps through the threshold and her mouth drops in awe, "Holy crap, Rizz. I knew you were rich, but I didn't think you were this rich!"

"My mother came into some money." I state closing the door.

"Can she adopt me," she begs.

"Trust me it's not all that great," I mutter.

I turn and head up the stairs as Charlene raises one of her perfectly shaped eyebrows at me. She stands there for a moment but then follows me up to my room.

The alarm reads eight thirty, as I finish the final touches on my freshly painted toe nails. Charlene sits at my vanity touching up her eyeliner and red lipstick.

"So what's going on with you and Charlie?" She asks dabbing her lips with a tissue.

"What are you talking about?" I screw on the top of the nail polish bottle and walk over to the vanity.

"Oh come on, Rizz. Everyone is talking about it. Did you guys do it or not?" She asks bluntly.

I arch an eyebrow at her, "No, Charlie's just some dumb jock who I have wrapped around my finger."

"I heard he's going to be at the party," Charlene says turning in the vanity chair.

"Then I guess we'll see him there," I say walking over to my closet, "How about you worry about finding me a top to wear."

Charlene glares at me before making her way to my closet doors, "I was just making conversation."

"Well let's talk about something other than Charlie, shall we?" I snap back.

Charlene sighs, and turns her attention to my closet. She rummages through a few of the hangers before pulling out one, "here, this is hot," she says holding up a bright yellow flow tank top, "You'll have Charlie eating out of the palm of your hand, and every other guy as well."

"Perfect."

Charlene drives her car past the thick rusted iron gates, and down the short driveway leading to a fork in the road. At the fork she turns right down the road leading to Nathalie's house. As we grow closer I can see the lights gleaming from the all the windows of her house and kids lurking outside on the wrap around porch.

"Tonight is all about letting lose," Charlene beams, "forgetting the past and moving forward."

"Whatever you say," I murmur as I watch kids stumble around on the porch.

Charlene hovers over the steering wheel as she searches for a parking spot in the open grass, "Kyle just better not be here. A break up is a break up. You don't show up at a party you know your "ex" is at. I mean seriously, it's like he's obsessed with me."

I roll my eyes, "You can't expect someone to put their whole life on pause just because you break up." I point to an empty spot in the grass, "There's a spot."

Charlene pulls the car up to the spot, "But still," she says.

"Watch out!" I exclaim as I reach my hand across her to honk the horn.

Charlene slams on the breaks as a black Ford Escape cuts in front of us and takes our parking spot.

"What an asshole," I say.

"Relax. There is a spot right next to them."

"I don't care if there was a spot right next to them or five spaces down, that was bullshit," I say as Charlene pulls up next to them.

Charlene turns off the ignition and I climb out of the car and lean up against the trunk crossing my arms over my chest. I scowl at the Ford Escape as I wait for Charlene. When she comes to stand next to me she says, "Please don't start any drama tonight, Rizz. Let's just have a good time."

"It's a little too late for that," I reply pointing to the two boys emerging from the car toward us.

"Great," she rolls her eyes.

"Hey," says the boy in khaki shorts as they approach us, "sorry about that. My friend here was in a hurry and couldn't wait any longer."

As he grew closer I began to recognize his shaggy brown hair, and tense jaw line. *I've seen him at school.* As his friend comes closer I can make out his dark black hair that just meets his blazing green eyes. I can't seem to place him. He isn't from Waverly High that's for sure. He looks much older than us; maybe he's a college kid? I notice the way his jeans hang off his hips as he walks, and how his black V-neck clings to his perfectly toned body showing only a glimpse of a small patch of chest hair, *yeah he must be a college kid.*

"What are you implying?" Charlene snaps.

I realize I'm staring at the older kid and pull my gaze away.

"That you drive like a snail," The shaggy haired kid laughs.

"Thom," the older boy scolds.

Charlene's eyes jump from the Thom boy to the older boy. Her mouth drops open and her eyes light up.

"Sorry," the older boy says, "I'm Lance," he points to the shaggy haired kid, "and this is Thom."

How do I know this Thom kid?

Lance goes on, "I'm hoping we can just look past this incident and just have a good time."

Charlene's lips quirk up into a shy smile as she gazes at Lance's warm smile. *How embarrassing.*

I push off of the car and say, "After you go back to Driver's Ed class and actually pass, we'll talk."

Both Charlene and Thom look at me with dropped jaws, but Lance stares at me with amusement. *How irritating.* I glare at him and stomp off in the direction of the house.

"I'm sorry about her," I hear Charlene apologize, "She's had a rough week," she lies.

Charlene catches up to me and says, "Way to be rude."

"Way to look like some sick love struck puppy dog back there," I reply.

"I did not," she gasps.

"You were basically drooling."

"Was not."

"Believe what you like."

Charlene stays silent until we get to the porch, "I get it. You think Lance is sexy and you want me to back off."

"No. Not at all," I snort walking up the front porch steps. *Although, he is pretty sexy. Stop it Rizz, and pull yourself together.*

"Oh, Rizz, when are you going to figure out that you can't pull one over on me?"

"Whatever, Charlene."

Entering Nathalie's house I watch as Charlene picks up a beer and takes off into the massive crowd of people. She doesn't miss a beat as she shimmies through the crowd in the living room dancing to the blaring music. From the corner of my eye I catch Nathalie coming toward me from the kitchen where Charlie and the rest of his football pals are playing an intense game of beer pong. Charlie glances up and waves, but my attention goes to Nathalie as she throws her arms around me, "Rizz," she slurs.

"Hey," I say, patting her on the back.

She gives me a broad smile when she pulls away from me.

I can't help but smile back at this girl with her untamed red curly hair falling over her shoulders. She takes a sip of the beer she is holding in one hand, and then a drag of her cigarette that is placed between her index and middle finger in the other.

I look into her bloodshot eyes and ask, "How much have you had to drink?"

"I don't know, Rizz, I wasn't keeping count." She slurs coming down hard on my name.

Nathalie was the one friend who looked to me for guidance and strength. I didn't understand it really, but in a strange way I pitied her. She was a small girl lost in a big world. The first day I had ever met her was in the bathroom at Lake Forest High during freshman year.

Walking into the bathroom to check if today was the day the janitors decided to do their jobs, I hear a low crying sound from the handicap stall. Curious, I push on the stall door and gently let it swing open to expose a petite red head sitting on the bathroom floor crying into her hands.

"You know," I say as her head shoots up, "everyone has their problems. You should just suck it up and move on."

Her swollen eyes grow large and her jaw drops. "You don't even know what I am going through," she says in a small voice.

"No, I don't," I reply my arm still outstretched holding open the bathroom stall door. "But it can't be that bad that you'll never get over it, so why bother being upset to begin with?"

"Because," she gasps, "if I don't take the time to acknowledge the hurt and pain now, then it will just come back to bite me in the ass later."

I shrug, "Suit yourself." I let my hand fall from the door and walk away. When I don't hear the slam of the stall door, I turn around and see the red head gawking at me. "What?" I ask.

"Don't you want to know what's wrong?" she asks, her face scrunched up.

"No, I don't."

"Well, why not?"

"I don't care."

She gives me a perplexed look before looking away as she wipes at her tear stained face. "What's your name," she asks when she looks back at me.

"Rizz."

"Rizz? That's..." she looks up at the ceiling as if in deep thought, and when her eyes dart back to mine they dance with joy, "That's unique."

It was my turn to look at her in puzzlement. No one had ever thought of my name as *unique*, only as *weird* or *silly*.

"It's nice to meet you, Rizz." She takes a step towards me and holds out her hand, "My name's Nathalie."

I take her hand in mine and give it a shake as she smiles at me with her bright blue eyes.

Later that year I found out that her parents and her used to live in a smaller town than Lake Forest, and when news spread about her father, some hot shot lawyer, cheating on her mother they packed up and moved here. They were the *social scandal* of the year Nathalie said. She said the scandal ruined her father's reputation, and he hoped moving to Lake Forest would give him a fresh start. It seemed to work out for him.

Over the years Nathalie began to become accustomed to my rude remarks, and straight forward answers. I even think she enjoyed them. It gave her a comfort knowing I'd tell her how it was. I became some sort of a backbone for her.

"Let's go up to your room and get you fixed up a bit," I say pulling on her elbow.

I weave Nathalie through the crowd of people talking on the stairs.

"Shit," Nathalie mumbles as she stumbles on the steps and spills some of her beer.

"Don't worry about it right now," I say grasping her hand in mine and tugging her up the stairs.

Once in her room I sit her down at her desk chair, "I'm going to fix your hair."

I pick up her brush from her dresser and tug it through her wild hair, "What the hell Nat, did you even brush your hair?"

"I was going for a certain look," She whines.

"What was that? Hot mess central?" I snort.

Nathalie lifts the bottle of beer to her lips and takes a swig.

I pull at her hair, and throw it up into a messy bun like mine. I shuffle around her so I am standing in front of her, and pull some strands of hair from the bun so they fall along her face.

"There, all better."

"I'm a mess," she says failing to stifle her tears.

"I can see that."

"It's Austin...he...wants...to see...other people," She says between sobs.

"Oh crap," I say more to myself.

"I know!" she exclaims, "What am I going to do?" she looks up at me with her now mascara marked face.

Frustrated I begin to walk around her room looking for a box of tissues. *This is just my night.*

When I find them, I pick up the box and throw them at her.

"Owe," she exclaims as the box bounces off of her and onto the floor. "You didn't have to throw them at me," she says picking them up.

"Here's what you're going to do." I scowl at her, "You're going to stop spurting water like a damn waterfall, get fixed up, throw a damn smile on your face, go downstairs, and walk right past Austin with your head held high. Then you're going to find that boy you invited and flirt like you never flirted before. You got it?"

Nathalie gapes at me as I kneel in front of her and pull tissues from the box in her hand. I grab the make-up remover from her dresser, pour it on the tissue, and dab the tissue at her face until her smeared make-up is cleaned up. I pull open one of her small dresser draws to her make-up and begin to reapply her cosmetics.

"There," I smile, as I sit back on my heels, "like it never even happened."

Nathalie eyes herself in the mirror and smiles. Then she finds me in the mirror and locks my gaze, "Thanks, Rizz."

"Yeah, well don't get used to it," I shrug.

Nathalie brings her bottle of beer to her lips, but I quickly take the bottle from her hands.

"No more of that crap."

Nathalie chuckles, "I wish I could be as hard as you are."

"Me too."

Nathalie laughs and embraces me in her second hug of the night. "Let's go," she says taking my hand in hers as she leads me out of her room and back downstairs to the party.

CHAPTER SEVEN: THOM

"Sorry about her," the blonde smiles at us, "She's had a rough week." She glances at me and then takes another longing look at Lance before skipping off after the brunette.

I notice my mouth hanging open and pick up my chin with my hand. *What the hell?*

"I guess Lance's charm doesn't work all the time after all," I say, throwing a punch at Lance's arm as he gawks at the girls walking away.

"Yeah, well we'll see."

"Don't even think about it man," I reply following his gaze. I watch as the blonde leans over the brunette's shoulder and say something, while the other snaps back at her. "Seriously, not even worth it."

"Who am I?" Lance asks, opening his arms.

I sigh, "You're Lance McCartney, he thrives for a challenge, and can get any girl he sets his sights on. Yeah, yeah, yeah."

"That's right," he smirks pointing his finger at me in a *"you got it"* gesture.

We head up to the house in silence before I begin to laugh to myself.

"What's so funny?"

"I just keep thinking about how you're going to get your ass handed to you by that girl."

Lance grunts, "I doubt that."

"Just you wait and see."

Lance's brows furrow as he grows frustrated, "You know, maybe she'd have acted differently if you hadn't distracted me."

I pause as Lance continues forward.

He looks to his right and notices I am not walking beside him when he stops and turns. When his eyes meet mine his face drops. *It's that look, the look I can't get out of my head.*

"Thom—"

"No," I say raising my hands for him to stop, "You're right."

"Thom, I was just messing around. I didn't mean anything by it," Lance says walking up to me and placing his hand on my shoulder. "I'm sorry. Let's just have a good time tonight."

His words echo in my head. *Let's just have a good time tonight.* It was his signature line that diffused any situation. I shake my head at him and get ready to lay into him when a high pitched voice calls from behind me,

"Hey good looking!"

Lance's hand drops from my shoulder as I turn to see Kayla strutting up to us. Her short red hair bobs as she walks in her stiletto heels. I imagine her falling in the grass; in fact I begin to wish for it to happen. Anything to take my mind off of that wretched accident. *Why does he always have to remind me of it?* I look at Lance. His facial expression has changed from sympathy to horror.

I smirk at him as I squeeze his shoulder and whisper, "You're on your own, bro."

Lance gazes at me in shocked horror. *Yeah, that's right.*

"Thom," Lance begs as I ignore him and walk toward the house.

I glance back and watch as Kayla envelopes her arms around Lance's unwelcoming body.

"I thought you'd be here," Kayla says loudly.

This was the thing with Kayla; she always wanted to be center of attention. She dressed up, talked too loud, and flaunted herself around. She even went as far as to altering her school uniform. She did anything for a small piece of recognition.

I can't hear Lance respond, but I see him grow stiff as Kayla runs her finger along his chest. *Yeah, I hope you squirm.*

I take the porch steps two at a time and walk through the threshold into the dome of loud music and partiers. I grab a beer from a nearby ice bucket and set out among the crowd. I glare at the couples lining the staircase as they lean into each other and whisper hushed words into each other's ears. I veer myself away from their sickening embraces and toward the living room where a mass crowd is dancing to the techno beat. *Lucky bastards, they have no care in the world.* More people come out from the back porch, and others emerge from behind closed doors. I snort. *Stoners, they hide their problems under a cloud of smoke. If only it were that easy for me. Dammit, why did Lance have to look at me like that?* I tighten my grip on the beer in my hand and bring it to my parted lips. *I need to get drunk, really drunk.* To my right, a small ping pong ball flying in the air catches my eye. Past the door frame of the kitchen I spot members of the football team playing beer pong. *Bingo.*

Another ball flies through the air as I walk up to the table. I reach out my hand and scoop it out of the air, "time's up boys."

"What the hell do you think you're doing," a tall, solid built football player glares at me.

"I think it's time you turned the tables over to someone else," I say squaring my shoulders.

"Do you now," he says walking from behind the table. He stands towering over me.

Damn, he's tall.

"Why don't you give someone else a chance to play pal," I say patting him on his shoulder.

He looks down at where I touched him and scoffs, "why don't you get lost before I kick your ass."

"Make me," I urge him.

He points down at me, "You better watch yourself—"

"Or what?"

"That's it," he says taking off his varsity jacket and throwing it to one of his football friends.

He wants a fight? Okay I'll give him one.

The football player fists his hand at his side and asks, "What's your smart mouth have to say now?"

"I hope you don't punch like a girl."

His face scrunches up as he pulls back his fist. I close my eyes and stand ready for the impact of his fist when a girl screams, "Charlie, no!"

I open my eyes to find the hot red head from school throw herself in front of me.

"Nathalie move out of the way, this kid is going to get what's coming to him."

"No, Charlie. You leave him alone," She says pressing her back against my front.

Hmm, under any other circumstances I think I'd enjoy this.

"Don't make me get one of my friends to move you for me," he threatens her.

The hell they will.

I place my hands under her arms and lift her from her spot on the ground in front of me to my side. "If anyone is going to man handle my girl, it's going to be me," I growl at him.

"Rizz," the hot red head pleads from beside me.

"Rizz?" I ask, glancing at the red head. I follow her pleading look to the brunette from outside. She approaches the football player and places her hand on his forearm.

"That's enough Charlie," she says sternly.

Rizz? What kind of name is that?

Charlie falls back, and I gaze in amazement. *What the fuck?* He looks at Rizz and gives her a small smile. *What the hell is he, her puppy?* She takes his hand and leads him out of the kitchen. *I guess so.*

"Thank you, Rizz, again," the hot red head says.

Rizz flashes the red head a smile as she leads Charlie into the sea of people dancing in the living room. I watch in awe, *what the hell just happened?*

"Now, about you man handling me?" The red head says.

I glance in her direction and watch as a smirk plays upon her lips.

"I'd rather it be me then one of them," I say giving her a wicked grin.

She smiles sweetly at me with her dazzling blue eyes, "The name's Nathalie."

"Thom," I gesture to myself. The tension from earlier begins to evaporate, and I find myself relaxing as I stare at this goddess in front of me.

"Yeah," she says nodding her head, "I remember you from school."

"You mean that prison they try to pass as a school?" I ask.

Nathalie laughs, "public school isn't shaping up to everything you had hoped it would be?"

God, she's beautiful when she laughs.

I find myself grinning, my face practically splitting in two, "well it's starting to look a lot better now."

Nathalie's cheeks begin to glow pink as she smiles.

"Want to play a round?" I ask nodding to the pong table.

"Sure," she says, "I have to warn you though I'm pretty much the queen of beer pong."

CHAPTER EIGHT: LANCE

I watch in horror as Kayla throws her arms around my neck. I shove my hands in my pockets, making no attempt at hugging her back, "Hi, Kayla," I mumble.

"I thought you'd be here," She says too loudly.

Geez, she's annoying.

"Here I am."

"I tried calling you earlier," she says running her finger along my chest.

I freeze instantly.

"I thought it would be kind of cute to show up together," she says looking up into my eyes.

I take a step back from her, "Oh, you mean like a couple," I ask gesturing quotation marks as I say the word *couple.*

Wow, she is impossible.

"Exactly," she smiles as she links her arm in mine.

"I don't think so, Kayla," I say unlinking her arm from mine, "We broke up remember?"

I turn away from her shocked expression and lilac perfume and head toward the house.

Without missing a beat Kayla catches up to me,

"Lance, I'm sorry," her voice low, "you're totally right, we broke up. I get it now. Can't we just be friends then?"

"Friends," I ask. I tilt my head to one side as if I'm contemplating its meaning, "I don't think you can do just friends."

"See that's where you're wrong," she pleads, "I can so do just friends."

"Ah, like you do with every other guy that crosses your path?"

"I'm just friends with Thom," she says as we walk up the porch steps.

"No," I chuckle, "you think you're friends with Thom, but you're really not."

I look into the crowd of people that liter the house, and wonder how I am going to get rid of Kayla. *She's like a damn leech. Just friends*, I snort inwardly. *She couldn't do just friends to save her life.* It was just a friend I caught her with at the café that night. I didn't even barge in and make a scene. *I should have.* The next day I just ended it. I told her I wasn't feeling it anymore, that we grew apart. She cried right there. *Like she even cared? It was probably just all part of her act.*

Staring into the crowd on the dance floor I spot the brunette from outside dancing around a tall, solid built guy. *He must be a football player.* I watch as her curvaceous body sways to the beat of the music. *She's mesmerizing.* The football player tries to pull her closer by putting his hands on her hips. She recoils, but plays it off as she turns to face him and puts her hands on his shoulders. He doesn't seem to be phased by her sudden rejection. He just continues to dance with her at arm's length, *enjoying the view, no doubt.*

I glance at Kayla who is also fixated on the brunette, "you want to be friends," I ask her.

Kayla peels her eyes away from the girl and back on me. "Of course," she smiles, although it doesn't meet her eyes.

"Then why don't you go find Thom for me. I'm sure he's gotten himself into some pretty deep trouble already."

Kayla gives me a hesitant smile, "Sure," and walks off toward the kitchen.

I look back at the dance floor as the song ends and see the brunette leaning into the football player on her tiptoes, whispering something in his ear. When she pulls away, the football player grins at her and nods his head. He heads off in my direction, and the brunette's eyes follow him. When her eyes jump to mine her face pales slightly, but she regains her composure and glares at me before whipping her body away from me. She carries herself confidently through the crowd of dancers as she heads to the sliding glass door behind the crowd. My eyes linger on her as I step forward and make my way through the crowd after her. I am intrigued, thirsting for more information about this strong confident girl trying so hard to hide the slightest hint of fear in her character.

I need to know her.

I walk quietly onto the back porch where the brunette stands with her elbows propped on the porch railing.

"You'd make a terrible stalker," she says turning around to face me.

"Don't flatter yourself," I say nonchalantly, "I wasn't following you."

"Oh right, you just stumbled out here to look at the stars all by yourself? What a romantic," She teases.

"Actually I came out here looking for my friend, but if romance is what you're looking for," my voice grows dark.

"Romance is for puss's," she says leaning against the railing and folding her arms across her chest.

I stand back and allow my eyes to fall over her. I make note of how she welcomes my obvious admiration of her body. I step toward her as a smirk forms across her lips, "I think you're mistaken."

"Oh?" she raises her eyebrows, her full lips still pulled into a smirk.

Damn she's sexy.

"Why's that?"

"A romantic can thrill you better than any other man," I whisper.

She unfolds her hands and pushes herself away from the railing. She walks around me, her eyes wandering up and down my body. She drags her hand lightly along my shoulder blades as she walks behind me. I close my eyes. *Damn she has a good effect on me.* When she comes back around she stands only inches away from me.

"You think you can thrill me?" she whispers into my ear.

I can feel her cool breath on my earlobe. She's good, too good. *Keep it together McCartney.*

"Is that a challenge?" I ask closing the gap between us.

"You tell me," she whispers, her blazing blue eyes staring right into me.

I grab her right hip with my left hand and pull her against the front of my body. She holds her breath as I lean into her face. Her full soft pink lips form a thin smirk again. *Damn those lips! I just want to feel them on mine.* I lean in a little more our mouths just barely brushing each other's. I stare into her steady blue eyes. *Damn, I want to kiss her right now, right here.* But instead, I lean my head to the right of her and whisper in her ear, "I don't think my friend is out here."

I back away as she scoffs, "unbelievable."

"What?" I chuckle.

"Is that your idea of hitting on a girl," her brows furrow.

"Who says I am?"

"Oh I see your game," she says pointing her index finger at me, "Let me guess, you're mister hot stuff. Girls hang on your every word and throw themselves at you. Well, let me tell you something, mister irresistible. I'm not some easy chick you can flash a smile at and expect to play your little games."

I stare into her artic eyes as I take in what she had said. *She couldn't be more wrong about me.* I let the silence drag on before opening my mouth and closing it again. I look at the porch ground and then back at her as I take a step closer to her. My eyes grow dark with amusement as I ask, "You think I'm irresistible?"

"Unbelievable," she scoffs pushing me away from her.

I laugh and she looks at me dumbfounded.

"I was only joking miss hard-ass."

"Excuse me," she asks defensively.

"You heard me," I say my face growing stern, "seriously you're like a glacier over there."

"A glacier?"

"Yeah, you know the large piece of ice."

"I'm not an idiot," she glares at me.

"Just specifying," I reply holding up my hands in surrender.

"You think because you're some college kid that you can just come in here and talk down to me? I'm not your average high school girl."

"I'm not a college kid, besides I was only suggesting that you let your ice act melt away and have some actual fun."

"Who says it's an act?" she snaps, her hands on her hips.

"Let me guess," I say mocking her, "you come off as the tough girl so no one will give you any crap. You're used to being in charge, always calling the shots. You're the popular girl and everyone likes you, or what they know of you. But you keep yourself distant in the hopes of not getting hurt. I'm not dumb, I saw you with that guy on the dance floor. Everything is just fine as long as you're the one in control."

I wait for the girl to say something back, but she doesn't. She just stares at me with bold blue eyes. *Could I have been right? Did I nail her to the wall? I wish I knew what she was thinking.* She takes a deep breath and then steps toward me. When she looks up at me, her lost expression is gone and is replaced by an "I own everyone" look and she says,

"I guess you'll never know."

I open my mouth to respond when Thom and some red head I don't recognize walk out onto the back porch holding hands.

"Hey man, what are you guys doing out here," Thom asks winking at me.

The brunette scowls at him, and the red head's face beams up at Thom.

"O-M-G, Thom. This is my friend from earlier. The girl who saved my night twice already. She is one great friend you know," the girl attached to Thom's side says.

The brunette gives the red head a small smile.

"Hi," the red head says turning to me, "my name is Nathalie. This is my place. You must be Thom's B-F-F Lance."

"Yeah," I say reaching my hand out to shake hers as I smirk at her text message dialogue.

"Oh! What a gentleman," Nathalie says freeing her hand from Thom's and shaking mine. I smirk at the brunette and she rolls her eyes.

"Looks like you found a good one tonight, girl," Nathalie addresses the brunette.

"Not exactly," she responds, "I was just leaving."

"Nonsense, you two have been talking out here for a while. We've been watching the flames go up between the two of you," Nathalie says dreamily.

Yeah flames did go up, just not any good ones.

"I'm afraid not," I cut in, "I don't even know your friends name."

"Well that's not very polite," Nathalie says, snapping her head to the brunette.

The brunette glares at me.

I know, I know, what a lame way to get someone's name.

Turning back toward Nathalie she says, "Well Nathalie, you and I know I'm not a very polite person." She glares at me one more time and says, "Enjoy the party," before heading back into the house.

"I'm sorry about that," Nathalie apologizes, "She's had a rough day. I better go check on her." She turns to Thom, "I'll be right back."

"Alright," Thom replies.

Once Nathalie enters the house Thom walks up to me and pats me on the back, "Jeez, that girl must have had one really shitty day. Just your luck, huh?"

"Yeah," I nod in agreement, "or her friends are just use to covering for her when she's rude."

"Either way, you've got your hands full with that one," He laughs. "Did you see Nathalie though? She's gorgeous."

"Yeah," I nod uninterested.

I stare through the sliding glass door into the party at the girls walking through the crowd.

"She might be worth dating," Thom whispers.

Eyes widening, I glance at Thom, "You think?"

"Yeah," Thom smiles, "I think so."

I place my hand on Thom's shoulder and squeeze it, "Well then, I'm happy for you Thom. Really, this is great news."

"Yeah, who would of thought," he smiles.

"Definitely not me," I reply, my attention getting drawn back to the girls walking through the crowd.

Things just got a little easier for me now. Tonight wouldn't be the last time I'd see this mysterious girl, and I'm glad. I want to know more about her. It's as if she's a mystery and I'm Colonial Mustard ready to find all the clues in order to break down those thick walls she has built around her. There is no turning back now, I'm hooked.

CHAPTER NINE: RIZZ

Unbelievable, that's what that Lance kid is. Unfreakin' believable. I make my way through the crowd of dancers, nudging them out of my way.

"Rizz, Rizz," Nathalie shouts from behind me, "Rizz, wait up."

I continue to walk out from the crowd and to a closed hallway door.

"Rizz," she calls again.

I stop, resting my hand on the doorknob, "What," I say in exasperation.

"What was that all about?" she asks as I face her.

"Nothing."

"Rizz," Nathalie raises her eyebrows.

"He's arrogant," I shrug my shoulders.

"Oh, really? 'Cause he seemed like a complete gentleman to me."

"You think every guy is a gentleman," I say rolling my eyes.

"Why do you do this?"

"Do what?"

"You always ruin your chances of having a real boyfriend," Nathalie pouts.

I lean against the closed door, "Did it ever occur to you that I'm perfectly fine without one?"

"This is perfectly fine?" she says pointing to me with her hand and moving it up and down as if she is Vanna White showing off some big prize.

I cross my arms over my chest.

"Yeah, being cynical is way better."

"I'm not cynical," I sneer. *Wow Nat grew a pair tonight.*

"Whatever you say, Rizz."

"You know what; just go back to Timmy…Teddy…or whatever his name is. I've had enough of people today." I open the closed door and step half way in, "And tell that stalker that his little girlfriend with the red hair is looking for him." I point to the girl starring at the two boys on the back porch. Nathalie turns to look and I slip into the room shutting the door behind me.

Seriously what is it with people tonight? This Lance kid walks into my life for one night and now everyone wants to act completely opposite. *Like seriously? What was it with Nat?* She knows I don't do the boyfriend thing. *And I am not cynical.*

This Lance character better keep his distance. I know I haven't seen the last of him. Nathalie never just "hooks up" with guys, and this guy she has her eyes set on right now is Lance's best friend. *Just great.*

"Razzle," my friend John greets me.

"Hey John," I reply reaching my hand out to him, "let me get a hit of that will ya?"

John extends his arms to me and I grab the blunt from him. I take a hit and let the smoke sit in my lungs before exhaling.

"It's pretty crazy out there isn't it?" A girl with a thin head piece around her forehead says.

"It sure is, Sarah," I say passing her the blunt.

"I can tell," she takes a hit and exhales. "Your aura is all out of whack."

I smile at Sarah, and take a seat next to John.

Sarah is a flower child although she describes herself as a free spirit. Her parents are to blame for her strange appearance. The 70's changed everything for them, and of course they passed it all onto Sarah. She was taught as long as she is at peace nothing bad would ever come to her. Sometimes I feel as if she isn't even in this world at all, but in her own little universe. This idea fascinates me. Maybe it's all the weed talking, but a world without harm sounds pretty good to me. My own oasis to escape to where you are able to float in mid-air and sleep on the clouds; where no one dies and you could live without fear. A world where you are able to walk on water and the clouds form into dancing men; where you can scream at the top of your lungs without anyone judging you; where the man on the moon is more than just a bedtime story, and where peace, love, and happiness truly exists.

"Razzle," John shouts pulling me from my fantasy, "pass that over here." He nods at the blunt between Sarah's fingers. She too has wandered off into her own universe.

I carefully grab the blunt from her trying not to pull her out of her daze. I am successful in my task, and take a few hits before handing it to John.

I watch John take in a sharp breath and then exhale. You never would have pinned him as a stoner. He had a baby face and a clean buzz cut. His eyes were big and brown, the kind that would make any girl's heart throb. I always pegged him for an army man; he held the qualities of a good-boy look, but I knew he was far from it. I watch as his thin yet strong exterior takes in another lungful. He was built, but you'd never know that by just looking at him. It was underneath his faded jeans and Beatles t-shirt that you saw the muscle he had.

***

It was last summer when I had gotten to know John. My mom was in town for a business function, but I was able to slip away with the girls and come to John's place. His parents were out of town so he decided to throw a party. The two of us spent the whole night sitting on the couch smoking as we pointed out every detail that we didn't like about the people walking by. It wasn't until later that he looked at me and said, "razzle me Rizz."

"Razzle?" I snort.

"Yeah," he smirks, "like dazzle, but with an 'r' because of your name."

"You want me to dazzle you?" I ask.

"Yeah," he says scooting closer to me on the couch and placing his hand on my thigh, "I do."

I just stared at him debating the odds of what had just come out his mouth. It wasn't that I didn't want to that made me pause. It was the fact that I wanted to. I really wanted to, but the problem was I liked him. John didn't annoy me like most people. He was the first guy that ever threw me off my game and made me think about the act I was putting on. If I did this with him it would be like pulling him into my web of secrets; letting him see into who I really am. And if I didn't he would just be like all the others. A minion in this screwed up game I have created.

All of a sudden there is a commotion and a dusty brown haired boy lands in my lap spilling his beer down the front of my top.

"Are you serious," I yell pushing him off of me so he thuds onto the ground.

The boy scrambles to his feet, "I'm sorry."

"New flash," I snap as I stand to my feet, "If you can't handle your alcohol then don't drink at all, you moron."

"It was an accident," the kid slurs raising his hands in defense.

"Why don't you just get out of here?" John says standing up and facing the kid.

I watch as the kid retreats sloppily into the kitchen and then look down at my shirt.

"Shit," I mutter picking at the beer-soaked front of my shirt.

"Let's get you something dry to wear," John says looking at the wet blotch on my chest.

"Thanks," I say as he grabs my hand.

John shuts the door behind us as we walk into his room. I look around his room as he rummages through his bureau. Band posters hang tacked to the walls; The Beatles, The Rolling Stones. I smirk at them as I linger over to a bookshelf that had been built into the wall. I drag my fingertips along the spines of each book as I take a closer look. Pulling one from the shelf I read off the cover,

"The Adventures of Tom Sawyer," I smile, "So you're a Mark Twain fan?" I ask scanning the rest of the books on the shelf.

"Yeah," John glances over to me, "He's a great writer. He was even very intuitional."

"Oh?" my eyebrows rise.

"He has a lot of fantastic quotes."

"Enlighten me," I ask placing the book back on the shelf.

John continues to rummage through his draws, "If you tell the truth, you don't have to remember anything."

My smiles fades as I stand looking at John dumbfounded, "What?"

John pulls out a shirt from the draw and looks at me.

"The quote," John explains, "It's one of his quotes."

"Right," I say giving him a small smile as my body begins to relax.

"Here," he says closing the space between us. "You can change into this," he holds up a Nirvana band tee.

"Alright," I say taking the shirt.

John turns his back to me and I begin to peel off my wet clothes. I toss my tight nude leather jacket and white tank top on his king sized bed, and look down at John's worn out band tee in my hands. Glancing at his back I think back to what he said to me in the living room. *Razzle him?* Then I remember the quote he recited. *How bizarre?* It was as if he knew my secrets, and that frightened me. I have to do something about it; to be back in control.

I look at the tee again before tossing it on the bed. I walk slowly up behind John and wrap my arms around his waist so they twist up his torso and my hands lay gently on his pecks. I feel his back muscles flex against my chest as he draws in a sharp breath. I rest my head between his shoulder blades and close my eyes as I listen to the rhythm of his breathing as he relaxes under my touch. John turns in his spot and I loosen my grip on him so he can turn in my arms. His eyes blaze into mine as he caresses my cheek with his hand. His soft lips press gently against mine as he pushes me back. Slowly, I move backwards until I feel the edge of the mattress against my bottom. His right hand snakes around my waist, down my backside and firmly cups the bottom of my buttocks as he pulls my groin against his. His left hand mirrors this act, and after pulling me against him again he lifts me up so my legs wrap around his waist and sets me on his bed. He sends sweet kisses down my neck as he pulls me further onto the bed.

***

"So what's going on out there?" John asks pulling me out of my memory.

"Huh?" I shake my head.

"What happened that got you all out of 'whack'," he says, using quote signals.

"Oh," I say, rolling my eyes, "this kid thinks he's the shit and tried to get at me. He was just repulsive."

"Thought you liked repulsive guys," John says coldly as he takes another hit.

"John," I say softly, "You know that's not why I did what I did."

John holds up his hand to stop me, "Nah, it's whatever. We said we'd never talk about it again. It's cool."

"That's why you always bring it up," I mutter under my breath.

We sit in silence as we exchange the blunt between us. I think more of the night with John, but as I do my mind wanders to the confrontation with Lance. I think about the feel of his strong hands around my waist. I picture the closeness of our faces as he spoke in his deep mysterious voice. I see his eyes flash across my vision and think of all the secrets hidden within the depth of that sea of green. He's like a puzzle and that thrills me. I want to know more. To pick up the pieces and put them together leaving me to enjoy what I am longing to figure out.

"He can't be that repulsive if he makes you smile like that," John cuts into my inner thoughts.

"He doesn't make me smile," I scoff.

"Right, because you're just the type to smile randomly," he says rolling his eyes.

"I smile when I'm around you," I say without thinking.

John looks up at me, glaring, and then shakes his head and takes a long drag of the blunt finishing it. His lips part to say something but he stops himself.

"John," I press.

"Don't, Rizz."

My mouth shuts as I sit back. *He's hurt, crap, really hurt.* That night changed a lot between the both of us. It left us on rocky grounds whenever we were around each other. I took advantage of him to keep up my façade. That night I made him promise me that he would forget it ever happened. That he wouldn't mention it to anyone. I made him take a night that meant a lot to him and act like it didn't even take place.

The silence is broken with a knock on the door. John and I both look at the door with raised eyebrows. It isn't like the room is on the second floor. By now people should have realized that this room is an open room to come and go as you please. No knocking required.

"Isn't someone going to get that?" Sarah chirps.

I had forgotten she was in the room with us. I wonder if she heard anything John and I were talking about.

"This isn't some shack to hook up in," I shout at the door.

The door opens and I watch as a strong rough hand clutches the side of the door. His Nike shocks are the first to come through the door. As my eyes float up his denim jeans and linger at the way they hang off his hips my body clenches. When he finally enters the room our eyes lock, and I narrow mine instantly.

"Crap," I mutter.

"So you are a stoner," Lance says grinning from ear to ear. He shuts the door behind him and waits for me to reply.

"You should lose the grin, you look like a fruit," I shoot at him.

"Is that your best shot?"

"I would try harder, but I was taught to never waste my breath on people who aren't worth my time."

"Ouch," Lance mocks, clutching his chest with his hand, "that stung."

"You two know each other?" John chimes in.

"Unfortunately, she hasn't had the pleasure to really get to know me," Lance says winking at me. He holds his hand out to John and says, "The name's Lance, nice to meet you."

"John," he responds taking Lance's hand hesitantly in a handshake.

"I think I've seen you around school before," Lance announces, "private school, right?"

"Yeah, you do look familiar."

What the hell is this, a reunion?

"This is the fool I told you about," I mutter to John trying to steer the conversation another way.

John nods his head in response.

"So you couldn't get me off your mind," Lance asks, grinning his stupid goofy grin.

"What can I say I was so disgusted by you that I had to tell someone."

Lance laughs, "You know, you still haven't answered my question."

"I'm not a stoner." I lie.

Lance looks around the room, his gaze pausing on Sarah who had fallen back into her daze. He chuckles at her and then looks at me, "You could have fooled me."

"I guess you're not as dumb as you look then," I reply getting to my feet. I lean over and kiss John on the cheek. I walk toward the door and stop in front of Lance, "If you don't mind I'm trying to leave."

"You know you should really try giving manners a chance," He smiles.

I hear John laugh from behind me. Choosing to ignore him, I say, "That's not my thing."

"That's for sure," John says under his breath.

I turn and look at John, "Do you have something to add, John?"

"Not that this is any of my business," John says swaying his finger from Lance to me, "But I'd get out of her way if I were you before she physically hurts you," John finishes, pointing toward his privates.

Lance clears his throat and gives John a small smile before raising his hands in defeat and stepping aside.

In a huff I open the door and walk out slamming it behind me.

"Hey," I hear Lance shout after me.

This kid just can't take a hint.

I take a few small steps forward before stopping and turning toward him. I stand with my hand on my hip, "What do you want?"

"I'd like to start over," He sighs.

"No thanks," I say turning away.

"Wait," he says grabbing my hand.

I turn half way toward him and look at his hand that holds mine.

He nervously lets go.

I stifle a chuckle, "Don't you have someone else to bother?"

"No, no one as interesting as you."

"You don't even know me."

"Maybe you should give me the opportunity to get to know you."

"Not a chance," I say walking away.

Lance speeds up and cuts in front of me. Now facing me and walking backwards he says, "You shouldn't keep yourself so closed off to everyone."

I scoff, "Don't pretend to know a thing about me."

"Okay, sorry. I know my first impression wasn't the best," He's rambling now, trying to find the right words, "I want to make that up to you. Just give me the chance to do it."

I give him a pointed stare as I continue forward.

"I mean it's the least you could do after insulting me."

I stop in my tracks. *The nerve.* Pointing my finger at him I echo his words, enunciating each one, "after insulting you?"

"Yeah, I mean—," he begins, but I cut him off with a wave of my hand.

"If anyone was insulted tonight, it was me. Not only was I insulted just once, but twice—twice," I say holding up two fingers, "So forgive me for wanting to get as far away from you as possible." I fold my arms across my chest and wait for his response.

"Let me make it up to you then," He says holding his hand out.

I look at it for a few short seconds.

Just say no, and walk away.

I look into his now calming green eyes, and my body begins to relax.

What is wrong with me?

I unfold my arms and place my hand in the palm of his.

Great, my mind thinks. While my heart and every hormone in me screams *finally.*

CHAPTER TEN: LANCE

Getting her to come with me was a lot easier than I thought it would be. I lead her through the house in search for an empty room. Walking through the kitchen, I pick up two Bud Light bottles. We wander a little more before locating the empty family room where I sit down on the couch and wait for her to follow in sync. When she does I hand her one of the beer bottles.

She shakes her head.

"So you smoke, but you're not a fan of drinking," I say as I put the bottle on the coffee table in front of us.

"It's complicated," she says.

"Tell me about it," I command.

"Nothing to tell," she shrugs.

I give her a weak smile before taking a sip of my beer.

"I have a question for you," she says changing gears and surprising me.

"Yeah?" I urge her to go on.

She swings her legs up on the couch situating herself in an Indian style position. She pulls her hair tie from her hair and lets her wavy brown hair cascade down her shoulders and over the top of her breasts.

I urge myself to stay relaxed as I turn toward her and rest my arm along the back of the couch.

The girl leans in closer giving me a clear view down her blouse.

She's playing.

I clear my throat and lean closer to her as well, meeting her gaze. "Comfortable?" I whisper.

Her eyes dilate slightly and then she composes herself, "So, who was the red-head stalking you?"

"Ah, so you weren't just talking about me, but you were watching me too," I smirk.

"Don't flatter yourself," She mutters.

I take another swig of my beer, "I'll tell you what. I'll answer any questions you throw at me if you answer mine."

"Sounds dangerous," she says into my ear, closing the gap between us.

I breathe in her sweet scent, "It could be," I whisper back.

She leans back, closing me off again, "Alright."

"Shake on it," I say holding my hand out to her.

"Don't you trust me?" She asks batting her eyes.

"Like you said," I say leaning against the arm rest of the couch, "you could be a serial killer for all I know."

"Do I look like a killer?"

"You never know."

"Guess you'll just have to wait and find out," she smirks taking my hand in hers.

I return her grip and shake her hand, "The red-head, is my ex-girlfriend."

"Oh?" she asks, retrieving her hand from my grasp.

"We dated for a little while."

"That seems right," she replies, tucking a strand of hair behind her ear.

"What?"

"It just makes sense two stalkers would find their way to each other at some point."

I laugh and take another swig of my beer.

"Did she break up with you?"

I give her a pointed stare, "No, I ended it with her."

"I knew that." She smirks.

My eyebrows arch.

"I just wanted to see how conceited you could get," she smiles.

Wow, she's beautiful. This isn't her usual 'I'm in control' smile, no, this one is genuine.

"So what happened?" She asks.

I part my lips to answer, but catch myself, "You're asking quite a lot of questions. I think it's my turn."

"Let's call them detail questions," she smirks.

Ah, snarky brunette is back.

"Detail questions?"

"Yeah, you know the questions following the beginning question. You can't expect someone to not have a question pertaining to your answer. Especially when you're obviously leaving parts out."

I look at her dumbfounded, "A detail question?"

"Yes," she says sitting up straight.

"Okay," I say uneasy, "Well honestly she became a nuisance. Thom, my friend, always said we broke up because I didn't know how to hold onto the good things in life." I chuckle at the memory. "He didn't know the whole story though."

"And that was?"

"Alright, "I say bringing my left leg onto the couch and tucking it under myself, "I was picking up some food from the store for my Pop, and as I'm walking down the sidewalk something catches my eye. I look into one of the restaurant windows and see Kayla, the red-head, sitting at a table with another guy. At first I'm just thinking it's her cousin or something like that, but then he reaches across the table and kisses her. Trust me, cousins don't kiss like that. So the next day I broke up with her telling her it just wasn't working out anymore."

"I would have walked in and made a scene."

"That doesn't surprise me."

The girl folds her arms over her chest, "I just wouldn't have let anyone make me feel like an idiot like that."

"I'd rather feel that way than look like it."

She tilts her head to the right as she assesses my comment, "Yeah, I guess you have a point there."

"Whoa," I say pretending to be taken back.

"What?"

"No snide comment and you're actually agreeing to something? I'm impressed."

"Yeah, well don't get used to it," She smiles looking down into her lap.

There's that smile again, gosh she's beautiful.

As she lifts her hand to her face and pulls back a strand of hair again I catch sight of a small circular scar on her left temple. Wondering how she got it, I lean in closer to have a better look when her eyes catch mine.

"What is it?" she asks.

"Nothing, you uhm, you have a scar on your temple," I motion to my own forehead with my finger.

I watch as she stiffens in her seat, "You're very observant," she tries to laugh off.

"What happened?"

"It was a long time ago, and I was little. I don't really remember it that well," She says quickly.

I nod my head slowly in response. *She's hiding again.* I eye her speculatively, but she sits opposite me like a stone wall no longer showing any emotion. *That has to get exhausting over time.* In the fear that I might lose her completely I decide to change tactics.

"So, I've been telling you my whole story and I don't even know your name."

Her shoulders slump a tad, and I can feel the tension dissipate from the air.

"Rizz," She says.

I raise an eyebrow at her, "Rizz?"

She doesn't say anything.

"Rizz? Rizz. Rizz!"

Her eyebrows rise in amusement, "Are you trying it out, or something?"

I smile, "Did you get that from Grease?"

"Her name was Rizzo, and she was badass."

"So I take that as a yes?"

"I was five."

"No complaints here," I assure her, and her face immediately softens.

Talking to her is like throwing darts. Unpredictable; I never know what I'll get. One moment she is communicating openly with me and the next she's hiding behind a barricade. She is like a ticking time bomb. One wrong question could set her off. It's being able to stop the clock and reset the time that makes it so thrilling. Each time I got a step closer to figuring her out.

"So your image is important to you?" Rizz asks.

"What makes you say that?"

"You broke up with a girl because she cheated on you, but you never made that clear to her."

"I didn't want her to know I knew," I state simply.

"You saw her kissing another guy, and you didn't even address it," She urges.

"Like I said she was getting on my nerves already, she did me a favor."

"Which was?"

"Giving me a way out."

"She doesn't even know that though. She thinks you just broke up with her because you lost interest or met someone new."

"So then let her think that."

"You don't want people to know the truth?"

"She doesn't need that title attached to her."

"So it's not your image your worried about?"

"Sounds to me like 'image' is pretty important to you."

"Why would you say that?" she says her eyes narrowing.

"You're the one harping on it right now."

"I was just curious that's all." She snaps.

I finish what's left of my beer and set the empty bottle on the table, "So who was that guy from earlier?"

"Who, John? He's just an old friend."

"And the guy before that?"

"That's Charlie," she snorts.

"Just another old friend?"

"No, more like an acquaintance."

"So what's the story with them?"

"Like I said John's just an old friend, and there is no story with Charlie."

"You like him don't you?"

"Oh gosh no, Charlie just doesn't know how to take a hint. I swear he has no common sense at all." She leans in closer to me and whispers, "he's a jock."

"That must explain it all."

She laughs as she leans back, "You would think."

"So then what's the story with John?"

"Like I said, he's just an old friend."

"So there is a story, you just don't want to share it?" I protest. I rub my chin with my hand and squint at Rizz, "That tells me you either like him or something happened between you two already."

"Aren't you the detective?"

"You're avoiding the question."

"And you're getting personal."

"Something has happened then?"

"I never said that," Rizz says as she digs out her ringing phone from her pocket. The screen lights up with an incoming call. The word 'mom' flashes on the screen. Rizz puts her thumb over the red button and drags it to the left to ignore the call.

"Aren't you going to get that?" I ask pointing to her phone.

"It's no one important," She says, setting her phone on the coffee table.

"You don't think she'll worry?"

"Trust me; I'm the least of her worries."

Rizz shifts in her seat and I can sense her discomfort. I reach toward the coffee table for the beer I brought for her. The beads of water wet my hand as I grab hold of it. *Good, it's still cold.*

"You sure you don't want any?" I ask, offering her the beer.

"No, I don't drink."

"That's right. You're a smoker not a drinker."

"Yeah, that's why," She rolls her eyes.

"What's the real reason?" I ask, opening the bottle.

"Hitler," she responds icily.

"I'll pass on the elaboration, thanks," I mutter.

"You weren't going to get one anyway," She sneers.

What bit her in the ass?

"You know, you shouldn't be so cynical," I say, annoyed with her attitude.

"I'm not."

"I beg to differ."

"You shouldn't beg, it makes you look less masculine," She snaps.

I try to stifle my laugh but fail to do so. "You know what I don't understand about you," I ask, "every time you come close to having a good time with me you always throw an insult or wise crack at me. Why can't you just enjoy our time together and stop closing me out? Maybe if you did that then you wouldn't be so…bitter about everything." I look at her blank stare, "You'd probably have a better time."

"Okay, Doctor Phil," She rolls her eyes.

I ignore her comment as I succinctly state, "I'm just saying I could try and help you be less cynical."

"Okay, stop there," she says putting her hand up, "I don't need anyone's help. There is nothing wrong with me. I'm not some toy you can just fix up and then be on your merry way."

"I never meant to imply that. You're taking everything out of context."

She opens her mouth to say something when her phone begins to buzz on the coffee table. Picking the phone off of the table she looks at the screen and then silences the phone.

As she stands up I look at her and ask, "You okay?"

Rizz clears her throat before answering me, "As much as I would love to sit here and discuss your Sally sunshine outlook on life I have to get home to Hitler."

I watch as Rizz clicks her heels together and salute me with Hitler's salute. I try to suppress the chuckle rising in my throat but I fail, and a smile forms on Rizz's face as she turns and walks away.

Rizz certainly has a strange sense of humor. I shouldn't have laughed. If I were anyone else they most likely would have been offended or disgusted by her act, but it was funny if only for a split second. I quickly connect the dots to the fact that she doesn't get along with her mother. What could she have ever done to be compared to Hitler? Her mother couldn't be that horrible, could she?

My thoughts are halted when a very drunk Kayla flops down on the couch next to me.

"There you are," she says.

"Here I am," I say, raising my beer to her.

"I have been looking for you all night," She slurs.

"Well, you've found me," I mutter.

"Don't look so glum, Lance. It doesn't suit you," she says, nudging my shoulder.

I take the remaining sip of my beer, ignoring her comment.

"You know," she says running her hand through my overgrown hair, "You should really keep your hair grown out. It makes you look sexy as hell."

"That's an idea," I agree.

Kayla slips her hand on my knee, leaning in closer. My body stiffens at her touch.

"I'm glad you agree," she smirks, and before I can register what's happening her lips are pressed against mine.

I try to pull back from her, but as I do she only moves further into me.

"Kayla," I muffle into her mouth as I raise my hands to her shoulders to inch her away from me.

Her eyebrows knit together as she looks at me.

"I have to go find Thom," I say, getting up from the couch quickly.

"Lance," She calls after me, but I make no move to look back at her.

I walk through the house in search of Thom, pissed at myself for letting Kayla get so close to me. *I hadn't even had that much to drink.* I knew that it wouldn't stay quite. Kayla had a way of using situations like that against you when you had least expect it, even if it was her who instigated the situation.

Why can't she just leave me alone?

I've given her more than enough hints that I'm not interested. Hell, I basically shouted it to the world. But she's relentless.

I round the corner of the kitchen doorway and look through the body of people dancing in the living room. As the crowd moves apart I spot Thom and Nathalie sitting on the couch.

I head toward them.

Nathalie sees me first and smiles at me.

Thom's gaze follows hers and lands on me, "Hey, man, what's got you all worked up?"

"We have to go," I say bluntly.

"What's the rush?" he asks, looking from me back to Nathalie.

"Do you want to end up walking home or not?" I threaten. I didn't want to tell him about Kayla. Not when Nathalie was sitting right there. I know how girls operate, and I wasn't planning on ruining my chances with Rizz.

"Alright, just give me a second."

"I'll meet you out by the truck."

Thom nods his head in agreement, and I head toward the front door.

CHAPTER ELEVEN: THOM

Annoyance courses through my body as Lance threatens me into leaving with him.

Can't he see I'm finally having a good time? Why does everything have to revolve around him?

Ever since Nathalie's brunette friend dragged that jock off, Nat and I have been inseparable tonight. In my courses to lure girls to the bedroom in order to help myself numb the pain and forget that one fateful night I had been successful, if only for the time being. When the girls began talking again, rage and annoyance would wash over me, and I'd want nothing more than to bask in the task again if only to shut them up and allow myself a release from the bottled up tension that radiated off of me.

With Nathalie, it was different. I watch the way her lips curl up into a smile as she talks on about her two best friends, and enjoy the small spark that glistens in her eyes as the light catches them. *She is intoxicating.* When her hand would lie atop mine, I would turn my palm over and begin to play with her fingers, gently stroking them with my thumb as she continues on. Her touch creating an exhilarating calmness, and what I want more than anything is to dive straight in and let the feeling consume me, erasing all the pain the last few years have brought me.

But as I watch my best friend walk in the direction of the exit, the calmness slowly slips away knowing that it is time to get back to reality.

"Hey, babe, I have to get going," I say to Nathalie.

"That's alright, I'll see you at school on Monday," Nathalie smiles at me and I begin to relax.

Damn, that smile. Maybe I could walk home? No, I know Lance has a good reason for up and leaving all of a sudden.

"I better go. He seems pretty shaken up about something."

"Okay, I hope he's alright."

I lean in and brush my lips against hers, "Don't worry about him, he'll be fine."

He always is

"Okay," she smiles, pressing her lips against mine.

I caress her cheek with my hand as I deepen the kiss.

"I'll text you," I say pulling away from her.

"Okay."

I walk up to the Ford that Lance is leaning against with his arms folded across his chest. He's staring up at the night sky, his forehead creased.

"What was that all about?" I ask, approaching him.

"Kayla," Lance says, unfolding his arms and reaching for the truck door.

"Okay?" I ask rounding to the passenger side, opening the door.

Lance climbs into the driver's seat, slams his door, and puts the key in the ignition. "She made a damn pass at me."

"That isn't surprising," I chuckle, slamming the door and reaching for my seatbelt.

Lance glares at me.

"I don't see the big deal," I shrug.

"She's freaking crazy. She just pounced on me, and I didn't get a chance to stop her," he whines as he backs out of the spot in grass.

I let out a small chuckle, "She scared you off so badly that we had to leave a party?"

"It's not funny," Lance mutters, turning onto the main road, "and she didn't scare me off. She's just like a damn leech and this is the best way to avoid her."

"Still always thinking of you, I see," I mutter.

"What's that supposed to mean?" Lance snaps, his knuckles growing white as he grips the steering wheel.

"It means, you couldn't even take one for the team," I snap back. "I finally find a girl I could remotely like, and my night has to get cut short because you can't handle your ex for one night."

"It's not like that Thom. Kayla's stunt could ruin everything with Rizz," He bites back.

"Rizz? What, is that code for something?" I ask, my anger beginning to subside.

"No, that's the girl's name from the porch."

"No way?" I ask, baffled.

Lance stops at a stop sign and smirks in my direction.

"I don't believe you. She wouldn't even give you the time of day."

"Yeah, well I got a lot more than that."

"Lance McCartney, my man," I say, slapping him on the shoulder.

"Not that," He chuckles, "I'm not you Thom."

"Yeah, well my ways might be changing."

Lance turns onto our street, "That serious, huh?"

"There is just something about her."

"I know that feeling," Lance agrees, as he pulls into his driveway. "Sorry, I cut your night short."

"Don't sweat it," I say climbing out of the truck, "You owe me one though."

"You got it."

"I'll see you tomorrow," I wave as I head in the direction of my house.

Lance waves in response as he heads up the walkway to the garage of his house.

The house is dark as I walk through the threshold. *I wonder if my mom even got up today.* When I reach the kitchen I flip up one of the light switches and a dim light cascades over the counters. A couple of unwashed dishes lie in the sink, hinting that my mom had at least dragged herself from her bed and fed herself. A chair at the kitchen table stands pulled out and I walk over to push it back in. I notice a bunch of papers spewed across the surface of the table, and begin to sort them into a neat pile when their contents catch my eye. I hold the paper out in front of me and read the words that cause my gut to wrench. I hurriedly spread the papers back out onto the table top and begin to look over them feverishly. *No, fucking way.* I rub at my eyes, willing myself to wake up from this nightmare. *This can't be real.* My breathing begins to grow harsh, and my vision blurs. I try to steady myself as I lay my palms flat out on the table and close my eyes. *Breathe Thom, Breathe.* I screw my eyes shut tighter. *This has to be some sort of misunderstanding.*

I hear the shuffling of feet from behind me. Startled, I whip around to see my mom standing in the doorway of the kitchen. Her small frame is engulfed with her baggy sweats and cream colored shawl that drapes around her shoulders. Her hair looks dull, hanging above her shoulders.

"I thought you'd be out later," she says, her tired eyes lingering on me.

"Lance wanted to leave early," I reply.

Slowly, she walks over to the sink and begins running water over the dirty dishes.

I turn back to the table and pick up one of the papers. "What is this?" I ask holding it up for her.

She doesn't turn to look at me. Instead, she begins to wash off the dishes in the sink.

"Mom," I say calmly.

She doesn't respond.

"Mom," I shout.

She jumps in her spot, and turns to look at me.

"What is this?" I ask again.

My mom looks at me with sad eyes, and puts the dish she is holding back in the sink. After wiping her hands off on a hand towel she says, "I'm selling the house."

My fist clenches at my side and I fight to keep a steady voice. "When were you going to tell me?"

My mother looks away from me, her intentions clear.

"So, what? I just don't exist anymore, is that it?" I sneer, balling the paper up in my hand.

"No, Thom," She gasps, "You'll be going off to college. It won't be like you're homeless."

"This is my home, not some crappy dorm room," I yell, "How could you not tell me this?"

"I was going to, when the time was right," She offers, as tears fill her eyes.

"Like you were going to tell me that you are divorcing Dad?"

"How did you know about that?" She asks defensively.

"So it's true then?" I hiss.

"Thom, I can't do this. I have to move on with my life."

"And what about him?" I scream at her, "Don't you think he wants to move on too? Don't you think this is hard for him too? God, he's the one rotting in the cell not you."

Silent sobs escape my mom as her chest heaves.

I look at her, stunned at the person I see in front of me. This person isn't the loving and supportive wife I had known her to be. How could she be so selfish as to turn her back on the one man who she vowed herself to?

A weight crushes down on me as realization dawns. This is my fault. My stupid mistake caused all of this.

I slam the crumpled up paper onto the table and storm out.

"Thom," my mother calls after me between sobs, "I have to do this."

"Do whatever you have to do, I don't care anymore." I snap.

I storm into my room and slam the door shut behind me.

How could this happen?

I pace my bedroom floor, pulling at my hair as I run my hands through it. This is my fault, all of it; the divorce, the selling of the house. I'm the reasoning behind all of it.

I grow angrier as my thoughts fill my head.

How could she do this to us?

Anger boils into rage, and I feel like I need to hit something, anything. I pace my room faster as each thought begins to collide into another. Her words echo in my head, *I have to do this. I have to move on with my life. I can't do this anymore.*

I pull at my hair again and screw my eyes shut.

"Ah!" I yell as I kick at my dresser. The items on top topple over as it shakes.

I walk over to the mirror behind the door and look at my reflection. I run my hand through my shaggy hair and still my hand halfway through. *This is your fault.* My eyes glare at my reflection, and before I have time to think about what I am doing, my fist smashes into the mirror. The pain and anger ripples through me and I thrust my hand into the broken mirror repeatedly. Huffing wildly I pull away from the mirror and look down at the shards of glass that had fallen to the ground. Examining my hand, I find small pieces sticking out from the cuts on my knuckles. Blood drips down my arm, but all I notice is the calmness that suddenly floods over me. The moment is lost when my bedroom door opens and my mother lets out a shriek as she hurries to my side.

"It's okay baby," she coos, "It's alright." She pets my hair, and kisses me on the forehead as I lean my head against her cheek.

CHAPTER TWELVE: RIZZ

I pull a box of Reese's Puff cereal from the cabinet and pour the contents into the bowl sitting on the counter. Walking into the dining room I sit down at the table letting my mind wander to thoughts of last night. I imagine the way Lance's breath felt on my skin as he whispered in my ear and the feel of his rough hands on my hip as he pulled me closer to him. My cheeks heat up as I remember our conversation that night. I smile at my cereal as I think of how he pushed me to open up to him. He wasn't afraid to push my boundaries, and he didn't let me walk all over him like most guys did. He surprised me and in all honesty, I look forward to seeing him again.

"Rizz," Hope exclaims as she rushes into the dining room.

I slightly jump in my seat as she pulls me from my thoughts. "What's up?" I ask scooping a spoonful of cereal and bringing it to my mouth.

"Guess what Daddy said I can do," she says her grin growing wider across her pixie shaped face.

"What did he say?" I ask, looking into her blue eyes.

"He said I can go to the park," Hope's brown hair bounces on her shoulders as she jumps up and down in excitement.

"I'm sensing a catch here," I chuckle as I finish up my cereal.

Chip never spent one-on-one time with Hope. He buried himself in his work. The only time he graced us with his presence was when my mother ordered him to take her out.

"He said I could go if you take me," Hope says, looking at me with pleading eyes.

I smile at her innocence, "You know I'm going to say yes."

Hope squeals and jumps on me as she wraps her arms around my mid-drift. "We can play on the monkey bars all day long."

"Well not all day," I say, "I have work tonight."

Hope's face falls slightly, but she shakes it off before excitedly saying, "Okay."

I always enjoy spending time with Hope. There wasn't a single moment of her childhood that I wanted to miss. Of course one day she'll realize I'm not the greatest example to look up to, but she'll see how much I cared for her and how often I was there to take care of her when our parents weren't.

"Let me just clean this up, and then get the keys from Dad," I smile at her as I stand up from the table and pick up my bowl.

Everything in the office looks the same as it had in every other house we lived in as we moved around. The walls, covered with bookshelves filled with law books, and his desk is piled high with paper work.

Chip looks up from the file in his hand, no doubt his most recent case, to acknowledge our presence. His slim structure is dressed in suit and tie apparel. We barely saw him in anything else. He removes his wire glasses and rubs at his tired blue eyes. He sets the file on the desk and runs his hand through his light brown hair.

Hope, a spitting image of him, runs up to him and throws her arms around his waist. "She said she'd take me, Daddy." She boasts.

Chip places his hand on her head and beams down at her. My heart tears in my chest as I watch his affection for her grow evident on his face. *Why couldn't he just spend time with her himself.*

"That's great, sweetie."

"I'm going to need the car keys," I cut in, walking up to his desk, holding out my hand.

"Alright," Chip says, digging into his pants pocket, "here you go." He sets them in my hand.

It was easy with Chip. I didn't have to fight with him or listen to any rude remarks. He just gave me what I wanted when I asked for it. I knew Chip loved us, after all we were his little girls, but I just never understood why he didn't do anything about the abuse. Why ignore it instead of protecting us from her?

"Let's go, Hope," I say smiling at her.

Chip gives her a squeeze before she detaches herself from his side.

"Have fun girls, be safe," He calls after us.

I stop at the doorway and turn to face Chip as Hope runs ahead, "You know, it wouldn't hurt to spend some time with her."

"I'm very busy today," he says, picking up the file, "and I spent time with her last night."

"Eating peanuts out of a dish at a bar and watching the Cubs play is a sad excuse for spending time with her. Why not try spending time doing something she actually enjoys. You know something that benefits her," I say with a sigh and walk out of the room after Hope.

I could never be rude to Chip whenever I confronted him. It helped that he always kept a level head. He cared about us. He just had a funny way of showing it. I wish he'd do more, but he didn't. He just didn't try hard enough. More reason for me to be there for Hope.

As soon as I park the car, Hope pushes the door open and runs for the monkey bars. I walk up to a bench and sit down watching as Hope swings herself across the open pit. I love watching Hope play. To see her smile and have fun, and enjoy what she has for a childhood makes me happy that she has more than I had at her age. More than anything I want her to stay pure. Hope has the ability to be someone great. I'll be damned if my mother ruins that for her. I don't want the life I was subjected to at her age for her. That's why I'm here to protect her. If it weren't for Hope, I would have left a long time ago.

"Can I ask you a question?" Hope asks, still hanging from the monkey bars.

"Sure can," I say, standing up and walking toward her.

"Why don't you like Mom?" she says, making her way across the open pit.

I grab onto one of the monkey bars and follow her across, "It's pretty complicated."

I wanted to tell Hope why I disliked our mother so much, but I couldn't. There were just too many reasons. I wouldn't have known where to start.

"You can tell me," she says, letting go of the bar and falling into the pit.

I let go and land in the pit after her. I couldn't tell her about the incident that changed everything. The reason I began to hand back everything my mother dished out to me. I couldn't tell Hope about that horrid day. She didn't need that burden.

I pull my phone from my pocket and look at the time, "It's noon. What do you say we go grab some lunch?" I ask changing the subject.

A flit of disappointment flashes across her face, but is soon covered with a smile as she agrees.

I look at the clock hanging in the diner and notice that it's almost two-thirty.

"Alright, Hope. I think it's time we get you home."

"Do we have to?" Hope whines.

"Yeah, I have to get to work. And I don't want any trouble tonight," I explain, knowing my mother would be awake by now.

"Fine," Hope moans, rolling up her sleeves to her plaid shirt.

My eyes catch a small burn on her arm, "Hope?" I ask squinting at her arm, "What's that on your arm?"

"It's nothing," Hope says quickly, rolling her right sleeve back down.

I grab Hope's arm and roll the sleeve back up. My heart crashes as I look at the circular burns that mark the inside of her right arm. I reach up to my temple and rub the slightly risen scar.

***

The smell of cigarette smoke consumes the dimly lit living room. I sit motionless on the couch next to my mother as she takes another drag of her third cigarette for the afternoon. Hot tears slide down my cheeks, but I make no move to wipe them from my face. I sit there in silence forcing back the cries I desperately want to let out.

Just stay quiet. Crying will only make it worse.

I glance at my mother as she brings the cigarette hanging between her fingers to her mouth. She takes the last drag and my body clenches as I watch the end of the cigarette burn. Her hazy eyes glare at me, and I lift the end of my tee-shirt exposing my stomach. Bringing the cigarette to my skin my mother stabs it into my flesh and I wince as the sting from the burn courses through me. When she's finished she pulls the cigarette away and flicks it to the living room floor. She fumbles with the pack of Marlboros on the end table and pulls out another, bringing it to her lips and lighting it.

How many more is she going to smoke until it's over?

Where is Daddy? Why isn't he stopping her?

My mother glares at me again and I pull down my shirt, hiding the three new burns she has added to the *collection.*

"You're a stupid little girl," my mother slurs at me, "and stupid girls get punished."

Punished for what? I wanted to ask, but I knew better. Engaging in any sort of way would only excel the situation, and all I wanted was for it to end.

Please, Daddy, come home soon. Make her stop.

Make her stop.

***

"Did that witch do this to you?" I seethe.

Hope looks down at her empty plate on the table and says, "She didn't mean to. It was an accident."

"Oh right? The cigarette just fell out of her hand and onto your arm?" My brows knit together, "This wasn't an accident. Stop making excuses for her to continue to hurt you."

"I don't want you two to start fighting." Hope argues.

"It's not okay for her to do this to you. It's inhumane. How long did you think you'd be able to keep this from me?"

"At least until they healed, and went away," Hope mumbles.

"They don't go away," I snap, "Scars never just go away."

"Rizz," Hope pleads as I stand up from the table, "Please don't fight with her."

I throw some money down on the table and shoot Hope a look that tells her to give up.

Hope opens her mouth to say something, but thinks better of it. Getting up from the table she follows me out to the car.

I was furious with my mother. I couldn't take her hitting Hope, let alone sticking a burning cigarette to her skin. That crossed all the lines. I wasn't going to let her get away with this. I wonder for a moment if I should tell Chip. Would he do something? He didn't when it was me. Did he even know what was going on when it was me? I shake my head. *It doesn't matter. It's over and done with.* This is about Hope now, and I was the only one who could do anything about it.

"How dare you do this to her," I shout, storming into the living room with Hope at my side.

My mother, lounging on the couch with a magazine in her hands, looks up, "Excuse me?"

"How dare you burn her."

"I have no idea what you're talking about," she says, focusing her attention back to the magazine. She turns the page and glances over an article.

Raging, I walk over to the couch and rip the magazine from her hands, throwing it to the ground. I grab Hope's arm and roll up the sleeve and shove it in front of my mother's glaring face.

"Oh, that," She states.

"Oh, that?" I repeat.

Bile rises in my throat, and I let go of Hope's arm. I hear Hope begin to cry as I point my finger at my mother and seethe, "How could you? She's only eight years old. She's not your damn ashtray."

"She handles it a lot better than you did," my mother snaps.

My face screws up in disgust, "What is wrong with you? Whoever let you have children?"

"You ungrateful little Bitch. I gave you life," She snaps in fake shock.

I snort at her response, "What a great life you've given me."

My mother stands up from the couch and I take a step back ushering Hope behind me.

"Come here, Hope," my mother beckons.

I push Hope further behind me, and my mother blazes her steely look into me.

"Get out of the way, you stupid girl."

You're a stupid girl, stupid girls get punished. Her words echo through my mind.

"Is that what you called Hope right before you stuck that cigarette to her arm?" I growl.

"That is none of your business."

"Is history repeating itself?"

"Shut up," She warns.

"You know she'll end up hating you for this, right? One day she'll grow up and realize how fucked up all of this is and she'll despise you for it, just like I did," I go on.

"You stupid girl," she yells as she reaches to grab for me, but I step out of her reach pushing both Hope and I away from her.

"At least she'll be grateful for having me here for her," I proceed, "When she looks back on her

life she'll remember me being there unlike you.
You're wasted every second of her life, and hitting
her whenever you get the chance." I wanted to stop,
but I couldn't the words kept spewing out like
projectile vomit. "I thought you would have shaped
up after everything that happened with Luke, but
hey, why stop now? One down, two to go," I snap,
tears falling down my face.

"Stop it! Stop fighting!" Hope says, stepping out
from behind me.

I go to reach for her as she walks up to our
mother, but she walks out of my grasp.

"Please stop fighting," Hope pleads, facing my
mother's cold stare.

My mother reaches up and gently runs her
finger along Hope's cheek. A wicked smile forms
upon my mother's lips and her hand disappears
from Hope's cheek only to connect with it again as
she backhands Hope across the face.

"This is entirely your fault," she venomously
says.

***

This is entirely your fault. My mother's words
echo through my mind. Suddenly I'm eight years
old again. I clutch to the living room's door frame

as I watch as my mother stares impassively at the fire place mantel, her face stained with dried tears. Tears stream down my own face as the truth of what happened sets in. A cigarette hangs from between my mother's fingers, and she brings it to her lips breathing in a long drag. As she exhales, her body heaves up with new tears. I run to her side to comfort her. Putting my hand on top of her own, I rub it softly and say, "It's okay, Mommy."

Her body stills and she glares at my hand as if my touch disgusts her. She pulls her hand from underneath mine and sets it in her lap.

"Mamma?" I ask.

Glaring, she meets my eyes, "This is your fault."

"But, Mama—"

Reaching up, she grabs the side of my face holding it still. With her other hand she brings the cigarette and shoves it into my left temple. I scream out in pain as my mother twists the stick into my skin deeper and deeper.

"You stupid, stupid girl," My mother sneers as I try to wriggle free from her but her grip remains strong, "This is your fault."

Finally she releases me and I fall to the ground, clutching the side of my face as the tears stream down my face.

I look up to see my mother relight her cigarette and take a long drag as if nothing had happened. Getting to my feet, I run from the room, knowing if I stayed the only thing I would receive would be more burns to my already scared skin.

***

I rush to Hope's side, pulling her face to mine and cradling her cheek in my hand. I know the blow Hope suffered was meant for me.

"You okay?" I coo to her.

Hope's hand clasps over her reddening cheek as she falls into my embrace.

I look up at my mother, who is towering over us, "You're pathetic."

My mother says nothing.

Directing my attention back to Hope I say, "Come on. Let's go get you cleaned up."

I grab a washcloth from the linen closet and head into the bathroom. Hope follows me and sits down on the toilet lid. I close the bathroom door behind us before turning on the faucet and wet the cloth with warm water.

"Jeez, Hope. When are you going to learn to stay out of a fight between her and me?" I say dabbing at the cut on her lip. I pull away so she can answer.

"I just wanted you two to stop yelling."

"Was it worth it?" I ask, my eyebrows rising.

I wipe the excess blood off of her chin. Pulling out a tube of Neosporin I squeeze some onto my finger and rub it into her lip.

"Rizz?" Hope asks.

"Yeah?" I ask, screwing the cap back onto the tube and placing it in the drawer.

"Who's Luke?"

I still at the mention of his name, but quickly compose myself as I fold the washcloth in half. Hanging it on the towel rack I hesitantly respond, "He's just an old friend. He was around before you were born."

"What happened to him?" Hope presses.

I swallow the lump rising in my throat before answering, "He passed away."

"Were you close to him?"

I smile weakly at Hope, "I didn't get the chance to get to know him."

"But you loved him?"

"Yeah," I nod, a tear rolling down my cheek, "I loved him."

I wipe away the tear with my thumb and stifle a small laugh, "look at me, I'm turning into a mess." I reach for the bathroom door and pull it open, "I have to head to work soon, so let's get you ready for bed, and then you can just play in your room, okay?"

Hope slides off of the toilet seat, "Okay," she agrees.

"Lock the door, okay?" I tell Hope as I walk out of her bedroom.

She nods her head, and I shut the door behind me. Standing outside the door I wait until I hear the small click of the lock, and then head down the hallway to my own room.

I pull my shirt up over my head and throw it into the dirty laundry basket sitting outside of my closet. Walking up to my dresser I grab my work shirt and throw it on. I tug at the hemline of the shirt as I look myself over in the mirror, the bold printed word "Javalicious" stares back at me.

Those are the perks of working at a coffee shop.

I roll my eyes at myself in the mirror, and head out of the room toward the staircase. Hurriedly, I make way to the bottom and bolt out the front door avoiding any further confrontation with my mother.

Once at the Coffee Café, I make my way around the counter and through the doors leading to the kitchen area. Grace, my boss is hunched over a tray of sweets, an icing bag in her hands.

"Hey, Grace," I call to her as I head back to the small office.

She looks up from her pastries and gives me a warm smile. "Hey, cookie," she calls back.

I return her warm smile as she calls me by the nickname she had picked out for me ever since I was that scared little girl who'd run away to the Café in hopes of escaping the life that waited for me back home. Grace owns the Coffee Café here in Lake Forest, and she probably would have hired me then if I were of age, but I wasn't, so she waited until I was of legal age to recruit me to her team. Of course things got a little complicated due to the moving around a lot, but I always had a job here whenever I came back into town.

Grace is the sweetest old lady I had ever gotten the pleasure to know. She has this warm glow about her, and when you're in her presence you can't help but feel like you're home. Grace treated me like family, of course she probably saw me grow up more than my own mother had. I spent a great amount of my childhood hiding out in the Café. I would bring in books from the local library so no one would wonder what a little kid was doing in a coffee shop by herself. I didn't know where else to go, and Grace had a way of making me feel safe.

I had a growing suspicion that Grace knew what went on back at *home*. Sometimes I would catch her looking at me with a sad expression fixed on her face, but she never brought it to the light. Not that I would have admitted it to her if she had. But I could just feel like she knew there was more to me than I let on, and sometimes I catch myself wondering what it would be like to just unload it all on her. What kind of support would she offer, but the thought leaves me as quickly as it came. It's my burden to hold. It's my screwed up life.

Besides, she's just my boss.

"Just set your stuff in the office, and go ahead on the register. Joel will be taking off as soon as you punch in," Grace says, returning to the pastries in front of her.

I nod and head to the office, setting my purse down on the desk. I walk back out to the front of the store and sign myself onto the register, clocking in as I do so.

Joel walks up beside me and nudges my shoulder with his. "You ready for a long night of hell?" He asks.

"Was it that bad?" I ask, nudging him back.

Joel graduated from Waverly High two years ago, and has been working at the Coffee Café to help pay for community college ever since then.

"Are you kidding me, if I have to hear one more complaint about how the coffee is too strong, or why an espresso shot is called an espresso shot if it does nothing to keep the average coffee junkie going, I'll rip my hair out."

I laugh as Joel tugs at his shaggy black hair and grunts in frustration.

"I guess I should brace myself then."

"I don't think you'll have too much trouble," He says looking me over as he runs his hand along the stubble growing in on his chin. "You girls seem to always get the easy customers. Maybe it's just because they get too distracted with the view."

I laugh as I playfully hit Joel in the arm, "Come on now, you know the rules. No hitting on the crew members."

"I've never been one to follow the rules," he smiles, rubbing his arm where I had hit him.

"Whatever, Joel," I say dismissing him with a wave of the hand.

Joel was cute, but definitely not my type. He had the whole coffee shop poet vibe going for him, and he even worked up the nerve to participate in an open-mic once. Luckily I was in town and was able to stop in for moral support, but that's all I'd ever be. I was the co-worker who leant a supportive hand here and there. Sure at school I enjoyed breaking the rules, but not here. I respected Grace too much for all that.

"Well, I'm headed out," Joel says, punching in his numbers on the register.

"I'll see ya," I wave, before directing my attention to the couple walking into the shop.

"Good luck," He whispers in my ear.

I smirk at him before shaking him off and addressing the customers, "Hi, what can I get for you?"

The last thing I wanted right now was to be working and pretending like I was in a cheerful mood when all I could think about was my altercation with my mother earlier and how old demons got dug up. It had been ten years since everything that has happened with Luke. I barely knew him, but loved him just the same. I visited him every day in the hospital of his short life, and then at the cemetery up until we moved. Things seemed to get better when Hope was born. It was almost like I was getting a second chance. A chance at protecting her and making sure she got the life she deserved, a life I couldn't have for myself.

"Hi, one mocha frappe and a chocolate scone," The middle aged man says pulling me from my thoughts.

"And will that be all today?" I ask, pressing his order into the register.

"Could I have a skinny iced latte with no whip cream," the woman chimes in.

"Sure thing," I reply, adding in her order and giving them their total.

After the man pays, I set to work making their drinks. Once finished, I place the drinks and the scone on the counter and shout out their order.

"Have a great day," I wish the couple as they come to the counter, plastering on a fake smile.

Yeah, tonight was going to be a long night.

CHAPTER THIRTEEN: LANCE

"Watch out for the hand grenade," Thom shouts.

"They're gaining up on me. I'm going to need some back up," I retort.

"Crap, I hate when they release the dogs," Thom curses, throwing down his control, "Damn it."

I stare at the flashing words "mission failed" on the screen, and toss the controller to the side.

"That's the third damn time," Thom huffs, standing up from the leather game chair.

"Relax man," I chuckle, "it's only a game."

"Yeah, yeah," Thom says waving me off, "What time is it?"

I look at my watch, "almost five-thirty. When do you have to get going?"

"I don't know, Nathalie just said she'd text me when she was on her way," Thom pulls out his phone and checks his messages.

I look at his bandaged hand that is holding his phone.

"How'd you say you busted up your hand again?" I ask, nodding to his hand.

"I didn't."

I raise my brow.

Catching my eye, Thom sighs, "Sorry, man. It's embarrassing; I may have overdone the drinking last night."

Bullshit, he wasn't even drunk when I took him home last night.

"When I got home, I thought it would be a good idea to be some kick ass karate master, you know how they do that breaking boards stuff?"

I nod.

"Yeah, well let's just say it's not as easy as it looks." Thom shoves his phone back in his pocket and picks up his controller, "Anyway, want to try again?"

I snort, "Yeah, right. You're getting a little too wound up."

"Guess you're right," Thom says, plopping back down on the chair, "Pop doesn't need a reason to kick me out."

"Now why would we ever consider doing that?" Pop's voice comes from behind us.

We turn toward the doorway and see Pop leaning against the door frame.

"Hey, Pop."

"Hey, Mr. McCartney," Thom says, jumping back to his feet.

Pop smirks, "One minute I'm Pop and the next I'm Mr. McCartney?"

"Sorry, Pop," Thom shrugs giving him a weak smile.

"What happened to your hand?" he says gesturing to his wrapped hand.

"Thom thinks he's some sort of karate expert."

Pop snorts, "I'm guessing it didn't go so well."

"Yeah," Thom shrugs, "Bit that dream in the ass real quick."

"So what're you boys getting into tonight?" Pop says, taking a seat on one of the leather game chairs' arm rest.

"Whatever life throws at us," I reply.

Thom winces.

"We were about to get some coffee," I continue, "Want one?"

"No thanks. You two go ahead," Pop says getting up from the chair, "and stay out of trouble."

"I'll meet you in the car," Thom intervenes.

My eyebrows knit together, "Okay?"

"Have a good night," Thom calls to Pop after returning the controller to the silver metal stand.

"You too, Son," Pop replies.

Thom winces again, before walking out into the hallway.

I get up from the game chair and place my controller next to the one Thom returned. Reaching for the Xbox, I press the power button, following the same motions for the flat screen.

"What has gotten into the boy?" Pop wonders aloud.

"It really depends on the day," I attempt to joke.

Pop's face grows serious.

"He feels guilty," I shrug.

Pop takes a deep sigh, "It wasn't his fault."

"I know that, but it doesn't matter. He thinks…"

"He was at the wrong place at the wrong time."

"They both were," I say referring to Thom and his father.

"She's in a better place," Pop says.

"I didn't…" I pause looking at Pop's distraught facial expression, "I better get going."

Pop nods, "you tell him that he has nothing to blame himself for."

I nod, knowing it will do no good, and head out into the hallway.

I start the engine to the Ford and pull out of the garage. Thom sits silently, staring out the car window.

"He doesn't blame you."

"He should," Thom says as he continues to look out the window at the passing scenery of houses.

My brows knit together and I tighten my grip on the steering wheel.

How could he say something like that?

"It's not like you were the one driving," I mutter.

Thom's head snaps to me, "So the truth comes out."

"It was an accident," I urge the words out.

"Is that what you really think?"

I stay silent, turning onto the main road.

"I don't know..." I shake my head, "it's just...the whole thing..." I sigh, "It just sucks."

Thom stares at me.

I turn down another road leading to the shopping strip.

"I know it bothers you too," Thom whispers, "And I know you don't want to blame him...but you do."

I swallow the lump in my throat forcing it down. He's right, I do blame his father, but I shouldn't. It was an accident.

"I'm just trying to move on."

Thom stays silent. I glance at him to see him staring out the window again. The streets are lit up with lamp posts that line the sidewalks. A few people walk along the stores, and others walk off the curb to get into their waiting vehicles.

Thom and I had never really addressed how the accident affected me. It was like I swept it under a rug in order to help Thom move on. But that was the thing. He wasn't moving on. No matter how many therapy sessions he attended, they didn't help. He was stuck, and I didn't know what to do to help him through anymore. With every push to help him, he'd only push back.

Thom's phone rings, and he digs it out of his pocket.

"Hey," he smiles.

I watch as Thom's rigid body begins to relax.

"Yeah…sounds good…okay…see you in a bit."

Thom hangs up, and pockets his phone in his jeans.

"That was Nat."

I nod my head, a small smile tugging at my lips.

"She wants to know what's going on with you and Rizz."

I snort, "What, now you're part of girl talk?"

Thom chuckles, "Something tells me that that girl doesn't participate in girl talk."

"That's probably true," I agree pulling into the parking lot of Coffee Café.

"She seems like a handful."

"Nah. There's something about her," I say as we walk into the café.

"Yeah, like her temper?" Thom chuckles.

I smirk, "yeah, that she does have." I walk up to the counter and signal for the elderly woman.

Thom leans his back against the counter.

"How may I help you, darling?" the woman asks.

"Two espressos, please," I say holding up two fingers.

The woman begins ringing in my order.

"Well tonight may be your lucky night," Thom says, smacking my shoulder with the back of his hand.

I look to where he is pointing and see Rizz bussing off a table in the café lobby. My jaw drops slightly as I take in her pale and swollen face, her eyes bloodshot and her hair thrown into a curly mess.

"You think she knows she looks like that?" Thom leans in, whispering.

"That'll be seven dollars," The woman behind the counter chimes in.

I pull my eyes away from Rizz, and look at the elderly woman's concerned face.

"Right," I say, pulling my wallet from my back pocket. I hand her a ten.

"Here you go, Hun," She hands me my change. "It'll be right up." She says eyeing me speculatively before walking away.

I look back at Rizz. She pulls out a chair and sits down throwing the rag on the table surface. Putting her elbows on the table she covers her face with her hands.

"Go talk to her, mister irresistible," Thom nudges me.

"I'm starting to wish I never told you that part," I growl at Thom.

He nudges me again, and I head in the direction of Rizz.

I walk up to her hesitantly. I never expected for her to seem so…*normal*. I look back to Thom who is talking with the elderly woman from behind the counter.

He seriously can strike up a conversation with anyone.

I reach Rizz and clear my throat, "Is this seat taken?"

She looks at me, startled. "What do you want?" She mutters.

I sit down across from her, not waiting for an invitation.

She wouldn't be giving me one anyway.

"To make sure you're okay," I answer her.

"I'm fine. You can leave now," She says, looking anywhere but at me.

I rub my hands together in my lap, unsure of what to say. This wasn't the girl I had met at the party. This girl sitting before me seems almost broken. As if she is holding on by a slowly fraying piece of thread.

"So you work here," I let the question hang in the air as a statement.

"Yeah…" she says wiping at her eyes, "Some of us aren't as fortunate to have parents who lavish money on their kids."

"What's that supposed to mean?" I ask, my eyes narrowing.

"Nothing," she says shaking her head, "Sorry."

Her apology throws me. *Who is this girl?* In the hopes to steer the conversation to safer grounds I smirk at her and say, "Nice shirt."

A small smile forms on her lips, and I can't keep my smirk from turning into a face splitting grin.

There's that smile.

"Do you need me to call someone for you?" I ask, turning serious again.

Rizz's eyes meet mine instantly.

Fear. That's what I saw.

"No," she practically shouts. Catching herself, Rizz clears her throat. "Sorry," she says now with a level tone, "They don't…No, it's okay."

I nod my head, concern now etched on my face, "Do you need a ride?"

"I'll be fine, thanks."

I seriously doubt that for some reason.

"My shift isn't over anyhow."

As if on cue the woman behind the counter calls out to her, "Cookie, you're times up. You can head home for the night."

I look at the woman who is giving Rizz a pointed stare.

"Are you sure?" Rizz pleads.

"I'm positive. Go have some fun with your friends."

"They're not…"

"Go," the woman says cutting Rizz off.

Rizz forfeits. She sighs throwing her elbow back on the table and laying her chin in the palm of her hand.

"Guess you're free then," I say matter of fact like, "Now what about that ride."

"I don't need one," She says pointing out the window to an Impala, "I drove."

It started to rain sometime during our conversation, and it was coming down hard.

I eye her curiously, "You don't look like you're in a hurry to go anywhere."

"Still observant, I see."

"You're not going home are you?" concern etched in my voice.

"You don't have to worry about me."

"Come hang out with Thom and me."

Her eyebrows rise.

"It'll buy you some time."

Rizz leans back in her seat, looking at me with disbelief.

"What?"

"You're so nice to me."

"So?"

"No matter how rude I am to you, you continue to be nice. Why?"

"You're not like the other girls," I shrug.

"How's that?"

"For starters, you're not falling all over me."

Rizz snorts, "And here I thought it was just because you couldn't get a clue."

I laugh, and for the first time she joins me.

"One question though," I say after settling down.

"Yeah?" she says, wiping at the tears under her eyes from laughing.

"You're not a mass murderer, right?"

Rizz laughs again, the light reaching her eyes, "You're not a stalker, right?"

"It's settled then," I grin at her.

She smiles back, and I'm not sure if it's the silly banter we just participated in or the fact that she was showing me a side of her I thought I'd never see, but one thing was for sure: I was falling for this girl fast, and she was falling for me too.

CHAPTER FOURTEEN: THOM

After Lance heads over to where Rizz is sitting, the elderly woman walks up to the counter, tapping me on the shoulder.

"What is his business with my Cookie?" She snaps at me.

"Whoa," I say holding my hands up, "I don't know what you're talking about, but whatever is going on with your "cookie" you should take it up with him. I don't want to get into the middle of that situation."

The elderly woman slaps me on the back of the head.

"Owe," I mutter reaching up to rub my head.

"No, my Cookie," She says pointing to Rizz.

"Well you should have made that clear."

She rolls her eyes at me, and then places her hands down on the counter top leaning closer to me.

"Well?" She prompts.

"He likes her, I guess."

"You guess?"

"I don't know, you want me to go ask him?" I say, turning away from the counter.

"Get back here," She demands.

I stop, leaning back against the counter.

"None of that smart business," she scolds.

"Yes ma'am," I say, saluting her.

The gold bracelets on her wrist clang together as she points her arthritis suffered finger at me in a warning manner, "Actions like that are what ask for another slap upside the head."

"Sorry," I mutter holding my hands up in surrender.

"They do look cute together," She says leaning on the counter, watching Lance and Rizz talk.

"I guess," I say, leaning back against the counter and folding my hands across my chest. "What's your interest anyhow?"

The woman's smile fades, "That girl's been through hell and back."

I look at the woman, and then back at Rizz. "Haven't we all?" I wonder out loud.

"Not like this one," She responds sadly. The woman backs off of the counter, her voice growing stern as she adds, "And she doesn't need some boy coming into her life screwing with that pretty little head of hers."

"You sound like family."

"Oh, Honey, I wish I were...I wish I were."

I glance at her as she turns around to finish fixing up our drinks.

"Do you know what happened to her?"

"I don't think anyone knows," she says setting the drinks on the counter, "But I've seen the scars."

"Scars?" I ask.

She pushes the drinks toward me, "Not all scars lay on the surface." She nods toward Rizz, "but for her? They lie not only on the surface but underneath as well ever since I could remember." Her face grows sad, "Now if you ask me, that's a true hell."

I take the drinks in my hands and take a sip of mine as I look over the edge of the cup at Rizz. *What could she have possibly gone through?*

"Cookie, you're times up. You can head home for the night," The woman calls to her.

"Are you sure?" Rizz pleads.

"I'm positive. Go have some fun with your friends."

"They're not…" Rizz begins.

"Go," the woman says cutting Rizz off.

Rizz sighs throwing her elbow back on the table and laying her chin in the palm of her hand.

I look at the woman, "what's your name?"

"Grace," She states, "And you better remember it, because if you two dare hurt that girl I'll be looking for you."

"He won't," I assure her.

She nods towards Lance and Rizz, "They really do look great together."

I watch as the two of them laugh together at the table, "Yeah, they do."

An awkward silence fills the Impala. I run my hand down my thigh repeatedly and stare out the window. Reaching up, I hold onto the handle as Rizz rounds the bend on two wheels.

What does this girl think this is, NASCAR?

I sit there silently praying tonight isn't the night I'll die. After all I'm meeting Nathalie soon.

"Turn right," I pipe up.

Rizz sharply turns the car as she almost speeds past the turn.

"Sorry," She mutters.

"Mind actually doing the speed limit?" I snap at her.

"What's wrong," she smirks, looking at me and taking her eyes off of the road, "You afraid?"

"Can you just watch where you're going?" I say pointing to the road with my eyes.

"Don't be such a baby," she laughs as she returns her gaze to the road.

The car begins to slow down slightly and my body starts to relax.

"Better?" she asks.

"Much," I grumble at her.

I catch a glimpse of the smile playing on her lips as she adjusts her grip on the steering wheel.

"So," I say, letting it sit in the air.

"Yeah?" She asks, looking at me again.

My eyes bulge and the tension in my shoulders reappears, "eyes on the road," I snap.

Rizz quickly looks back to the road, "Jeez, what's your problem?"

"Nothing. Sorry," I mutter.

"No seriously, what freaks you out so much about me just looking at you for a second?"

"It's nothing. Just watch where you're driving, okay?"

"Yeah, right," She says doubtfully, "What happened to your hand by the way?"

"Nothing, turn left here."

Rizz takes the corner sharply again, and my body temperature begins to rise, "Seriously, can you not kill us?"

"Will you stop acting like we are going to get into an accident? I know what I'm doing."

"Clearly."

Why the hell did Lance make me drive with her?

"Why are you even coming back with us?" I snap at her. I was going to kill Lance for this. This girl isn't only crazy but she has a death wish as well.

"It wasn't my idea."

Damn Lance.

"Well why the hell did you agree?"

"Have you ever tried telling that kid no? It's like the word has completely been erased from his vocabulary."

Freaking Lance.

"Yeah," I growl, "He's impossible...go right."

Rizz turns the car slowly onto the road causing my body to thaw. My anger begins to subside slightly although I'm still going to chew Lance a new one for having me drive with this maniac.

"Do you know why he's like that?" She asks.

"Like what?"

"Never taking 'no' for an answer."

I shrug, "Do you like him or something."

Rizz shakes her head, "I don't do boyfriends."

"I didn't ask if you wanted to date him."

"Do you like Nathalie?" she counters.

"I think that answer is obvious."

"She doesn't do hook ups."

"Really?" I ask in fake shock.

"Just don't hurt her, okay?" She snaps at me.

"Scouts honor," I remark, holding up my two fingers.

Rizz stays silent and I direct my attention back to the passing scenery outside the passenger window.

"Lance is stubborn," Rizz says, "and arrogant. He says what he feels and I respect that. But his optimism and need to help annoys me."

I let her statement linger before answering, "Lance thinks he needs to fix everything and help everyone. It's his way of coping."

"Coping with what?"

"Turn here," I point to our street.

Rizz turns onto our drive, and slowly creeps down the street.

I swallow the lump in my throat and answer her question, "His adoptive mom, Ann."

"He was adopted?"

I nod in confirmation, "Maybe you should cut him some slack."

"Why? Is mister perfect not so perfect?"

I point to the driveway where Lance's Ford Escape waits, "he lives there."

Rizz pulls into the driveway and puts her car into park.

My hand pauses on the door handle and I look at Rizz while she unbuckles her seat belt. When her eyes rise to mine I say, "He's never been perfect. He's had a tough life."

Rizz's eye widen slightly. Slowly I pull my gaze away from hers and get out of the car.

Walking up to the garage where Lance is waiting, I stuff my hands into my front pockets. Why did I bring her up, and to Rizz of all people? But Lance trusts her, right? So shouldn't I? I mean it's only a matter of time until he tells her everything. Then she'll tell Nathalie and Nathalie won't even want to look my way again. *Shit*. What the hell is wrong with me?

A hand clamps down on my shoulder. My brow furrows as I look up at Lance's worried look.

"Hey man, what's going on?" Lance asks in a hushed tone.

I give him a weak smile, "Nothing, it's cool."

Lance squeezes my shoulder slightly, "You sure man? You've got this look…"

I glance at the grey cement driveway, shaking my head. I turn away from Lance and look toward Rizz who is now walking up the driveway to us. I force a sly grin and then look back at Lance.

Loud enough so Rizz can hear me I say, "If you were driving with her, you'd be wearing the same look, man."

"Oh, quit being such a baby," Rizz snaps as she reaches us, "It wasn't that bad."

Lance chuckles.

"Let's just say that this girl here has a death wish, and next time I don't want to be a part of it."

"I'm sure there won't be a next time," Rizz mumbles.

Lance gives her a quick look before clearing his throat.

"So, just follow me," he says.

Lance turns toward the garage and walks through the doorway.

Holding my hand out for Rizz to go in front of me, I say, "Soon you'll find that you'll want to come running back here, sweetheart."

Rizz grunts, "don't call me sweetheart."

"Not a problem," I mutter.

I follow Rizz through the hallway and into the kitchen. Peering over her head I spot Pop sitting on a bar stool at the island looking over paperwork in a manila folder. Noticing us, he looks up from the information in front of him and closes the folder as he gets up from the stool and smiles at us.

"And who's this?" Pop asks instantly.

"Hey, Pop," Lance says leaning against the island bar.

I walk up to the island and sit down in the stool Pop has stood from.

"This is Rizz," Lance says, motioning toward her.

Pop extends his hand to Rizz, and she slowly takes his hand in hers.

"It's nice to see a pretty girl around after all this time."

I tense as Rizz's cheeks grow pink.

"Uhm, thanks," She says.

Releasing her hand from his she adds, "It's nice to meet you, mister…"

"You can call me Pop."

Rizz smiles politely, "I don't think I'd be comfortable with that, I mean—"

"Everyone calls him that," I cut her off, a little edge in my voice.

"Really, it's fine," Lance agrees, lifting himself from the bar and eyeing me suspiciously.

Rizz smiles sweetly at Lance and then gives me a pointed stare before directing her attention to Pop, "Like I was saying, I don't feel comfortable with that. I mean after all, I am just meeting you."

I roll my eyes, which earns me another pointed stare from Rizz.

"Fair point," Pop nods in understanding, "Then for you it's Mr. McCartney."

Rizz smiles.

"But feel free to use Pop whenever you're ready," He smiles.

"It's nice to meet you, Sir."

"Likewise."

"Got a new case here, Pop?" I ask motioning to the manila folder sitting in front of me.

Pop's lips form a small smile as he slides the folder out from in front of me and into his hands.

"Yes, nothing serious though. Just some broken bones. Skateboarding accident."

I nod my head.

"Thank goodness neither of you boys ride a skateboard, all my hair would be grey from worrying so much."

"It's getting there," I joke.

"As a matter of fact, I think I see one right...here," Lance says, plucking a hair from Pop's head.

Pop flinches away from Lance and rubs his hand through his hair. Lance and I laugh as we torture the poor man a little bit more. I glance at Rizz and see a smile playing on her lips. Catching Lance looking at her, I turn to Pop to get his attention in order for Lance to have his moment.

"Anyway, you don't have to worry about us, we'll be just fine."

"Yeah," Lance agrees, "You have nothing to worry about."

"Oh, I worry about you boys a lot more these days after everything that happened."

I immediately tense up again, balling my hands into fists on the counter. It always came back to this. No matter how great everything would be going, we always ended back where we started. The accident that changed all of our lives.

Turning my back from everyone, I close my eyes trying to even my breath. *Just take deep breaths Thom, just like the doctor said. In, out, in, out.*

I hear Rizz clear her throat, but I keep my eyes shut and my back to everyone as I sit at the counter trying to calm every last nerve in my body. *Why couldn't I just get past all of this? Oh yeah, because it's my fault.*

"Are you a doctor?" I hear Rizz ask.

"He's one of the best surgeons out there," I grumble, still not looking at anyone.

Deep breaths, Thom, deep breaths.

"They have me working in the E.R. at the moment. The graveyard shifts."

My body trembles as Pop says graveyard.

"I'll take what I can get though. I'm just thankful they took me back at all."

I screw my eyes shut tighter. *Why is he making this so damn hard?*

"They'd be crazy not to, Pop," Lance comforts.

"So what happened?" Rizz asks.

I turn and face Rizz, my breathing still slow. I watch as she looks from Lance and Pop quizzically.

My brows furrow and then her eyes meet mine. I stiffen further at the unwelcoming thoughts of why Pop stopped working for the hospital. How was it that everything connected to that treacherous afternoon? I couldn't catch a break. I was being tortured every single day.

Rizz's stare bores into me like a hot iron and I can't bare it any longer. I look away from all of them as I stand from the chair. Without a word I head down the hallway to the front door.

"Where you going?" Lance calls after me.

I stop walking.

"I just…" my phone vibrates in my pocket and I reach into it, retrieving my phone. Looking at the text, my body finally relaxes. I smile at the screen. Turning to face the three of them, I hold up my phone and shake it in front of them.

"Sorry, man, time to go. My lady will be here soon."

I wink at Rizz and she rolls her eyes at me.

Pop's brows furrow as he looks from me to Rizz.

"He's referring to my friend," Rizz explains.

"Ah," Pop says. Directing his attention to me, "You treat that girl good now you hear me, son?"

"You got it, Pop."

Reaching down, I pull my phone out of my pocket and begin scrolling through my messages.

Without looking up from my phone I say, "I gotta get going, though. She'll be by soon."

"Alright," Lance says running his hand along the island's counter top, "You coming by tomorrow for our morning run?"

I look up from my phone, "I'm not sure yet, I'll text ya later and let you know."

"Alright, man."

I nod at Lance and then at Pop, "See ya later, Pop."

"You be good now, Thom."

"Always am, Pop, later, Rizz. Try not to castrate him, alright."

Rizz's eyes bulge slightly before glaring at me.

"Thom," Pop scolds.

"Sorry, Pop," I laugh as I make my way to the front door, "See you guys later."

Walking out of the garage, I cut across the lawn to my front stoop. After pulling my phone back out of my pocket, I sit down on the step and open up my messages. I open the message from Nathalie that reads that she'll be there in five minutes. Smiling, I pocket my phone.

Leaning back on my hands and staring out into the street, I think about the way Nathalie's red hair cascades around her face and how her piercing blue eyes still my entirety. Thinking about her sing-song voice physically relaxes me and puts my mental state at ease. She is like a drug to me, my own sedative to ease my over rapid mind and my racing insecurities of the accident. She stops the visions of that afternoon from replaying in my head and erases the engraved look of torment and lost that was etched across Lance's face as he fell to his knees; that same look that appears at the worse moments, causing my insides to tear me apart repeatedly. Nathalie makes all of that go away whenever I think of her or stand in her presence. She isn't an angel sent for me, no, she is her own sort of goddess with the power to heal any broken soul.

Headlights beam down our street as a car turns onto the road. The car slows down and signals to turn into my drive. I stand from the stoop as the head lights click off and the driver's side door opens to reveal a red head climbing from the car.

Walking up to her, I wrap my arms around her waist and pull her into me. I breathe in her honey scent as she entwines her arms around my waist, hugging me back.

"Well, that was the best hello I've ever received," She smiles as she pulls away.

Slowly letting go of her I respond, "You ain't seen nothing yet baby."

Placing my finger under her chin I tilt her head up slightly and slowly cascade down meeting her lips with my own. I push against her lips and she opens them welcoming me into her heavenly mouth. Bringing my hand to her cheek, I gently lean her against the side of her car as I close the driver's side door without leaving her lips. Cupping my hand on the back of her head I run my fingers through her soft red curls and deepen the kiss. A smile forms on her lips as she continues to press against my own, pulling away slightly she says,

"I could get used to this."

I chuckle before brushing my lips against hers. Between kisses I reply, "Good, this may happen often."

"Is that so?"

I nod my head and lean down pressing my forehead against hers. Staring at her crystal blue eyes, I open my mouth to speak, but the porch light flicks on distracting me. The front door opens and the tension shoots back up through my body as I look at my mother's small frame standing in the doorway.

Squinting into the darkness my mother asks, "Thom? Who's your friend?"

"Shit," I mumble.

Nathalie looks at me with furrowed brows.

I give her a small smile and take ahold of her hand, "Come on. Let me introduce you to my mom."

Nathalie willingly comes with me wrapping her hands around my bicep holding it in the small valley between her breasts. At the feel of her body against me, the edge begins to evaporate. Stopping at the stoop I wave my hand from Nathalie to my mom and back.

"Mom, this is Nathalie. Nathalie, my mom."

"It's nice to meet you Mrs. Downey."

My mom flinches, but covers it with a small smile, "Oh, honey, why don't you come on inside. Seriously, Thom is just like his father." My mother gives a small laugh, "The stories I could tell you about that man, me, and driveways."

My stomach lurches at the mention of my father. Ignoring the queasy feeling in the pit of my stomach, I place my hand on Nathalie's lower back and lead her through the front door.

"Now, tell me darling, has my boy been treating you right?" My mom asks as we follow her into the kitchen.

"Mom."

Nathalie reaches for my hand and gives it a small squeeze, "He's been a complete gentleman."

"Is that so?" My mother pulls out a chair from the kitchen table and sits down.

Nathalie follows in suit.

Running my hand through my hair, I grab the back of one of the wooden chairs and pull it from the table.

"Oh, sweetie," My mom says, "why don't you cut up some fruit for us to snack on?"

Nodding my head I saunter over to the fridge and pull a cantaloupe from it, placing it on the counter. As I rummage through the cupboards in search of a cutting board, my mother begins to talk again.

"He gets that from his father, you know?" my mother laughs, "That man was the definition of a gentlemen."

My head perks up from under the cabinet next the sink. *What the fuck?*

"Thom always wanted to be just like his Daddy." My mom finds my gaze and smiles. "You should have seen him growing up. He'd put shaving cream on his little face and pretend to be just like his father." Her eyes begin to water, and she looks away from me.

Nathalie giggles, "Did he now? Please go on."

I glance at Nathalie who sneaks a peak at me from the corner of her eyes. A warm smile spreads across her face as my mother continues to tell Nathalie about the time my father pretended to teach me how to shave. I turn my back to them and stiffly rummage through the cupboards.

"He was a good man," My mother says, "He loved Thom so much."

He was? Loved? He still is that good man. He's still fucking here.

Finding the cutting board, I slam it down on the cupboard. My mom and Nathalie jump.

"Sorry," I mutter as I pull out a knife from the drawer.

My mom shakes her head and directs her attention back to Nathalie.

"As I was saying though, I see so much of his father in him. His father was very respectful, but he had his wild side too, if you know what I mean. There wasn't a day that would pass by that I didn't feel loved by that man. Thom is like that too."

"He sounds like a great man," Nathalie says, "Thom was very lucky to have a father like that."

"He still is a great man," I growl into the cantaloupe.

"Oh," Nathalie perks up, "I'm sorry, Thom, I was getting the intention that he was...well...that he passed away."

"I know," I take the knife and stab it into the cantaloupe.

"I'm sorry, honey, that was my fault," my mom pipes up, "His father is still very much alive. He's just...away for the time being."

"Oh," Nathalie says quietly.

Cutting the cantaloupe into small slices, I feel Nathalie's stare on me. I close my eyes and take a deep breath, trying to focus on her blue eyes.

"Thom looks just like him too, you know?"

"He does?"

I grip the knife tighter with my right hand and the cantaloupe with my left.

"Oh yes, my husband was a very handsome man, and respectable. That's what I loved most about him. Not to mention the fact that he could always make me feel like I was the only girl in the world." My mom giggles, "I know that sounds so cliché, but he had that gift, he would just look at me, and I knew, I was the only girl he saw."

"It sounds like you really love him."

"Oh, I did…he was…an extraordinary man."

My body clenches, anger boiling inside of me. I turn to my mother and snap,

"If he's such an extraordinary man then why get the divorce?"

Shocked, "I told you why."

Angrily, I slash the knife through the cantaloupe and accidentally slice my thumb. Numbness begins to rush over me as I close my eyes allowing the pain to fill me, but the numbness quickly subsides to the anger raging inside.

"That's bullshit. You sit here and say all this shit and expect me to believe that that's it. That you just can't do it anymore."

"Language, Thom."

"Is he not respectable enough for you anymore? Is that it?"

"Thomas!"

Pulling my injured hand from the cupboard, I begin speaking with my hands, flailing my injured thumb around, "Are you afraid people are whispering behind your back? That you have this bad reputation now?"

"Thom," my mom whispers.

I walk toward my mom, "That's bullshit. You and I both know it, because no one knows. No one is allowed to know. That's what Pop did for us, in order to protect our reputation."

Nathalie and my mom jump as I slam my injured hand on the table.

"No one fucking knows." I growl.

My mom gasps, "Thom, your hurt."

I pull away as my mom reaches for my hand.

"It's fine."

My mom stands from her seat, "Let me see it, Baby."

My mom steps toward me, but I push her away softly.

Tears well in her eyes, and I look at the ground.

"Excuse me," she whispers.

After she leaves the kitchen, I walk over to the kitchen sink and turn on the water, running it over my wound.

Small hands glide over my shoulders, and my body begins to relax. *Nathalie.* Closing my eyes to hold back the tears forming, I lift my shoulders to shrug her hands from me. Her hands leave my shoulders, only to be replaced on either side of my hands under the running water. I open my eyes to watch her gently massage my open cut.

"You don't have to stay, I'll understand."

Nathalie reaches for the hand soap on the edge of the sink. Squeezing some in her palm she begins to lather it into my open cut.

I hiss at the sting of the soap.

She rinses the cut out, and then reaches for a towel.

As she dabs at my cut she says, "Look at me, Thom."

I pull my eyes to her clear blue gaze.

"I'm not going anywhere. We all have baggage."

I close my eyes and lean my forehead against hers.

"Where's your father, Thom?"

I open my eyes, meeting her warm gaze again.

"He's in jail," I say, the words bitter in my mouth.

Nathalie's eyes widen as she lets out a small gasp.

You've done it now, Thom. Now she'll be gone for good.

Nathalie reaches her hand to my cheek and caresses it as her eyes soften, and then she wraps her arms around my neck and pulls me into her embrace.

"I'm so sorry," she whispers.

Unsure of what to do, I wrap my arms around her waist, allowing her touch to physically relax every muscle in my body. As it works, I hold her tighter.

"Thank you," I whisper hoarsely.

CHAPTER FIFTEEN: RIZZ

I look around Lance's kitchen, taking in the large yet homey room. Empty water glasses line the sink's edge. A half-eaten sandwich sits on a piece of paper towel on top of the island's wooden counter top. *Men.* Papers are scattered across the top of the island, a newspaper lying open to the business section hides beneath them. All reminders of the detachment of my own home and its clinic feel with Clorox wiped down countertops, white cupboards and clear island tops. I grow comfortable taking in the surroundings of this lived in kitchen; so unfamiliar to my own, but comfortable—oddly enough. Oak furnished cupboards line all but one kitchen wall. The far end of the kitchen the wall turns from plaster to brick, opening up into a large wood burning oven.

"Pretty cool, huh?" Lance asks me.

I pull my gaze from the oven, "Yeah."

"My mom always wanted one, made her feel like she was in Italy."

"Was she from there?"

Lance chuckles, "No, but she had an Italian background."

I nod my head in response, unsure whether or not to press on.

"Do you want me to show you around?" Lance asks.

"Lead the way."

Lance takes me from the kitchen into the living room where his father had presumably run off to after Thom had left. He sits leisurely on the couch with the manila folder in his lap. A Mac Book Pro sits on a nearby coffee table, the screen dimming due to the inactivity. Pictures flit across the muted television screen across from where Mr. McCartney is sitting. The pillows on the couch are worn down from being used over the years, and indentations make themselves known on the couch cushions. Pop looks up from his file and gives me a warm smile.

"Showing her around?"

"Yeah," Lance replies, "Just making our way through."

Lance walks through the living room and I follow in sync, smiling at his father as I pass him. Following Lance up the stairway, we hang a left and walk into a room that could be titled as nothing less than a man cave. A large plasma flat screen TV hangs on the far end of the wall. Underneath it, a sleek silver television stand holds the game consoles of a PlayStation 3, Xbox, and a Wii, a DVD player and a plethora of games and movies. Set in front of the big screen are two leather game chairs and a couch. Unlike the other rooms, this one is kept tidy. The chairs look brand new and the controllers are tucked away in the stand. Movie and game cases line the stand neatly.

"Very organized in here," I observe.

"I like to keep things in good condition."

On the opposite side of the room, a dart board hangs from the wall. Next to it a pool cue rack hangs, holding cues, chalk, and the pool ball rack.

"No pool table?" I ask.

"Not yet, it's a new addition."

"Making the ultimate man cave, huh?"

Lance chuckles, "I don't know about man cave, but I do call it the game room."

"I'm pretty sure this," I gesture to the room, "is the definition of a man cave."

Shaking his head, Lance smiles and says, "Come on, I want to show you something."

We head out of the "game room" and down the hallway until we reach a sliding glass door at what I assume to be the back end of the house. I follow Lance as he steps out onto a stone built terrace. A small round table and two bamboo chairs sit to the right, overlooking the balcony's edge. I walk up to the black iron railings wrapping around the terrace and grab hold as I peer over the edge into a crystal clear in-ground pool. Beyond the pool is a flower bed filled with stargazer lilies, tiger lilies, fancy crown lilies and lemon stardust lilies. The yard goes far back and is lined with cherry trees.

"It's beautiful," I gasp.

"This is one of my favorite places," Lance says as he stands next to me overlooking his yard.

Unable to reply, I nod my head.

"I like coming out here to play the guitar—"

"A hidden talent?" I smile.

"I could play something for you."

Turning toward him, "That's okay, I believe you."

"Are you afraid?" He asks arching a brow.

"Of what?"

"Falling for me," he smirks.

"Like that would ever happen."

Of course it would happen. It's happening right now.

"I guess it's for the best actually."

I know he's only teasing, but part of that sticks with me. *He's right, it is for the best. He's just some guy, Rizz. Some really sweet and caring guy with smoldering emerald eyes and tight muscles—snap out of it, Rizz. Gosh, get a grip.*

"You're right," I say more harshly than I intend, "It is for the best." I turn away from him, "What's next?" I ask, heading back into the house.

After closing the sliding glass doors, Lance cuts in front of me shaking his head as he leads the way back down the hall to the stairs and out the back door of his house. Cautiously, I follow behind him as he shimmies with the iron gate surrounding the pool's patio.

"Need some help?" I mutter.

"I got it," Lance snaps.

Whoa, what bit him in the ass?

"Yeah, I can see that."

Lance jiggles the gate one last time before turning on me and saying, "What's your problem?"

Taken back, "I don't have a problem."

"You seriously are the most frustrating female I have ever met."

"Thanks...I think."

Lance groans and shakes his head in annoyance, "Seriously, frustrating."

"I don't know what you want me to say," I reply, "And honestly, I don't even know what we are talking about."

"Just..." Lance rakes his hand through his lengthy black hair, "nevermind...just forget it. Sorry."

I nod my head in agreement, and step around him to attempt opening the gate. My hand brushes against his and he flinches slightly.

"Sorry," I mutter, reaching that same hand up to pull a loose strand of hair behind my ear.

Lance closes his eyes and takes a deep breath before reaching out to re-tuck the strand of hair I failed to keep behind my ear. His hand lingers, and the soft pad of his thumb brushes against my cheek.

"Don't be," Lance whispers.

A shiver runs through me. Leaning into his touch I close my eyes and try to steady my rapid heartbeat. All too soon his touch is gone. I open my eyes to find him staring at me with want, but he holds great restraint as he reaches back around me, and opens the gate to the pool.

"Come on," He whispers, motioning with a jerk of his head to follow him.

"What? Are we going skinny dipping now?"

Lance smiles, "As much as I'd love to do that with you right now, I think it would be safer if we didn't."

"Safer?" I ask, unable to stop myself.

Ignoring me, Lance walks up to the edge of the pool and kicks off his sneakers.

"No socks?" I ask.

"They're restricting."

"That's disgusting. Your feet probably stink."

"Want a sniff?" He smirks as he eases himself down onto the ledge of the pool, submerging his feet into the water.

I scrunch up my face in disgust and say, "No thanks."

"Yeah, didn't think you the kind for a foot fetish," Lance pats the concrete next to him, "join me?"

"If you insist," I smile as I tug off my Chuck Taylors and black socks.

I squat down next to him. Slowly I reach my foot out into the water to test the temperature. I dip my toe into the water and quickly remove it.

Lance laughs, "It's not that bad, I promise. Only the top is cold."

"And I'm supposed to just trust you?"

"Yeah, you are," He says matter-of-factly.

And I do. I sit down and dip my feet into the water, shivering as I pass the cold top layer and get to the slightly warmer under-layer.

"That wasn't so hard, now was it?" He asks, nudging me with his shoulder.

"What wasn't?"

"Trusting someone."

My eyes widen as I begin to feel completely exposed to him. How could he make me feel like he could see right through everything—my whole façade?

"Don't get over excited," I manage.

"I wouldn't dream of it."

I snort as I circle my legs slowly in the water. There is something about the smooth motion of the water against my skin or the fresh smell of chlorine that just relaxes me. But neither of those is helping the knotted feeling in my stomach as I look from the corner of my eye at Lance's thigh only inches from my own.

Trying to ease the knots in my stomach, I lean back onto my palms and say, "So, why do you like it out here so much?"

Mimicking me, Lance leans back too. Flipping his hair from his face he says, "It's a great place to get away."

"I think you need a haircut," I laugh.

"You don't like it?"

"Oh, no, you definitely have that long-haired hot mysterious look going for you, but I'm concerned your neck will get a spasm if you keep doing that."

"You're probably right," he laughs, "Then I'd have to turn my whole body to steal glimpses of you in the pool light."

I open my mouth to say something back but falter when I catch his gaze. He's studying me intently. My mouth goes dry, and I force myself to keep his gaze. *Don't start being a girl now, Rizz.*

Breaking away, I ask, "What do you possibly have to get away from?"

"I have plenty."

"It doesn't seem like that. I mean look around, your house is amazing."

"Thanks."

"Don't tell me you don't think so?"

"Not everything is how it seems to be all the time."

"Right, you've had a hard life."

Lance narrows his eyes at me.

"I didn't mean that anyway," I quickly say, "Thom had mentioned it in the car on our way over…sorry…"

"Did he now?" Lance smirks.

I bet he just loves seeing me squirm. Damn it, why am I acting like this? Oh yeah, that's right, because he keeps looking at you like he wants to rip your clothes off and you damn well want him to.

Lance's eyes light up with humor, "What else did he mention?"

"He said you were adopted."

Lance nods his head, "That's right."

"He also mentioned a woman named Ann…I think."

I watch as Lance grows rigid. Sitting up straight he runs a hand through his hair. My brows scrunch together as I study him.

He clears his throat and says, "He did, did he?"

"Yeah…" I reply hesitantly as I watch his jaw lock up, "he said she was your adoptive mom."

Lance nods his head slowly, "She was. I was in and out of foster homes when I was young…" he clears his throat, "Pop and Ann adopted me when I was about six or seven."

"Well…where is she?"

Lance swallows staring blankly into the pool water. He grows distant as he doesn't answer, but I want answers. I want to know him, so I reach up and place my hand on his shoulder,

"Lance?"

He snaps his head towards me and the sorrow etched on his face rips the knots from my stomach leaving a hollow feeling. *I know that look.*

"What happened to her?" I ask, knowingly.

Clearing his throat, "She…uhm…she was involved in an accident a couple years ago."

I brace myself, waiting for the words to leave his lips.

"She was in a coma for six months, but couldn't make it out of it. So, we...uh…we had to…Pop had to…" Lance clears his throat again, "she passed away."

Gently, I ask, "What sort of accident."

"She was struck by a car."

"Lance," I exclaim as I scoot closer, "that's terrible, I'm so sorry."

"Trust me, enough people are sorry about it, you don't need to be too." He says, growing bitter.

"Right." I say, starting to scoot back into safe territory.

Lance reaches out and stops me by putting his hand on my thigh. My whole leg tingles as the warmth of his palm seeps through my jeans.

"Sorry," he says, "I didn't mean it like that."

I nod my head and settle back down next to him. I look down at his remaining hand on my thigh. He makes no move to retreat it. This causes me to smile at my lap, but my smile fades as he asks,

"What happened to you earlier?"

I lift my weighed down thigh slightly, and he removes his hand from it. This was why I didn't get close to people, because they wanted to know things about you too. I'm not sure if I'd ever be willing to tell Lance everything or anything at all. I like him, every hormone in my body was pointing to that, but enough to share my deepest secrets? Enough to show him how fucked up my life truly is. No, I wasn't ready for that. I'd never be ready for that. I had to end this, and I had to end it now.

I look up at Lance to find him staring expectantly at me. His sea green eyes bore into me, and for once, I feel safe. My breath hitches in my throat, and I find myself unable to speak. *I'm gawking, holy crap, I'm gawking at him.*

"Rizz?" he asks gently, as he palms the side of my face with his hand. Closing my eyes as he brushes his thumb along my cheekbone, I hear him whisper, "What happened?"

Slowly, I open my eyes and meet his gaze, "I got in a fight with my mother."

"Ah, Hitler?"

I smile and laugh to myself as I remember the night of Nathalie's party, "Yes, Hitler."

"Why Hitler?"

I look away, but Lance drags my face back towards his. I stare at him and say, "Because she's a terrible person."

Choosing not to ask me to elaborate, Lance asks, "What did you two fight about?"

"The question is more like what didn't we fight about."

"You two fight often?"

"More like every time she lays eyes on me."

"I'm sorry."

"Don't be, I'm not. Not when that's all you've ever known." I look at the ripples in the pool water as I drag my legs through it, "One time I thought everything was going to get better." I still my legs and look up at Lance, "I was wrong." *God was I wrong.*

"Was that what your fight was about?"

"Sort of," I shrug, "Someone who…there used to be someone who I thought would turn everything around for us, but they were taken from us. My mother…" I scoff, "blames me."

Lance stares silently at me.

"I was wrong anyway," I add quietly, "About things getting better." I think about Hope how everything I went through she is beginning to go through. *God, how could I think Luke would be able to save us, to put the broken pieces back together?* It was impossible to put something that shattered back together when you didn't or couldn't even understand what shattered it in the first place.

"We knew the driver…" Lance says suddenly, "he was a friend of the family—Pop's best friend actually."

My heart falls as I sit staring at Lance with my mouth open.

"He ran a red light—he was distracted by a passenger," Lance's eyes fill with tears as he continues on, "I want to hate him...to be pissed off..."

"To stop pretending everything is all right," I whisper.

Lance's red stained eyes look at me, "exactly."

"Why can't you?" I ask, directing my attention back to the water.

"It's complicated," He mutters.

"Trust me, I know complicated."

Lance places his finger under my chin and gently turns my head to face him.

"Sometimes," he says, "complicated can be intriguing."

"And sometimes," I reply, "it can be a burden."

Lance drops his hand in his lap and clears his throat.

Recoiling into myself I drift to thoughts of Luke. I begin to remember wondering why I never saw my mother that often while she was pregnant. For long hours of the day she would be locked away in her bedroom. I envied all the little girls on TV shows whose mothers adored them and let them rub their little hands over their baby bumps. How I just longed to feel the life inside of my own mother, but every time my mother would shoo me away with hateful comments. When she became pregnant with Hope, I didn't even bother to try. All I thought was maybe if I didn't show my love for her like I had with Luke then my mother wouldn't have shortened her life like she had with him.

"What happened?" Lance asks, pulling me from my thoughts, "to the person you thought would make things better?"

Beginning to stir my feet in the water again, I manage, "He...uhm..." I clear my throat, "He left us," I lie slightly, unable to let Lance see that far into me this soon.

Lance nods his head, "I know the feeling."

I jolt my head up to look at him, nervous that he saw through my half-truth, but he shows nothing but understanding for me. Suddenly I remember that he was abandoned when he was young and lived in and out of foster homes before finding his father and Ann.

"Do you know where they are?" I ask, referring to his birth parents.

Lance sighs, "My mother's dead," Lance snorts, "and my father? He's some rehabbed junkie who wants to make amends…like that's going to happen."

I reach over and clasp my hand on his, "Don't say that."

Lance turns his hand in mine and holds it firmly.

Ignoring the shivers that surge through my body, I add, "When someone you are genetically programmed to love leaves you, you find yourself wishing you could have at least tried to have known them no matter how terrible they may turn out."

I look down at our intertwined hands and whisper, "The regret gets to you."

Lance leans forward, tipping my chin up.

Dragging my eyelashes up, I inspect his chiseled jaw and strong check bones until my eyes are level with his.

Starring at me, Lance cups my cheek in his palm, "Rizz," he whispers leaning in closer.

My entire body stills as he inches closer, closing the gap between the two of us. The tip of his nose brushes against mine, and he stops his slow procession.

I stare at him in anticipation.

"What is your real name?" he asks.

I'm taken back for a moment by the unexpected question. I bite my lip.

Sliding his hand from my cheek to my chin, Lance runs the pad of his thumb along my bottom lip. His eyes flicker from my eyes to my lip and back to my eyes. Gently, he tugs on my bottom lip causing me to release it.

"Please," he whispers, "don't bite your lip."

"Why?" I breathe.

"Because, it makes me want to devour you right here and right now."

I gasp breathlessly at his honesty. Composing myself, I smirk, getting ready to hit him with one of my snide remarks.

Yeah having him want to devour you makes you start acting like yourself again is that it? But I thought we wanted that. We wanted to taste every inch of his maculate body.

"But first," he says, interrupting my lust, "I'd really like to know you're real name."

My smirk fades, and I know that this is it. That by telling him my name, all my walls will begin tumbling down. But looking into his eyes at his want for not only me, but for me to trust him and allow him to understand, I fold. The walls began falling the moment I slipped my hand into his the night of Nathalie's party. I was his then, before the realization even hit. That's why the next thing to come out of my mouth was,

"Laura."

Searching my eyes, Lance asks, "Why do you have everyone call you Rizz?"

"Because, I hate my mother's name," I respond, holding his gaze.

The moment the words leave my lips, I scold myself. I know what is coming next. The same question I avoided with Hope. *Why do you hate your mother so much?* It wasn't something I was ready to elaborate on, but that was the thing with Lance. He made it so easy; one look into his understanding eyes and I was putty in his hands. It didn't help that he had secrets of his own, or the fact my hormones went on a rampage every time we were near each other and then rabid every time we touched. This though, I couldn't, not now. I wasn't ready to tell my earth shattering secrets to someone I had just met—to someone who could easily take those shattered pieces and turn them to dust, leaving me to sweep the tiny particles up with nothing but my own hands.

Lance tucks a strand of hair behind my ear and leans in, his lips lightly brushing against mine before pulling back to hover millimeters from my own.

"I hate it too," Lance says, surprising me and closing the gap between us.

His lips softly push against mine, until I give in, opening to his curious tongue. I let him explore my mouth as I do his, savoring the warmth of his sweet taste mixed with my own. Leaning in closer to him and reaching my hand to the back of his head I tug on his too long hair, and push out all the thoughts of the last few hours. As he deepens each kiss, I begin to shove out memories of the past years. All that is real to me is this moment. This is my reality, my safety.

Slowly Lance leans backward, bringing me with him so I am lying on top of him. His fingers brush lightly up my arm and along my shoulder. As they dance over my collar bone, my stomach flutters in anticipation. I tighten my grip in his hair and pull softly causing him to let out a low groan. Swiftly, he rolls me over so he is now on top, pressing his length against my hip. The blood races to my rapidly pounding chest as I pull him closer, devouring his mouth with my own. I close my eyes letting the feel of him take over—the smoothness of his hands against my skin, his warm breath mixing with my own, and the soft yet firm feel of his lips against mine. I'm all but lost in his lingering syrupy smell when the slam of a door jolts us apart breaking the spell and allowing the bad memories to roll back in like storm clouds on a hot summer's night.

Lance pulls away, looking up at the house. I sit up, brushing my hair from my face as I catch a glimpse of a light on the second floor turn on. I look out across the pool and notice the sun setting behind the line of cherry trees.

Shit.

Quickly getting to my feet, I begin to pull my socks back on. Lance stands next to me, confusion etched across his face.

"Sorry," I say pulling on one of my converses, "I gotta go."

Lance runs his hand up the back of his neck and through his hair exposing his muscular biceps. His shirt rides up allowing me to catch a glimpse of his happy trail, and my thoughts wander to the realization of the happiness that trail leads to. I turn away from him as my cheeks grow hot by the memory.

"Let me walk you out," He sighs.

"Okay," I agree pulling on my other shoe.

Lance leads me from the pool to a stone pathway that wraps around the house. Following it, we reach a tall wooden gate which Lance pushes open to the driveway.

I pull my keys from my jeans' pocket and press the door lock button causing my car's lights to flash as the locks pop open. Walking to the driver's side, I play with the keys in my hand.

"I guess I'll see ya around?" I ask.

"Yeah," Lance smiles, "here, let me get your number."

I pull my phone from my back pocket, and hand it to him, "just put your number in, and I'll text you," I smile at him.

Taking my phone from me, he begins typing in his information. Once he's done he hands the phone back to me. As I'm about to hit the button to start a new message, my phone pings. Opening the text I read the message from John, "Pick up at the station in five."

I click off of the message and open my car door, "I'll text you," I tell Lance as I climb into my car.

As I go to close my door Lance catches it. Dipping down into the car his mouth meets mine again. This time his kiss isn't devouring. He kisses me tenderly, sending me a silent promise. When he pulls away from me, he gives me a sexy smile and closes my car door.

I stare at him through my windshield as he waves goodbye. I give him a small wave before putting my car into reverse and backing out of the drive.

Holy crap, what was that. In no more than an hour I had let Lance in more than I had anyone in my life. I told him things my own sister never knew. Strangely enough, it was like he saw right through my half answers—like he knew there was more to what was being said. But he never pushed. He let me share when I was ready and he let me be in control—something I so desperately need. But I'm not in control. I opened up to him because of the way he looked at me. The way his eyes penetrated into the deepest corners of my soul. And I lost all forms of control when his lips pressed against mine devouring me and opening me—leaving me standing there raw and naked to his perception.

As I pull up alongside John's parked car at the gas station, my nerve endings stand at attention. *I need a fix now more than ever.*

John walks out of the convenience store and I roll down my window for him. Leaning against the door, John peers in at me.

"Damn, Rizz," he says, "you look like hell."

I roll my eyes as I dig through my glove compartment. "Thanks," I mutter as I hand him a ten.

"What's going on?" he asks.

Holding out my hand, I let out a breath of annoyance, "will you just give me the stuff?"

"Whoa, chill," he says, dropping the baggy in my upturned palm.

I close my hand around it and pocket it. Feeling the baggy in my jeans I begin to relax.

"You look like you need it."

"It's been a long day."

John smiles, "Well that stuff will turn your night around."

"Good," I say as I start my car to back up, "I'll see you around."

"Sure thing," John says, tapping the side of car before strolling around to his.

I pull out of the parking lot and back onto the streets. Unsure of where to go, I pull into the parking lot of the Super market. Finding a parking spot, I put my car in park and pull out a half used pack of Zig Zag cigarillo wraps. Pulling out my baggy, I set to work breaking apart the leaves from the stem and picking out the seeds. *One of these days I'm going to invest in a grinder.* Finished, I sprinkle the leaves into the wrap evenly, and begin rolling the blunt. After sealing the blunt, I light the end and take a hit, allowing the herb to settle in my chest. As I exhale, the edge begins to slip away and I lean back in my seat allowing myself to drift off with each hit.

CHAPTER SIXTEEN: THOM

I pick at the cuticles of my fingers as I lean back into the green leather couch. A Persian rug lies beneath my bouncing feet. Across from me sitting in one of those large new age leather swivel chairs is my therapist, Dr. Connors, scribbling notes onto the pad in his lap. His pen, stuck between his fingers, suddenly stops flicking across the paper and he looks up at me.

"How have you been feeling, Thom?" he asks.

"Just dandy," I mutter, slumping back into the couch cushions.

"Now, Thom, I have told you several times before, it's important to express how you are feeling."

"What's the point?" I scoff.

"It helps to give me a better understanding what is going on and how I can continue to guide you through this difficult time," he gestures to me, "Now, how have you been feeling?"

I sigh deeply, folding my arms over my chest. Dr. Connors begins jotting notes into his notepad.

Rolling my eyes, "I've been feeling fine, I guess."

"You guess?"

I clear my throat as I readjust my seat on the couch. I lay my arm along the back of the couch. Looking from my lap to his gaze, I shrug my shoulders, "I've felt fine."

"And how have things at home been going?"

"Fine."

"What is fine to you?"

I shrug my shoulders and look to the clock on the wall.

"You'll have to help me out here, Thom. You won't get anything from these sessions if you aren't honest with me."

I run my fingers along the bridge of my nose before looking at my therapist again.

"They've been shitty, okay? Is that what you wanted to hear?"

"How have things been 'shitty'?"

"My mom's leaving us."

"Us?"

"She's getting a divorce."

My therapist nods his head in understanding, "And how is she leaving you?"

"She's selling the house when I go away to college."

"How does that make you feel?"

I look up at him in angered shock, "How do you think it makes me feel?"

"It's not my job to think for you, Thom. Please, how does this information make you feel?"

"It makes me mad," I say jumping to my feet.

"Thom, please sit down."

Running my hands through my hair, I take a steady breath and sit back down.

"I don't understand," I say into my hands.

Crossing his legs, "What don't you understand?"

"Why she would do all this. I mean I know why this is all happening, but not why she is doing it."

"We all have our own ways of coping with situations. Some of us take avenues that allow us to face our demons, some put the blame on themselves until it gets too overbearing and others run away from their demons allowing them to dictate their lives."

I stay silent as my therapist continues on.

"You have to understand, Thom. Your mother and you are both coping in your own ways. What did you do when you found out she was filing for a divorce?"

"I kept it to myself."

"Why?"

"I don't know."

He nods his head, "and what about when you found out she was selling the house?"

"I yelled at her."

"What caused you to yell at her this time?"

"I was already pissed off—she walked into the room when I found the papers—I just snapped."

"What did she tell you?"

"That she couldn't do it anymore, that she was sorry."

"And how did that make you feel?"

I squirm in my seat as his gaze falls on me, penetrating me, "I felt like it was my fault."

"Why did you feel like that?"

"Because it's the truth, this whole fucking mess is my fault."

"Deep breaths, Thom," He reminds me, "It's important that you express yourself without getting worked up."

I run my hands down my thighs as I even out my breathing. I look up to see my therapist watching me intently.

"After you fought with your mother, what did you do?"

"I went to my room—I was trying the breathing techniques you gave me."

"How did the exercise work?"

I look away.

"How did you get those bandages?" he asks referring to the bandages that cover my right arm and left thumb.

"Out of a first aid kit," I mutter.

"What do you plan on getting from our meetings, Thom?"

"I don't know, closure, I guess."

"In order to get that closure, you have to work with me."

I nod my head.

"So, how did you get those bandages?"

I point to my hand, "I punched my mirror while trying those breathing exercises." I then point to my thumb, "I was cutting up a cantaloupe while my mother was comparing me to my father."

I continue to stare at the Persian rug beneath my feet. Dr. Connors' voice reaches me, "And how did it feel?"

"It hurt…at first…at first it hurt," I begin to meet his gaze, "and then I—I felt calm."

"Have you ever purposely cut yourself, Thom."

"What? No," I yell as I jump to my feet.

"Thom, please sit down. It's my job to get all of the truth."

"Why would I ever purposely hurt myself?" I continue to yell, standing in front of Dr. Connors. I begin racing my hand through my hair repeatedly.

"Thom," he begins, but his words fade out as I begin focusing on my rapid breathing.

It's okay, Thom. Just breathe. In, out, in, out.

I struggle to steady my breathing. *In, out, in, out.*

I begin pacing in front of Dr. Connors as I try to get my emotions under control. His mouth is moving but nothing forms into words. I don't hear him, I can't. I'm on my own. His voice is gone; unable to coach me through the episode I am experiencing.

I have to do something. Focus, Thom. Get yourself under control.

I lean my forehead against the wall and slam my open palm against the wall. The memories of those two nights flood into my mind and take over my vision.

Just fucking breathe and get yourself under control, Thom.

But I can't. The sight of me in the mirror scowling back at me takes over. *This is your fault.*

The wind gets knocked out of me and I struggle to catch my breath. Suddenly my mother sitting at the kitchen table penetrates my sight and her words ring through my eardrums, *my husband was a very handsome man; respectable; what I loved most about him; I was the only girl he saw; he was an extraordinary man.* I close my hand into a fist and pound it against the wall as I fight to keep the tears at bay and my breathing under control.

"Think of something...happy," Dr. Connors' voice breaks through.

I try. But the memories are strong. The smashing of my fist against the mirror; the quick slice of my thumb; the blood; the broken glass; my broken soul, but then I see it; her smile, her piercing blue eyes and her long full curly red hair cascading down her shoulders. I feel the warmth of her hands around mine, and as her words begin to drift through me, my breathing begins to even. *Everyone has baggage.* My fist unclenches and I back away from the wall. *I'm not going anywhere.* Slowly, I stumble back but catch myself. Turning, I look at Dr. Connors who is smiling at me. I nod my head as a small smile forms on my lips.

"Very good, Thom," he points to the couch, "Take a seat."

I do as he says and sink back into the couch completely relaxed.

"What pulled you back?"

"More like who."

Dr. Connors raises his eyebrows as he waves his hand in front of him for me to go on.

"Her name is Nathalie."

"Is she someone of significance to you?"

"She's…" I pause, unsure of what to say. We had never made anything official.

"She must be pretty significant to you if she can pull you back to yourself."

"She is."

"I'd like to meet her."

My head snaps to his, "What?"

"It will prove quite useful to meet with the both of you here."

"Why?"

"She obviously has quite the impact on you, Thom. It would be beneficial for you to bring her here, especially if you plan to start a relationship with her."

"But—"

"She has caused great progress for you in a short amount of time. Look how relaxed you are— the most I've seen you since you walked into my office two years ago."

I nod my head.

Dr. Connors looks at his wrist watch, "Our time is up for today, but before you go let me leave you with this."

I nod for him to go on.

"The breathing exercises are obviously not working as well as they have been. This may be because you are facing more challenges than you were after the accident." Dr. Connors crosses his legs, "Whenever you feel like you are losing yourself or like you want to hurt yourself, I would like you to try to focus in on Nathalie. She seems to be your center. Focusing on her brings you back to yourself. So for now, we will use her as your anchor."

"What if it stops working?"

"Then we will consider other avenues, but for now it seems to be working immensely."

I stand from the couch, "Okay."

Dr. Connors stands and heads for the door, opening it, "And remember, Thom, I would like you to bring her to your next session. She is obviously of importance to you. Don't keep secrets from her if you plan to keep her."

"I'll talk to her," I say, walking past him out into the waiting room.

"I will see you next week."

I walk out of the office onto the sidewalk. A gust of wind hits me, and I pull my jacket closer around me to block the slight chill of the wind. Walking down the street past shops, I think of how I will tell Nathalie about my therapy sessions without telling her everything.

I wish I could, but I can't. Pop made it that way. We all had to stay tight lipped about the accident in order to protect all of us. I know Pop was only thinking about my mother and me, but keeping this secret—hiding the most important piece of information from not only strangers, but each other is the worse punishment I could endure.

It is eating me alive—holding this secret. Every day it weighs me down with guilt and regret, and I can share that with no one but myself and Dr. Connors. So how, how could tell Nathalie about my sessions without telling her the whole truth? It was impossible, and she would see right through me.

What if I did tell her everything? Would Pop turn around and make everything public? Surely he wouldn't do that? What if I told Nathalie everything? Would she look at me the same knowing the truth about my father—about me?

My phone goes off in my pocket. I retrieve it and look at the screen.

Lance.

Unwilling to deal with him at the moment, I hit the ignore button and pocket my phone. I have one thing to do right now. I have to tell Nathalie as much as I can.

CHAPTER SEVENTEEN: LANCE

Walking into the kitchen I pull open a cabinet, taking a glass from the shelf and begin filling it with water. As I take a long sip, I think back to the feel of Rizz's lips on mine, the smooth feel of her skin against my own, and the small tremble of her body as she slowly began to let herself go.

Her guard was slowly coming down. I could feel it in her kiss. I allowed her to come out of hiding to be able to breathe the air that the world was sharing. As she leaned into me her body relaxed as if she was finally letting go. But as her mouth glided against mine it felt almost as if I was the oxygen she needed to grow stronger.

Slowly, she was pulling me closer and allowing me to pull down the walls she threw up at every corner. It was only a matter of time before her secrets began spilling out of her, allowing her to crumble and for me to be there to catch her as her tired limp body gives out. And I would be. I would be there to hold her and to be the oxygen she needs to begin over. To grow strong again—leaving her past where it belongs—behind her.

I take another sip of water before pouring the rest down the drain and setting the glass along the side of the sink. Exiting the kitchen, I turn off the lights and head upstairs. I pause outside of Pop's closed bedroom door.

The regret gets to you.

Looking at the bare door, I let Rizz's words continue to fill me. *You find yourself wishing you could have at least tried.*

I rap on the door. After a moment, Pop opens the door in pajama pants and a white tee-shirt.

Shocked to see me so late he asks, "Lance?"

"Hey, Pop."

"What's wrong?"

"I…uhm….I just wanted to let you know I'll meet with Jack."

Pop's hand falls from the door knob, "Are you sure?"

I clear my throat and nod my head, "Yeah, I owe it to myself to know who he is."

"Okay, I'll make the call tomorrow."

I nod and turn toward the direction of my room. I walk a few steps and stop, turning back toward Pop.

Meeting with Jack means opening closed doors of my past. Some of which I may find were better left shut. But most of all meeting with Jack means allowing him to be some sort of father at some point of my life.

I look at Pop, tears forming, "He may be my father, but you'll always be my Pop."

"Come here, boy," Pop says, reaching for me.

I walk to him and allow him to take me in his arms like he had when I was a child.

"I'm not worried. You deserve the answers to the questions you've been asking all your life."

I pat Pop's back and give him a squeeze before stepping back.

"Lance, look at me," Pop says.

I look up at Pop through glossy eyes.

"You don't have to be the strong one all the time. You're eighteen years old, allow yourself to cope—to feel—to hurt. It's not your responsibility to take care of everyone else."

"I know."

Pop wraps his arm around the back of my neck and pulls me back into him, "Take care of you first, son."

"I'm trying."

"I know, and this is a good first step."

I pull away from Pop, and nod my head in agreement.

"You go get some sleep now. We'll talk more in the morning."

I nod and head down the hall to my room. Pulling off my shirt and throwing it into the laundry basket sitting in the corner of the room I allow myself to think of all the scenarios that could happen during my visit with Jack. *My biological father.* What if I don't like him? Or worse, what if he doesn't like me? But what if we both get along? Where does that leave Pop?

I pull back the covers on my queen sized bed and crawl in, settling myself under the covers.

It wasn't that long ago Jack came back for me before. *You're my kid.* The anger etched across Pop's face when he saw Jack then was evident, but maybe this time would be different. After all, Jack

was doped up back then. *What if he relapses?* All
this meeting and getting to know each other would
be for nothing. He'd be gone again. *What if...what
if...what if...*

Getting up, I pull on a pair of basketball shorts
and a plain grey t-shirt. After tying my Nike shocks,
I pick up my phone from my nightstand table and
dial Thom's number. The line rings a few times
before being directed to his voicemail.

He must not want to come.

I pocket my phone and grab my headphones
from the desk on my way out of the room.

A rush of cool air hits me as I emerge from the
garage. I place an ear bud in each of my ears and
press a button on my iPhone allowing Imagine
Dragons to fill my eardrums. I walk down the drive
way and pick up my pace as I turn onto the street.

Two days.

In two days I'd be meeting my biological father.
I would be sitting down with him, and talking to my
actual father; my own flesh and blood; the man who
left me on a stoop for someone else to find and take
care of.

I push myself forward harder as the drums of 'Radioactive' pound on.

How could someone leave their own child like that?

I run faster as I turn off onto the main road toward the cemetery.

In less than forty-eight hours, I would be sitting face to face with the man I never got to know, the man who never saw me grow up, who never taught me how to throw a curve ball, or give me the "talk" about girls, the man who I never got the chance to call father.

The song changes to a slow ballad, and I begin to slow down as I turn into the entrance of the cemetery.

Maybe he left me, because he knew I deserved better? Maybe he didn't want to give me up, but he had to. He had to in order to give me a chance.

Yeah, right, pull your shit together, Lance. Either way, he left you.

I pull my iPhone out and skip over the slow ballad to an upbeat song. My feet pound against the concrete in sync with the rhythm. I round the bend. Sweat beads down the side of my face as I breathe in through my nose and out through my mouth.

He left me, but he's back now, and he can give me answers.

I jog further down the path, weaving around patches of gravestones. In the distance I can see the large Oak tree—the half-way point. A smile breaks out across my face and I pick up my pace, eager to reach my check point. As I grow closer, a figure catches my eye. I squint into the distance trying to make it out. The figure comes into view the closer I get, and as comprehension sets in I begin to slow down my pace.

I slow to a walk as I reach the tree. Walking off the path and into the grass I quietly make my way to her, trying not to startle her. She is staring off into the distance and I can tell she isn't here. She's somewhere else. Tears roll down her cheeks and suddenly I feel awkward being here. As if I am spying on her. Unwilling to turn around and leave, I reach out for her, softly calling her name.

CHAPTER EIGHTEEN: RIZZ

I stare at the gravestone, reading the inscription: *Luke James Murphy, May 5, 2004 to May 6, 2004, beloved son and brother.* I stare off into the distance remembering the day the truth came out, the day realization of how much of a monster my mother truly was hit me like an avalanche.

***

I walk into my mother's room to find her lying on the bed. I crawl on top and lay down next to her. She rolls over and her icy eyes meet mine. I smile at her, unaware of the cold way she looks at me.

"Can I feel him?" I ask.

My mother grimaces, "You'll give him some sort of disease."

"I can wash my hands, please, Mommy. I want to feel him kick."

"Washing your hands won't help. You are filled with disease, you disgusting stupid girl."

Tears fill my eyes, and my mother pushes me from the bed.

As I fall to the ground my mother mutters, "You're pathetic."

I get to my feet and watch as my mother opens a pill bottle. Pouring a handful of pills down her throat and washing them down with a glass of a clear liquid, she leans back onto the bed.

"You'll never get to touch him if I have anything to say about it."

The vision fades out, and I am sitting in the hospital waiting room. Chip walks through two large white doors, his eyes rimmed red and his chin speckled with scruffy grey and black hairs. When he reaches me, he kneels in front of me and envelopes me in his arms. My body sinks against his as grief and fear flows over me.

He pulls away and looks at me. His eyes filled with unshed tears. He speaks, words forming into unfamiliar sentences. As I slowly piece the words together tears escape me and stream down my cheeks. I am Chip's undoing, as his tears follow in suit.

A few days later I am watching my mother silently from the door way. I watch as my mother stares impassively at the fire mantel, her face stained with dried tears. Tears stream down my own face as the truth of what happened sets in. *She did this. She killed him.* A cigarette hangs from between my mother's fingers, and she brings it to her lips breathing in a long drag. As she exhales, her body heaves up with new tears. I run to her side to comfort her. Putting my hand on top of her own, I rub it softly and say, "it's okay, Mommy."

Her body stills and she glares at my hand as if my touch disgusts her. She pulls her hand from underneath mine and sets it in her lap.

"Mamma?" I ask.

Glaring, she meets my eyes, "This is your entire fault."

"But, Mama—"

Reaching up, she grabs the side of my face holding it still. With her other hand she brings the cigarette and shoves it into my left temple. I scream out in pain as my mother twists the stick into my skin deeper and deeper.

"You stupid, stupid girl," My mother sneers as I try to wriggle free from her but her grip remains strong. "This is all your fault."

Finally she releases me and I fall to the ground, clutching the side of my face as the tears stream down my cheeks.

I look up to see my mother relight her cigarette and take a long drag as if nothing had happened. Getting to my feet, I run from the room, knowing if I stayed the only thing I would receive would be more burns to my already scared skin. But she follows me. She grabs me by the hair and pulls me back into the room. I scream for my father, but it is no use. He isn't home. It's only me and her.

My mother throws me to the ground, "Where do you think you're going?" she sneers.

I let my tears break out into sobs, not caring what she will do to punish me for crying.

"What did I tell you about crying? It's pathetic."

My mother kneels down and pulls my shirt up above my head. I squirm under her trying to get away, but she is quick and the cigarette digs into my skin. I curl up as I let out a scream.

"Stop it, Mommy, stop it."

She pulls the cigarette from my skin only to thrust it into a new area.

I cry out again.

Pulling the cigarette from me my mother takes a drag shifting her weight to the side. I take the chance to pull my shirt back down and move from under her.

"You stupid girl," my mother yells, as she reaches for me with the cigarette.

I slap her hand causing the cigarette to fall to the ground. As my mother looks to the ground with shock where the cigarette had fallen, I quickly get to my feet.

"Please stop, Mommy."

My mother turns her glare on me. She pulls back her hand and smacks me across the face. I fall to the ground again, but quickly scramble to my feet to keep her from getting back on top of me.

My mother lunges at me, but I duck under her and run pass her out of the room. Hurriedly, I run up the stairs to my room. I hear my mother's footsteps behind me, and dare not look back.

Running into my room I slam the door behind me and lock it, but I don't stop. As the knob begins to jiggle violently, I run to the side of my dresser and push on it, urging it to move. It's heavy, but I don't give up. I take the socks off of my feet so I can get a better grip on the floor, and push hard on the dresser until slowly it begins to move. Finally I am able to get it in front of the door. A loud bang hits the door and I jump back, frightened.

The pounding continues and I slowly back into the corner on the opposite side of the room. I sink to the floor, pulling my legs into my chest. I stare at the barricaded door and begin to sob uncontrollably as the pounding finally fades out and I can't hear anything but my rapid breathing.

***

Tears slide down my face as I remember the night I finally fought back. She probably would have had killed me that night—she was out for blood, and I was at the top of her list. She was a monster then, she still is. But I never understood, even now, what I had ever done for her to be filled with so much hate for me.

What did I ever do to her? Why does she hate me?

The tears flow quicker down my face as I ponder all the unanswered questions. Suddenly, I feel the soft touch of skin on my elbow and hear a soft voice saying my name.

I jump back and face my intruder to find Lance standing behind me with a sweat stained grey t-shirt and basketball shorts. Ear buds hang from his ears—one ear free of a bud.

"Lance?" I ask, "What are you doing here?"

"I come here to jog." His brows furrow, "Are you okay?"

I wipe at my face as I nod, "Yeah. I…uhm…"

Lance looks down at the gravestone in front of me, "Did you know him?"

I let out a snorting laugh, "You could say that."

"Who is he?" Lance asks, as he reaches my side.

I kneel down on the ground and gently rub my hand along the gravestone. A small smile pulls at my lips, "He was my brother."

Lance kneels down next to me, "He's the one, isn't he?"

I look at him and his eyes search mine.

"The one who left you."

I nod, "He didn't even live longer than an hour."

"What happened?"

"My mother."

Lance stays quiet as I try to maintain my temper. I think back to all the times I had tried to feel my baby brother's kick, and how my mother would push me away. I showed her that I loved him before he was even born and she did the one thing she could do to take him away from me—to ruin any happiness I could have.

Suddenly it all made sense. *You'll never get to touch him, if I have anything to do with it.* Her words like knives to my already bleeding heart. All the nights she spent locked away in her room, getting high off of pills or drunk until she felt numb.

"She did this, all because I loved him."

"What?"

"She killed him, because of me," I whisper, "It is my fault."

I feel my body begin to crumble slowly, but before I hit the ground strong arms reach out to catch me. Lance pulls me to him so I am sitting my back to his front.

"Rizz, what are you talking about?"

"I showed her that I loved him, and she took him from me."

Lance's grip tightens around me. He lays his head against mine as I continue,

"I signed his death sentence without even realizing it. She took him from me, because she hated me that much. I killed my brother."

Lance takes in a sharp breath, "No, you didn't."

"But I did."

"No, you're mother's actions were her own, her reasons may have been screwed up, but they were hers."

"When she got pregnant with Hope, I didn't bother her, I didn't show her how happy I was or how excited I was to be a sister again. I saved her— I could have saved him too."

"You can't put the blame on yourself. Whatever happened is all on your mother, not on you. You couldn't have done anything."

"I never got to know him, Lance." I tilt my head to look at him, "I didn't even get to see him. It's like he never existed."

Lance wraps his arms around me tighter, hugging me, "I'm so sorry." He kisses the top of my head, "I'm so sorry you had to go through that."

I nuzzle my head into his chest. We lie there for some time, before the storm clouds roll in and thunder breaks out.

"We should get going," Lance says, "Come on." He helps me to my feet, and wraps an arm around my waist.

I lean into him as we walk down the path to my parked car. A raindrop falls and splats on my forearm, several follow as thunder growls out again followed by the strike of lightening. Lance grabs my arm, pulling me into him, and before I can protest he sweeps me off of my feet and into his arms making a quick dash to the car. Quickly he opens the passenger side door and sets me onto the seat. After closing the door, he rushes to the driver's side and jumps into the car.

I wipe at the water that covers my exposed skin, "Great weather, huh?" I mutter.

Lance looks at me with amusement and chuckles, "The best for May."

I dig through my pocket and hand Lance the keys for my car. He turns it on and I mess with the controls for the heat.

"This should help dry our clothes."

"As well as give us a heat stroke."

I lean back in my seat as I laugh quietly at his quip.

Lance studies me for a moment, his brows drawing together, "What did you mean by saying she *took* him from you."

I fidget with my hands in my lap, "My mom," I clear my throat, "My mom's an alcoholic…and…a drug abuser."

Lance places his hand over mine, stilling them.

Shock courses through me as I look down at our hands, "She would lock herself in her room at times. One time she didn't and I saw her, but I was eight, and I didn't think anything of it." I grab Lance's hand, "I didn't know."

Lance gives my hand a squeeze, "And with Hope?"

"She stayed sober. After Luke, everything changed. I stayed as far away from my mother as I could, and she stayed sober throughout the pregnancy."

I look up at Lance, "I think my ignoring the fact that she was pregnant saved Hope. She became my second chance."

"Second chance for what?"

"To save someone, to redeem myself, I guess."

Lance looks at me quizzically.

"My life is beyond screwed up, Lance, but that doesn't mean Hope's has to be too. I can make sure she gets the sort of life she deserves, not the one I've lived."

"You didn't have to live this one either."

I shake my head, "Yes, I did. I had no choice. These were the cards life dealt me.'

"You could have chosen differently."

"Maybe, but I'd always be on this track. I'd always be this girl."

"I disagree—."

I shake my head, raising my hand to cut him off, "you don't understand, Lance. And that's okay, I don't expect you to."

He didn't understand, because he wasn't getting the full story. He didn't know about the abuse I endured throughout my childhood. How my mother destroyed me. He doesn't know why it's important for my walls to shoot back up every second I grow remotely close to someone. In the end I would get hurt, and this kind of hurt, this kind of pain—it would ruin me.

"We come from different worlds, Lance. You've been much luckier than I have, and therefore you can be saved. But me, I'm already ruined. I can't be saved."

"I don't believe that."

"Well believe it." I say, willing the words that will push him away forever out of my mouth, "I'm just the cynical pothead who only cares about herself because that's all she's ever known, and you're Mr. Perfect with a father who will swoop in and save you from harm at a moment's notice. Your life is perfect, and it has no place for me."

I pull my hands away from his and look straight into my lap, knowing the instant I look into his eyes I would cave.

Lance is silent, but I sit there patiently for his response or for him to leave my car. When he does neither, I take the risk and look up at him.

He is staring at me with anger sketched across his face.

My mouth opens slightly in shock at his expression.

"I thought," he begins, "we were past these false accusations."

I knew what he meant. How could he be mister perfect when he lost both of his moms, or when his real father was a recovering junkie? He was far from perfect and I knew that, but I had to do this. I had to push him away. It was the only way to ensure that I remain somewhat in tack.

"You know I'm right," I lie.

"Shut up."

"Excuse me?" I say, my fire starting to pick back up.

"I'm not perfect."

"Lance—"

"I said, shut up, Rizz."

I am taken back by the forcefulness of his words.

"My life has been far from perfect. I was bounced from foster home to foster home. You couldn't even begin to imagine what that's like. How some homes were good, and the people were kind. While others couldn't care less about you or whether or not you got fed or if the bigger kids beat

you up. Then I found my parents and at that
moment I finally felt like I was happy and my life
was close to perfect, my mother got taken away
from me, and by a friend no less. I can't even—"
Lance shakes his head stopping himself from going
on, "Then, to find out that my real father is alive,
and has known where I have been all my life, but
did nothing to contact me. Yeah, I'm the definition
of perfect."

"Lance, I—" I try.

"You what? You're sorry? You didn't realize?
That's the thing, Rizz, you make assumptions. You
don't bother trying to get to know someone."

"I'd only be setting myself up to get hurt."

"So what? At least you tried."

"And where would that get me?" I ask, growing
angry.

"One step closer from not being alone," He
snaps out.

"So you're saying I'm going to be lonely?" I
snap.

Lance groans, "What the hell is wrong with
you," he curses before grabbing my face and pulling
me to him. Our lips collide. He kisses me hungrily,

his hand skimming down my cheek and to my neck. His other hand explores down the side of my body to my hip. He tightens his hold, pulling me over the console so I am straddling him. I dive into him, meeting each one of his starved kisses with my own.

The instant our lips meet, my walls are struck by the wrecking ball known as Lance. And I let them fall around me leaving me naked to him, because right here in this moment I feel strong. I feel empowered by him; he gives me the energy to try and his kiss reminds me that I don't have to be alone; that I can allow myself to be loved; that it is okay.

He pulls away and rubs his nose along mine, "You are the most frustrating woman I have ever met."

"Is that a problem?' I ask.

"Never."

"Good," I smile before covering his mouth with my own.

Lance kisses me tenderly before pulling away again. Holding my head at the nape of my neck, he presses our foreheads together.

I look into his pleading eyes and grow curious as to what lies behind them.

"You have to trust me," He says.

"I'm trying." I reply, slowly pulling away from him. I reach into my pocket and pull out my phone. I begin to tap on the touch screen when Lance asks,

"What are you doing?"

I type out a few more keys and then tuck my phone away.

"What I should have done, yesterday," I say, as his phone rings from his pocket.

He opens his phone, and smiles down at the message on his screen.

"You're pretty perfect too," he replies aloud.

I kiss him softly before moving off of him and back into the passenger seat, "It stopped raining." I notice.

"Very observant," he smirks, throwing my own words back at me.

I jokingly punch him in the shoulder, "Hey!" I laugh.

Lance shrugs, "You asked for it."

"Yeah…yeah," I say waving my hand in the air, "get out of my car and finish your run."

"You're cute when you're fussy," he says, leaning over to console, capturing my lips with his own.

My face flushes, and when he pulls back a large grin spreads across his face.

Damn him, and that breathtaking smile.

"This," he says, pointing to my cheeks, "Is the sexiest damn thing I've ever seen."

My face grows hot and the warmth shoots through my whole body.

Damn him.

He reaches for the car door and exits the car, "I'll text you."

Unable to speak, I nod my head.

Once he turns and heads down the path with his ear buds now in place, I crawl over the console into the driver's seat and shut the door. I stare off after him.

He glances back at me and waves.

I smile and direct my stare back to the front windshield, but find myself glancing back toward him.

Yeah, I'm a goner.

I pull into the garage, cutting off the engine. Looking at my reflection in the review mirror I rub at the smeared mascara under my eyes.

Thank God I wasn't wearing any eyeliner.

I'm steps closer to opening myself fully to Lance. Talking to him about Luke was the first step in the right direction, and it was terrifying yet liberating at the same time. Sharing my deepest secrets with him was like lifting a boulder from my chest; allowing me to breathe again.

I rub at my red eyes one more time, before giving up and opening the car door and heading into the house.

I walk through the foyer pass the living room where my mother is sitting on the couch, wine glass in hand, watching the television screen.

I catch her eye and she looks up from the television, "Get back here," She calls.

I stop and walk back to the living room entrance. I lean against the doorway crossing my arms over my chest.

"Where have you been?" She slurs.

"At a friend's." I reply flatly.

"A boy no doubt, you little whore."

I shake my head in disbelief and push from the doorway, "I'm not the one with the problem of keeping their legs closed."

My mother gets up from the couch, setting the glass of wine on the coffee table, and stalks toward me, "Don't you dare talk to me like that."

She grows nearer, but I don't flinch from her.

"What? You can't handle the truth?"

My mother snorts, "The truth? You know nothing of the truth."

"I know enough."

Her eyes narrow as she looks at me. Suddenly, she begins to laugh, "You stupid girl, are you high?"

"What? No," I reply.

"Don't you lie to me," her stare grows cold.

"So what if I am," I yell at her, "what are you going to do about it?" I step closer to her, "Absolutely nothing."

My mother's hand flinches at her side.

"Go ahead," I seethe, "Do it. See what I care. I stopped caring the minute you killed Luke."

My mother's fist connects with my jaw and I stumble back against the door frame. A sharp pain shoots up my back as the corner of the door frame digs into my spine. My head falls back against the wall, bouncing off. I let out a low groan.

My mother wraps her boney fingers around my throat and holds me against the wall. I meet her steely glare and roughly say, "Go ahead," I say tears forming in my eyes, "finish what you started all those years ago."

My mother pushes her hand harder against my throat. Slowly my airways begin to constrict, and my breathing becomes weaker. My eyes flutter, and my mother's hand suddenly releases from my neck. My legs give out and I fall to the ground.

My mother squats beside me, and grabs my face in her hand tipping it up so I am looking at her.

"I own you," she sneers, "Don't you ever forget that."

She violently releases my face letting it fall back against the living room rug. She stumbles over to the coffee table and picks up the wine glass, downing the rest of its contents.

She glares down the wine glass at me, and then everything goes black.

CHAPTER NINTEEN: THOM

Taking a burger from the heated chute and placing it on my tray, I move down the line toward the cash registers in the school cafeteria. I grab a couple cookies from the display rack and hand the lunch lady an extra fifty cents before exiting the line.

I scan the round tables surrounding the cafeteria until I land on Nathalie's turned down face at one of the round tables near the vending machines. Once reaching the table, I pull out the empty chair next to her, set my tray on the table and sit down.

She looks up from her salad and smiles at me, "Hey, sweetie."

"Hey," I smile as I unwrap my burger, "Got you a cookie."

"Thanks," she says, picking the cookie up from my tray.

I remove the crown of the bun from the burger. Opening the packet of ketchup, I squeeze it onto my bare burger.

"So," I start quietly, "I wanted to talk to you about something."

"Yeah?" she encourages.

"Yeah," I pause as someone passes behind us. "It's kind of serious…and I don't…" Another classmate passes our table and I wait for them to get a good distance away before beginning again, "I don't really want anyone to know."

Nathalie puts down her fork and places her hand on my forearm, "What is it?"

"A couple years ago, I was involved in an accident."

Nathalie grows worried, "What kind of accident."

"A bad one," I tell her, "I had to—I have to attend therapy sessions every week to see…" I lean in a little closer as a peer approaches our table, "how I'm coping."

I watch the peer from the corner of my eyes as they walk past us, "Anyway, I was in a session yesterday, and well, my therapist—Dr. Connors—he'd like to meet you."

"Me?" She asks pulling away a short distance, "Why?"

"He thinks…well…that you're the cause for all the great progress I've been making."

"Why do you have to go to…therapy," she whispers as she looks around her.

"The accident was traumatic for everyone involved, it was recommended."

"Who was involved?" she asks, leaning in.

I hesitate, "Lance and I."

"Does he have to go to therapy?"

"He…uhm…he declined."

"Then it must not have been that bad."

I look down at my burger, "No, it was…" I look up at her, "It's more complicated for me."

"You can tell me, Thom."

I look away from her and attend to my food again, placing the crown back onto the burger.

"Just…just come to this session with me first."

Nathalie rubs my forearm before pulling her hand away, picking up her fork. Stabbing a piece of lettuce, she asks, "When is it?"

I look from my burger in my hands to her, "Friday, after school."

"Okay," she shrugs, bringing her fork to her mouth, "I'll be there."

My mouth hangs open as I look at her.

She chews on her lettuce. Noticing me staring at her she looks at me, "What?"

"Will you be my girlfriend?"

Nathalie stops mid chew and stares at me. Swallowing, she opens her mouth to respond but I cut her off,

"Wait, don't answer that. Wait until after the session. Then tell me."

Nathalie gives me a smile and nods her head, "Okay."

I pick up my burger and take a bite. Feeling Nathalie's eyes on me, I steal a glance at her and smile as she directs her eyes back at her salad, a blush blazing across her face.

Breaking off a piece of the cookie I brought her, she pops it into her mouth and turns to me, "So...how is Lance?"

I snort to myself at her subtleness. Knowing her real intentions of bringing him up, I dodge it and reply, "Good, mostly because of Rizz."

"Wait, what?" she exclaims.

"Yeah, I guess they have been talking lately."

"No way," she says straightening in her chair, "You have to tell me."

"I don't really know much, Nat."

"You are such a tease," she pouts.

"All I know is that they are talking and it seems to be helping him."

"What do you mean?"

I wave my hand in the air, "I don't know, he just seems...more focused on him."

"I don't understand."

"I know," I say, taking another bite of my burger.

"I can't believe she didn't tell me," she says sitting back in her chair.

"I'm sure she was going to," I say wiping my face with a napkin, "I just beat her to it."

"Beat who to what?" A female says as she sets her tray on the table.

I look up to see Charlene and Rizz settling into the chairs across from Nat and me. Rizz pulls the scarf she is wearing tighter around her neck. I watch her quizzically. Her eyes meet mine and for a moment her eyes hold mine.

Sadness.

All too familiar with the feeling hidden in her eyes I look away.

Nathalie opens her mouth to speak, but the clearing of my throat stops her from saying anything.

"Nothing," she says, "we were just talking about our college applications, looks like he beat me to the deadline."

"Oh, yeah? For what school?" Charlene asks me.

"Columbia," I answer.

"Weird," Charlene says, "I could have sworn you already handed that one in, Nat."

"Yeah, I had to resubmit it. Forgot to attach my references," she says, eyeing me.

Rizz catches Nat's lie and smirks at us.

"What?" I ask her.

"Oh, nothing," she says nonchalantly, as she begins to take apart her chicken wrap.

"What other schools did you apply to?" Charlene asks.

I look away from Rizz, meeting Char's gaze, "Well Columbia is my first choice, but I also applied to the University of Chicago."

"Only two?"

"Yeah, I didn't really want to go anywhere else but Columbia, so if I don't get in there I might as well just stay in Chicago."

"You must be pretty confident then."

"That I am."

"Well, Columbia is a great school," Nat says, "They'll be stupid not to enroll you."

I smile at her, "Thanks. What about you, Char?"

"Oh I applied all over California."

"California?"

"They don't know it yet, but that state is dying to have me added to their population. Hollywood here I come."

Rizz rolls her eyes at her chicken wrap as I stifle a laugh.

"What?" Char asks, "You guys laugh now, but when I'm married to Liam Hemsworth we'll see who is laughing then."

"Yeah, you keep telling yourself that." Rizz quips.

"Whatever. You guys will see, and I'll be more than glad to skip down the streets yelling 'I told you so, I told you so.'"

Nathalie shakes her head as she laughs at her friend's ridiculousness. Directing her attention on Rizz she says, "That is the cutest scarf, Rizz."

Rizz brings her hand to the scarf and gives Nat a small smile, "Thanks."

"I love all the spring colors."

Rizz smiles and nods her head before taking a bite of her wrap.

I watch Rizz as she chews her food. Nathalie continues to talk to Char as if her best friend wasn't acting remotely strange. Pulling my gaze from Rizz, I look to Nathalie and say, "I've got to go take care of a few things."

"Okay," she says, "I'll walk with you." She looks back at her friends, "I'll see you ladies later tonight."

Rizz gives Nat another smile.

"Okay, Doll," Charlene chimes.

I wave to the girls before heading out of the cafeteria. Stopping outside of my locker I begin putting in the combination as Nathalie leans against the lockers and eyes me curiously.

"What?" I ask, opening my locker.

"Nothing."

"That look, isn't nothing. Something's on your mind, so out with it."

I exchange the books from my bag for new ones as Nathalie stands up straight.

"I just…"

I close my locker and lean against it, facing her.

She looks at the ground for a moment and then meets my eyes again, "Do you…visit your dad?"

I look around us before answering in a hushed tone, "Not anymore."

"Why not?" She asks, her brows coming together.

"It's complicated, Nat. Just...I'll explain everything...I just ... I can't right now, okay?"

I plead with her to let it go. I couldn't tell her. Not right now. I just had to see how the therapy session went first before spilling not only my secret to her, but my best friend's too.

Nathalie slowly nods her head, "Yeah, okay."

I pull her into my arms and wrap her in a hug, "Thank you." I mutter into her hair.

Kissing the top of her head I say, "I promise I will tell you soon. It's just complicated."

"How?" she asks, pulling away from me.

I look down at her as I let out a sigh, "It's not just my story I'd be telling you."

She nods her head in understanding and wraps her arms tightly around me and nuzzles her head into my chest.

"When you're ready, I'll be ready to listen."

CHAPTER TWENTY: RIZZ

I flop down on my bed, unraveling the scarf from my neck and discarding it on the floor. Staring at the ceiling I think of how Thom was watching me in lunch today.

What the hell was his problem?

I gently rub at my neck massaging the tenderness of the muscles, and flinching every so often at the dull pain from the light bruises that line my neck.

After waking up from passing out the other night, I found myself alone lying on the living room floor where my mother left me. Chip must have been working late at the office, because his home office light was off, which it rarely ever was. I found my way to my room, discarded my clothes and ran a hot bath which I eased myself into letting the scalding heat replace the pain and anger of that night.

I turn over onto my stomach and rest my head in my crossed arms. My neck grows stiff, so I slowly roll back over onto my back and continue staring at the ceiling.

I own you.

My mother's words ring over and over in my head, and the more I think of them the angrier I grow. Standing, I walk to my vanity and sit down in the chair. I ball my hands into fists as I look in the mirror at the lightened bruises of my mother's handiwork.

One day, she won't stop. One day, she'll finish what she started.

I bring my hand to my neck and gently stroke it with my fingertips. My bedroom door slowly opens and I scramble to pick up the scarf from the floor, but am too late as Hope walks through the doorway.

"Rizz?" she asks, "What happened?"

"It's nothing," I lie, wrapping the scarf around my neck.

"No, let me see," she says, tugging on my arm.

Sighing, I undo the scarf letting it fall to my side as I kneel on my bedroom floor in front of my dresser.

"Did mom do this to you?" Hope asks quietly as she looks at my bruised neck.

I lower myself so I am now sitting crossed legged.

Hope joins me, "She did, didn't she?"

"Don't tell me you're surprised?" I ask, picking the scarf up and playing with it in my lap. Holding it up I say, "I had to wear this stupid thing to school today." I throw it to the side, "Who the hell wears scarves in the spring?"

"Lots of people do. I saw a woman just the other day."

"Yeah, I bet she was old."

Hope giggles as she nods her head, "You're an old lady."

I swat my hand at Hope's arm teasingly, "Hey, that hurt."

Hope falls back, clutching her stomach as she bursts out into a fit of giggles, "My sister," she laughs, "the old woman."

"Okay, I think something is seriously wrong with you," I smile, "It's not that funny."

"Yes it is," she insists, "I'll show you." Hope, now lying on her stomach reaches for the scarf lying in front of my dresser, "Just let me see—Rizz?"

Rolling my eyes, "I'm not going to put it on, if that's what you're planning."

"Rizz?" she repeats.

"I'm serious, Hope, I had to wear that damn thing all day. I felt so constricted."

"Rizz," Hope shouts.

"What?"

"What's this?" she asks pulling out my ashtray from under my dresser.

Shit.

"It's just an ashtray," I say calmly.

"But…what's the stuff in it?" she asks, her brows pulled together, "those don't look like the things mom uses."

"That's because mom smokes cigarettes. Those are different."

"How?"

"They are a different type of cigarette except without all the harmful chemicals."

"Chemicals?"

I sit awkwardly on the floor, holding the ashtray in my lap, "Yeah, the ones you always...*see*...mom smoke have a lot of harmful chemicals in them. So it's important that you never ever smoke those, okay?"

Hope clutches her arm to her body in horror, "Do they seep in through your skin?"

I chuckle, "No, Hope. The chemicals are exposed through the smoke."

Hope relaxes letting her arm fall into her lap, "what makes that stuff better?" Hope asks, pointing to the ashtray.

"Well, this stuff is a plant. There aren't any harmful chemicals put into it—it comes from nature."

"Can I try those?"

"No," I say quickly.

Hope crosses her arms in front of her chest, "Why not?"

"Hope," I sigh, "smoking of any kind isn't good for you."

"Then why do you do it?"

Why do I smoke? Because it eases the annoyance of everyone around me, it allows me to forget.

I open my mouth to answer when my phone begins vibrating on my dresser. Getting to my knees, I lean up and grab my phone.

"Hello?" I ask, after pressing the answer button.

"Hey, Doll, we still on for tonight?" Char's voice comes across the line.

I pull my phone away from my face and look at the time displayed in the top right corner: 3:30 p.m.

"Yeah," I reply, putting the phone back to my ear, "Come over around five."

"Okay, we'll see you then."

I end the call.

"You're not coming?" Hope whines.

I look to her to find that her face has fallen.

"You know I don't go to those anymore."

Every spring, my mother hosts an extravagant business party at her office in the city. Past years, she would drag me to them and then when Hope was old enough, she would drag her too. The more I began to challenge my mother though, the more she pushed me away—allowing me to never have to attend one of the horrendous events again.

I look at Hope's jutted out lip and smirk,

"Come here," I say, opening my arms to her, "Don't pout."

"You sound like Mom."

With those four words I stiffen up. I feel as if I had been struck repeatedly by my mother.

Hope pulls away, looking up at me in horror, "Rizz, I didn't mean it."

I force my body to relax and crack out a small smile. Nodding my head, I pull her back into my arms, "I know, I'm nothing like her."

Squeezing her one last time, I pull away from her, "You should probably go get ready. You guys will be leaving soon."

Hope nods and gets to her feet, "Rizz?"

"Yeah?"

"Will you come help me?"

I smile at her, "of course."

I get up from the floor and follow Hope out into the hallway to her room. Once in, I make my way to her closet and begin pulling at the clothes on the hangers, searching for the right outfit for her to wear.

"You have to look presentable," I tell her, "after all, there will be very important people at this function."

I unhook one of her fancier dresses from the hanger and hold it out in front of her. Crinkling her nose, she shakes her head.

"Too fancy for ya?" I ask.

"Way to fancy," she nods.

I return the dress to its rightful place and begin rummaging through again.

"I'm going to be a business woman just like mom one day," Hope says.

"Oh, yeah?" I ask, "Then we better pick you out something very businesslike. Who knows, your future boss might be at this party."

"Isn't mom the boss?"

"You don't want to work for mom," I tell her as I pull another dress from the rack.

"Why not?"

"You should never mix your personal life with your business life," I state matter-of-factly.

I hold the dress up to her, and she smiles. Stepping from the closet I lay the dress out on her bed.

"Okay, first thing first, your hair," I grab Hope's shoulders and steer her toward her own vanity and sit her down.

Picking her brush from the table top I ask, "How do business woman wear their hairs now-a-days?"

"A tight bun, please," Hope orders.

"You got it," I say, as I gather her hair in my hands.

After finishing up on her hair, I leave her to change into her dress.

"Hurry up; you have to get down stairs in like five minutes."

"I know, jeez," Hope says waving her hand dismissively at me, "I'm hurrying."

"Well, hurry faster," I smirk, heading back to my room.

Walking back into my room, I spot the ashtray lying in the middle of my bedroom floor. Picking it up, I slide it back under my dresser. Making my way to my desk, I pick up my sketch book and bring it back to my bed. I flop down and flip open the pad to the sketch of Swallows I began drawing before our permanent move back to Lake Forest.

I etch my pencil along the smooth outlines of the birds, darkening the lines. Rubbing my finger along the lines, I smudge the granite into one of the bird's middle creating a grey scale effect. Drawing these birds was a tattoo idea, knowing the light sense of freedom and hope they gave me. They—to me—represented the freedom I would one day have. They represented the day I would be able to leave— to never look back, and until that day, that's all the birds would be—an idea.

A light knock comes from the door, followed by Hope's entrance. Standing in front of me in a navy blue dress, she spins around.

"How do I look?" she asks.

"Like you'll get the job."

"Rizz," she laughs, "I can't be a businesswoman right now. I'm eight."

"Well they'll be missing out. You ask some pretty direct questions, and you don't stop until you get answers. Now that I think of it, you could probably make a pretty good lawyer."

"Rizz, I'm eight." She says again matter-of-factly.

"Right," I smile, "You look great Hope. Like the ultimate businesswoman—for an eight year old."

Hope beams at me, clasping her hands together in front of her, "Perfect."

"Now get downstairs," I wave her out the door, "and try to enjoy yourself."

"I will," she exclaims, walking out the doorway.

"Yeah, you're one weird eight year old," I call after her.

Hope gives me one last wave before moving out of view. I direct my attention back down to my birds and smile to myself as I trace the outlines and add shadows under the bird's wings.

One day, Hope and I will be free—free from her; our mother.

An hour later, I'm sitting in my room with Nat and Char lounging around my bedroom floor. Nat flips through the latest issue of Cosmopolitan, while Char adds a new coat of red polish to my finger nails.

"Why does it have to be red?" I ask.

"Because," Nat pipes up, "red is sexy. Plus," she holds up the Cosmo magazine for me to see, "it's the latest style tip."

"It reminds me of hookers."

Char snorts, "Is that where you've been lately? Hanging with hookers?"

"Oh shut up." Nat defends me, "She's just been busy."

"And what about you?" Char says, directing her attention on Nat now, "You've been M-I-A more so than this one." She points to me with the polish brush.

Nathalie's cheeks grow pink, "I've been hanging out with Thom."

Charlene's hand stills as she dips the brush into the bottle. Letting go of it she looks at Nat, "Are you two dating now?"

"He asked me."

"He what?" I ask, staring at her with wide eyes.

"What did you say?" Char asks.

"He told me not to answer yet?"

"What?" I ask.

"Why not?" Char adds.

"I—I—I can't say."

"Nat, come on, we are your best friends."

"I know, I just—I promised him he could trust me."

"Seriously—" Char starts.

"Well do you want to date him," I ask, cutting off Charlene as I notice Nat's uneasiness.

Detecting when someone is trying to keep a secret has become my specialty since I've been keeping several my whole life.

"I want to say yes."

"But?" Char asks.

"I think he's hiding something from me."

"So find it out," Char states, "That's what I do with you two. I keep pushing until I get all the details."

I snort under my breath, but Charlene notices and says,

"What, you don't think so?"

"Oh, no, you definitely get all the details," I say, rolling my eyes.

Nathalie chuckles into the magazine.

"I hate you guys, you know that," Char quips.

"I'd die before I saw that day," I say.

Char rolls her eyes at me and turns to Nat, "Well if you like him, go for it. Soon enough, whatever he is hiding will come out."

"You never know," I add, "Maybe he wants to tell you, he just doesn't know how."

"Or maybe," Char adds, "He can't tell you. He's forbidden. Ooo, your own tragic love story."

"Shut up, Char," I beckon.

"I'm just saying," she exclaims, placing her hands on her hips.

"Well, don't."

Catching Nathalie's shocked expression, I ask, "What?"

"Since when do you give such insightful advice?"

"What are you talking about?"

"You never talk boys with us."

"Yeah," Char chimes in, "You always change the subject. Are you sick?"

"Would you both just shut up?" I say. Nodding to my hands, "You have some nails to finish."

"And she is back," Charlene mutters.

Nathalie laughs as she reopens the magazine and continues to flip through the pages.

Nathalie was right though, since when do I ever involve myself with their love lives—I don't. I steer clear of any kind of conversation relating to anything remotely close their relationships. Maybe it was because it was Nathalie. The one person who always looked to me before doing anything and here she was making decisions without watching the way I responded. Or maybe it was because the guy she was interested in was so close to the one guy who could cause me to lose myself with just one brush of his skin against mine.

My phone begins to buzz on my bed. Charlene pulls the brush away from my nail, allowing me to stand and retrieve my phone. Picking it up from the bed, I look at the caller I.D and smile at his name appearing across my screen.

Answering, I ask, "Hello?"

"Hey, it's Lance."

"I know, caller I.D."

"Right," he laughs.

"What's up?" I ask.

Nathalie and Charlene eye me curiously.

"I want to take you somewhere."

"You want to take me somewhere?" I ask, looking at Nat and Char.

"Yup, tonight."

"Where?"

"It's a surprise."

"I hate surprises," I say flatly.

At this, Nat and Char perk up.

Char mouths, "Who is it?"

I roll my eyes at her and turn my back to them as Lance responds,

"Trust me. This one will be worth it."

"I don't know…"

"I won't take no for an answer, I'll pick you up in twenty."

"Twenty minutes!" I exclaim, "Lance, I have friends over."

"Lance?" Charlene and Nathalie exclaim.

I grimace as I turn to look at their shocked and excited faces.

"Oh, we can leave," Charlene says loudly.

"Hi, Lance," Nathalie chimes.

I wave my hand violently at them to shut them up.

"Sounds like you're free," Lance chuckles.

Sighing, "Alright, twenty minutes."

"Great, see you in a bit," He says, before disconnecting.

I hang up the phone, throwing it back onto my bed. Charlene and Nathalie, both standing, look at me with their hands on their hips.

"Is that why you're suddenly 'Miss Advice Giver'?" Charlene jokes.

"I have to get changed," I say ignoring her.

"Since when are you two talking?" Nathalie exclaims, "And when were you going to tell us?"

"It's no big deal."

"No big deal," Nat shouts, throwing her hands in the air, "it's the biggest deal ever."

"Fine," I cave, "We've been talking, I guess. Now will you two stop gawking at me and help me get ready?"

"No offense," Char says, "but I like this new you a whole lot more."

"Whatever," I mutter, pulling open my closet.

"Do you know where he is taking you?" Nathalie excitedly asks as she steps up to the closet.

"It's a surprise," I reply.

"Okay, then you should wear something that is dressy yet casual," Nathalie rummages through my closet, "Char, do something with her hair."

"Oh, no," I reply, "I can manage my own hair."

"Some things, I guess, will never change," Char mutters as she makes her way to Nathalie's side and helps her rummage through my clothes.

Fifteen minutes later, my room looks as if a tornado had hit it. Clothes are thrown all over the room covering the floor, bed, and vanity's chair. I stand in the middle of the chaos in only my bra and underwear.

"Try this," Nathalie says, handing me another shirt from the back of my closet.

I take the tribal printed tank top from her and slip it on.

"With these," Charlene says handing me a pair of blue jeans.

Sliding into the jeans, I button them up and look into the mirror.

Nat claps her hands together, "That's the one."

"It's perfect," Char agrees.

I smile at the two of them, and then back at my reflection in the mirror.

"Okay," Nat says, "We are going to get out of here, but you better give us details, or you're dead."

"I'll keep that in mind," I chuckle.

Nat and Char grab their bags and head out of my room. I look at my reflection one more time and think how weird it was to actually care what Lance thought. I always cared what people thought about me, but what was different was the feeling of confidence I had around him versus other people.

I walk over to my vanity and put more makeup on the now lighter bruises on my neck. Knowing that the girls hadn't noticed the bruises made me feel comfortable that Lance wouldn't either. As I touch up the make-up, I hear the front door open followed by chatter.

"Crap," I exclaim, picking up a white cardigan from the pile of clothes. I grab my bag from the clothes rack in the far corner of the room and head downstairs.

As I reach the bottom of the stairs, Lance's eyes lock with mine from over Nat and Char's heads.

"Hey," He smiles.

"Hi," I sigh.

"So, like we were saying," Nat says, "We were just leaving."

"You two love birds have fun now," Char adds.

Nathalie slaps Char's arm and scolds her.

Lance laughs, and I roll my eyes at the two of them.

Nathalie shoots me an apologetic look as she leads Char around Lance and out the front door.

I shake my head as the two walk down the pathway.

"You ready?" Lance asks.

I nod, "Let's go."

We drove for an hour where we filled the time talking about our lives. I told him more about Hope and how she wants to be a businesswoman like our mother one day, but how I felt she would be better off being a lawyer like our father. I told him more about John and our past relationship, and how I pushed him away. Lance was sympathetic when it was welcomed and understanding when it was necessary.

There was something about talking with Lance. I wanted him to know me, to truly know everything. I didn't want to hide from him, but some things I couldn't say. I couldn't tell him everything, not in one sitting. I needed more time in order to bare my whole soul to him. For some reason I had a feeling he knew this, but he never pushed. He just sat back and listened, laughing when I was being sarcastic and nodding politely when he didn't have anything to say.

He shared with me how his adoptive mom would teach him lessons through stories she would make up. He explained that his Pop had a private practice before the accident, but afterwards gave it up. Now his Pop works for the ER in order to build up his practice, which takes time to re-establish the former reputation.

Lance pulls off onto a dirt path as I tell him how Charlene and I met.

"She was friends with Nat already, she was a package deal I suppose, but I liked her fiery spirit. I guess she liked that in me too, because we clicked right away."

I look out the car window and the tall grass surrounding the edge of the dirt path, "Uh, Lance?"

"Yeah?"

"Where are we going?"

"You'll see."

We drive down the path a little ways before we come to a stop in the middle of nowhere.

Lance puts the car in park and turns off the ignition, "We have to walk the rest of the way."

"Why?" I ask, as Lance rummages through the glove compartment.

Pulling out a blindfold and holding it out in front of me he says, "Don't want to ruin the surprise.

I look at the blindfold in horror, "You really are a serial killer aren't you?"

"Trust me," Lance states.

"Do I have a choice?"

"Not really."

I take a deep sigh before turning my back to him and allowing him to tie the blindfold on my face. When his hands disappear from behind me, I hear his car door open and shut. A moment later, mine opens and I feel his fingers lace with my own.

"Okay, come on," Lance says, "I'll be your guide."

"This is the part where you take me to a man dug hole and leave me to starve, isn't it?"

"You should stop watching criminal shows. Seriously, you're going give yourself a heart attack someday with all that worrying."

"You're the one blindfolding helpless girls," I mutter.

"You're far from helpless."

I stay silent as Lance leads me forward. Five minutes later we stop, and Lance reaches up to undo my blindfold.

"Okay," he says, "We're here."

The blindfold falls from my face exposing my eyes to pure natural beauty. In front of me stands a large weeping willow tree with its vines hanging low around the trunk creating a private shaded area. Lying under the tree upon the green grass is a red and white-checkered blanket and picnic basket full of food and drinks.

My jaw drops as I look from the tree to Lance.

"I thought you'd like to watch the sunset," He explains.

"You did all this?" I manage.

He nods his head as he squeezes my hand, "Come on."

I follow him to the blanket and sit down as Lance pulls Tupperware dishes from the basket,

"Some potato salad, turkey sandwiches, crackers," Lance pulls a bottle from the basket, "and some sparkling apple cider for the lady who doesn't drink."

Lance pulls two plastic cups from the basket, "Couldn't bring the good glasses, hope you understand."

I nod as he pours some cider into the cup and hands it to me.

"Thank you, kind sir," I smirk.

"My pleasure," he smirks back.

"How did you find this place?"

"Pop told me about it."

"Oh?"

"I found this old photo of my Pop and Ann under this very tree. I guess he used to take her here when they were our age."

"It's beautiful here," I say looking up at the tree's vines surrounding us.

Lance leans forward, brushing a piece of loose hair from my face.

My eyes lock with his, and he says,

"No, it's gorgeous."

I smile as I feel my cheeks grow hot.

The hell with my walls.

We sit under the tree sharing stories and memories as we eat and watch the sunset. Lance leans against the trunk of the tree and I snuggle in between his legs, my back to his chest. Wrapping his arms around my torso, he kisses me on the cheek.

I turn my head so I am looking up at him and say, "So does this mean we are together now?"

"So blunt," he jokes.

I elbow him softly in the ribs.

"And feisty, I like that."

"Lance," I scold.

Lance chuckles before looking into my eyes with seriousness, "You are the most challenging person I have ever met and you are mine," he says, before devouring my lips with his own.

CHAPTER TWENTY-ONE: LANCE

I walk into the diner and wait for the hostess to seat me. Once in the booth, I place a drink order and flip open the menu as the waitress leaves. I keep my head ducked down behind the menu as my eyes glance over the pictures of burgers and the blood red writing of the font, but I'm not really seeing them. Instead I think back to that day where my biological father came to my front door, grabbed my arm in his rough hands and spoke those three words that I wish I could erase from my mind. *I'm your father.*

I hadn't talked to my biological father after telling Pop that I would meet with him. Pop handled everything over the phone talking to *him* or maybe it was his therapist—either way that one phone call is how I find myself sitting in this retro looking booth in a diner on the outskirts of Lake Forest. Pop had asked to accompany me, but I told him this was something I needed to do on my own. I wasn't sure what I was going to say or even do, knowing the mixed feelings boiling inside of me.

The bell above the door chimes and I perk my head up toward the door only to see a woman and her daughter being greeted by the young hostess. She looks about my age, maybe older. She's probably working this minimum wage job to help put her through college—something I won't have to worry about doing seeing that I won't be going to college. Instead, I'll be traveling the world and actually living. The hostess leads the woman and her daughter to a booth a few behind me. As the hostess walks back up to the podium, I observe her small wiry figure and her brown hair pulled into a loose bun on top of her head. As I watch the hostess go about her work I wish I hadn't come alone as Rizz begins to fill my thoughts. She would have understood what I was going through, but I couldn't pull her into this—my fucked up world.

The bell chimes again and a tall man who looks in his thirties comes walking through the door. Black shaggy hair hangs over his forehead which he removes from his eyes as he flips his head back. Reaching the podium he flashes a smile at the hostess and her face flushes as she meets his eyes. He says something to her and she nods her head before motioning back toward me. He brings his head up and scans the room until his emerald green eyes land on my own. I stare back at him stunned.

It's like looking in a mirror—twenty years from now.

He gives what I guess is his thanks to the hostess and makes his way back to me. He has put on weight since the last time I had seen him four years ago. I set down the menu and splay my hands out on the table top.

He stops at the side of the table, one hand stuffed in his back pocket. He gives me an awkward smile and nods his head, "Lance."

I nod my head in response, unable to find my voice, as I gesture to the empty booth across from me.

The waitress comes up to the table to take his drink order.

"Just water, thanks," he says.

"Okay," she chirps, "You gentlemen need more time to look over the menu?"

I nod my head, still unable to find my voice.

"Okay, I'll be right back with your drinks," she says.

My *father* picks up the other menu and looks it over, his brows furrowed as he concentrates on what he's reading.

I continue to stare at him. Wrinkles are forming at the corners of his eyes, and his face is covered in stubble. I wait for him to bring the back of his hand to his nose, like he had done so long ago, but he doesn't. He just continues to look over the menu. No doubt, knowing I'm staring at him, he looks up and gives me a small smile.

"It's like looking in a mirror, right?" he asks.

My jaw tightens as I nod.

He gives me a sad smile, "I know this must be hard…it's hard for me too."

Anger ripples through me, but I do my best to contain it. I pick up my menu again, opening it.

"What," I clear my throat, "What should I call you?"

"Jack would be fine."

I nod again before directing my attention to the menu. I look over the choices, but nothing catches my eye as I find myself unable to think of eating. Questions fill my head making it hard to think about anything but this man sitting in front of me.

The waitress comes back with Jack's water, setting it on the table in front of him.

"You two ready to order?" she asks, pulling her pad from her apron and clicking on her pen.

"I'll just have a cheeseburger and some fries," I mumble.

"Cheddar or American?" she asks.

"Cheddar is fine."

She scribbles in the pad and then turns her attention to Jack.

"I'll have the same," he says handing her his menu.

"Coming right up," she smiles, taking the menus and heading back toward the kitchen.

"I'm a simple man," Jack comments as he catches me watching him again.

I stay silent as I nod my head. I run my thumb along the condensation on the glass of my water as I rack my head with something to say. But what is there to say? This isn't a normal meeting. It's not like we know each other, like we're family. He's a stranger—something he chose to become. And before I can stop myself, the words spill out,

"Why did you do it?"

Jack looks at me in confusion and says nothing, waiting for me to clarify.

"Why did you give me up?"

Jack takes a deep breath before answering, "I—I didn't know what else to do."

"Raising me never crossed your mind?" I snap.

Jack's eyes sadden as he looks at me.

Anger rages inside, but I try to control it so I can make some sense of what must have been going through his head.

"You have to try to understand—"

"That's why I'm here," I cut him off, "To understand how someone could give up their own flesh and blood."

He sighs again as he rubs his index finger between his brows. Looking back up at me he quietly says, "I was scared."

I open my mouth to say something, but with a shake of his head he stops me.

"Let me explain."

I snap my mouth shut and slam my back against the back of the booth, crossing my arms over my chest.

"You were only a year old when I made the decision to give you up. I admit, I was scared, here I was just barley an adult, my wife dead, a child, and a nasty addiction to drugs."

Jack rests his elbows on the table top as the woman from earlier walks down the aisle with her daughter. I watch them as they make their way to the front of the diner to the restrooms.

Jack leans in closer and continues, "At that point it wasn't just weed or cocaine that I craved. My addiction grew to heroine and I couldn't stop. My mind was so foggy and days ran into each other and then one day the haze separated and I heard your cries from the next room and I began to panic. I couldn't remember what day it was or how long it had been before the high faded."

My jaw tightens, and Jack notices.

"I know I wasn't father of the year or anything like that. And that day, I realized it. Panic surged through me and I knew I had to do something, anything to give you a better life."

Jack pauses as he hears the chatter from the woman's daughter coming back down the aisle. Once they take their seats back in their both he picks up where he left off,

"So I wrapped you up in as many blankets as I could find and I took you to the nearest group home I could find and I…I left you there."

"So you did it for my best interest?" I say evenly trying to stay calm.

"You needed a father, Lance, not a junkie."

"I didn't have a father for six years."

Jack hangs his head as he looks at his water glass in his hand, "I know you don't think so, but by putting you in that group home, I was able to save you."

"Yeah, a lot of saving you did as I was bouncing between foster homes."

"It must have been hard."

Taken off guard, I nod my head, "It was."

The waitress arrives at our table with our plates in her hands. Setting them on the table she asks,

"You boys need anything else?"

"No, we are okay," Jack says, "Lance?"

"Yeah, I'm good," I nod.

I look at my food and find myself growing hungry the more I stare at it. I reach over and grab the ketchup from the bin. Jack grabs the salt and vinegar and I wait until he is finished to apply them to my own fries and then slowly pour the ketchup over the fries.

"What happened?" I ask as I pick at my fries, "To my mom?"

Jack takes a bite of his cheeseburger. Setting down the burger, he wipes his hands off on a napkin.

"She was in a car accident."

The knife stabs into my heart as I think how I lost both of my mother's to a car.

"I know," I clear my throat, "I meant what happened in the accident?"

Jack's eyes glaze over suddenly as he stares off behind me, no doubt remembering that day.

"It was winter," he recollects, "We were driving home after visiting with her parents," his smile warms his face, "Her parents loved seeing you," he snorts, "You're probably the only thing her father—your Grandpop—liked about me."

"Did he know about the drugs?"

"If he did, he didn't say anything about it."

I stay quiet as I think about the fact that he couldn't pull himself together enough to take care of me, but instead he chose the drugs over his own son.

"Anyway," Jack says taking my silence as a cue to go on, "We hit a patch of black ice and I lost control of the car. The car spun right through a red light, and the car coming through the cross section didn't have time to stop." He takes a deep breath trying to steady himself, "Claire—your mother—was hit right on...she...she died on impact."

The knife turns at the realization that she couldn't be saved. *Just like Ann.* I sit back in the booth again and staring down at my plate. Looking back up at Jack I ask,

"The other driver?"

"He was in a coma for a couple days, but pulled through."

"And...us?"

"I had a few cuts and bruises and I broke my wrist, but you didn't have a scratch on you. The damage was more toward the front end of the car."

I duck my head and look at my plate unsure of what to say. I didn't know her, but even so, a piece of me feels empty and I can't help but think that I'll feel like that for the rest of my life.

"Why didn't you drop me off with my grandparent's?"

"Your grandparents—the accident had a toll on them...they didn't want to be...involved with anything or anyone that would remind them of their daughter." Jack rubs his hand along the chin, "They didn't want anything to do with us after the accident."

"So it pushed you further away?" I mumble.

Jack looks past me as he hesitates to answer. "Yeah," he says finally meeting my eyes. He chuckles, "father of the year, huh?"

I sit at the diner with Jack for an hour longer falling in and out of awkward silences and strained small talk. He asked about school and my plans after graduation. The bitterness I was feeling toward began to ebb as I talked with him about my plans to travel. He thought it was great, but also said that an education is important. I ended up straying toward conversation of Rizz, and the more I talked about her the more I began to relax. Jack would look at me with a knowing look and then it would turn to a look I didn't quite understand, like he knew exactly how I felt and strangely that made me feel connected to him. As if we shared a similar understanding that I couldn't share with anyone else.

After our goodbyes Jack asked if we could meet again. I stand outside the diner and stare at him contemplating his request, and in the end I found myself agreeing to meet him again.

I was still angry toward him, but after all, he was my father, and he was trying. And despite everything I wanted to know more. I wanted to know him.

Walking down the school hallway all I can think about is Rizz. Lately she's the only thing on my mind. I can't get her face out of my head. Rizz shows me the real her when we're together. Although she still is hiding from me, she is close to breaking through, and I can feel it each time I learn something new about her. She is a strong, caring woman who only wants the best for her sister. She has lost and had the courage to face it and continue forward. But she was a girl who was frightened too. I saw that each time she grew close to opening up only to shut back down. She's afraid to let people in only to be let down in the end. It made sense now, but the more time she spends with me, the closer she comes to letting me be the one to break through those walls she so desperately holds onto.

My thoughts halt as Kayla walks up to me, latching onto my arm, "Hey, Lance."

I pull her hand from my arm and angrily say, "Get lost, Kayla."

"Don't start acting like that kiss meant nothing," she says smiling.

"It did mean nothing," I say, pulling open my locker. I toss my books into it and then close the door. "Look, Kayla. We had fun when we were together way back then, but it's over. I have someone else in my life."

Surprised, Kayla asks, "Who?"

Detecting the jealousy in her voice, I knew she'd never leave me alone unless I told her. Behind her, I catch sight of John walking toward us.

Shit.

"Who?" Kayla demands.

"Can we do this later?" I ask her in a hushed tone.

"No," she shouts, "I want to know who won the heart of Mister Lance McCartney."

"Stop being so dramatic, Kayla, and keep your voice down."

"Why, are you ashamed?"

"Of course not," I shout.

"Then spill it."

Damn, Kayla.

As John grows closer I knew this was going to be bad. He was already staring, his eyebrows narrowing as he zones in on me.

Sighing, I reply, "Her name is Rizz."

"You're dating the stoner girl?" Kayla shouts in disbelief.

I grow stiff at the condescending tone Kayla uses as she bashes Rizz.

"Why don't you just back off, Kayla. She's more the woman than you'll ever be."

"Fuck you, Lance," Kayla spats.

"So you're with Rizz?" John says coldly as he reaches us.

"Yeah," I confirm.

"Good luck with her," John snorts, "She can be hard to handle, especially in bed. Give me a call and I can give you some pointers. After all I know how she likes it," he adds smugly.

"I know you're just angry so I'm going to let that slide," I say, holding back my rage.

"So she told you? You know that's all she's good for."

"That's not how I heard it," I retort.

"She's only good for a hit it and quit it—"

My fist connects with his jaw, cutting him short. I grab his jacket and push him against the lockers. Kayla screams and jumps away from us.

"Don't ever talk about her like that again," I sneer.

"Or what?" he says egging me on.

I ignore him and release his jacket, pushing him against the lockers as I do. I turn and begin walking away when John shouts,

"Hey, you forgot something."

I turn to face him only for my jaw to meet his fist. A crowd finally forms and the throwing of punches excel. I grab his jacket again and throw him to the ground where I climb on top of him, pinning him to the ground and repeatedly throw punches at his face. Soon Principal Turner and a few of the P.E. teachers break up the fight. One teacher pulls me off of John and another pulls John off of the ground. John and I glare at each other as the teachers hold us a safe distance apart.

"Both of you, to my office, now," Principal Turner says.

I sit in the chair opposite Principal Turner's desk. Next to me is Pop, who look less than pleased to be here.

"We take fighting very seriously here," Principal Turner tells Pop.

"Will he still be able to graduate?" Pop asks.

"Yes, but I'm afraid he won't be able to walk the stage."

"What?" I exclaim.

Pop gives me a pointed stare and I sit back into my chair.

"We have strict rules on fighting here."

"I'm sure there is something we can do to work this out. No one should be robbed of their graduation experience, don't you agree?" Pop asks Principal Turner.

"I suppose not."

"What do you propose?"

"Seeing as this is the only outburst we have had from Lance, he can walk the stage if he apologizes to the boy, but they both will have to serve a two day suspension."

"But there is only three days left of school."

"I see here that you have completed all your course work in advance, so two days off school grounds won't harm you."

"Academically, maybe," I mutter.

Pop gives me another pointed stare, causing me to change my tune. I give Principal Turner a tight smile, "I suppose it won't."

"Do I have to apologize though? He was the one who started it."

Pop gives me another look as if to say be quiet, but I ignore it and look at Principal Turner who is studying a few papers on his desk.

"It says here that a Miss. Kayla Jones reported you as the one to throw the first punch."

"I mean, yeah, but he instigated the fight. Why should I—"

"Lance," Pop says.

"But, Pop—"

"But nothing. You will apologize to the boy and that's that. End of story."

I sit back in my chair scowling.

Principal Turner nods his head at Pop, before picking up his phone and calling his secretary.

"Yes, send Mr. John Thomas in."

A moment later, the door opens and bruised up John walks through the doors. He scowls at me and I scowl back. Pop looks from John to me in amazement.

Catching Pop's expression, I shrug my shoulders.

"Sit down, Mr. Thomas," Principal Turner says.

John takes a seat next to me.

Principal Turner raises his brow at me, pointing to John.

I take a deep breath and then turn to John, "I'm sorry for beating the shit out of you." I mumble.

"Lance," Pop scolds.

"What?" I exclaim, "I said I was sorry."

"Good enough," Principal Turner says, "John is there anything you'd like to say?"

"I'm sorry I didn't get enough punches in."

I chuckle as I watch Pop cover his face with his hand and Principal Turner look up at the ceiling.

John joins me in my laughter as he notices this too.

"You are dismissed," Principal Turner tells all of us.

John gets up from his seat first. Pop and I follow him into the hallway. John turns to face me. I stop and wait for him to spit out whatever it is he wants to say.

"I am sorry though," John says.

"I'm not sorry for sticking up for her," I reply, "But I am sorry for how far it went."

John nods and walks off toward the school's exit.

Once alone, Pop asks, "You did that to that boy?"

I shrug my shoulders, "At the time, he deserved it."

"How could you be so irresponsible?" Pop says in a low tone.

"You should have heard the things he said about Rizz. I wasn't going to let him get away with that."

"So this was all because of Rizz?" Pop asks angrily.

"You're the one who told me to stand up for the ones I care about."

"Yes, but not to wail on the person you are standing up to. Nothing like this has ever happened before you met her."

"That's not fair and you know it," I say growing angry.

"I don't have time for this right now. I have to get back to the ER. We'll talk about this when we get home." Pop says, walking off toward the exit.

"Wasn't it you who taught me how to be a gentleman and treat woman with respect? And if I ever saw someone who didn't, I should teach them a thing or two?"

"Yes, son, but not like this."

"If this situation was reversed, if you had to stand there and listen to all the shitty words he spewed about Rizz but for Mom, you would have reacted the same way."

"We'll talk about this later," Pop repeats. "Now get home." he says, heading out the school's exit.

I knew I was getting through to Pop. He knew in that moment that I was right, he would have reacted the same if it were him and Ann. It didn't matter if he felt I was right though, he would still act like the adult; the parent. This angered me. For Pop to act is if I were wrong when he knew deep down I was right.

I reach into my pocket and pull out my phone, dialing Rizz's number.

"Hello?" her voice comes across the line.

"Hey, it's me."

"You do know it's the middle of the school day, right?" she asks, concern etched in her voice.

"I got suspended."

"What?" she asks in a shocked whisper.

"Yeah, for two days."

"Why?"

I hesitate for a moment, but then decide to tell her, "I got into a fight."

"You did what?"

"With John."

"Oh my God."

"Look, I'll explain everything. Do you think you could ditch?"

"And put a dent in my attendance record? I don't think so, but I'll work something out."

"Okay, thanks."

"I have to go, someone is coming."

"I'll see you at my place in twenty," I say before she disconnects the call.

I pocket my phone and head out to the school parking lot. Climbing into my Escape, I start the truck and pull out of the lot.

Pulling into the driveway, I throw the car into park and rush into the house, leaving the front door unlocked. I'm angry at Pop for not taking my side. For being the parent in a situation he would have reacted exactly the same way if he were me.

Two fricken days without school? I'm going to go mad.

The last thing I want right now is to be alone; to dwell on the fact that I will have absolutely nothing to do these next few days and no one to keep me company, because they will all be finishing up their school year.

I head up to my room and throw on some normal clothes and dispose of my bloody uniform in the laundry hamper. Soon I hear Rizz's voice call for me through the house.

"Lance?" she calls, "The front door was open. Where are you?"

"I'm up here."

I hear the echoes of Rizz's footsteps as she walks up the stairs.

"Lance?" she calls as she reaches the top of the stairway.

"In here," I shout.

"What are you doing?" Rizz asks, standing in the doorway of my room.

"Just moving things out of the way," I reply, moving my bed against the wall on the far side of the room.

"For what?"

"You'll see."

"Not another surprise," Rizz moans.

"Would you just get over here and help me."

"I kinda like the view from here," She says, leaning against the doorway.

"Yeah?"

"Yeah, very masculine. I can see every muscle as you move."

I smile at her from over my shoulder before pushing on the chest that stands at the end of my bed.

"Why are you doing this again?" She asks.

After pushing the chest out of the way, I walk over to my iHome and put on *Wonderful Tonight* by Eric Clapton.

"Come here," I say, holding my hand out to her as I walk back to the center of the room.

Rizz places her hand in mine and I pull her close to my body as I wrap my arms around her waist.

"What's going on?" she whispers to me in concern.

"Dance with me," I whisper back.

"Lance—"

I turn Rizz in a spin, "Just dance with me, okay?"

Rizz looks at me quizzically, but gives up, "Okay."

Her face breaks out into a smile as I glide her across the floor.

"Where did you learn to dance?" She asks.

"Ann taught me before my first school dance," I smile sadly at the ground between us.

"She did a good job," Rizz says, ducking her head to catch my eyes, "is that what is bothering you?"

"Not exactly," Lance says, "If she were here this whole suspension situation would be different. Pop would have acted differently."

"How so?"

"She would have fought for me."

"And your dad didn't?"

I twirl Rizz around, and sway with her for a while before asking, "How did you get out of school?"

"Ah, the famous subject change," Rizz calls me out.

I give her a small shrug of my shoulders as I smile slightly.

"I made a note," She says laying her head against my chest, "I've become a pro at forging my mother's signature over the years."

"That's illegal you know," I smirk as I set my chin on the top of her head, and look across the room at the mirror hanging on the wall. I watch as we dance to the music. Everything about Rizz memorizes me; how her smile reaches her breath taking blue eyes, the way her hair flows along her shoulders, her sing-song voice and the way her body moves confidently through a crowd. I always thought I was making her strong, but in reality, she was making me strong. With each touch or every smile she causes a swarm of emotions to run over me, making me feel full; complete and in control of myself. She put me at ease.

Rizz pulls away from me and says, "What happened between you and John?"

"It doesn't matter," I say pulling her closer to me as jealousy courses through me.

"It matters to me," she says sadly, looking up at me.

I gently push her away and walk to the window. I grit my teeth and turn to look at her. I don't understand why she even cared, why she would even want to know the remarks he made about her. I was pissed all over again thinking of the words that spewed from his mouth in the heat of the moment. I couldn't imagine how one who cared for her so much could stoop so low to say such cruel things about her. I was jealous that there was something between them, but I was more pissed off that he would talk of it as if it was cheap and dirty. If only she knew, but I couldn't say those things to her. I couldn't be the cause of that hurt.

"He said cruel things," I say sitting on the bed, "That's what he did. He got what he deserved." I look away from her at my hands.

Rizz pads over to me and kneels in front of me. Taking my head in her hands, she lifts it so I am looking at her.

"What were you thinking?" she says, weakly.

My face contorts up in confusion.

What was I thinking?

I stand from the bed and storm across the room.

Rizz stands up and watches me.

I look at her, struggling with what I am about to say. Pacing back to her, I gently grab her elbow with my right hand.

"You are mine, and I will never let anyone disrespect you. I'll always protect you, Rizz. From your mother, from him, and from yourself."

Rizz's eyes begin to tear up.

"You deserve one person to show you how much they care for you."

Rizz clasps my head between her hands and kisses me.

Pulling her to me, I place my left hand on the small of her back and cradle her head in my right. Tenderly kissing every centimeter of her neck, I lift her up so she is straddling me. Her small hands lay on either side of my cheeks as she passionately kisses me while I carry her around to the side of the bed.

Setting her gently on the bed, I pull off my shirt and lay atop of her, leaning my weight on my side. My thumb glides lightly over her soft pink lips before I embrace them with my own. I glide my hand down the side of her body rubbing her covered breasts along the way and teasing her. Wanting more of her, I slide my hand underneath her shirt. As I glide my hand up her torso, I feel slightly raised bumps. I pause to trace the bumps with my fingertips, counting each one.

Rizz's hand caresses my neck and makes its way to my belt buckle. Forgetting about the bumps on her torso, I kiss her again before lifting my hips to make it easier for her to undress me. After slipping out of my pants I make quick work at undoing her own and sliding them down her long legs. I slide my hand up her thigh before cupping her center. Rizz tilts her hips into my touch, welcoming it. She wraps her hand around my neck, pulling me to her lips. Smoothly, she shifts her weight and throws herself so she is now on top and I am lying under her.

Rizz gives me a devilish grin as she lifts the hem of her shirt up and over her head exposing several small circular burns along her torso. Shocked, I meet her sad eyes. Slowly, she descends to me and nibbles at the side of my neck. Her cool breath lingers against my ear as she whispers,

"I want you to see all of me—to know all of me."

Her face hovers over mine. I reach up to tuck a piece of her hair behind her ear before guiding her lips down to mine.

Finally, she is all mine.

CHAPTER TWNETY-TWO: RIZZ

Lance and I lay cuddled up under the covers of his bed. I examine our clothes spewed all over his bedroom floor as I listen to the rhythm of his breathing. I lay my hand on his chest and snuggle in closer to him. Closing his hand around my shoulder he pulls me closer, and kisses the top of my head.

Lance is different from the other guys. His touch is gentle yet strong, but the biggest difference is that when he looks at me he truly sees me, not the girl I so desperately hide behind.

Lance shifts to his side, meeting my eyes with his own as he slowly pulls the covers down as if asking for my permission. I stare back at him encouraging him to reveal my body to him.

I want him to see me, to really see me.

Lance rests his hand on my stomach, spreading his fingers out before beginning to trace each one of the scars with his fingertips like he had earlier. Only, this time it's different, this time he's really seeing them.

"These scars," Lance speaks quietly, "They're from a cigarette, aren't they?"

I rest my arm behind my head and smirk, "Someone looks a little pensive."

"Don't do that," Lance whispers, looking at the scars. His eyes jump to mine, "Don't shut me out."

I take a deep breath as I look at the ceiling.

This is what I wanted. I wanted him to know me. That meant telling him everything that made me who I am.

I clear my throat as I begin speaking to the ceiling, "They're my mother's handiwork."

I feel the bile rising inside, but hold it back. I hate my scars; always reminding me of my past and of the life I can't seem to escape. I want nothing more than to forget it all and be free of it.

"Why did she do this to you?" Lance asks, softly.

"My mom is an alcoholic and a drug addict, Lance, why do they do half the shit they do." I reply bitterly.

Lance remains silent, giving me the time to calm down.

"I was six when she first stuck a cigarette to my skin. Before then she would only hit me."

I continue to talk to the ceiling although I can feel Lance's eyes on me.

"She was smart about it too, never doing it where someone could easily find it."

"Where was your father?"

"I don't know. At the office I guess. He always seemed to be missing."

"The scar on your temple?"

"I was eight. I went to comfort my mother after losing Luke," I turn and look at Lance, "And you know what she did? She blamed me for it all, and that's when she didn't care if what she did to me could be hidden or not. She was out for blood then, and that's the day I started fighting back." I swallow the lump forming in my throat, "I used to stick up for her. She was my mom, so I would hide everything she did, but after that moment, it got harder to hide. Luckily, we didn't stay put in a city long enough for anyone to start asking questions."

"When was the last time?" Lance asks, holding back his anger.

I look back at the ceiling, "three days ago." I run my hands along my neck, "she choked me."

Lance sits up, and pulls me to him.

"You have to tell someone."

"I just did."

"No, like the police."

My eyes wide with fear jump to his, "I can't."

"What do you mean you can't?" His arms tighten around me as his face scrunches in confusion and anger.

"I promise it doesn't happen as often anymore. Ever since I began to fight back she backed off. She knows I can ruin her, just let it be."

"Rizz—"

"Promise me, Lance, you won't say anything."

"You need to tell someone."

"I can't, Lance, no one will believe me."

"Why not?"

"Because, my mom is the most successful businesswoman in Chicago. They won't believe me and then I'll be dead. You can't tell anyone."

"But you have proof."

"No, Lance, all I have is scars that I could have inflicted on myself. I wouldn't stand a chance against her."

Lance looks unconvinced.

"No, Lance. I won't. The only thing keeping her from harming Hope is me. The moment I fight against her through the system is the moment I sign both mine and Hope's death warrant. I won't do that to my sister."

"Rizz," he begins to plead.

"I told you, Lance, because I trust you, because I wanted you to know who I really am."

"I love you, Rizz." Lance says as he wraps me into his arms, "If I see even a scratch on you, there's no stopping me. I'm going to the authorities and reporting her."

Pulling myself to my knees, I kneel in front of him. Grabbing his face gently in my hands I kiss him chastely. Pushing back some of his hair from his eyes, I look into them. Concern and love is etched in them. I smile sweetly as I run my hand along his cheek. I try to urge the words from my lips, but they won't form. Those feelings are so foreign to me, but I know that deep down hidden somewhere that they are there desperately trying to crawl their way into the light. So I do the only thing I can to show him how much he means to me and I meet his lips with my own allowing us to get lost in each other and his sheets again.

CHAPTER TWENTY-THREE: THOM

I stare at the wrinkled piece of paper in my hands as I sit limply at the kitchen table. It's Friday and I am waiting for Nathalie to come over so we can head to my therapy session. Waiting for her, I decided to sort through the mail on the kitchen table where I found a letter addressed to me in my father's scrawled hand writing. Ripping it open I unfold the letter and begin to read. Now I sit here staring at the letter in my hands re-reading it for the third time trying to suppress the feelings burning inside of me fighting to burst through.

Thom,

I understand why you have ended your visits with me, and I want you to know that no matter what happens in our lives that I love you and I'll always love you. You are my son, and because of this, I will always wish and hope the best for you.

I find myself constantly thinking back to that day—the day of the accident. And I have come to the conclusion that there was nothing we could have done differently. Do you believe in fate, son? I do.

And I believe that it was fate that turned its head and decided that it was her time and that I would be at fault. And I accept that. But now it is your turn to accept this fate. I see the toll the accident takes on you and I am sad to admit that it is why you have stopped visiting.

If there is one thing I hope to come out of all this is that you will grow strong. That you take this awful experience and grow from it. But most of all I hope you do not turn ill towards fate. For, fate can be ugly, but it can be beautiful too. It was fate that brought your mother to me and soon after, you into this world.

I know you may have a hard time believing this because your mother has asked for a divorce, but know that this is what she must do to move on with her life, and I accept this too because more than anything I want nothing but happiness for the both of you. I ask only one thing of you and that is to look after each other. Live your lives and move on, but most of all don't lose each other in the process of your healing.

You are my son Thom, and I will always do my best to protect you no matter how far I am from you. And that is why I am writing this letter—as a reminder that that day was inevitable and nothing could change its outcome. So stop blaming yourself,

because it is not your fault, Thom. So grieve for
your losses and move on, because that is the only
thing you are responsible for—for moving on.

I love you, son.

I grow numb as I re-read the letter for a fourth time. He wants me to accept and to move on, but how can I do that when my whole world is falling apart. When my best friend and his father want to do nothing but forget rather than admit what happened. I'm living in a lie and there is no coping with that—no healing from that.

I crumple the letter in my fist and slam it down on the table.

No, I can't accept this.

The doorbell rings and I jolt upright. I look back at the letter under my flattened palm and begin to uncrumple the paper and fold it, slipping it into my back pocket. The doorbell rings again and I pull myself from the chair and head toward the door. I open it to Nathalie's beaming face and some of the edge dissipates as she walks into my open arms.

"You ready to go?" She asks, pulling away from me.

Unsure if I can keep the edge from my voice I simply nod and step out onto the front porch shutting the door behind me.

Sensing something is wrong she asks, "Are you okay?"

I simply nod and give her a small smile.

Backing off, she slips her arm around my waist and I lay mine along her shoulders bringing her into my body. I kiss the top of her head breathing in her scent letting it settle my nerves.

I sit on the couch next to Nathalie as Dr. Connors begins to ask questions about Nathalie and her social life. Hesitantly she answers his questions, but soon her curiosity catches up to her.

"No offense, but what does anything about me have to do with Thom?"

Dr. Connors smiles as he crosses his legs, "You are an important part of Thom's life, so naturally it is beneficial to find out why."

Nathalie nods her head as if she understands but the clueless expression on her face tells me she doesn't. I want to laugh at her confusion but thoughts of my father's letter run through my head and overtake any emotional feelings pumping through my veins. I pick at the tacky green leather couch's arm rest and bounce my knee trying to calm myself. As always Dr. Connors picks up on these small actions and directs his attention to me.

"And how does this meeting make you feel, Thom?"

"I feel fine," I snap.

Dr. Connors' eyebrows raise, and Nathalie looks at me in concern. I bow my head in shame at my sudden outburst.

"And having Nathalie here? How does that make you feel? Anxious?"

I look him directly in the eyes and answer in all honesty, "A little, but…it makes me feel good."

"And what about having her here makes you feel good?"

I look at Nathalie now, "Because I am being honest with her, and that feels good."

Nathalie moves her hand on top of mine and squeezes gently causing my knee to stop jumping.

Dr. Connors takes notice and writes in his notepad.

"How does this make you feel, Nathalie?"

She looks at him confused as if wondering why she is now being the one analyzed, but she shakes it off and answers anyway, "It makes me feel good too."

"I'm glad to hear this." Dr. Connors says as he writes into his pad, "It's important that the two of you learn to accept each other for who you are. A relationship is built on honesty, trust and acceptance."

At the word 'accept' my head snaps to my therapist and my body begins to boil. I pull my hand from under Nathalie's and run it through my hair.

"Thom?" she asks.

Dr. Connors catching the concern in Nathalie's voice looks up at me.

The anger itches as it crawls over my skin. I try to calm down with the breathing techniques, but it is impossible.

"Thom," Dr. Connors says, "It's okay, deep breaths."

I lean over resting my arms on my knees trying desperately to take in steady breaths but they become quicker causing me to feel overwhelmed.

"Nathalie," I hear Dr. Connors say, "Could you try to work through this with him? He needs to know you are here."

I don't hear her response, but from the corner of my eye I catch her hand reaching for my arm. I flinch away from her and get to my feet.

"Please don't touch me right now," I try to say in an even voice.

Her hand drops back to her side as a flash of hurt crosses her features.

Something tears at my heart, but it is soon forgotten as flames shoot up my body. I walk over to the window and lean against it. Pressing my face against it, I pray that my body will calm down. More emotion sweeps over me as I realize that Nathalie is witnessing this all and I worry what she will think of me afterward, but most of all I think of the letter and my father and how fucking pissed off it makes me.

Acceptance. That is all my father wants, for me to accept everything that happened.

"Thom," Dr. Connors' voice breaks through to me, "Let's talk this through, okay?"

I nod my head as I turn and lean my back against the window. My eyes are shut but I slowly force them open to look at my therapist sitting calmly in front of me and a frightened Nathalie.

"Can you tell me how you are feeling right now?"

I snort as I think how everything comes back to how I am feeling. I want to make a snide remark, but then I remember what he told me just last week. I need to be honest in order to get closure.

I need to try.

"Angry," I choke out.

"And what triggered this feeling?"

"Accept—acceptance," I mutter.

Nathalie sits back into the couch no doubt confused out of her mind.

"And what about acceptance made you feel angry?"

"A letter," I whisper.

"A letter?"

I nod, pulling the letter from my pocket and holding it out to him. I don't dare to move in fear that I will begin to lose the control I am slowly gaining back.

Dr. Connors gets up from his chair and retrieves the letter from me. Opening it, he scans it.

"This letter is from your father?"

I nod in agreement.

"When did you receive this?"

"Before coming here."

Dr. Connors nods his head as if the pieces are slowly coming together.

Worry flashes across Nathalie's face and she begins to say something, but Dr. Connors gives her a look that advises her against it.

"Why does this letter make you feel angry?" he asks.

My head snaps to his and my eyes grow wide. I look at him as if he is insane. As if he should know that the answer to that is blatantly clear. That is when I am no longer able to hold it all back. The anger is spilling over and I need to release it.

"I'm angry with everyone." I push away from the window and begin to pace the room between Nathalie and Dr. Connors.

"I'm angry at my best friend because every fucking day he hides how the accident makes him really feel thinking he is making it "easier" for everyone involved if he just ignores it. I'm angry at my mom for giving up on my father, for abandoning him and for abandoning me. I'm angry with Pop for covering the whole fucking thing up." I pull at my hair as I pace in front of them, "Who the hell does that? I'm angry with him for making it impossible to talk about. I'm angry with myself for distracting my dad just long enough to miss the signal and to kill his best friend's wife—my best friend's mom."

I pause, trying to catch my breath and watch as realization washes over Nathalie's face. Her hands go up to her mouth as her eyes fill with tears.

"But mostly," I go on, "I am angry with my father for writing that letter. For telling me that it is okay and that he *accepts* it all. I'm angry that he doesn't blame me and that through all of this he is still the loving parent I so desperately need."

I let out a long breath as I sag against the wall to the ground.

"I'm angry," I say quietly, "That it's my dad rotting in jail and not me."

Nathalie's tears slide down her cheeks as she looks at me in sympathy. She inches closer to the edge of the couch and looks at Dr. Connors. He nods his head and she rushes over to my side.

Sitting next to me she pulls my body into her and I rest my head into her chest as I slowly let myself break apart and finally I am able to let myself cry in the arms of the one person who I have come to care about more than myself.

CHAPTER TWENTY-FOUR: RIZZ

I spent the weekend with Lance sitting alongside his pool as I watched him do laps while I soaked in the sun's rays. Lance was bummed when I wouldn't strip down to a bikini and join him, but I just wasn't ready for that. I spent years hiding my scars and I wasn't ready to walk around with them on display for anyone else to see. So I made sure to find my shortest shorts and my spaghetti strap tank top to wear as I lay out on one of the pool chairs a safe distance from the water.

I have my Ray Bands on and I'm beginning to doze off when I hear the slosh of water in the pool. I smile up into the sun thinking of the way Lance's muscles must be moving as he works his way through the water. I turn my head as I begin to nod off and smile when suddenly I feel something wet on my skin. Drowsy, I begin to pull myself from my sleep. My eyes bulge open when I notice I am being picked up, but before I can protest cool water consumes me and I am sinking. I flail my hands around and when my feet reach the bottom I kick off of it and emerge to a laughing Lance on the edge of the pool. I gasp for air, running my hand down my face as I wipe away the water.

"Lance," I yell, "I'm going to kill you."

Lance gives me a sly smile before backing away from the edge only to run straight toward the pool. He kicks off of the edge, jumping over me, and pulls his legs to his chest, wrapping his arms around his knees. Water splashes up and hits me. When he emerges, he is laughing.

"You think you're so funny, don't you?" I scold him.

Lance smiles at me as his swims over to my side, and pulls me into his arms.

"What if I didn't know how to swim?" I ask, wrapping my arms around his neck.

"Then I would have saved you."

"And what if I went psycho on your ass for throwing me in here?"

"I think I would have been able to handle your crazy ass."

"Oh yeah?" I smirk leaning in to kiss him.

Lance smiles as he moves to close the gap between us, but I quickly jump up and dunk his head in the water.

"That was dirty," Lance exclaims once he pops up from the water.

"Payback's a bitch," I laugh.

A glint flashes across Lance's eyes as he makes his way toward me. I begin to splash him with water to detour his path, but he captures my wrist in his hand and pulls me close to him. Before I know it his smiling lips are on mine and I wrap my legs around his waist, getting lost in his kiss.

We spend the rest of weekend either at his house or at the field under the old grandmother willow tree—as I call it. Although I wish I could spend Sunday with him too I have a shift at the Café soon and Lance has something he has to take care of. I assumed it had something to do with Thom, but Nathalie called earlier saying she was spending the day with him and wanted to know if Lance and I wanted to join. When I told her he was busy she asked with what and I didn't have an answer.

"Well, I wouldn't worry about it," she said, "I'm sure it's important."

"Yeah, I guess."

"He'll tell you about it when he's ready."

"I know."

I hate knowing he is keeping something from me. Something he can't trust me with, and to be honest, it kind of hurts. But I know if it wasn't serious he'd tell me, so I let it go.

Instead I take this time away from Lance to find out for myself what Lance and John's fight was all about. Lance did a pretty good job trying to make me forget about the whole fight and the fact that John said something so horrible that Lance wouldn't even repeat it to me. I know I should just let it go, but I can't. It's not in me. I need to know what happened. Not only because the words that were said were about me, but because John, who I considered a friend, had said them. This was more than just a fight between two guys. This was personal and that's why I find myself outside John's house with my fist centimeters from the wooden door.

I close the distance between the two and knock three times. I step back as the front door opens and a petite woman in a pencil skirt and a blazer stands in front of me.

"Hello?" she asks.

"Hi," I respond, "Is John here?"

"Yes," she nods as she waves me in, "come on in sweetie and I'll go get him."

I step over the threshold and plant my hands in the back pockets of my jeans as I rock back on my heels. I look around the front foyer and am reminded of camping as I take in the wooden furnished walls.

"Johnathan," his mother calls, "there is someone here to see you."

She directs her attention back to me, "I'm sorry, honey, I didn't catch your name."

"Rizz," I reply, "I'm a friend of John's."

I hear John's footsteps moving across the floor above us as he makes his way to the staircase.

"Well, it's great to meet you," she smiles. Her phone goes off and she looks down at it, "Sorry," she says, "I have to take this."

I nod as she heads out of the foyer to the kitchen.

"Who is it mo—" John says, but stops as he reaches the top of the staircase and sees me standing at the bottom.

I cross my arms over my chest and poke my hip out as I stare at him with an arched brow.

Slowly he descends the stairs. He takes a nervous swallow once reaching me and says, "Hey Rizz."

"That's all you have to say to me?" I question, hoping this will draw answers from him.

"I'm sorry, Rizz. I'm guessing he told you everything?" He says shamefully.

I throw my hands up in aggravation, knowing that pretending to know is going to get me nowhere.

"No," I groan, "he won't tell me anything. All I know is you said something about me to piss him off and that you guys decided to work it out with your fists."

"It wasn't one of my finest moments," John admits.

"Seriously, what the hell where you thinking?" I scold him.

"Why do you even care? You're with him, not me," he snaps.

"I want to know what you said," I demand.

John's eyes gleam as he takes a step toward me, "No, I don't think that's why you're here."

I sigh in exasperation and put my hands on my hips, "Of course it is."

"No, I think you're here because deep down you know there is something between me and you and you don't want to lose that."

"You're my friend, John."

"You belong with me, Rizz," he says, inching closer and placing his hand on my hip.

I shake my head in protest and back away from him. In this instant I feel conflicted. I know I have feelings for John, but my feelings for Lance trump those for John. Those feelings grew out of a place that is buried deep inside me—the old me—the me that I am trying so hard to overcome. My feelings for John all began that night a few years ago, but I was a different person then. I realized my mistake, but I was selfish and I couldn't lose the one person I had finally felt somewhat comfortable around.

***

I lie on John's bed and watch him as he puts his clothes back on. His back muscles flex as he moves, and I feel chills flow down my spine. John turns toward me and I can see his tight abs. He catches me looking and smiles. I return the smile as I bunch up the sheets around me to cover my exposed body.

Once he is fully dressed, he crawls onto the bed and makes his way up to me, kissing me on the forehead. A warmth fills me as my eyes flutter close at the feel of his lips against my skin.

"You're beautiful, Rizz," John tells me as he pulls away.

"I doubt that," I reply, thinking of the scars on my torso.

"You're the most beautiful girlfriend anyone could have," he says and kisses me.

I stiffen at the word 'girlfriend' and pull away from him.

"What's the matter?"

I look at him as my stomach begins to tighten, "I'm not your girlfriend, John."

Pain flashes across his face and I fight to keep my expression level.

John leans back and slumps down beside me on the bed.

"Then what are we?"

"We're friends," I state.

John gets up from the bed and says, "Friends don't do what we just did."

"Some do," I mutter as I watch him pace the room.

I wanted to do something to make this better. To run into his arms and tell him that I was only joking, but I couldn't. Fear rippled through me at the thought of a relationship. I didn't do boyfriends. I was the fucked up girl who used guys and then pushed them away when I got what I wanted. I wasn't girlfriend material.

"Listen, John," I say in an even tone, "trust me when I tell you that I enjoyed it, but we'd be better off as friends. It just wouldn't work out."

John narrows his eyes at me, "How do you know if you don't try?"

"I just know."

"I'm not going to stop trying to win you over."

I shake my head, "You'll be wasting your time."

"It's time worth wasting."

***

John reaches for me, but I step out of his grasp. His face falls, but I stand my ground.

"I belong with Lance," I state firmly.

John's expression turns up into anger as he says, "He'll never be right for you."

I scoff at his insinuation.

"You have a past, Rizz."

I look at him in shock.

"He'll never understand it, you know? But I do, I understand it. I have seen the scars and I know how you get scars like that."

"Shut up, John," I warn in a low tone.

"You get them from being burned," his voice breaks, "Burned by cigarette butts."

"Shut up," I sternly warn again.

"I won't let you hide from me anymore," he says, grabbing my hand in his.

"I'm not hiding," I say choking back the tears as I pull my hand from his.

"Yes, you are and you'll just continue to hide from him, but you don't have to with me," He grabs ahold of my shoulders as he pleads with me, "Pick me, Rizz. Not some pretty boy who will never understand you."

"He knows," I blurt out.

"What?" John asks in disbelief as his grip loosens on me.

"I told him…everything." I look at John through watery eyes, "I can't hide from him."

John's hands fall from my shoulders and to his side.

I bite back my tears, "I told you…you'd be wasting your time."

"Why him?" he whispers.

I open my mouth to respond, but close it as I think about my answer. Since the day I met Lance I was instantly attracted to him in a way I hadn't been attracted to another before. I didn't even want to pursue him because I found him aggravating—because I found myself begin to feel again, feelings that were so foreign to me. But the more he didn't give up on me the more those feelings came out in full force and I found myself becoming someone else—growing strong and being able to feel again, to really feel.

"Because…" I look up at John, "He makes me feel real."

I smile as I think about our past weekend together and how I didn't shut him out like I had with so many before him.

"Then what are you doing here?" John asks, quietly.

"I—I have to go," I say, realizing that it doesn't matter what John said that day. All that matters is that Lance stuck up for me—he protected me. I walk out of John's house and to my car. Looking back at the front door, I see John standing in the doorway. He gives me a sad smile and waves. I wave back, climb into my car, and pull out of his drive.

"Lance," I shout as I walk through his kitchen entry way. I found out they never lock the door in case Thom needs to "get away" as Lance put it. From what, I'm not sure, but from what I conclude things are a little stressed at his house.

"Lance, where are you?" I call, "I have something to tell you."

I walk through his house, but there is no sign of him anywhere. I trot upstairs to his room, but he isn't there. I pull my phone from my back pocket and put in the password before opening up my messages and sending him a "where are you?" text. I wait, but don't receive a reply.

I think where else he could be and decide to check with Thom. I rush down the stairs and outside to Thom's house. I knock on the front door and wait for someone to answer. No one does, so I knock again, this time harder. I wait and then the door opens and I find myself staring at Nathalie who is standing with the door half way opened and a shocked expression on her face.

"Rizz?" She asks.

"Who is it?" I hear Thom call.

"It-it's Rizz," She shouts back.

Thom emerges from behind a small Nathalie in a red bikini.

"Rizz?"

"Yes, it's me," I say exasperated, "Do you know where Lance is?"

I'm losing my patience as I look down at my phone screen to see he still hasn't responded. Nathalie and Thom exchange a look which raises my suspicions.

"I don't know," Thom shrugs, "Haven't talked to him since last night."

"Do you want to hang out?" Nathalie offers awkwardly.

"You can wait here for him," Thom adds equally as awkward.

I look at them with a raised brow, "Uh, no. I have to get to work."

"He probably just stepped out to get something," Thom offers.

"Uh..yeah..."

Nathalie sinks back behind him as if she knows something I don't.

"Are you okay, Nat?" I ask.

"Yeah," She chirps, plastering on her signature fake smile.

I open my mouth to say something when Thom beats me to it.

"I'll let him know you were looking for him if he comes by."

I nod and give them both one last suspicious look before heading down the porch steps and back across the yard to Lance's.

I rush into the café and past the counter to the back room. Pulling the strap of my bag from over my head and plopping it down onto the desk I rush back out to the front counter to punch in my numbers.

"Whoa, slow down there speedy Gonzales," Joel chuckles.

"I'm never late," I mutter under my breath as I reach the counter.

"I wouldn't worry about it. You're like Grace's soft spot, she won't even take a second glance."

"I'm still late."

"Joel," I hear Grace scold him, "What did I tell you about distancing yourself from my cookie."

I glance up at her and smile at her protectiveness.

"Get over here," She points at him with her finger and then to where she is standing.

"See what I mean," He mutters as he walks toward her.

I smile to myself as I finish punching my numbers into the register, and get to work.

Pulling an apron from the hooks on the far wall, I wrap it around my waist and tie it behind my back. I grab a rag and head out to the dining area to wipe down tables. Overhead, the song *You Had Me At Hello* plays and I find myself singing along. As I sing, I begin to find truth in the lyrics. I never thought I would fully trust anyone again—not after the life I have lived. I have seen how people hide things from one of another and fill each other up with broken promises and heartaches. I didn't want any of that. I always kept an eye out for those kind of people. I watched my back, because at the end of the day I knew the only person I could trust was myself, but Lance changed that for me. He came into my life like a damn wrecking ball and broke down my walls, and surprisingly I find myself able to breathe easier. From the moment I met him there was an instant connection—he literally had me at "hello" no matter how hard I tried to fight it.

"What has you in a fine mood today?" Grace calls from behind me.

I jump at the sudden intrusion of my thoughts. Placing my hand on my chest, I breathe, "Oh, Grace, you scared me."

"Sorry, Cookie."

I smile at her as I bend over a table to continue to wipe it down, "It's okay."

"So what has you smiling from ear to ear? I haven't seen you this happy since that day I told you, you could stay here as long as you'd like." She whispers.

I face Grace and play with the rag in my hand, folding it up in a neat square.

"I'm just in a really good mood."

"Does a certain boy have to do with this?"

I look at her in shock as my face heats up.

"Ooo, it does."

I walk over to another table and begin to wipe it off, "His name's Lance." I stand up straight and face her, "I think I might...I really like him."

"Oh, Cookie," she coos, "I can tell."

"It kind of scares me," I whisper at the floor, "But it also makes me feel really good."

Grace places her finger under my chin and lifts my head so my gaze catches hers.

"Teen love is like that, sweetie. It lifts you up and scares the bejeezus out of you at the same time. You just be careful, Cookie. You've been through too much already."

My eyes widen at her hidden acknowledgment of my home life.

"You're secret's safe with me," she winks, "You make sure that boy treats you right now." She calls over her shoulder as she walks back up to the counter.

I stand there in shock as the truth hits me. All this time, Grace knew. The one woman I found to be more like family than my own two parents, knew. How could I have been so foolish to think she wouldn't figure it out? All the scars and bruises—she saw them all. The sad looks she would direct my way when she thought I wasn't looking weren't just looks of worry, they were looks of a sad knowledge. As I stand here, I think of how much Grace had done for me over the years. She wasn't just my boss. She was more of a mother figure than my own would ever be.

I sit at my desk in my History class—my hardest subject—and write down the notes from the board into my spiral notebook as my teacher Mr. Watson continues to talk about our government. My forehead creases as I try to comprehend the words coming out of my teacher's mouth.

I can feel a headache coming on.

There is a knock at the classroom door and all heads turn in that direction as a student walks through the doorway and hands Mr. Watson a slip of paper. He looks it over and then looks up at the classroom, scanning the faces. When his eyes land on me, he clears his throat,

"Rizz, Principal Tucker would like to see you."

All eyes suddenly turn to me as I nod and begin to collect my books. A couple girls nearby begin to whisper to each other, but stop once I shoot them a look.

Yeah, think about who you are whispering about.

I grab my bag from the floor, throw it over my shoulder and head for the door. Once at the office, I walk past his secretary who looks up and smiles at me as I knock on his office door. Opening it slightly, I pop my head in and say,

"You wanted to see me?"

Principal Tucker looks up from his file, "Ah, Rizz, please have a seat."

I walk in and shut the door behind me before taking a seat in one of the plush leather chairs.

"What's going on?"

Principal Tucker sits back in his chair, "I got a call from Princeton today."

I perk up at the mention of Princeton. It was my number one choice of colleges to get into and Principal Tucker was doing everything he could to help me, academically, to get a full scholarship.

"And?" I ask.

"They'd like to have a meeting with you."

I perch up at the end of the chair, "What kind of meeting?"

"It says here that they have reviewed your application and they would like to talk to you about attending their University. Congratulations."

I sit back a little, "What about the academic scholarship?"

"That's something that should be brought up at the meeting, but I wouldn't worry. You are a straight A student, Rizz. The only class you seem to be having difficulties in is History, so just keep working at it and ace your exam and you should be in good shape." Principal Tucker flips through some papers in the file, "Even if they don't give you a full ride, I'm sure they would give you a room and board scholarship which will lessen your total tuition costs."

I slump back in the chair, "I need that full ride."

Principal Tucker closes the file, "Then focus on acing your History exam and we will see from there."

I nod as I reach for my bag.

"We'll figure something out, Rizz."

I give Principal Tucker a small smile before opening the office door and heading out into the hallway. I make my way to my locker and open it, setting my books on the shelf.

I have to get that full ride, I have to.

I pull my History book from the shelf and set it into my bag. I'm searching through my bag for my cellphone when from the corner of my eye I see Nathalie and Charlene approaching me.

"Hey, love," Charlene chimes as she reaches me.

"Hey," I mutter still searching through my bag.

Nathalie leans against the lockers as she scans the faces in the hall.

"I don't think he's here today," Charlene says, as she watches Nat.

"Yeah, that's what I was afraid of," Nat sighs.

I give up looking through my bag with a huff before turning my attention to Nat.

"Are you two alright?"

"Yeah," Nat says, "Why wouldn't we be?"

"Oh, I don't know, because you guys were acting really weird yesterday."

"Yesterday? When did you see them yesterday?" Char asks.

"She was looking for Lance," Nat explains, "And came by Thom's to see if he knew where he was."

Char nods her head.

"Then what is causing you two to act so strange?"

"It's nothing," Nat reassures, "He's just going through stuff."

"Well don't let him drag you through it too."

Nathalie shakes her head, "Look, I'm having a pool party next week to help him get out of his head, and you and Lance are invited." She looks at Char, "And you too, of course."

"Well I'm down," Charlene exclaims.

"I'll be there too," I agree, "I'm not one to miss a party."

"Oh we know," Char jokes.

I roll my eyes as Nathalie's phone goes off. She looks down and reads the text.

"I have to go. I'll text you guys with the details."

CHAPTER TWENTY-FIVE: LANCE

I tinker with the engine of the Jaguar as I duck under the hood. Country music blares in the background of the shop, Ray's favorite music and the only music that is allowed to be played during work hours. I hum along to Blake Shelton's *Sure Be Cool If You Did* as I replace a broken belt. I started working at Ray's Garage a few months after Ann died. It served as a good distraction, and it was the only place I could find solitude from everything that was going on—is going on.

I finish up with the belt and close the hood of the Jag. Wiping my hands off on an oil stained rag, I head over to the shop entrance to let Ray know the Jag is ready to go.

I usually only worked at the shop on weekends or during breaks throughout the school year. But since I got suspended I told Ray if he needed me I could start up sooner because working at the garage was better than sitting at home all day and losing my damn mind like the frickin' mad hatter.

I walk through the glass doors to the main entrance of the shop. A couple customers sit on the black leather couch staring up at the flat screen television hanging on the wall as they wait for their cars to be finished. Ray's Garage was a small town shop, but because of his loyal customers he was able to fix the place up from the old garage atmosphere to a well-run shop. I don't think the customers would have cared either way considering Ray's going above and beyond for his customers.

I walk up to the counter where Ray is typing some information into the computer and hand him the keys for the Jag.

"Jag's all set."

"Alright, get Seth to do a test run on it and we'll be all set."

I nod in agreement and turn on my heels to find Seth. I would have done the test drive myself, but I was banned from test driving the fancier cars a week or two after first starting up work at the garage. I had a lot on my mind then since it wasn't that long after the accident. I was on a test drive, but my mind wasn't focusing on listening to the car or even paying attention to the cars in front of me. I was lucky Ray didn't fire me after smashing up a customer's Mercedes. I guess it helped offering to work for free until the cost for the damage was covered. Plus, I think he knew I was going through some rough stuff and knew the job would help.

I head back out to the garage and when I get to the Jag, I find Thom leaning up against it with his arms crossed over his chest.

When he sees me he lifts himself from the car and meets me halfway.

"What's up?" I ask as I glance around the garage.

"I need to ask you something," Thom says calmly.

"It couldn't wait 'till I got off?"

Thom runs a hand through his hair and tugs at it.

"Thom, what's going on?" I ask, concerned.

"I need you to stop."

"Stop?"

"Yeah, stop—" Thom looks around the garage too and then looks back at me, "Stop pretending like you are okay and that everything is just fucking dandy."

I push past him and pull the hood of the Jag up, "I don't know what you're talking about."

"Yes, you freaking do," He sneers in a low tone.

I hold the hood up with my extended arm and look at the parts under the hood without really seeing them.

"I need you to stop, Lance. It's killing me. Stop avoiding it all."

"I'm fine."

Thom snorts, "Yeah, I know what 'fine' is like."

I pull away from the car and get in Thom's face, "I'm fine, Thom. I dealt with my shit months ago. Maybe you should start dealing with yours."

Thom grimaces as he shakes his head at me, "Whatever, man." He turns to walk out of the garage, but turns back, eyes narrowed and says, "Oh by the way, Rizz stopped by looking for you the other day."

I snap my head up to meet his glare, "Did you tell her where I was?"

"No, I kept your secret," Thom snaps as he turns on his heels and heads out of the garage.

"Thom." I call after him.

"Forget it." He calls over his shoulders, "It doesn't even matter." He spins on his heels and begins walking backward, "And tell her, or I will."

"It's not that easy."

Thom stops, "Why, because you'll have to admit what you're feeling?"

I shake my head in denial.

"She'll figure it out, you know?"

"Then I will tell her when she does. She'll understand."

"Yeah," Thom snorts, "Good luck with that."

"Thom," I call after him as he turns to leave again, "This is the only way I know...how to...to cope."

Thom stops, but doesn't turn to face me. He shakes his head and softly says over his shoulder, "It's not healthy...for you or me."

I turn back to the Jag and lean my wrists against the hood as I look aimlessly into the life of the car. The thing was, I knew Thom was right—about it all. I had to deal with things better. I just didn't know how. Not when everyone else around me was hurting. The moment I saw Thom at the funeral, I knew I had to be the one to keep it together—for his sake. I had to put on the strong front and let Pop's rules take over. She passed away, and I had to move on. That's what she would have wanted. She would have wanted me to live my life—to be happy. And I am, even with the lingering empty feeling that made a permanent home in my heart the minute I laid eyes on her body lying there in the crosswalk.

Rizz helped ease that pain every day I spent with her. She numbed the emptiness, and part of me feels as if Ann brought her to me. That Ann is continuing to be that guardian angel she told me she was the day she and Pop adopted me. The only thing Ann wouldn't be proud of is my keeping secrets from Rizz. I know keeping things from Rizz isn't a good idea. She is smart and it doesn't take her long to notice things, but I'm not ready to share that part of my life with her yet. I barely knew anything about him, or whether or not I'd be seeing him repeatedly. I have met with him two times so far, and each time all I felt was a strong anger toward the man who was supposed to be my father. I couldn't let her know about him yet. She would want to get involved and I wasn't ready for that.

I sigh into the Jag, before closing the hood and making my way through the garage in search of Seth. As I walk through the garage, I think of Rizz and keeping secrets from her.

I'll tell her about him in a couple days, just not yet.

I run my hands through Rizz's long chestnut curls, twisting the ends around my finger as she leans into me while we watch reruns of *Breaking Bad* on Netflix. I study her as she becomes entranced in the television screen. Everything about Rizz enthralled me, from her soft hair which I loved to play with and she loved letting me, to her porcelain skin, small hands, and her honey smell. When it comes to Rizz nothing else matters. Rizz laughs at something Jess says, and I smile as I watch her cheeks bunch up. I run my hand down her arm and pull her closer as I kiss her on the forehead.

She looks up at me and smiles, pressing her lips to mine. When she pulls away she smiles and I run my nose along hers as I whisper, "I love you."

A blush forms across her cheeks and I place a chaste kiss on her temple before directing my attention back to the show.

Feeling Rizz's intense stare on me I peak at her through my eyelashes and smirk, "It's not polite to stare."

A blush creeps over her face as she grips her bottom lip between her teeth in order to keep the corner of her mouth from turning up.

"I saw that," I smirk.

A chuckle escapes her as she shakes her head and lowers it to my chest. As she nuzzles her face into my chest, she mutters,

"I was looking for you the other day, but I couldn't find you."

"I know," I reply, running my hand lightly up and down her arm, "Thom told me."

"I thought it was weird that he didn't even know where you were."

"He's not my keeper," I chuckle.

"I know, I just thought—never mind," she says shaking her head. "Where were you?"

"I had to run some errands for Pop," I say as I inwardly cringe at the lie. "He's been working overtime a lot, so I've been trying to help out."

Rizz nods, analyzing my half lie.

"What did you need to tell me?" I ask, trying to throw her off my trail.

Suddenly, Rizz stiffens in my arms.

"Babe, are you okay?"

"Yeah, why?" She asks, trying to keep her tone level.

The more time I spent with Rizz, the more I was able to get her to throw down the walls of hers. Now I was able to know exactly how she felt in any moment. Sure there were times when her walls went back up—usually when we got more into the heavy stuff, but she's working on it and I'm doing my best in order to help her.

"Because you just went completely stiff," I say, shifting myself so I can look at her.

"Oh, sorry. I just—I was caught off guard."

I raise an eyebrow at her.

"It's nothing," she says as she shakes her head again, "I was just looking for you and I couldn't find you…and you didn't respond to my text…you always—what?" she asks as she looks at me.

I'm smiling at her with no doubt the dumbest grin on my face, because I know what she wanted to tell me but there was no way I was going to steal that moment from her—from myself. So instead of telling her 'I know', I say, "You sound like a girl."

I chuckle and rub my side where Rizz has just elbowed me.

"Shut up," She says.

"It's kind of cute."

"Whatever," she mumbles, crossing her arms over her chest and settling deeper down into the couch.

"Don't be embarrassed," I laugh as I pull her back into me.

"Whatever," She says again, nudging my chest with her cheek.

"I love you," I whisper, kissing her on her head.

"I know," she whispers back, kissing my chest.

I give her a small squeeze to hide the small tug at my chest when she didn't say it back. She needed more time, and I know that. After everything she has been through. Getting her to say those three words to me was going to be hard. I know she was going to have to get her nerve up again. That day she had it, but she couldn't find me, and now she was put on the spot and that made her nervous. I had to wait until she found that nerve again, and I would.

It's been two days since we both graduated and walked the stage at our schools. I graduated at the top of my class as was expected by Pop and as always I never let him down. Rizz also graduated as one of the five top students in her class. She walked the stage even after the car had a mysterious malfunction on the way to school. Luckily I was able to show Rizz a few things under the hood of a car, and even more luckily she was the type to really pay attention. She suspects it was a plot of her mother's—to take something special from her once again. Rizz still hadn't heard a word about her scholarship standing. Apparently, Princeton had some more "looking into" to do. I try my best to keep Rizz's mind off of it—I can tell it stresses her out—and what better way to do that than to take summer on at full force.

I pluck at a few chords on the acoustic guitar that rests in my lap as I sit on the patio couch on the back terrace. Rizz sits next to me, her back against the arm rest and her feet lying on my lap wedged between my stomach and the guitar.

Rizz laughs, "You better watch out. George Harrison might come back from the dead and start hitting you over the head for playing that thing like that."

"Ha. Ha," I reply. I look at her with a smirk before strumming the guitar and begin singing badly, "Oh, Rizz. You're just the chizz bizz. You work me up in such a tizz. Oh Ri—"

Rizz wraps her hand around the neck of the guitar and laughs, "Okay, okay, so you're no smooth singing John Lennon either."

"Now my feelings are hurt," I say, clutching my chest.

"Maybe," Rizz says removing her feet from my lap and sitting up on her knees, "this will make you feel better." She leans over me, and her shirt hangs loose allowing me a clear view to her perky breasts hiding underneath her bra. I place my hand on her collar bone and slide it up along her neck as I lean the guitar against the couch on the floor. Rizz makes her way onto my lap, straddling my lap with her strong long legs. Placing my hands on her hips, I pull her closer to me and cover her mouth with my own and let her sweet taste mix with my own.

Rizz pulls away, setting her forehead against mine, "Lance?"

I run my hand along her thigh, "Yeah?"

"I want you to meet Hope."

"Are—are you sure?" I ask, caught off guard.

She nods her head against mine, "I trust you."

I capture her mouth with my own again as the severity of Rizz's request settles in. I know meeting

Hope meant a big step in our relationship. It's only been a short amount of time since I had met Rizz, but from the moment I laid eyes on her I instantly felt a pull toward her. I couldn't have let her out of my grasp even if I tried.

Guilt rushes over me as I realize the courage she mustered up in just the idea of me meeting the one person who means more to her than me. She wasn't just spitting out an idea though, she was making a plan, and I couldn't even let her into my own life completely. I've been hiding my meetings with Jack from the one person I trust more than anyone. I've been making excuses and telling white lies to the one person who just told me she trusted me— something she doesn't take lightly. I was—I am a coward.

CHAPTER TWENTY-SIX: THOM

I bounce my foot up and down as I hunch over the top of the metal table in the contained room. I hated coming here. It made me feel guilty— nervous. It made me feel like crimes could be contagious. As if I would be next to get locked away in this damn place if I took a wrong step and looked at a guard the wrong way.

I chuckle to myself at my idiocy, but that doesn't stop my leg from going rabid.

It's been weeks since I have come to see my father. I couldn't handle it, but right now there was something even more dominating that I couldn't handle. I knew why I was here. I had to get straight answers. I had to try to understand what my brain obviously wouldn't let me comprehend. I had to know his reasons for writing those strings of words down on that paper. *That fucking letter. God. Why couldn't I just get it out of my head?*

I clutch my fist as the words continue to spin through my head.

Dammit, get ahold of yourself.

Attempting to steady my breathing I think back to that day in Dr. Connors office.

I catch a glimpse of her wild red hair bouncing on her shoulders as she rushes to me. She falls to her knees beside me and her warm welcoming arms wrap around me. The aroma of cinnamon reaches me and I allow her to pull me into her as I rest my head on her chest and begin to even out my breathing. As my breathing evens, I pull back from her and try to protest, but she wasn't having it.

"No, Thom, this is you and I accept that. Don't tell me to leave by saying you expect it. Let me make my own decisions."

I just stare at her trying to muster any excuse to get her to leave before I hurt her too.

"You're not getting rid of me. I'm your girlfriend, Thom."

My eyes widen as her words begin to seep in.

"I choose you," she whispers as she brings her lips gently to my forehead.

Burying my face into her chest I whisper, "Thank you."

I straighten up in the metal chair as my body slowly relaxes. I drum my fingers against the table top and focus on the beat of my fingers as they hit the surface.

The door opens and my father is led through the door. He waits for the guard to uncuff him before sitting down in the empty chair.

"Hey, Son," he says as he runs his hand over his balding head.

"Hey, Dad," I reply, stopping my thrumming against the table's surface, "How are you doing?"

"I should be asking you that question?" he says, staring at me pointedly.

I raise a brow at him and look around the room, "I'm pretty sure the question came from the right person."

"How are things at home? With school?" he asks, avoiding my question.

I choose to not respond about home. I can't bring up how Mom has made it her life's mission to break the world record of packing up a house the fastest or how the only time she leaves her room now is when she's packing or when Nathalie is over. "I got into Columbia," I say instead.

Not that I would be going.

"That's great news, Son. Full ride like we had hoped?"

"Yeah, I got the academic scholarship like you said I would."

"You're a smart kid, Thom. You must know that by now."

I blow out a deep breath as I look to the side shaking my head.

"Then why can't I understand."

"Understand?" my father asks perplexed.

I meet his gaze, "How could you say it's not my fault?"

"Thom," he says, almost a whisper.

"No, Dad, everything about that day was my fault—"

"You have to stop blaming yourself," he says, hunching over the table.

The guard knocks on the small door window and my father sits back in his seat.

"You weren't even supposed to pick me up."

"Thom—"

"No, Dad, we weren't supposed to be there! It was my fault. I missed my ride, I distracted you."

"Thom," My father says sternly trying not to raise his voice.

"It's my fault Mom is packing all the shit up, it's my fault she asked for a divorce and it's my fault you're in here."

"God help me, Thom! You cut it out right now!" my father says slamming his palm on the table.

The door opens and the guard rushes in pulling my father into his hold and re-cuffing his hands.

"Times up," the guard yells to me.

My father fights against the guard's hold so he faces me as he says, "You need to stop this Thom. Nothing was your fault, it's time you accept it."

And those were the last words spoken as my father is led out of the room and down the cold hallway back to his cell. I sit back in the chair and fight to keep the emotions at bay.

I walk through the front door and slam it behind me. There is clattering coming from the kitchen so I make my way toward the noise to find my mother taking dishes from the cupboards and wrapping them in newspaper as she places them into boxes labeled "kitchen."

She must hear me, because she turns slightly to acknowledge me, "Oh, hi honey, grab some paper and help me, would you?"

I walk up to her and take the plate that she just finished wrapping in the Sunday comics from her. Without taking my scowl off of her, I un-wrap the plate and place it back into the cupboard.

"We aren't moving," I say, almost a whisper.

My mother looks from me to the plate I had just put back with wide eyes, "Yes, we are."

"No, we aren't," I reply steadily.

"Thom, we've talked about this."

"No," I say slamming my hand onto the counter.

My mother flinches.

"You told, and expected me to be okay with it."

"Thom."

"You expected me to be okay with it all," I now yell as the tears begin to stream down.

My mother flinches again as my voice raises, "Thom we have to do this."

"No, Mom, you have to do this. But what about me, huh?" I now scream in her face as I slam my hand against my chest. "What about me?"

"It's not like you will be homeless, Sweetie. You'll be living on campus, and there will be a room for you at my new house."

"Oh, that's a relief," I sneer at her, "I'll have a strange home to go to as you hide away in yet another room as the therapy sessions continue to fail you."

Pain flashes across my mother's face, but I go on.

"I need a mother," I yell, "I need my father, and you're taking that from me! You're trying to erase him from your life and from mine."

I slam my hand down on the counter and a stray fork penetrates through my palm, but I barely flinch as the blood trickles down my palm.

"What will you do next when you find out you can't erase him from your life either?"

My mother stands silent as she stares at me as if she can barely recognize me.

I shake my head in anger and frustration and storm thorough the kitchen and up the stairs to my room. I slam my door with a huff, slamming my palms against the closed door. Unsatisfied I ball my hands into fists and pound at the wooden door as I kick at the base of it repeatedly. The wood begins to shard and I continue to kick. A moment later I give up, and pace my bedroom, trying to catch my breath. I think about Nat and her wild red hair, but the rage ripples through me. I knock over my desk chair and wipe the objects sitting on top onto the floor with one quick motion. As a glass hits the floor it shatters and I stare at the broken pieces on the ground.

I hold up my palm and look at the four small holes in my palm then back at the glass. I walk over to where the glass lays on the floor and drop to my knees. Tears continue to streak my face as I grab ahold of a large broken portion and press it to my palm. Slowly I apply pressure and push the glass into my flesh. Blood trickles out and I begin to feel the weight leave my soul. I let out a small sigh as I glide the glass through the flesh of my palm and stop just above my wrist. Releasing the glass from my hand I fall back on my bottom as I let the sweet pain take over all emotion and slowly I relax into the wall and drift off into a weightless sleep.

CHAPTER TWENTY-SEVEN: RIZZ

I glance over at Lance fidgeting with his hands in the passenger seat as I turn off of the main road and onto my street.

"You okay?" I ask.

"Yeah, why?"

I arch a brow at him and nod toward his lap where he is wringing his hands in his lap.

"I'm just a little nervous," he chuckles.

"To meet an eight-year-old?" I reply flatly.

"It has more to do with what she means to you than anything."

"She'll love you, Lance. You don't have to worry."

"How do you know?"

"Because of the fact that she is eight. She likes everyone."

Lance chuckles and looks out the window, "thank you for this."

I look out the windshield as I speak my next thought, "You mean something to me, Lance, something important. I want the two most important people in my life to know each other."

Lance is silent as I pull into the driveway. After putting the car in park I steal a glance at him to see that he is watching me.

"You trust me?" he says after a beat.

"Of course I do," I say in all honesty.

"Thank you," he says before opening the car door and stepping out.

I continue to stare at his empty seat.

What the hell?

A tap comes from my window. Whiping myself around I find Lance standing outside my door with his hand outstretched to his side,

"Are you coming?"

"Uhm, yeah," I say as I get out of the car and shake away the feeling that he is hiding something from me.

I had the feeling before that Lance wasn't telling me something. He was constantly telling me he was going to "hang out with Thom" and never did so. Of course he didn't know I knew this, and maybe I should have said something to him about it, but whatever he was keeping from me I knew he wanted to tell me. He just didn't know how, or at least that's what I keep telling myself. The truth is he's keeping something from me and I'm continuing to let him keep it from me, but not anymore. It has to stop.

I get out of the car and walk up to the house with Lance at my heel. As I pull out my key and begin to insert it into the lock, I turn toward him and ask,

"What's been going on with you lately?"

"What do you mean?" He asks, his brows creasing.

"Well first off you're acting really strange," I say, pushing open the door and walking through the threshold.

Lance follows behind me as he rubs the back of his neck, "I've just been going through a lot with Pop and Thom. It's not a big deal."

"You know you wince every time you tell me a lie, right?" I say turning on him, "Tell me what's going on Lance."

Lance's body grows stiff and his face grows pale as he focusses on something behind him.

"Lance," I say, putting my hand on his forearm, "You can tell me anything, you know that."

"Ahem," someone clears their throat from behind me.

I turn and find my father standing in the foyer staring at us with tired eyes.

"Dad," I exclaim.

My father looks at me with a shocked expression as I clear my throat and try to find my words again, "Lance, this is my dad. Dad, this is Lance." I wave a hand between the two of them.

Lance moves from his immobilized stance toward my father and reaches out his hand. My father takes it as Lance says,

"It's nice to meet you, sir."

My father takes Lance's hand and shakes it, "It's nice to meet you too." Turning his attention to me he says, "I was headed out to the office since your mother is out, but…" he continues as he glances at Lance, "I think I can work from home today."

"What about Hope?" I ask, squaring up my shoulders.

"She wanted to come with me," he explains, "She has been showing a great interest in the law, mostly the illegal narcotic department."

"Why would she be interested in that?" I ask dumbfounded.

"I have no idea. I guess she must have seen something on television," he says.

I nod my head slowly, not believing him.

"Where is Hope? I wanted her to meet Lance."

"She's upstairs, putting on her shoes."

"You know she is supposed to carry them down and put them on down here."

"Your mother isn't home, Rizz."

"It doesn't matter," I snap, but stop myself as I remember Lance is watching our whole interaction. "I'm going to take Lance to see her," I say changing subject.

I grab ahold of Lance's hand and lead him around my father and up the front staircase and to Hope's bedroom. I knock on the door and wait.

"Hope, it's me," I call through the door when she doesn't answer right away.

A moment later the door flings open and Hope glares at me. I'm taken back by her reaction to me and am unable to find any words.

Hope glances over my shoulder and notices Lance, "Who's that?"

Finding my voice I say, "This, is Lance."

Hope's eyes lock with mine again and I can see them begin to soften as well as her facial features.

"I wanted you two to finally meet," I smile at her.

Lance steps in front of me and squats down to Hope's level. He holds out his hand, "It's nice to finally meet you, Hope. Rizz has told me a lot about you."

Hope looks at his extended hand and without taking it she says, "I haven't heard much about you." she pauses as my jaw drops slightly at her rudeness. I open my mouth to say something but then she takes two of his fingers in her hand and shakes them vigorously. "It's nice to meet you anyhow."

Lance laughs, "That's quite some handshake."

"Thank you," She says sweetly.

"Did you think of that all on your own?" Lance asks with a grin.

"Sure did," Hope boasts.

"You're on the right track to being able to make up your own secret handshake."

"What kind of secret handshake?"

"Well," Lance says pretending he is in deep thought, "It can be anything you want."

Hope thinks for a minute and then says, "Alright, I know."

"Well let's see it," Lance exclaims.

"I can't."

"Why not?"

Hope attempts to secretly point at me without me noticing. I smile at this as Lance says,

"Oh, right," And then winks at Hope.

Lance looks up at me and smiles. I smile back unsure why he would ever think Hope wouldn't like him since he is doing so great with her.

Backing from the doorway I say, "I'll just be downstairs. Remember to carry your shoes down, Hope."

Pain flashes across Hope's face, but Lance doesn't see it as he is still looking at me. Soon it is erased from her face and I turn to head down the stairs.

I head back into the main foyer at the end of the staircase and find my father still standing in the archway. He leans against a wall with his arms folded over his chest and his legs crossed at his ankles.

"You know you never took your shoes off," Chip chuckles.

I shoot him a glare, "I can take care of myself. Hope is helpless."

"I think you are overreacting Rizz."

I scoff at his remark and begin to push past him, "I don't know why I even bother trying to get you to see things my way."

Chip sighs as he pushes himself from the wall, "Your mother has a temper, but she has never let it go too far."

I spin on my heels and face him, "How would you know? You were never home. You never heard my cries, my pleas for you to walk through that door. You have no idea how bad it was."

Chip pinches the bridge of his nose, "This boy, Lance, he seems good for you."

I scoff as I shake my head.

So typical.

"Is that so, because you've known him all of what, two seconds? You're such a great judge of character *Dad*."

"I haven't heard that in quite a long time," Chip says straightening up.

I feel the tears begin to burn my eyes as they form in the beds of my eyelids. I take a sharp swallow and say, "Yeah, well I wouldn't get used to it."

"Rizz," my father presses, "I wish you would just tell me what it is your holding back."

I look away from my father as the memory of my mother jabbing the cigarette butts into my stomach and wishing for my father to walk through the front door, pick me up, and save me from the misery that was my mother. But he never did. The door never opened, and he never whisked in to my rescue. No, I endured the pain. I hid the scars, and never spoke of the torture that would take place when he was working late at the office.

"Rizz," my father pleads. He takes a step closer as I fight to keep the tears at bay, "I can't help you if you don't tell me."

He reaches up and gently places his palm on my cheek.

I close my eyes as the feel of my father's strong hand radiates through me. As I finally feel the safety I had always dreamt of having from my father. I open my eyes to return my father's gaze and part my lips to speak as I hear Hope's laughter followed by Lance's sail down the staircase, and the moment is lost. I step back from my father and his hand falls at his side right before Lance and Hope turn the corner of the staircase.

"Hey," Lance says as he looks between me and my father. Concern etches across his features and I give him a small reassuring smile.

He raises an eyebrow and I only smile once again as I look away from him and to Hope as she says, "We are going to go play on the monkey bars at the park."

Hope swings her and Lance's joined hands and continues, "Are you going to come with us?"

I smile at her as I squat to her level and reply, "Are you kidding? Watching you be a monkey is always the highlight of my day."

I watch as Hope and Lance play on the monkey bars. Seeing the two of them together makes me think about Lance's and my short future together. I begin to think what it's going to be like after summer. Lance will be traveling the world and I will be headed to New Jersey to further my education at Princeton. I didn't think about our future really when we began our relationship. Where will we stand at the end of the summer? I don't want things to change between us and honestly I'm afraid. I'm afraid that losing him—the one person I have trusted with my soul—would cause me to fall back into my old routines completely. I was wrong before when I thought Luke and Hope were supposed to save me from myself. It wasn't them. Instead destiny had a different plan for me—Lance. And within a few months we would be apart. I will be alone again, and left to hide behind the mask I know so well.

Hope runs up to me and takes the seat next to me on the bench. I can sense the distance that is sitting between us and I'm confused as to how it got there. Lance soon comes running up to us and hunches forward putting his hands on his knees.

"She is quite the monkey," Lance huffs, "You weren't kidding about that."

Hope beams up at Lance and it causes my insides to tighten. I don't want this to end. I can see little flashes of a future with Lance. A future where we continue to take Hope to the park and we stroll along holding hands and smile in the direction of the little girl climbing on the monkey bars.

My thoughts are halted when Lance's phone goes off.

He reaches into his back pocket and pulls it out, checking the caller ID.

Looking up he says, "I'll just be one second." He begins to saunter off as he answers the phone, "Hello…I told you not to call me…I can't. No…yes I know that…I'm with her right now…" Lance looks toward me and gives me a reassuring smile.

I half smile back as he begins to walk further away out of hearing distance.

"I like him," Hope says, as she breaks my concentration of trying to listen.

"Me too," I smile back sadly.

"What's wrong?" Hope asks as she draws her brows together.

I squint at Lance as he leans against the swing set on the far end of the playground, "He's hiding something from me."

"How do you know?"

"He's being secretive."

"How do you know?"

I shake my head not wanting to explain, "It's just a feeling."

"I know that feeling," she says, looking away.

Looking at Hope, my jaw slack I begin to ask her what she is talking about when Lance walks up and asks, "You ready to go?"

Bringing my attention to him I ask, "Who called?"

"It was just Thom," Lance says, looking away.

I say nothing as I wait for Lance to meet my eyes, but he doesn't.

Without saying anything to Lance I stand up and push past him to the car. Calling back I say, "Let's go Hope."

I hear Hope's footsteps behind me as she runs to catch up to me, and then I feel her small hand slip into mine.

I give her hand a small squeeze, and smile slightly, "I know you're mad at me about something," I whisper to her, "But thank you."

Hope says nothing but squeezes my hand in response.

We drop Hope off at the house and make our way back to Lance's house so I can drop him off. We sit in silence, and I wonder if he'll ever tell me what's going on. I ponder the thought and know that he isn't going to say anything, and in the end it's going to pull us apart. So I make the decision to say something.

I pull into the driveway and put the car into park.

"So what did Thom want?" I ask, resting my arms on the steering wheel.

"He just wanted to hang out, but—."

"Do you really want to continue with this lie right now?" I ask, cutting him off.

Lance looks at me with wide eyes and his mouth hanging open slightly, but he makes no move to begin telling me the truth.

I shake my head as I pull open the car door, get out, and walk to the side of his house. As I walk around the side I admire the vines with little colorful flowers creep up the side of the house. Everything about Lance's home was beautiful. I walk in his gazebo that sat in the middle of the garden in the yard and sit on one of the benches that overlooked a small handmade pond. I hear Lance's hesitant footsteps as he enters the gazebo after me.

"What aren't you telling me?" I ask, staring out at the pond.

"What?" Lance asks.

I look up to see his brows furrowed. He wasn't angry, but he wasn't surprised either. He was continuing to try to hide.

"I'm not stupid Lance," I say jumping from my seat, "I know you haven't been hanging out with Thom when you say you have been. If you haven't noticed he's dating one of my best friends."

I pause, allowing him to say something but he doesn't.

"Are you cheating on me? Is that what it is, part of your game? You got the cold cynical bitch to open up to you both mentally and physically so now you're on to your next target?"

Lance looks at me with huge eyes and the vein in his forehead begins to pop. If he wasn't pissed before he certainly is now.

"Last I knew, I wasn't the one who played the games." He snaps.

I take a step back as I let the sting of that comment settle. I knew I deserved it, but it still stung.

"I'm sorry," he says his voice calmer now, "I would never do that to you and you know that. That's not who I am."

I choke back the tears that are building, "I know," I say and look away from him.

Lance closes the gap between us and lifts my chin with his finger so I am looking at him.

"I'm not seeing any girl behind your back, Rizz."

My eyes widen at the fear of—

"Don't even start thinking like that," Lance says sensing my thoughts. He quickly goes on, "I haven't been hanging out with Thom either. I wasn't ready to tell you and that's why I have been lying to you, and I am so sorry for that Baby."

"Just tell me what's going on."

"I've been lying to you because I wasn't ready to tell you that I was meeting with my biological father."

A wave of relief washes over me as I let the information sink in and suddenly I feel foolish for thinking what he was doing was worse than the reality and I begin to laugh. I begin to laugh hysterically as I think of my foolishness.

"Why are you laughing?" Lance asks with a pain in his voice.

Looking at the hurt in his eyes I try to calm my laughing which doesn't take long as a rush of anger bubbles inside of me and I punch him in the arm.

"Owe, shit, what was that for," Lance asks, rubbing his arm.

"You should have told me, you jackass."

"I'm sorry, alright, I just…"

"You what? Wanted to worry the shit out of me? 'Cause you succeeded. Wow, you are such an ass sometimes."

"I didn't want to give you more than you could handle. I knew you had a lot going on back home."

"That doesn't mean I can't be there for you too, you idiot. I mean I'm not a pro at this relationship thing, but I'm pretty sure that's what couples do. They be there for each other and tell each other things." I grunt as I raise my hands in frustration, "damn, I want to hit you again."

"Please don't," Lance says quickly, "you have one mean swing."

"Yeah, and you better remember that," I teasingly threaten him.

Lance looks at me with a smirk and then begins to laugh.

"What's so funny now?"

"We are probably the most insane people ever. If only the neighbors could have seen us."

I crack a smile as he clutches his stomach.

"If you don't cut it out I might have to get Pop out here to commit you to the looney bin."

Lance immediately stops laughing and straightens up. Looking at me with a devilish grin he says, "Pop isn't home, and won't be until tomorrow morning."

I return Lance's devilish grin as he grabs my hand and guides me back to his house and we enter in through the back door.

CHAPTER TWENTY-EIGHT: LANCE

"Rizz," I whisper into her ear before gently nibbling on it, "Rizz," I coo, "Wake up."

Rizz nudges her head as my lips continue to play along her earlobe.

"Come on, Rizz," I coax her again.

She lets out a small moan as she rolls on her side, placing her head on my shoulder and her hand snakes up my bare chest.

I chuckle as I run my fingers through her soft brunette bed head.

"What time is it?" She mumbles.

"Seven," I whisper as I glide my thumb along her cheek, "We fell asleep."

Rizz moans as she tilts her cheek into my touch. Then suddenly her body grows ridged. With a gasp Rizz sits up clutching the covers to her chest and looks out at the room with large eyes.

"Oh my God," She gasps, "Pop's going to think I'm some sort of hussy."

I chuckle and Rizz shoots me with daggers at she whips her head around to stare me down.

"It's okay," I assure her, "He isn't supposed to get back until eight. Besides," I add, "He'd never think so shallow of you."

"I'm pretty sure we are playing with fire."

"Ah, but the burn feels so good," I muse.

"Ha ha," she says as she lies back down on the bed, "You won't be saying that when the third degree burns bite you in the—."

I cut her off with a deep kiss, "Good morning," I say as I pull away.

Rizz smiles and brushes the back of her hand against my cheek, "Good morning."

I pull Rizz into my chest and kiss her on her forehead before pulling away and getting up from the bed. The covers fall from my naked body as I make my way across the walkway to my bedroom bathroom.

"Now that's a sight I'll never get tired of seeing," I hear Rizz quip.

I look over my shoulder to find her scoping out my backside. Smirking, I walk through the bathroom doorway and shut the door behind me.

I turn on the facet and cup my hands under the cool running water. Leaning over the sink I bring the puddle of water forming in my hands up to my face and splash it up at my skin and run my hands over my face. Shaking my hands, I reach for a towel and dry off my hands and face.

Stepping back out of the bathroom I find Rizz sitting on the edge of the bed with her back to me as she slips on her bra.

I walk over to my chest and pull open a drawer, retrieving a pair of boxers. After slipping them on I walk over to where Rizz is now standing in only her undergarments.

Running my hands along her bare arms, I take in the sight of her lean figure.

"Now this," I say admiring her with my eyes, "I could never get used to."

Rizz rises up on her toes and places a chaste kiss on my jawline, "Too bad I have to leave."

She smirks as she sidesteps me and my hands fall back to my side.

I swing back around and grab her hand, pulling her back to my chest.

Rizz's eyes smile up at me as I cherish her features. Leaning in, I brush my lips lightly against hers,

"We still have about fifteen minutes before we really have to start getting dressed."

Rizz chuckles, "oh, is fifteen minutes all you need?"

I let out a laugh and lean my forehead against hers, "You really know how to emasculate a guy, don't you?"

"It's one of my many talents," she jokes.

I smile as I place my hands on either side of her face and place one final kiss on her lips before pulling away.

"Okay," I say, "Get cleaned up at home and I'll swing by to pick you up at ten."

Rizz's eyebrows pull together, "What's at ten?"

"Coffee with Jack," I say simply as I make my way back toward the bathroom.

"Wait, what?" Rizz says as she rushes in front of me, blocking my way to the bathroom, "I get to meet Jack?"

Placing my hands on her hips, I lift her up and set her down so she is clear of my path.

"Of course you do."

"I'm going to ignore the fact that you just man-handled me only because I really want to meet your biological father."

"Good choice."

"Hey," she scolds as she smacks my arm, "Don't start acting all cocky. We both know who wears the pants in this relationship."

I raise my brows at her challenge.

"Don't even think—."

I scoop Rizz up in my arms and throw her on the bed as I jump on top of her. Rizz lets out a squeal,

"You jerk," she laughs.

Pinning her hands down on either side of her head I say, "Now, I thought this relationship was a democracy not a dictatorship."

"That's what I wanted you to think," she smirks.

"Oh, yeah?" I egg her on.

"It was all part of the greater scheme."

"Ah, but now I know your secret."

"I'm so diabolical you won't be able to do a thing."

"Is that so?" I say with a half smirk.

Rizz's eyes grow larger, "Lance, Don't you even dar—." She ends with laughter as I begin to tickle her sides.

"I know your weakness," I say in an evil voice followed by an evil laugh.

Rizz begins to laugh harder as she jerks around on the bed.

"You...won't get...away with this," she says between laughs.

"Oh, I think I will," I smile.

I stop tickling her and jerk up, "Did you hear that?"

Rizz stills beneath me as I hover over top of her and listen.

"Shit," I say jumping up from the bed, "Pop's home early."

Rizz jumps up from the bed as I scoop up her shirt from the floor and toss it to her.

"Get dressed."

"No, I was just going to go say hi to your father in my bra and panties," she says throwing her shirt on over her head.

Rizz bends over to gather her pants from the floor and I smack her ass as I head back toward the bathroom.

"Ouch," She whispers, "What the hell was that for?"

"The smartass comment."

She rolls her eyes as she pulls up her jeans and I head for the bathroom.

"Where are you going?" she asks.

"To brush my teeth."

"Really? After kissing me all morning, you are now just going to brush your teeth?"

"Morning breath will only bring us closer."

She rolls her eyes again.

"And what do you suppose I do to get out of here? Shimmy down the drain pipe."

"Well, there is an idea," I say tilting my head.

Rizz picks up my shirt from the floor and throws it at me.

"Screw your morning breath, your ass is walking me out now. Chances are your Pop went straight to his room to freshen up. That gives us about five minutes to sneak me out and save your ass."

"I love when you get all secret agent on me."

"Oh please," she says rolling her eyes. "Now, put that on and lets go," she says pointing to the shirt in my hands.

I throw it on over my head and then grab my shorts from the floor and stumble into them as I follow Rizz to the bedroom door.

She peeks out and motions for me, "The coast is clear."

"It's almost like having my own Mrs. Smith. Do you have any heavy artillery hidden in your—."

"If you don't want to get kneed in your privates, I suggest you don't finish that sentence."

I let out a low chuckle and follow her out into the hallway. I grab her hand and bring it to my lips. She meets my gaze with shock.

"I love you," I mouth.

Her eyes grow soft and a smile spreads across her face.

Knowing she wouldn't respond, I lace her fingers with mine and begin to lead her down the stairs.

Opening the front door, I lead her out to her car. Rizz leans against the car door and smiles at me. I tower over her, placing a hand on the frame of the car and the other on her waist as I lean down and kiss her goodbye.

"See you at ten," I say pulling away from her.

"Ten," she confirms.

I step back letting her into her car. Watching as she backs out of the driveway and onto the street, I wave to her before going back inside.

As I shut the door behind me and turn toward the foyer I find Pop standing in front of me with his arms crossed over his chest.

"Have a late night?" he asks.

"Uh…" I hesitate as I point back at the door with my thumb.

Pop raises his hand to silence me, "I hope you were cautious."

"Pop…" I say running my hand through my hair and avoiding all contact.

"I got a call from Oxford. They want you to come and get a feel for the place. They even offered to pay for the airfare."

"I told you already, Pop, I'm taking the year off to travel."

"Where better to travel then in London."

"You and I both know I won't have time to travel if I go there for school."

"Lance, you'll be living in a different continent and experiencing a whole different culture, what could possibly be better than that?"

"Look Pop, we talked about this. I want to travel the states before you ship me off to London."

"Don't do that. Don't make it sound like I am forcing you to go."

"It's starting to feel like that," I say as I push past him and into the kitchen.

"Oxford is a great school and they are offering you a full ride. Lance, you can't pass this up."

"I'm not going," I say as I pull a glass from the cupboard.

"I don't understand you. You'd rather travel in a place you are so familiar with than a whole new world."

"I don't see it like that. There is so much on our own soil I have yet to see—to experience. We have so much history I haven't even discovered yet," I say placing the glass on the counter and facing Pop. "Why would I leave my own home to learn about another culture's history when I'm not all that familiar with my own?"

Pop pinches the bridge of his nose, "And this has nothing to do with Rizz?"

I shake my head in disbelief, "Pop, we've talked about this before I even met Rizz. This decision is mine and mine alone."

"You need an education, Son."

"And I will get one. Afterwards."

"You know what the statistic is of those who say they will go back to school and never do is?"

"Pop, you and I know I have never been one to be part of some statistic."

Pop sighs, knowing he has lost this battle then points at me, "I hope you know what you're doing."

"I do," I nod.

Pop turns and begins heading out of the kitchen.

I slump against the counter and grab the glass.

Over his shoulder Pop adds, "No more late nights with Miss. Murphy. You hear?"

"Loud and clear," I say rubbing my thumb against the glass and setting it back onto the counter.

I head back upstairs and throw on some deodorant and brush my teeth before heading back downstairs and to the garage where my truck sits.

I push the button on the garage's wall to open the door. As the door ascends upward I walk over to the car's side and slide in.

I back the car down the driveway until I am centered in the middle, put it in park and hop out of the truck.

Grabbing a pail and sponge from inside the garage I make my way to the hose atthe side of the house and fill the pail with soap and water. Once the pail is filled, I take the hose and spray water over the Ford and begin to wash my truck.

"Hey, man," I hear from behind me, as I jump up and send suds of soap in the air as well.

I turn around to see Thom strolling across the yard to where I am now standing with sponge in hand.

"Someone looks a little startled," Thom chuckles.

"You know I hate when people sneak up on me."

"You have always been jumpy," Thom smirks, taking a sponge from the bucket.

"You taking Rizz out or something?" Thom asks as he begins to help wash the truck.

"We're going to meet Jack for some coffee," I say, turning back to the truck.

Thom laughs to himself as he forms circles of suds on the truck's back window, "So she figured it out, huh?"

"What makes you think I didn't just tell her like you told me to?"

"Like you do anything I say," Thom mumbles, "Plus, she looked pretty pissed off when she was dropping you off last night."

I stop the sponge in mid stroke and gap at Thom.

Noticing, he turns and says, "Hey, I was on my way over but turned on my heels as soon as I saw the flames shooting from her eyes. There was no way I was getting involved in that."

I snort as I direct my attention to the sponge in my hand and mumble, "Yeah, she figured it out."

"You've never been a subtle person," Thom quips.

"Whatever," I laugh as I throw the sponge at him and reach for the hose to begin rinsing off the truck, "So what were you coming over for?"

"Oh, yeah…right," Thom says as he fidgets with the sponge in his hand.

I glance at him for a moment as I hose off the truck.

Thom tosses the sponges into the pail, "I went to see my dad yesterday."

I stop spraying the truck and look at Thom in shock, "By yourself?"

"Well you weren't there so I guess so," Thom tries to play off as a joke, but the harshness in his tone isn't hard to miss.

"Thom—" I start to say, but he waves me off.

"Yeah, I went alone," he says as he gives me a shy look, "I got this letter from him..." Thom shakes his head. "I got accepted to Columbia," he says changing the subject.

"That's great, Thom," I say, "That's your first choice wasn't it?"

"I don't know if I'm going to go."

"What do you mean?" I ask.

"It's just all too much," Thom says.

"Dude," I say, "Stop being so cryptic and just tell me what's going through your head."

"Everything just happened so fast you know. The accident, my dad, my mom, you, Pop, changing schools, getting accepted to a school my dad and I hoped I'd get into. It's just all so much."

"So what are you saying?"

"I don't think I can handle it all," Thom admits.

"But, man, that's you dream school. I mean that's all you ever talked about before…"

"Before the accident," Thom finishes for me.

I give him a sheepish look, "Sorry man."

"See, that right there. You can't even expect me to keep it together by just mentioning the accident, and I can't. I cringe every time thinking about it. So, how am I supposed to keep it together going to a school that my father dreamed of me going to when he's sitting in a jail cell?"

"You can't look at it that way."

"But I do, and whether or not you want to admit it, you do too."

"You know that's not true." I say throwing down the hose.

"Then why stop talking about it all? Why cut off your sentences? Why—"

"Because, Thom," I say raising my voice, "I know how it affects you. I know the stress it puts on you, and I'd do anything to help ease the pain or alleviate the stress."

Thom begins to speak, but I cut him off.

"Maybe you're right, maybe you shouldn't go to Columbia," I say in a soft tone, "Maybe, you should take some time off. Find yourself again. Take the year off and travel with me, maybe it will help rid some of the stress you've built up."

Thom stops and thinks about what I said. Picking up the hose he begins to finish rinsing off the suds.

"I don't know," he shrugs, "maybe."

But I know his mind is made up. I hear the doubt in his voice. There is no way he'd give up going to Columbia, because now it serves a new purpose. In his mind it now serves as a way to make up for the fact his dad is sitting in a jail cell. It's the only way Thom can make it up to his father.

I sigh as I dip down to pick up a rag from beside the bucket. Thom sets down the hose and I toss him the rag.

"Help me dry this bad boy off?" I ask.

Thom shakes his head and begins wiping at the truck as I scoop up another rag and join him.

I drive around the bend that leads to Rizz's house and feel the anxiousness grow stronger with each turn of the wheels. I didn't know how this was going to go. How Rizz would react or how she would just act in general. I knew how things set Rizz off and how she always had some sort of sarcastic remark to counteract the situation. I knew this and these where things that I loved about her. I loved how she wouldn't let people take control of her and how she handled herself in situations, but this was different. This was still so new to me and I didn't want the one person who means the most to me and the one person who could potentially become a huge part of my life to dislike each other. It wasn't just Rizz. It was Jack too, because Jack had this edge to him as well—maybe from all the drug abuse—but it was there and it was evident. My worse fear though, is that Rizz would be reminded of her mother the moment she looked at Jack. That Jack would remind her of something her mother would never do, of what she will never be: a parent who cares enough about their child to get better— not just for themselves, but for their child too.

I pull up to Rizz's house and put the car in park. Reaching for the door handle, I catch a glimpse of movement through the living room window of the house. I stare at the two beings arguing inside the house and find myself unable to move. I knew barging in would only make things worse for Rizz, and at the moment it only looked as if they were arguing. I try to steady my slightly raging breath as I continue to watch the two argue. Slowly, I pull myself from the car and slam the door shut.

Rizz's mother's attention turns to me and she locks her cold glare on me as she stares out the living room window. Rizz's eyes follow her mother's and I see the panic in her eyes as she realizes that her mother has "spotted" me.

I catch a glimpse of Rizz rushing from the living to what I assume to be the front foyer and her mother following after her as I turn to make my way to the front door.

Rizz never wanted me to meet her mother, and I knew why. I understood it and honestly, I was glad I would never get to meet the woman who would harm such an amazing individual such as Rizz.

The front door opens quickly and is slammed shut. Rizz rushes down the front steps and grabs ahold of my hand.

"Let's go," she mutters.

I pull on her hand to stop her, "Rizz stop."

"We can't, come on," she says without making eye contact.

"Rizz," I say tugging on her hand gently, "look at me."

Rizz hesitates as she slowly faces me and tilts her head up for me to see.

I pull my brows together as I stare at the red handprint flushed across her face.

"Rizz," I whisper as I palm her cheek gently.

Rizz closes her eyes as she tries to hold back the tears she forces herself to never show, "Lance, we have to--."

A loud smash causes Rizz's head to jerk up back at the house.

"Hope," Rizz whispers and rushes around me to the front door.

I quickly follow after her into the house and grab ahold of her shoulders pulling her back against my chest as a glass vase flies past us and smashes against the wall.

"You okay?" I ask her as she looks up at me with wide eyes.

Rizz shakes her head silently as she pulls herself away from me and quietly walks around the broken pieces of the vase and to the opening of the living room.

Rizz's hand shoots up to her mouth as she gasps. I rush to her side and look into the living room with amazement as picture frame lay smashed along the living room floor, and cushions are turned up on the couch with the stuffing pulled from them.

In the corner a small cart is standing with an array of glass bottles filled with liquids. Standing over the cart is a petite woman with her back turned to us.

"Lance," Rizz whispers, "Let's go."

Rizz backs away from the living room and heads for the stairs. Taking them two at a time, I follow after her to Hope's room.

Rizz tries the knob, but has no luck.

Knocking quietly Rizz whispers through the door, "It's okay Hope, It's me. Open up."

The lock clicks and Rizz tries the knob again. The door opens to a crying Hope who rushes into Rizz's arms.

Rizz falls to her knees and starts to coo to Hope in order to calm her down.

I step back into the hall and lean against the wall next to the bedroom door. I let a deep breath out as I rest my head against the wall. I close my eyes tightly in order to keep my own tears at bay. I can't let Rizz go through with this anymore. I have to do something.

"Come on," I hear Rizz say to Hope, "You can come with us. Right, Lance? Lance?"

I pull myself together and reappear in the doorway.

"Yeah, she can come with us."

"Will Jack mind?" she asks, with pleading eyes.

"He won't mind. I'll tell him to meet us at the playground."

"The?"

"I think someone owes me a rematch on those monkey bars," I say, smirking at Hope who finally begins to crack a small smile.

Rizz pulls Hope into her and gives her a hug, "Let's go."

I take Rizz and Hope to the park and call Jack to let him know we would be meeting him at the park instead of the café shop.

"Why the sudden change?" he asks.

"Rizz is here to meet you…and well we had to bring her younger sister too," I pause, "She likes the park, so I thought it would be a good idea to come here."

I watch as Rizz helps Hope across the monkey bars, not that she needs it, and furrow my brows.

"Lance, what's going on?" Jack asks.

"What made you want to come clean?" I ask point blank.

"I told you this. I wanted to be a part of your life. This was the only way."

"Do you ever wish you could go back to how you were before?"

"I never wish that, Lance," he pauses, "But I would be lying if I told you I didn't struggle with it every day. It's a battle, one I hope to win."

"If you lost, would you want someone to turn you back in?"

"Where is this coming from Lance?"

"It's nothing," I pause as I look back over at Rizz and her sister, "I just want to understand."

"That's the thing Lance, I don't think anyone who has never lived the life I lived would understand."

I nod as I say nothing.

"I'll see you soon."

"Yeah," I say, "Okay."

Hanging up the phone I pocket it and head back to where Rizz is now sitting on a bench watching her sister play along the monkey bars.

"She really likes those things," I say as I sit down next to her.

"Thank you," Rizz says, looking at the wood chips, "For taking her here to calm her down."

I give her a small smile as I rub the back of her neck.

"I'm sorry you had to see that…I never wanted you to be a part of that."

"But I am, Rizz," I say with more edge in my voice than I intend.

Rizz looks up at me with wide eyes.

"Sorry," I say looking away from her, "I just…I can't understand why you would ever continue to put yourself and your sister in harm's way."

"I—"

"You need to tell someone. You need to turn her in. Stop running away and actually call the police."

"I can't."

"Why not?" I say trying to keep my voice low.

"No one will believe me."

"They will if they see the evidence."

"Lance, just please stop. There is no winning with her."

"This isn't a game, Rizz. This is your life."

"I know that, Lance," Rizz yells.

We both glance to Hope who is now looking at us.

"It's okay Hope," I say.

"We're just talking," Rizz assures her.

Hope goes back to playing on the monkey bars and I look at Rizz with anger and concern coursing through me.

"You have to do something. You can't let this continue on your whole life."

"Why do you think I want to get into Princeton so badly?" Rizz says.

"And what about Hope? Are you just going to leave her here while you get away?"

"I'll take her with me."

"And you'll be the one in jail for kidnapping your own sister," I spit out.

"You don't understand," Rizz says shaking her head.

"Then help me to understand."

"It's the only way. I can't call the police, because my mother owns them, I can't tell my father because there is no proof and without proof he'll never believe me." Rizz breaks into sobs as she tells me everything finally, "I can't tell anyone because no one will believe me, and then my mother won't just beat me anymore. She'll try to finish what she started the day she returned from the hospital after losing Luke. And this time I might not be as lucky as I was before."

I pull Rizz into my arms and rest my chin on top of her head as she struggles to pull herself together.

"We'll figure it out," I whisper into her hair as I kiss her, "I promise."

A car door slams in the distance and I lift my head slightly to see overtop of Rizz. Coming toward us from the parking lot is Jack. I look down at Rizz and whisper into her ear,

"I'll give you a moment."

Rizz nods her head slightly as I get to my feet and head toward where Jack is approaching us cautiously.

Looking over my shoulder I see Rizz make her way to her sister playing on the monkey bars and as I watch them interact with each other some of the edge begins to dissipate and I feel my shoulders begin to relax.

Jack comes to a stop as I reach him with concern etched across his face.

"Hey, Jack," I say.

"Lance," he says with a nod as he slaps a hand on my back in greeting, "You going to tell me what's going on? Or keep acting like everything is okay?"

I scratch at my temple trying to think on my feet real quick for a cover up for her, but Jack sees right through me.

"Don't even think about it, Son."

A small pang hits my heart as I dart my eyes quickly up to his and then away again.

Jack shuffles on his feet, obviously uncomfortable with the slip up.

Knowing I didn't want to lie to the man I'm trying to create a relationship with and not giving away Rizz's secret, I look up at Jack with strained eyes.

"Something happened, and as much as I want to say something...I can't...it's not my story to tell."

Jack places his hands on my shoulders and looks straight at me, "As happy as I am to hear you aren't the one in trouble, you can't keep something to yourself if it's a matter of life or death, Lance."

I struggle with myself before I make eye contact again and say, "I can't."

Jack lets his hands fall from my shoulders and nods his head in understanding.

"We do a lot for the people we care about, Lance, but sometimes what they think is best is only going to hurt them in the end. Just think about it."

I nod before turning and leading him back to the playground where Rizz is cheering Hope on as she makes her way across the monkey bars two at a time.

I smile at them both as we approach them and Rizz meets my gaze, smiling back. She says something to Hope causing her to jump from the monkey bars and to the ground. Placing her hand around Hope's shoulder Rizz leads the both of them to where Jack and I are now standing waiting for them.

"Hi," Rizz says, putting her hands on Hope's shoulders as she stops behind her.

"You must be Rizz," Jack says, holding his hand out in front of him for her to take.

She takes it and gives him a smile and a shake.

"Now who is this?" Jack says, squatting down.

"I'm Hope," She boasts.

"Well isn't that a beautiful name? It's nice to meet you, Hope."

Hope eagerly grabs Jack's outreached hand and gives it a shake.

"Do you like monkey bars? I love monkey bars. I can go two at a time now. Want to watch?"

"Well that's quite an accomplishment," Jack says with good natured amazement.

"She must really like you," Rizz says before Hope can respond. "She had to warm up with Lance when she first met him."

"Yeah, I got the once over from an eight-year-old," I laugh.

"Serves you right," Jack jokes before directing his attention back to Hope.

"Why don't you show Lance so I can chat with your big sister for a moment? Then you can show me how talented you are at the monkey bars."

Hope beams at Jack, "Okay," and grabs a hold of my hand, dragging me to the monkey bars."

I look back at Rizz helplessly and she gives me a shrug of her shoulder as an unmistakable look comes across her face.

Crap.

I know that look—her arrogant look. She's going to try to give him a run for his money, because no one ever confronts Rizz without things going her way—no matter who the person is.

Hope and I begin to reproach Jack and Rizz slowly. Their backs are now turned to us. Deciding I want to know a little of what Jack is saying to Rizz, I kneel down to Hope's level and ask,

"You want to play a game?"

"Sure," She chirps.

"Let's play the slow motion game."

"The what?"

"The slow motion game. Here's the rules. We both have to be absolutely silent and move in slow motion. The person who can move in slow motion the slowest is the winner."

"How do you know whose slower?"

"The last one to approach Rizz and Jack is the winner, but if they turn around then we both lose."

Hope gives a little laugh before agreeing to play my game.

"Okay you ready?" I ask.

She nods her head and I lift three fingers and mouth the numbers as I put down each finger. Then we are off.

As we slowly approach Rizz and Jack I can hear that Rizz isn't digging into him as I had expected she would be.

"You know," I hear Jack say to her, "I wasn't sure if Lance would ever want to meet me."

Rizz says nothing, and Jack goes on,

"I'm glad I am getting to know him. He's a great boy. Does what he can for the people he loves. He has this protectiveness about himself." Jack chuckles, "I'm pretty sure he gets that from his mom."

Rizz turns her head to him, surely interested in the mention of my birth mother.

"What was she like?" Rizz asks.

A sad laugh escapes Jack, "She was the definition of beauty. Not just outside beauty, but inside beauty. She had this huge heart—always wanted the best for people and never gave up on anyone. To her, no one was a lost cause."

"That's hard to believe," Rizz mutters, "That no one is a lost cause."

Jack looks at Rizz with kind eyes, "We all have secrets, Rizz. Sometimes those secrets can tear a person apart until it seems like there is no hope left for them. That was the beauty of Lila...she never lost hope in anyone."

Rizz diverts her eyes saying nothing.

"It's okay to have secrets, Rizz. Just don't let them ruin who you are in the process of trying to hide them from the world."

"What makes you such an expert?" Rizz snaps.

Crap.

Jack just smiles and replies, "Take it from someone who was one of those lost causes—who had ruined his life with secrets. It's better to tell the ones you care about all about your secrets and to let them help you instead of keeping it...well...a secret...before you end up losing them for good."

Rizz looks at him in wonder. Her mouth opens to say more but before she gets the chance Hope launches herself at her exclaiming,

"I won, I won."

Rizz looks at her in shock and I have nothing left to do but smile at Hope and say,

"You sure did. Let's hear it for the champ."

I begin to clap my hands together and encourage Jack and Rizz to join along. They do and as Rizz claps her hands together she asks Hope what game we were playing.

"We were playing slow motion," Hope says.

At Rizz's confused face, Hope goes on.

"We had to be quite and move in slow motion."

"Is that so?" Rizz says, eyeing me.

I rub the back of my neck, knowing I was caught.

"Yeah, well…I just thought I'd make the walk back a little interesting."

"I'm sure," Rizz says with amusement in her voice.

Jack lets out a low chuckle, "I have something for you, Lance."

Thankful for the subject change I turn to him and follow him back to his car.

Jack leans into the passenger side door and pulls out a book, handing it to me.

I look at it with confusion until realization comes over me.

"It's a scrapbook?"

"Yeah, it's your mom's. She made it for you before you were born. I thought you would like to have it."

"Are you sure?" I ask, dumbfounded.

Jack gives another low chuckle, "I'm sure. She would have wanted you to have it."

I run my hand along the leather scrapbook, but don't open it.

"Thank you," I say in almost a whisper.

"Lance, I know this may be too early to say. Hell, it might even be the wrong time to say it."

I look at him silently as I wait for him to continue on.

"I know I was coked up most of the time. I was there, but I wasn't really there, but the one thing I knew for sure is that your—Lila loved you. She would have been proud of the man you are becoming." Jack takes a deep breath. "It must be hard growing up without a mom even the second time around, but I—I don't know—I just hope that what you find in there will help you realize that no matter what your moms are always with you."

I look down at the scrapbook with furrowed eyebrows unsure what it would be that I would find in here to remind me that everything will be okay— to remind me even though the two women who were supposed to be my mothers are still with me anyhow.

I swallow back the lump in my throat and look at Jack with glossy eyes, "Thanks."

"You're welcome, Lance," he says as he places his hand in between my shoulder blades and walks me back to my car where Rizz and Hope are waiting for me.

CHAPTER TWENTY-NINE: RIZZ

The house is dark as I walk through the front door. Hope runs up the stairs to her room as I flip on the front hallway's light. Squinting, I look around to find everything still intact from earlier that evening. Stillness eases its way through the house the further I walk down the hallway. As I reach the living room. I glance in to find my mother passed out on the couch. She is spread across it on her stomach with a bottle of Brandy hanging from her hand.

***

I gasp and rush toward her, taking the bottle from her hand and set it on the table beside her. I search for a pulse on her wrist, but am having trouble finding one.

"Mom," I shout, "Mom, can you hear me?"

I feel the tears fall as I shake my mother's motionless body. My head spins as the pounding of my heart grows louder, "Mom," I cry again, "Please get up."

Finally she grunts and I let out a sigh of relief.

"Mom," I exclaim, as I help her get off of the couch, "Come on, Let's get you upstairs."

I grab underneath her, wrapping her arms around my neck and allowing her to lean on me as I lead her up the staircase and to her room. Helping her into bed, I tuck her in under the covers and kiss her on the forehead. As I turn to leave she grabs hold of my wrist causing me to turn back to her.

"I hate you, you know that," She sneers, "You ruined my life."

I stare at her stunned as she releases my wrist and turns over.

Making my way to Chip's home office I slump down in his leather chair. Kicking at the hidden door in his desk, I open it and pull out one of his cigars. Taking a pair of scissors from a drawer, I slice open the cigar dumping the tobacco into the nearby trash can. I reach into the desk and pull out an old stash that Chip had long forgotten about after I had found it in the neighbor's yard and set to work lining the wrapper with the leaves of the plant. After rolling the amateur blunt, I light it, breathing in the steady calming effect of the plant.

***

I stare at my mother lying on the couch, and feel sick to my stomach. The last time I found her lying there I was twelve years old. I was so afraid for her, but not anymore. Now, as I stare at her all I think is hopefully this time she won't get up, but I know I wouldn't be that lucky. I grimace at her and turn to leave when I hear her voice come across the room.

"You're home," she calls, "Good."

I face her, placing my hand on my hip.

"I have news," she exclaims into the couch as she attempts to get up, but her hand slips and she falls landing face first into the cushion.

I stay put, not making a move to help.

She gives up and stays sprawled out on the couch. She rests the side of her head on the cushions so she is looking straight at me.

"You're not going to Princeton," she slurs, raising her Brandy to me, "Cheers." She takes a swig, dripping some onto the couch. Then, she sets the bottle onto the floor and smirks at me.

I roll my eyes, "Yes, I am. I already have the acceptance letter."

My mother's smile grows smug, "I'm not paying for it."

Straightening, I say, "You're lying."

"I spent the money on a new home," she boasts, "It's a cute little place right on the beach."

"You lie," I say, holding back the tears that well inside me.

My mother snickers as she takes another sip of her Brandy.

"I'll get a scholarship, you can't keep me here."

"Not enough to pay for it in full," she smirks.

"This is so predictable," I sneer, "every time something good happens to me, you take it from me."

My mother attempts to stand from the couch, but fails.

"Maybe if you showed a little more respect—"

"Respect?" I shout, "How could I ever have respect for someone like you?"

"How dare you," my mother exclaims, "I gave you life and raised you—"

"And what a great life that is. You have done nothing but abuse me all my life. You are the saddest excuse for a human, and I will always hate you."

My mother stares at me with cold eyes.

"I don't know what I ever did to you for you to treat me the way you do, but I will get out. I will find a way to get as far away from you as possible and when I do, you'll be sorry."

I break her stare and walk out of the room. As I walk down the hallway I pick up my pace allowing the tears to flow down my cheeks. I find my way to the garage; stopping outside of the car I try to steady my breath. All the hate boils up inside of me and I kick at the car's tire repeatedly until I feel a slight bit of calmness. I climb into the car and set the keys into the ignition slot.

Why me? What did I ever do to deserve this life?

Balling my hand into a fist, I punch the dashboard. Unsatisfied, I kick the closed door and hit the steering wheel with the palm of my hand. I can't take it anymore. I need to let it all out—to escape. After running my hand through my hair I start up the car and back out of the garage.

Entering the party, I take a beer from the ice bucket by the door. I let the coolness of the bottle sink into my hands as I walk through the partiers in the main foyer. I smile at the people I recognize from school as I make my way through. The thing about Lake Forest was that there was almost always a party—especially during the summer.

I make my way through the crowd in search of John. I needed a fix, and I needed one now. I didn't care if he had gotten into a fight with Lance over me, he was my friend and my dealer, and right now, I needed him more than anything.

I walk into the kitchen only to find it empty aside from a girl sitting on the kitchen counter, and her choice of the night leaning into her as he kisses her neck. I turn to walk back out, but walk into something solid.

"Shit," I mumble, as I stumble back.

"Whoa," the male says, "I've gotchya," he says grabbing ahold of me to steady me.

"Thanks," I say, looking up at him.

Crap.

"Charlie," I spit out.

"Hey, Rizz, didn't think I'd see you here."

"It's a party, isn't it?" I snap.

Charlie reaches his hand to rub the back of his neck, "Yeah, I mean…hey, you need help opening that?" he asks, pointing to the un-open beer in my hand.

"Uh, yeah…sure," I say handing it to him.

"These damn tops can be a bitch sometimes," He says, hooking the rim of the bottle cap on the counter and slamming down onto it with his hand. The bottle cap pops off and he hands me back my beer. "I prefer the twist tops."

"Have you seen, John?" I ask, taking the beer.

Charlie walks over to the fridge and takes out a beer for himself. Repeating the same pattern, he opens his own and takes a swig.

"No, haven't seen him all night."

I nod, as I turn my head to look out into the crowd of people outside of the kitchen.

"You gonna drink that?"

I look back at Charlie who is pointing to the beer.

"Oh, right," I mumble, "Bottoms up…or whatever," I say, before taking a swig. I scrunch my nose in disgust as I swallow the liquid. Holding the bottle out in front of me I look at in disgust and wonder how people actually drink this stuff.

Charlie chuckles at my discomfort, "Not your brew?"

I look at him in confusion, "Uh…no it's fine." I take another sip, this one better than the first as my taste buds begin to adjust to the yeast I am pouring down my throat.

"I've got some, you know. If that's what you're looking for."

I meet Charlie's eyes, "Huh?"

"Weed. I have some; I can smoke you up if you want," Charlie shrugs.

"Let's go," I say grabbing his arm.

"One sec," he says, as he turns back to the fridge, pulling a few more beers from it. "Alright, let's go."

An hour later, I am feeling relaxed from both the weed and the four beers I had consumed. I lay on the floor of the room with my hands folded over my stomach and stare at the ceiling. Charlie is sitting in a chair across from me, talking about his full ride to college on a football scholarship.

The more he talks about his scholarship the angrier I become that I hadn't gotten a full ride from Princeton. I worked my ass off all four years of high school to get straight A's, and yet here I was lying on a stranger's floor drunk and high and scholarship-less all because I couldn't ace my History exam.

Sitting up on my hands, I stare blankly at Charlie.

What the fuck was I doing here?

I had walked straight into my mother's trap and I knew it. She wanted me to feel like this, like I had nowhere else to turn than to that same bottle hanging from her cold boney fingers. All my life I had refused to be like her or to let her get the best of me, and look at me. I'm drunk in a stranger's home with a guy I used.

I stumble to my feet and grab ahold of the back of a chair to steady myself.

"I have to go," I slur.

"What?" Charlie asks, midsentence.

"I have to get out of here."

"I don't think you should be driving," he states.

I dismiss him with my hand, as I shuffle to the door, "I'll call a cab."

Charlie jumps from his chair, "Here, let me help you."

"I'm not a child," I snap at him.

"No," he agrees, "but you've clearly never drank before either."

"Right," I mumble, as I fall against him, letting him guide me down the stairs.

Fifteen minutes later, Charlie helps me into the cab he called for me and waves goodbye as he shuts the cab door.

"Where to, Miss?" The driver asks.

"Lance's place, please," I slur.

"Where is that exactly?" he asks.

"I don't...I don't know."

After arguing with the driver for a few minutes about not knowing the address to Lance's home, he finally settles on letting me give him directions as we drive.

This was just my night.

Another unnecessary fifteen minutes later I am standing outside Lance's front door. I knock lightly at first, and when no one answers I knock harder.

The door swings open, exposing a handsome Lance to me.

"Lance," I exclaim as I all but jump into his arms, wrapping my own around his neck.

"You're drunk," Lance states as he wraps his arms around me.

I pull away from him, "Yup."

"You don't get drunk," he says, concern etched across his features.

"I did tonight, and boy was I missing out," I sarcastically say.

"What's wrong?" Lance asks, as my eyes begin to well with tears.

"She's killing me, Lance. My mother is slowly killing me."

Lance pulls me into him, and I bury my face into his chest allowing myself to cry.

Rubbing my back soothingly, he says, "No, she's not. I won't let her get that far."

Lance pulls away and bends down.

"What are you doing?" I sniffle, as he scoops me up into his arms.

"Shh," he says, "just relax."

And so I do. I lean my head against his shoulder as he carries me up to his room and lays me down on his bed. He pulls at the hem of my shirt and I lift my arms, allowing him to dispose of it. At his dresser, he pulls one of his own shirts from a drawer and returns to my side, slipping it on over my head. I allow the scent of him to cocoon me and I instantly feel at ease.

I should have come here.

His fingers descend to my jeans and he undoes the button and zipper before tugging at the ankles pulling them down my body.

"Lay back," He orders as he discards the jeans onto the floor.

I lay back, and he brings the comforter up around me. Removing his own clothes, he slips on a pair of plaid pajama pants and crawls into bed beside me. He pulls me into him and I rest my cheek on his chest.

"Sleep," he whispers, "You're safe now."

And I do. For the first time, I am able to sleep knowing that I am safe, that no one can hurt me.

CHAPTER THIRTY: LANCE

I feel the heat of the sun's rays shine on me through the window and slowly open my eyes to see Rizz's innocent looking face lying next to me. She looks so peaceful as she sleeps and I begin to wonder how her mother could have abused her all those years or how Rizz could let it go on for so long without telling someone.

A tinge of guilt eats at me as realize that I am no better. All I am doing is helping her cover up her mother's actions. I'm helping her life spin out of control. If I wasn't a coward before I am now.

"I can feel your eyes on me," Rizz whispers, her eyes closed.

I reach my hand out to her face and trace the scar on her temple. My brows furrow as lay my palm against her face and tangle my fingers in her long brown hair. I push a few strands back as I look at her.

"You know your forehead wrinkles right here," she says pointing to the scrunched up skin between my eyebrows, "When you are feeling a little pensive. What's wrong?"

I run the pad of my thumb along the scar and meet Rizz's gaze,

"Pop isn't going to be happy that you spent the night."

Rizz looks at me with sad eyes seeing right through me. I wasn't worried about Pop. I could always handle him. What I couldn't handle was what was happening to Rizz and knowing I wouldn't do anything about it as long as she asked me to, because I would do anything for her.

Rizz looks away, "I know."

I lean in and give her a light kiss on the forehead.

"Go take a shower. I'll talk to him."

I slink off of the bed not waiting for Rizz to get up and make her way to the bathroom.

"Wait," Rizz calls after me.

I sigh and turn to look at her.

She slides to the edge of the bed, picking up the leather scrapbook on the bedside table.

"I think you should look at this now," Rizz says, motioning at the book.

I look from her to the book and nod slightly after a beat. Taking a seat next to Rizz I take the book from her hands and flip open the cover to find a picture of a younger Jack and a very pregnant woman whom I assume is my mother, Lila.

"They look so happy," Rizz observes.

I flip the page to see a picture of Lila lying in the hospital bed. On the page opposite is a picture of a small naked baby.

"Look at you."

I nod and turn the next page. A note falls from the page and into my lap. I go to pick it up as Rizz says,

"Look how cute you were," she points to the picture of Lila holding me.

"I'm not anymore?" I chuckle.

Rizz scrunches up her nose and shakes her head.

"I don't think so," she teases.

I nudge her with my elbow and she laughs.

"What's that?" She asks, pointing at the note paper in my hand.

"I'm not sure."

"Well open it."

"I will later," I say shutting the book and standing as I slide the piece of paper in my back pajama pocket.

Rizz looks up at me quizzically.

"You should take that shower. Nat's party is today and I'm sure we'll be late if we kill any more time."

"I don't need to take a shower," Rizz says, eyeing me, "I just need to brush this gross taste out of my mouth."

"There is some Listerine in the bathroom."

Rizz slides off the bed and walks to the bathroom, picking up her clothes on the way.

I change as I wait for Rizz to come from the bathroom. When she emerges I take the note that I set on my dresser top and put it in the back pocket of the new pants I changed into.

"You ready," I ask.

"Yeah," she says as she follows me out of the room and downstairs to the living room where we see Pop reading the newspaper and drinking a glass of coke.

"Lance," Pop says as he folds the paper in his lap, "Rizz."

"Hello Mr. McCartney."

I turn to Rizz, "Why don't you go wait by the truck. I'll be right out."

Rizz gives a small nod and then exits out to the garage.

"Want to explain why Rizz has spent the night?" Pop asks once Rizz has left.

"She was a mess," I reply, "Something happened at home and she had nowhere else to go."

"There seems to be a lot happening with that girl," he says tucking the newspaper under his arm as he walks into the kitchen.

"It's complicated," I reply, "Her mother has some issues and well it's not safe at the moment."

"If her home isn't safe then you need to tell someone, Son."

"It's not that easy."

"It may not seem that way, but it is. Lance, if that girl is in danger you need to tell someone. You can't help her by staying quiet."

I shake my head in frustration, "You don't think I know that?"

Pop sets the paper down on the counter and strides toward me. Placing a hand on my shoulder he says,

"Lance, what is going on?"

I look at Pop wanting to tell him, but knowing I can't. Knowing that telling him would only hurt Rizz. She trusted me, and I couldn't let her down.

"I can't," I say as I turn to walk back to where Rizz is waiting for me.

"Lance," Pop calls after me, "You can't hold onto someone else's secrets without them ruining you too…just think about that before you decide to keep doing what you are doing."

I walk down the front hallway toward the foyer as I try to compose myself again. Taking a beat, I lean against the wall and run my hands over my face. Staring off into nothingness I remember the note I found and pull it from my back pocket.

Unfolding it, I hold it out in front of me and begin to read.

To my handsome baby boy,

Her hand writing comes out all squiggly and loopy. I sink down to the floor as I continue to read the words my mother had written me.

I just came home from the doctor's office today and found out that I will be having a healthy baby boy. You'll be due soon and I can't wait to see you and hold you close to me. I didn't want to know the sex right away, but I got impatient not knowing. So of course I folded, and now I know I will be having a boy. Oh, gosh I'm so excited to meet you. I love you already.

I tear rolls down my cheek as I pause and reread those three words until I can't take it anymore.

I will always love you. As you grow I will be there for you to help you through the tough times and to enjoy all the good times with you. At some moments I won't be able to be there for you, but you will be okay. How do I know you'll make it out okay? Because I have hope. You, my baby boy, have two great gifts. Your father and I, we will make you strong.

We will teach you how to overcome the greatest struggles life can throw at you. You might not understand what I mean now, but one day when you are older I will tell you all about your father's and my path and the struggles we have made it through and then you will be able to understand.

But sweetie, one day you'll have to be able to learn how to stay strong on your own when neither of us are there to hold you up. You won't have the gentle touch of your mother or the strength of your father to lean on. You'll have to figure out that strength for yourself so you can stand on your own.

I want you to know I will always be there for you through every step. I will always be looking out for my baby boy. So stay strong my little man.

I love you,

Mom

I wipe at my face as I fold up the piece of paper and slide it back into my pocket. I have felt so lost since the accident. Slowly I have been able to pull myself back together, but I always had a feeling deep inside me that wondered why the women in my life had always been taken from me. I never knew my real mother; at least not that I could remember.

I wasn't sure why all this was happening now, but somehow I knew I needed to read that note. I needed to know that she loved me and cared for me.

I needed to know that no matter what happened to her that she was a part of me.

As I continue to dwell on the fact that all the women in my life tend to be ripped from me I think of Rizz. Suddenly, the thought occurs to me.

I have to do something.

We drive around the bends to Rizz's house so she can get her swimsuit for the pool party. I glance at Rizz wanting to tell her I am going to say something, but unsure how to get the words out.

"So why can't you just borrow a bikini from Nathalie or Charlene?" I say instead.

"They can't know anything that's going on at home."

"Why not?" I ask, turning around another bend.

"They've never met my parents. They have no idea what is going on. If I show up without a bathing suit they will be curious and I'm not in the mood to dodge any questions."

"They are you're friends, Rizz, I think they would be understanding."

"You don't know them like I do. All they know is my image."

"Don't you ever get tired of lying to them?"

Rizz is silent as she stares out the window. I pull into the driveway and Rizz climbs out of the car.

"Just keep the car running," she says as she shuts the car door.

I rest my elbow on the door as I wait for Rizz to come back out. A few moments later the front door opens and she rushes out. Quickly she hops into the car and gives me a hesitant smile as she pulls the seat belt across her body and buckles it.

"What's going on?" I ask.

"I'll tell you, just get us out of here first," she says watching the front door.

I catch movement from the corner of my eye and look in the direction of the garage. As I watch her mother struggle around the corner of the house with a golf club tightly clenched in her hand I throw the car into reverse and squeal out of the driveway.

As I speed away I glance quickly at Rizz, "Did she hit you?"

"She missed."

I throw the car into park when we are about to exit the development.

"What are you doing, Lance?"

"We are telling someone," I blurt out at her.

She looks at me with wide eyes.

"Either you are telling someone about everything or I will report it myself." I make no move to touch Rizz as tears begin to fall from her eyes.

I try to soften my voice, "I have lost the only two women in my life that meant something to me. I will not lose you too. You say something or I will."

Rizz looks out the window and wipes at her face. Shortly, she begins to nod her head.

"Okay," she peeps, as she looks at me, "You're right." She nods again as if beginning to believe what she was saying, "After the party."

I nod in agreement and reach out for her hand. I give it a squeeze and shift the car back into drive and head into the direction of Nathalie's.

"It'll be okay," I assure her.

Nathalie's backyard is full of people as we walk through the back doors. Her in-ground pool is decorated with a waterfall and a slide on the far end. Beach balls are hung along the fence and some float in the pool along with other blow up toys and rafts. Tables full of food are set up along the fence. In the yard several games are set up including Kan Jam, croquet and the ball and ladder game.

I glance down at Rizz as she looks around the party no doubt searching for Nathalie and Charlene.

I spot Thom and Nathalie near the side of the pool where they are talking to a group of kids they must know from school.

"Have I ever told you how uncomfortable public school parties make me?" I whisper into Rizz's ear.

Rizz nudges me, "And here I thought you could handle everything and anything thrown at you."

"Yeah, knowing absolutely no one is cause for a good time."

"In some cases," Rizz says as she stands in front of me, "those are the best parties. You can be anyone you want."

"Ah," I say leaning down, "but you already do that," I smirk.

Rizz lets out a small laugh as Charlene comes up behind her.

"Hey doll," she chimes.

Rizz turns and smiles at Charlene, "Hey. Where's Nat."

"Over there," I point.

Charlene smiles at me, "keeping tabs on the group, huh?"

"What?"

"Just ignore her," Rizz laughs, "Let's go over there."

"I'm just going to use the bathroom real quick," I say hooking my thumb back at the house.

"Okay," Rizz says, "I'll actually come with. I want to get a soda from the kitchen. You want anything?" she asks Charlene.

"No," she says, "but I will come with to keep you company."

The three of us head back into the house. I leave the two of them in the kitchen where Charlene begins to tell Rizz about some guy she has been off and on with, and make my way to find the bathroom.

I step out of the bathroom and into the hallway and smack right into Kayla.

Shit.

I hold out my arm to steady her, "Sorry about that."

Kayla looks up at me and smiles, "Oh it's quite alright."

I smile and nod at her as I try to side step her, but she only moves with me.

"Where have you been lately?" she asks, "I haven't seen you at any parties lately."

"Yeah, hanging with the girlfriend tends to keep you grounded a bit."

"That sounds boring," Kayla pouts, "remember how we used to have so much fun going out. You and I were the life of the party."

"Yeah, well that's history," I say trying to step away again.

Kayla grabs hold of my hand and pulls me toward her. Without letting go of my hand she says, "You know, I haven't been able to do anything but think about that kiss we shared. I can still taste you on my lips. Isn't that funny?"

I open my mouth to respond when I hear someone behind me clear their throat.

I turn to find Rizz standing behind me with her arms crossed over her chest.

"Oops," Kayla smirks.

I pull my hand from Kayla's, "It's not what you think." I stutter.

Dammit, Lance, you sound like you did something wrong.

Rizz raises her eyebrow at me and scoffs as she turns and walks away.

"Rizz, wait," I call after her.

I follow her into a study and wait for her to turn on me to let me have it, but she doesn't. She doesn't even turn to look at me. Slowly, I walk up to her and place a hand on her shoulder,

"Rizz?"

She shakes my hand off, letting it fall back to my side.

"Rizz, I swear nothing happened."

"You lied to me, Lance."

"What? No, never."

"You told me you would never fall for any of her bullshit again, and yet you kissed her."

"I never kissed her, Rizz," I say turning her around to face me. Tears streak down her face as she glares at me. "She kissed me at the party where I met you."

"It doesn't matter, Lance. You let her kiss you, you didn't stop it."

"I don't understand why you are getting so upset. She threw herself at me catching me off guard. It wasn't like I invited her to kiss me, Rizz," I say growing angry.

Rizz stays silent.

"Why are you being so damn irrational?" I growl. "She's just some stupid girl who wants to tear people down and here you are letting her, because when things get tough you just accept them and let it continue to happen instead of doing something about it."

"What is that supposed to mean?" Rizz asks, offended.

"You know exactly what I'm talking about. You spent your whole life just accepting what your mom did to you instead of acknowledging it."

Rizz shoves at my chest, "You know what, Lance. Forget it. Forget it all. Just pretend like you never met me."

Anger courses through me at her comment.

"You aren't going to do anything about it are you?"

"I'm sure you already know that answer since you know me all so well," she snaps.

"Don't be so damn stubborn. This isn't just about you anymore. She came at my car with a golf club."

"Yeah, because I was in it."

"I'm still reporting her, Rizz."

"Go ahead. No one will believe you."

I shake my head in tired frustration.

"Don't do this, Rizz."

"I think you should leave, Lance," she says pointing to the door.

"Rizz, please, you know none of this should have ever happened."

"Just leave Lance," she says with a sigh, "I can't deal with this right now."

I run my hand through my hair and let out a groan, "Sometimes, I just don't understand you." I shake my head in frustration and walk out of the study, through the house and out the front door.

I reach for my truck door when I hear someone come up behind me.

"You know," her shrill voice comes, "You shouldn't have led her on like that."

I spin around to face Kayla and walk toward her causing her to step back until she hits the side of someone's car. I get as much in her face as I can and growl,

"Do you think this is funny? Do you think messing with my relationship is funny? That hurting Rizz is just so damn funny?"

"This isn't about *her*, Lance," she says getting right back in my face, "this is about you and me."

"There is no you and me," I shout at her, "I don't care what you do, but there will never be a you and me ever again."

I push off of the car and turn back to my own.

"Why not, Lance? What did I ever do to you?" she yells.

"You broke me," I yell at her, "you tore me down and now you are tearing down the one person I actually ever cared about. Do you realize you just took her away from me?" I say pointing back at the house.

I dig my finger into her chest, "You are the one who cheated. You are the one who messed up. So do me a favor and stay the hell out of my life."

"Lance," Kayla calls as I climb into my truck.

"No, Kayla," I snap, "I think you did enough damage."

I slam my door shut and take off for anywhere that is not here.

CHAPTER THIRTY-ONE: RIZZ

I walk out of the study and make my way to the family room where I sit down in one of the leather couches. I slouch in the couch urging myself to keep it together. I can't lose it, not here. I wanted to be angry at Lance, but I knew he was right. I just couldn't admit it to him.

I really hate that girl.

I shouldn't have reacted the way I had, but I was so used to being hurt that I threw my walls back up. I would be damned if I let someone tear me down, let alone in front of a crowd.

I rest my head on my hand as I daze off. How did things get so out of control?

"There you are," Charlene exclaims as she walks back into the house, "Where's Lance?"

"He left," I reply.

"Without you?" she asks.

She takes a seat next to me, "Honey, what happened?"

"Nothing. It's over. He left. That's that."

"It's never that simple," Charlene rolls her eyes, "Come on, tell me what happened. Maybe I can help."

"Yeah, I don't think anyone can fix the mess that is Rizz Murphy," I mutter.

"What are you talking about?"

"Nothing," I say sitting up, "Can you give me a ride home?"

"Of course," She says getting up from the couch. She holds out her hand for me to take, "Let's ditch this place. I wasn't having fun anyhow."

I step out of Char's car and head up the drive to my house.

"Hey, Doll," Char calls after me.

I turn around to see Charlene hanging half way out of her car window.

"Yeah?"

"John's having a party tomorrow if you want to go. We'll both go out as new women ready to take on the world."

I give her a shrug, "Sounds great."

"I'll come by at nine," she says as she climbs back into her car and takes off.

I wave after her before heading back up the path to my house. I stop at the welcome home mat and grimace. This house has never been close to home for me. Just a reminder of my childhood and the disastrous life I've always lived. This place wasn't anywhere close to a home. After all a home is supposed to make you feel safe and secure.

I take a deep breath and open the door and stare into the darkness consumed by all the lies and hatred. With the pressure and tension rising, my eyes burn and I feel the boulders tumble off the cliff trapping me inside this dreaded house. There is nowhere else for me to go. I'm doomed for disaster.

I walk up the stairs and enter my room. I shut the door behind me and throw my bag onto my bed. Kneeling on the ground I take the grate off of the wall by loosening the bolts. I take the baggie from its hiding spot and take the half smoked joint from the bag. Leaving the bag on the ground I flop back onto my bed and light the end of the joint. As the smoke fills my lungs I let all the horror of what has been my life rush over me.

I stare at the ceiling as I replay each attack my mother made on me in my head.

I take another hit and then another until the joint is out. Unwilling to move I hold the butt end of the joint in my hand and close my fist knowing all too well the feeling of the heat that stings my palm. I continue to stare at the ceiling as a tear slides down the side of my face.

This is what my life will always be like.

My bedroom door opens and I jump up as I see Hope step into the room.

"What is that smell?" hope asks scrunching her nose.

"It's nothing," I say, rushing to where she is standing.

"What's wrong?"

"Nothing," I say, ushering her back out the door, "I just need to be left alone for a bit."

"What happened?"

"Nothing, Hope," I snap, "I just want to be left alone, okay?" I say, pushing her out into the hallway.

"Just go into your room," I wipe at my face. "And lock your door," I say before shutting my door and locking it.

I rush back to the baggie sitting on the floor and pull out my grinder as I fill it with pieces of weed. I grind the bits and dump them out onto the blunt wrap and start to roll. When I finish I return back to my bed, lie down and light up letting the smoke settle over me as I begin to fade away into nothingness.

CHAPTER THIRTY-TWO: THOM

I wait in the cold metal seat again as the guard goes to bring my father to meet with me. I needed to convince him that his letter was insane—that he shouldn't be taking the blame. Not when it wasn't his fault. I need to let him know and make him understand that everything that is happening is my fault. He needs to know that mom plans on divorcing him. That she's leaving—of course he knows these things, but he needs to know he can't let them happen. We are a family. We need to be a family.

The guard opens the door to the small private visiting room and leads my father through the door. He unlocks my father's cuffs and my father pulls the chair out taking a seat.

The guard shuts the door, but stands inside the room next to it.

I lift my brow in question.

"You two now get the same kind of privileges as the other inmates since your last visit got a little heated."

"He wouldn't have hurt me."

"Privileges are revoked. You're lucky you are even allowed to visit."

"I thought this was supposed to be the private visitor room," I challenge.

"Thom," my father warns, "Its fine."

"Just pretend I'm not even here," the guard says with a smirk.

I glare at the guard before turning my attention to my father.

"Dad, I need to talk to you about something."

"I figured that, Thom. What is it?"

"It's about your letter. You can't take the blame for something that wasn't your fault."

"Not this again, Thom," my father says exasperated, "I already told you. It was not your fault. It was an accident."

"But it was. I caused the accident. I distracted you."

"Thom," my father scolds, "You were not the one driving. You are not the one who took their eyes off of the road. You are not responsible for the action I made."

"But I am, Dad. If I didn't distract you, you wouldn't be here. If I didn't—"

"What do you want me to say?" my father says angrily, "Do you want me to tell you it's all your fault? Is that what you want? Because I won't. It was an accident. The fault belongs to no one. Now it's about time you accepted that and moved on."

"How can I accept anything when my life is falling apart? Mom is divorcing you."

"Yes, she is. I signed the papers today."

"What?" I ask, jumping from my chair.

The guard takes a step forward, but my father raises his hand for him to stop. I begin to back against the wall breathing deeply.

"Just give him a moment. Touching him is going to make it worse."

"What's his problem?" the guard asks.

"It's anxiety."

I clutch at my chest and silently wince when I touch the freshly new cut on my hip that I put there just the other day.

"Thom, are you okay?" My father asks when he notices me wincing.

I place my hand on my hip and press it against the cut in order to feel the pain in order to calm myself down. The pain helps and I am able to take deep even breaths. I don't move from the wall and just stare at my father.

"Thom, what's wrong with your hip."

"Nothing," I lie.

"Thom," my father says sternly, not believing me.

"It's nothing," I shout.

I shake my head in frustration as my eyes begin to water, "How could you sign them?"

"She needs to move on, Thom. She deserves that."

I shake my head in angered frustration unable to take everything that is happening. I can't handle it anymore.

"I have to go," I say, "I have to get out of here."

"Thom."

"No, Dad," I shout, "This is all my fault."

My father looks at me his eyes sad, but I say nothing as I walk past him and to the door.

My father grabs my arm as I pass and I let him hold it as I avoid his gaze.

"This is all my fault," I whisper as I jerk my arm from his hold and walk out the door.

I walk out to the prison parking lot and head toward my truck. I hop into the bed of the pickup truck and pinch the bridge of my nose as I try to calm myself. The pain in my side is starting to feel numb and I know soon I will need a new outlet. I open up the glove compartment looking for something—anything that will be able to penetrate my skin and give me the release I so desperately need.

I shove a few pieces of random paper around and find nothing to give me solace.

"Dammit," I shout as I slam my hand against the steering wheel.

I need to do something. I need to get out of here to get any sort of release I could possibly get my hands on.

I think back to earlier this afternoon when Nat reminded me of a party that is going on tonight. I look at the digital clock on the dashboard that reads eight. The drive back to Lake Forest is about a half hour drive. By the time I get to Nat's it would be close to nine and the party is out in the boondocks so the timing is just right. Making up my mind, I send Nat a quick text to be ready by nine and then put the truck into gear and pull out of the visitor's parking lot and through the gates.

I grab another beer from the fridge and make my way into the living room in order to find Nat. People are crowded around the back doors and I head that way to see what all the interest is for. I push past strangers and friends and finally make it to the opening where I see Nat with her feet in the air and her holding herself up on the keg. Two football players stand beside her in order to catch her if she were to fall. The crowd begins to cheer her on as she continues to chug beer from the tap. Finally Nat pulls herself down and the guys help right herself before sending her off in my direction.

"Thom," Nat slurs with a lopsided smile, "Did you see that?"

I nod my head still shocked with what I had seen. I never knew Nat to be the one to do a keg stand. Pulling myself together as I take a pull of my beer I say,

"Actually, it was kinda hot."

Nat's eyes snap to mine and a mischievous smile crosses her face.

"Slow down there boy," Nat says closing the gap between us. Leaning in, she rubs her chest against mine and whispers, "Good things happen to those who wait."

With that she takes off in the direction of the kitchen where a group of guys and girls are doing body shots.

Nat looks back at me with a glint of lust in her eyes and lifts at the hem of her shirt tugging it up and over her head. Biting her lip she tosses the shirt back at me and winks.

I definitely like this girl.

I tuck her shirt into my back pocket and scurry of to where she is now sitting on the counter.

Gage, a friend from one of my classes, begins to sprinkle salt along my girl's hot body and places a lime in her mouth before filling her belly button with tequila.

Damn she's hot.

I lick the line of salt from her chest to her belly button where I suck up the tequila and then lock my mouth over hers as I suck on the lime. I pull away and Nat sits up, pulling me back into her. I taste the lime on my lips and get carried away as I lift her ass off of the counter and begin to walk away from our friends in the kitchen, but Nat stops and squirms in my arms.

"No, Thom. Not yet," she whines.

I growl in aggravation and set her down.

"Come one Babe," She says tugging on my hand and leading me back to the kitchen, "do some shots with me."

She pulls two shot glasses from the cleaning rack that sits on the side of the sink and grabs the tequila bottle from Gage's hand.

"Could I borrow this for a sec?" she asks sweetly.

"Have at it," Gage smiles.

Nat pours one for me and then one for her. Setting the bottle down she picks up one of the extra salt shakers and sprinkles a bit on her hand. Handing the shaker to me I do the same thing.

"Cheers," She says holding her shot glass up to me.

I grab mine, tap it against hers and throw it back without licking the salt from my hand.

Damn that was good.

Nat squeezes hers eyes together and gives her head a little shake before reaching for the tequila and pouring us another round.

After three more shots I wrap my arms around a very drunk Nathalie and pull her toward me.

"I think I've waited long enough," I whisper into her ear.

She shivers as my hot breath falls over her ear and travels down her neck.

Nat smirks at me and picks up the tequila bottle and pours us another shot. Handing my glass to me she clinks the glasses together and says,

"Cheers to a good night."

We both take the shot back and then I sweep her up off her feet and carry her across the kitchen and living room.

Our drunken friends shout out cat calls and whistles, but I ignore them. There is only one thing I want and care about right now—losing myself in this girl—the only girl I ever cared for.

I carry her up the stairs as her fingers play in my hair and she presses light feathered kisses against my neck.

Throwing open one of the upstairs doors I turn on the light to find a vacant bedroom.

Perfect.

I slam the door shut behind me with my foot and walk to the side of the queen sized bed where I set Nat down.

Pulling off my shoes, I climb on top of her trailing kisses up her body as I reach her mouth. Nat wraps her hands around my neck and pulls me in closer to her. I let my hands wander along the side of her body and across her chest. I begin to make my trail to the back of her bra when the door flies open. I jump up covering Nat with my body and look to the doorway where I see Rizz standing there with large eyes as she looks from Nat to me.

"Sorry," she mumbles, "I was looking for John."

"Your drug dealer is down stairs," I snap at her, "You of all people should know that happens on the first floor."

Rizz looks at me with a shocked expression.

"I'm not stupid, Rizz. I know a druggie when I see one."

Nat sits up and looks past me at Rizz, "I saw him in the kitchen a while ago," she slurs.

Rizz looks at Nat in concern, but says nothing.

"I've got this," I try to assure her nicely.

Rizz hesitates before turning, "yeah, thanks," and walks out the door, shutting it behind her.

I look back down at Nat who is now biting her bottom lip and that's enough for me to dive back in for more. I continue my exploration of her body and am about to undo her bra when she suddenly flips me over as she whispers, "I love you, Thom."

I kiss her harder as I let her words sink into me and pull her against my chest. Nathalie's hands begin to snake down to the top of my pants. Her fingers work the button of my pants until they undo. I close my eyes and wait for her expectant touch, but it doesn't come. I open my eyes to find Nat siting up holding her head as she sways slightly from side to side.

"Nat?" I ask hesitantly.

"I—I—" she tries to say, but she falls to my side and her eyes roll back in her head.

Panic begins to strike through me and I place my hands on her shoulders.

"Nat?" I shout as I gently shake her, "Nat, wake up. Nathalie?"

As fear begins to rush over me I jump from the bed and re-button my pants as I rush out the door in search for Rizz.

I rush down the stairs and Gage blocks my way.

"Hey man. Must have put her to bed, huh?" he chuckles.

I just look at him in fear as I shout at him, "Where is Rizz?"

Gage's smile fades replaced with worry, "Dude, what's wrong?"

"Dammit, Gage, just tell me which room Rizz is in."

"I don't know man. She and John headed upstairs not too long ago."

I turn and run up the stairs taking them two at a time. Rushing down the hallway I throw open every door on my way down until I reach the end of hall and throw open the last door to find John and Rizz face to face with about an inch between them.

Ignoring the nagging feeling of seeing my best friend's girl with another guy, I burst in. The two jump apart and stare at me in shocked worriment.

"Rizz," I breathe, "It's Nat."

CHAPTER THIRTY-THREE: LANCE

The café seems busier today than it usually is when I meet Jack. There is a line of people forming from the counter to the door. The clerks work feverishly behind the counter to complete each order within a few minutes. I decide that I'll wait until they slow down to get a cup of coffee, and search the café for Jack.

I spot him in the back sitting in a booth by a window facing the parking lot. His head is tilted down, and as I come closer I can see that he is reading a book that is lying upon the table.

"Hey," I interrupt as I slide into the booth opposite him.

Jack closes the book and smiles at me, "I see you decided to skip the line too."

I give him a weak smile back, "I'll just go up when they slow down."

"My thoughts exactly," he says, setting the book aside. "So, how are you today?"

"Alright."

"You're a terrible liar, you know?"

I look at Jack.

"You have the same tell all sign as me."

"Rizz left," I reply as I look out the window and then back at Jack, "Trust is huge with her, and she thinks I lied to her."

"Did you?"

"No," I all but yell.

Jack puts his hands up in surrender, "Calm down there, fella, it's only a question."

"I didn't lie to her," I say more calmly, "It was just a huge trap my ex put me in."

"An ex, huh?"

"Unfortunately," I say resting my elbows on the edge of the table.

"You should try talking to Rizz."

"I did. She won't have it though. She's too damn stubborn."

Jack snorts, "You two remind me of your mother and me."

"In what way?"

Jack leans back in his seat, "In every way."

I wait for Jack to go on, but when he doesn't I ask, "Care to go on?"

Jack smirks, "Your mother and I got into a fight once. I was the one to leave though, but I did everything I could to get her back in the end."

"What was the fight about?"

"Your mother and I had been dating for a year. Her father, a round stump of a man, boy did I hate him." Jack chuckles, "he didn't approve of me. He thought I was no good, and he had no problem voicing his opinions of me." Jack leans forward in his seat, "Well, one day it all caught up to me. It got to be too much, so I told your mother I was leaving, that we weren't right for each other, and then I left."

"Where did you go?"

"California. Started a new life, well I tried to. Every day I thought about her. It was unbearable. I couldn't stop thinking about her, so that's when I got into some bad things to attempt to erase her from my memory, but nothing worked. No matter how high I got, she was still the center of my mind. So I came back for her."

"You got hooked on drugs because you were trying to forget her?"

"We do a lot of dumb shit to ease the pain of being alone."

"But you weren't alone, you chose to be," I say, growing angry.

"I know that now, Lance, and I regret it every day."

"Did she forgive you?" I ask, holding back the anger.

"Eventually," Jack says, and then motions to me, "You're living proof of that."

"We could have had a different life, you know? If you didn't leave."

"We could have. But who knows if I didn't leave if you'd be alive? We can't live dwelling on the 'what ifs', we have to make do with what is in front of us."

"So what should I do?"

Jack shakes his head and sighs, "I guess what I'm trying to say is that sometimes being apart is all it takes to realize you belong together."

I look down at the table and think about how hurt Rizz was when she had found Kayla and I like she had. I think back to how afraid she was to let the world know the truth about her—to come clean about the abuse she endured all her life.

At that moment I knew that no matter how badly I don't want to, that I would have to let her go. I would have to let her cool off and figure things out. I just need to give her a few days, because I already know we belong together. I will never let her go.

CHAPTER THIRTY-FOUR: RIZZ

I find John down in the kitchen talking with this kid, Gage, from school and approach the two of them.

"Hey," I say nudging John's side.

John looks at me his brows furrowed and says, "Hey."

"Can we talk?" I ask.

He hesitates, but nods in agreement, "Yeah, come on," he says as he guides me out of the kitchen. Over his shoulder he calls back to Gage, "Catch you later."

"Later," he replies.

John leads me back upstairs to the end of the hallway where his bedroom is. Everything inside looks the same as it had the first time I stepped foot in it. Band posters fill the walls, his bed is made and any stray objects are stored away in draws and the closet.

John pulls his stash from one of his dresser draws and motions for me to sit on the floor.

I take a seat and watch as he pulls an already rolled blunt from a cigar papers packet.

"So what's going on?" he asks as he lights the blunt.

I begin to tell him about the pool party and Kayla. He hands me the blunt and I take it, taking a drag. I cough a bit at the first hit as it settles in my chest.

"Why are you telling me all this?" John asks as I take my hit.

I look at him shyly. "I don't know…I guess…well…you're my best friend."

"No," he says, "Nathalie and Charlene are your best friends. If you even know what a friend is."

"What is that supposed to mean?" I ask, offended.

I take another drag, pissed at his attitude.

"Friends don't use each other. They don't mess with each other's heads, which is something you enjoy doing," John says pointedly as he takes the blunt from me.

"You keep talking to me like this I might just need one of these for myself," I say reluctantly giving him the blunt.

John chuckles, and the mood begins to lift a little.

"If we aren't friends, then what are we?"

John takes a drag, blowing the smoke back out into my face.

"We are two completely fucked up people."

I crack a smile and shake my head slowly, "You ever think we could change."

"We aren't the changing type, Razzle," he says, and points the blunt at me, "Look at you, you tried and now look at you."

"I don't think I was really trying. It just happened."

"Either way," John says, "You hit a bump in the road and you're right back to where you started. It's inevitable. You and me, we're pushers. We push everyone we care about away from us."

"I push you away," I comment.

John's eyes dart to me as he takes another drag.

"But I always come back to you," I go on.

John inches toward me with the blunt between his lips. He takes a deep drag and reaches his hand up to the blunt, removing it from his mouth.

I lean my head back and open my mouth allowing him to blow the smoke into it.

"That's because..."John says inches from my face after slowly blowing the smoke into my mouth. "We are two screwed up people who are way too comfortable with each other." He looks from my lips to my eyes and says, "And besides, I'm your drug dealer."

I smile at him as he begins to lean in a little more than I had planned him to when the door slams open. I jump apart from John and look to the doorway to find a freaked out looking Thom standing in the doorway.

He looks from me to John and back and finally says, "Rizz, its Nat."

Suddenly alert I ask, "What do you mean, Thom?"

"Something's wrong. She passed out and now she won't wake up."

"Is she breathing?" I ask as I get to my feet.

"I think so—barely." Thom exclaims.

I rush to the doorway as Thom turns down the hallway. I follow him to the room down the hall and gasp as I look at Nat's motionless body lying on the bed.

"I don't know what happened," Thom stutters, "One moment she was fine and the next she's—"

My eyes begin to water up as I make my way to the side of the bed, "Nathalie?" I touch her arm.

She's warm, good.

I place two fingers on the inside of her wrist and am relieved when I feel a small pulse.

"How much has she had to drink, Thom?"

"I don't know…a lot," He says, shrugging.

"We have to get her to a hospital."

"No, we can't. If Pop is working I will never here the end of it."

I snap my head at Thom and narrow my eyes at him.

"Your girlfriend is lying here unconscious most likely with alcohol poisoning and you're worried about what Pop will think?" I shout at him.

Thom squeezes his eyes tight obviously fighting with himself. He begins to nod his head slowly and opens his eyes, "Help me get her to your car."

I put my arm under Nathalie's small frame as Thom grabs her legs. Once we have her propped up on the bed and with her shirt back on, Thom scoops her up in his arms and follows me out of the room and down the stairs.

I spot John on the way out and nod my head in his direction. He gives back a knowing nod and I walk out the front door with Thom at my heels.

This wasn't the kind of life I wanted to live anymore and I wasn't going to keep putting myself in these situations. Lance had been right all along. If I wanted things to change I was going to have to be the one to make the first move.

I open the back door for Thom and he lays Nat down and crawls in beside her. Shutting the door I walk to the driver's side and climb in. Putting the car into drive I take off for the hospital as Thom whispers to Nathalie,

"I'm so sorry. I love you, Nat. it's going to be okay. I promise."

My grip tightens around the steering wheel as I hold the tears back. We finally reach the hospital and I pull up to the ER section. I put the car in park and rush through the ER doors as Thom gets Nathalie out of the car.

"Help," I shout to the nurse sitting behind the counter. "My friend she won't wake up. I think she has alcohol poisoning. Her pulse…it's low. Please, you have to help her."

The nurse rushes from behind the counter and calls a few nurses to help her.

It isn't long until they are transferring Nathalie from Thom's arms to a hospital gurney. The nurse begins asking questions about Nat as other nurses attend to her. What's her name? How old is she? What is her parents contact information? I try my best to answer all the questions I can. The nurse scribbles down all the information onto a chart and then tells us to wait in the waiting room. As they begin to roll Nat to the back room, Thom takes a step toward them.

"You have to stay here," the nurse with a mole on her cheek says to Thom.

"I can't leave her," Thom protests holding Nat's hand.

I walk over and put my hand on Thom's forearm.

"Come on, Thom. She'll be okay and when she wakes up she'll want to see you. Don't get yourself kicked out." I nod my head toward the waiting room, "Come one let's go sit down."

"I hate waiting," Thom says.

"I know, me too."

Thom looks back at Nat through the window of the ER room. I nudge him, and he follows me as I head to the waiting room.

CHAPTER THIRTY-FIVE: THOM

I bounce my leg repeatedly as Rizz and I wait for any news about Nathalie. I wring my hands in my lap and try to still my leg as I catch glimpses of an annoyed Rizz from the corner of my eye. She looks like she's about to jump on me at any minute. At least that's better than the looks I was getting when I was pacing the waiting room. I'm pretty sure I saw her fist ball up.

The seats are uncomfortable hard formed plastic that the hospital was trying to pass off as chairs. The aroma of cleaning products is stinking up the whole room, the waxed floors began to cause my eyes to water from the harsh glare and the nurse was pounding on her keyboard as she typed. Every single one of my senses is heightened and it is driving me to the edge. I was nervous and afraid, but most of all I felt guilty. Maybe I should have continued pacing and let Rizz kick my ass just to get some of the edge off.

"I'm going to get something to eat," Rizz says suddenly, getting up from her seat and standing in front of me.

I look up at her without saying anything. *Yeah, I was getting to her.*

"You want anything?" she asks.

My eyes light up as I look past her to the doctor who just walked through the door. I sigh in relief when I notice it isn't Pop.

Rizz turns to look at what caught my eye and her shoulders begin to relax. I stand up and walk past her meeting the doctor half way.

"Nathalie is stable," the doctor says.

Everything in me begins to relax slightly.

"Can we see her?" Rizz asks.

"I'm not supposed to be telling you anything or even allow you to see her," the doctor responds looking at Rizz. He directs his attention back to me, "But seeing as how her parents didn't answer and you two were the ones who brought her in, I'll make an exception just this once."

"Thank you," Rizz says.

"She's in recovery, so only one at a time."

"Thank you," I say this time, reaching for the doctor's hand.

The doctor shakes my hand and gives Rizz a polite smile before walking to the nurse's station.

I turn to Rizz who gives me a small smile and says,

"Go ahead."

I nod my head and turn in the direction of Nathalie's room.

Opening the door I walk into the room with my head down. Shutting the door behind me I make my way to the bed and slowly lift my head to see my beautiful goddess lying in the hospital bed with an IV in her hand.

"Hey," she smiles.

"Hey," I say, pulling up a chair next to her, "How are you feeling?"

"A lot better actually," she admits, "I guess I drank too much."

"You really scared the shit out me tonight."

Nat reaches for my hand and I give it to her.

"I'm sorry, Babe. I never meant for that to happen."

"Don't be sorry," I say, my eyes reaching hers.

Nat looks at me quizzically.

I bow my head in defeat and press her cool hand to my forehead as I whisper, "This is all my fault."

"What are you saying?" Nat asks trying to pull her hand from my grasp.

I hold her hand firmly in my hand and press it against my face as the tears begin to stream down my face.

How could I have been so stupid?

"I should have stopped you."

Nat pulls her hand from my grasp and I look at her pained face.

"I shouldn't have let you drink as much as you did. I should have noticed. I should have stopped you."

"Don't you dare to that, Thom," Nat snaps.

"This is my fault. You are here because of me."

"No, Thom. You listen to me right now," Nat says sternly, "I chose to drink. It was my choice not yours. This is my fault. Not yours. If you weren't there then I may not have been able to get the help I needed."

"You're here because of me."

"No, I am here because of me," she says grabbing my hand, "I'm awake and alive because of you."

I bow my forehead on our joined hands as I try to believe the words she is telling me.

"I won't hurt you anymore," I mutter, "I promise."

I feel Nathalie's fingers in my hair, "You never hurt me in the first place and I know you never will."

I stand up from the chair and place a chaste kiss on her forehead and then her lips.

"Rizz is waiting outside," I say.

Nat nods her head in understanding.

"I love you," I say squeezing her hand.

"I love you too," she smiles, squeezing my hand back.

I walk away letting our hands fall apart and reach for the door. Taking a deep breath I open the

door and step out into the hallway and make my
way to where Rizz is waiting.

CHAPTER THIRTY-SIX: RIZZ

It's dark. My eyes flicker letting in streams of light as I hear a voice from afar. My eyebrows come together and my eyelids open slowly letting the light in fully. I moan as I feel someone shaking me; waking me up.

"Rizz," Thom's voice comes, "You can go see her now."

I sit up and rub my eyes with the back of my hand.

"How long were you in there?"

"Not too long," he says, "You must have been tired."

"How is she?"

"She's alive," he says blankly, "I'm going to head home."

"Alright, do you need me to call you a cab?" I ask.

"I'm sure I will manage."

"Right," I mumble.

Thom begins to turn to leave, but stops himself, "What was going on with you and John?"

I look at Thom with a raised brow, "What?"

"What's going on with you two?"

"He's my dealer," I say in a hushed tone.

"There's more though isn't there?"

I think about the moment in John's room when he was about to kiss me and how I didn't want him to—not even to keep up appearances.

"No," I reply, "and there never will be."

Thom runs his hand through his hair as his jaw tightens.

"You should call Lance."

"Don't," I warn him.

Thom scoffs at me, "He needs you and you need him." He scoffs again, "You two make each other better."

"You sound so happy about that," I mutter.

"With you he was able to face shit, shit he didn't want to face."

"Yeah, well he can learn to face things on his own."

Thom shakes his head and turns to leave, "You know," he says facing me again, "Maybe if you took your head out of your ass you'd realize that she probably planned the whole thing."

I look at Thom, taken back. Narrowing my eyes I say, "I don't know what you're talking about."

"We both know you damn well do."

I stay silent.

"Believe what you want." He goes on. "But you know I'm right. You two are good for each other. It's like you make him face his problems and then make him forget them. Something we both wish we could do."

He gives me one final glare and then walks away; leaving me.

I stand up from the waiting room chair and head to Nathalie's room. The room looks bland. A chair sits beside the bed where a flushed Nathalie lays, her body hidden beneath a hospital gown.

"What the hell is wrong with your boyfriend?" I ask, hooking my thumb back toward the door.

"Hey to you too," she smiles.

The corners of my mouth rise slightly, "I think it's time you quit drinking. You can't go turning into Lindsay Lohan on me."

"Better her than Charlie Sheen."

I laugh as I walk to the chair and sit down, "But seriously what's up with Thom? It was like he loved Lance and hated him at the same time."

Nat gives me a sympathetic look, "I heard about the break. I'm sorry."

I roll my eyes, "I was the one to break it off."

"Well you're an idiot then," she smirks.

I laugh quietly.

"Honestly though," Nat says growing serious, "I thought it was sort of weird that you broke up." Nathalie reaches for the glass of water sitting next to her on the nightstand. "I thought you two were kind of destined for each other."

She takes a sip of the water and sets it down.

"What do you mean?" I ask.

"In a way you made each other…well…better. It's like neither of you could function without the other."

"You sound like Thom," I snort, "But you sound like you actually mean it. I don't know what you're boyfriend's issue was."

"Thom is dealing with a lot."

"Aren't we all?"

"It's not the same." Nathalie says slowly, "He's struggling with not only everything around him, but with himself too."

"What do you mean?"

"He blames himself every day."

"For what? You just ended up in the hospital tonight."

"Not me," Nathalie says shaking her head, "But I'm sure he's blaming himself for this now too."

I give her an arched brow as she hesitates.

"How much do you know about Lance's adoptive mom?"

"Ann? Just that she was in an accident and didn't make it."

"That accident didn't just affect Lance, Rizz. It affected Thom too…on a whole different level."

"What do you mean? She was Lance's mom—that doesn't make…any sense." I finish as the dots slowly begin to connect.

"The friend," I mutter in shock as I meet Nat's sad eyes.

"Was Thom's father," Nathalie finishes for me.

I stand from the chair and begin to pace the hospital room.

"Why wouldn't he tell me?" I wonder to myself more so than to Nat.

"Lance was probably protecting Thom."

I continue to pace as I rethink every conversation Lance and I had about his mother.

Why hadn't I figured it out earlier?

"I know how the accident affects Thom. He blames himself, and although I worry about him, I worry about Lance too."

My thoughts pause as I look back at Nathalie.

"He doesn't show any emotion about the accident at all. He avoids it. He won't talk about it with Thom at all."

"He just wants to move on."

"And Thom thinks he was."

"How?"

"By being with you. You were saving him, Rizz. It was like he was slowly facing what really happened that day."

"What?"

"You, as Thom put it, were causing him to face it all and that was saving him."

"Then why is Thom so angry with him?"

"Because even though Lance was facing it all on his own, he was still hiding from Thom, and in order for Thom to move on Lance needs to be able to face everything with Thom."

"Do you think he will?"

"I don't know," Nat says sadly.

CHAPTER THIRTY-SEVEN: LANCE

"Lance," I hear Thom's muffled voice.

I turn over on the couch, snuggling into the cushions, thinking it's only in my head.

"Lance," his voice comes again, louder.

Groggily, I sit up on the couch and reach for the television remote. Picking it up, I point it to the TV and press the power button. I sit there for a moment and wait, but hear nothing. I set the remote back onto the coffee table and run my hands over my face.

"Lance," I hear Thom shout.

I look at the time on the cable box to see it is three in the morning.

What the fuck?

Walking to the front window and looking out I see Thom waving his hands over his head in victory before walking up the pathway to the front door.

I open the door, "What are you doing here? Do you know what time it is?"

Thom steps around me and into the house, "What are you still doing up?"

"Couldn't sleep," I reply, "Why didn't you just use the doorbell?"

Thom nods his head and says, "Didn't want to wake Pop." Thom walks into the living room. I take in his disheveled hair and wrinkled clothes.

"So you just decided to wake up the whole neighborhood instead?" I say, shutting the door.

Thom doesn't respond as I follow him into the living room.

"You okay, man?" I ask.

"Yeah, why?"

"You look like you got hit by a train."

"I'm good."

"How was the party?"

Thom stops dead in his tracks.

"What's wrong?" I ask, stopping behind him.

"It's my fault," Thom sniffles.

"What happened?" I ask, beginning to panic, "Is Rizz okay?"

"You would think that, wouldn't you? What did you do to Rizz, Thom?" he snaps as he turns toward me.

I notice the dark circles beginning to form beneath his eyes.

"What are you talking—?"

"Your precious girlfriend is fine. It's mine that almost died tonight," Thom yells.

He collapses onto the couch, his face in his hands, "I should have stopped her."

"Thom."

"I knew she was drinking too much. I knew and I didn't stop her. I should have stopped her," he says, looking at me.

"You can't blame yourself," I say taking a seat next to him.

"I can't? Then why do I feel so bad? Why do I feel guilty? It's just like Ann's accident. I was the one who distracted my dad. I was the one to cause him to look away from the road. It was my fault."

"Thom," I whisper.

"No," Thom shouts, jumping from the couch, "don't act like you don't wish things turned out differently. Like you don't wonder what life would be like if she was here? I do? Did you know that? Every damn day."

"It's not your fault."

"Don't lie to me," Thom shouts.

I look at Thom with complete fear. This was my best friend who couldn't let go of the past. Who was letting an accident destroy him, and I couldn't help him.

"Thom," Pop's steady voice comes from behind us.

I turn to see Pop in his pajamas standing in the hallway.

"I think it's time you get home and get some rest."

Thom shakes his head as he smirks dangerously to himself before walking past Pop and me to the front door.

I turn to chase after him, but Pop blocks my way.

"Just let it go, Son."

I glare up at Pop and push his arm out of the way before pushing past him and running to the front door, "Thom," I shout after him as I walk out of the house and onto the grass, "Thom."

Thom stops in the middle of the yard and turns toward me.

"I don't blame you," I say slowly, taking a few steps toward him, "you're my best friend, I could never blame you."

"Stop lying to me, Lance," Thom yells.

"What do you want me to say?" I say raising my voice, "That I wish Ann were here? Yeah, of course I do. I hate that the accident happened. It was shitty we both know that. I hate that it was your father who was involved and I want to hate him for it."

"So you admit it then?"

"But I can't hate him," I continue, "because I know it wasn't intentional. Nothing about that day was intentional."

Thom says nothing so I go on, "I'm sorry Thom, I'm sorry I never said anything before. That I just pushed it away. I thought I had to be strong for your sake. I could see you struggling, and I didn't want to make it any harder. But you have to believe me, I don't blame you."

Thom clenches his fists at his side. "Well you don't have to be strong for me anymore." Thom sneers before walking away.

"Thom," I shout, "Don't do anything stupid."

I watch as Thom walks into his house. No last glance, no comment, just the back of his head and the repeating last words in my head.

Don't do anything stupid.

CHAPTER THIRTY-EIGHT: THOM

Knowing my mother was out of town house hunting, I slam the back door behind me not caring if the glass shatters.

I pace the living room as everything begin to collide together and explode inside my head.

I look at the floor ahead of me and see blood. I look down at my body not aware that I had hurt myself, but as I search my body I can't find the cut. There is nothing new on my body. I look back at the floor and the blood is gone.

I close my eyes and kneed my fingers in my head as I try to get my shit together, but the voices begin to flood through my head.

It's not your fault Thom.

It was an accident.

We have to take her to the hospital.

What Pop will think...

Don't you dare blame yourself.

What is your problem?

I hate that it was your father.

I wish Ann was here.

I'm leaving your father.

She deserves better.

Take care of each other.

I love you son...son...son...

I open my eyes and blood covers the walls. It's everywhere. I feel the sweat pour down my face as I look frantically around the room. I try to blink it away, but nothing works.

I have to get out of here. I have to stop all the noise...the pain...I need to make it all go away.

CHAPTER THIRTY-NINE: RIZZ

The lights blur blue and red, the siren flares, and the cool handcuffs dig into my skin. The neighbors all walk out of their gingerbread homes to watch the latest gossip unravel before their eyes.

After returning home from the hospital, I walk into the living room to find my *family* patiently sitting on the couch. My mother stares impassively at the fireplace.

Upon entering the living room, I notice the cops standing nearby. My heart skips a beat as I begin worrying what the monster must have done to Hope, but the feeling sinks to the pit of my stomach as the male officer approaches me. He begins to read me my rights, asking me to turn around and place my hands behind my back. Stunned, I do as I am told.

The female officer holds up a bag of weed in front of me, and explains that they had a warrant to search the premises due to an anonymous caller.

My eyes dart to my mother who is still looking at the fireplace, to Chip's sorrow filled eyes and then to Hope whose face is marked with tears.

I am led outside, where I see neighbors huddled in their doorways and holding back curtains peering out their windows.

The cop places his hand on the top of my head, guiding me into the back seat of the car. The door thuds shut and I stare out the window at my mother, Chip and Hope. My mother walks back into the house, her face cold as ice. Chip places his arm around Hope's shoulders as she attaches herself to the side of his leg.

I look forward at the gate keeping me caged in. My stomach tightens and I begin to feel dizzy as claustrophobia takes over my body.

Trapped, I'm trapped.

I think of my mother's cold stare as she turned back into the house and panic courses through me.

No, no, no, I have to get out of here.

I thrash my back against the seat and kick at the car door.

"You have to let me out," I scream, "I have to save her."

I continue to kick at the door. The male officer rushes to the car door with his gun drawn. "You have to calm down," he says through the glass of the window.

I stop kicking at the door as my head grows dizzier. "I have to save her," I say breathlessly.

"I have…I have to…" I say, as I slowly fall back onto the seat before everything grows dark.

I wake up, and I am lying down on a stretcher in the middle of the street. More blue and red lights blur around us. I feel groggy, but begin to sit up. A petite hand falls on my shoulder, gently pushing me back down.

"Don't get up," A female's voice says.

"What happened?"

"You passed out."

I look around me to see that we are still outside my house.

"I'm fine," I say, as panic begins to reside again.

"We just have to check your vitals."

"I'm fine," I repeat, trying to get up from the stretcher.

"Laura, you have to let them check your vitals," the male officer from earlier says from my side.

"Rizz," I snap, "My name is Rizz."

"Rizz," he nods.

I look at his name tag reading Tate. "I'm fine. Just take me to the station, please," I beg. "You're making an unnecessary scene. I'm fine, just please, take me to the station," I plead as I glance back at the house.

Appearances are everything to her.

Officer Tate follows my gaze to the house, and then nods his head.

"Is there something you're not telling me, Rizz?" he asks.

I shake my head, "Just please take me to the station."

He eyes me skeptically before addressing the paramedic, "I'll take her now."

The paramedic nods her head, and the officer wraps his fingers around my bicep. I hop of off the stretcher and follow him to the police car.

"No kicking, okay?"

I nod, and get into the back seat. As he pulls onto the street, I lean my head against the window, looking out at my house.

Whispering to myself I say, "I'm sorry, Hope."

At the station, the officer hands me a cup and points to the ladies room across from us. When I finish, I hand the female officer standing outside my stall the cup and follow her back into the foyer of the station. Officer Tate motions me to the counter where he begins to finger print me. Following the fingerprints, are the photos, and then I am placed into a holding cell where a few others sit.

A girl, not much older than me with multi colored hair and a nose ring sits next to a middle aged woman wearing a skintight leopard printed dress which exposes her assets. I smile sheepishly at them before walking to the bench opposite them and sitting down, leaning against the back wall.

I don't belong here.

I lean my head back against the wall and begin to wish I had Lance here; to be able to see him or touch him, and have him whisk all the fear running through me away. But he's not, because I pushed him away. I did what I did best.

"Miss. Murphy," Officer Tate calls.

I sit up straighter and look at him through the bars.

"You have a visitor."

"I can have one of those?" I ask.

He nods his head as he opens the door. A second cop stands close by watching the two other women carefully.

Officer Tate cuffs my hands again, and leads me from the cell to a small room with a table and two chairs.

"No plastic window and phone?" I ask.

"I think you watch too much T.V." he laughs.

I shrug, "I guess you can't believe everything you see on T.V."

Officer Tate guides me to one of the chairs. After he unlocks the cuffs, I rub at my wrists and take a seat.

The door opens again and I see Chip being led in by a female officer.

"You have five minutes," the female cop says.

Chip nods and takes a seat across from me.

"What are you doing here?" I ask.

"You have to know, that I was the one to call the police."

"You what?" I exclaim, jumping from my seat.

Officer Tate clears his throat from behind me.

I look back at him and he points to the chair.

Sitting back down I ask in the most even tone I could muster, "Why would you do that?"

"I had no choice."

"Everyone has a choice," I snap.

Chip runs his hands over his face, "You had it in my house, and when Hope came to me with a bag of that crap—asking questions—she's too young to be stained with all of this—I had to do something."

"Hope knows?"

"You have to understand that I am doing this for the both of you."

"Doing what?"

"I won't stand by and watch you throw your life away on drugs, and I won't allow you to follow in your mother's footsteps."

"What—"

"I'm not dumb, Rizz. I can see your mother is struggling. I can see that Hope looks up to you, and I can see you throwing away your life. When Hope came to me and told me what you had told her about this stuff I knew something was going on and I had to do something. I had to get you help."

"Hope did what?"

"This was all because Hope and I love you, and we don't want to see you fade away into nothingness."

"But—" I begin as the door opens again.

An officer leads Hope into the small room.

"Hope," I gasp.

"I'm sorry, but I had to do it," she cries.

I move to get up, but stop and look up at Officer Tate. He nods once, and I go to Hope, pulling her into my arms.

"It's okay."

"I need you," she whispers into my shoulder.

"Shh," I try to calm her, "It will be okay."

The female officer places her hand on my shoulder, "Times up."

I nod my head as I pull away from Hope. I grab her hand in mine and give it a squeeze before Chip places his hand on her shoulder and leads her from the room.

Guilt suddenly rushes over me as realization dawns on me. I opened a whole new world to Hope. I destroyed the little bit of innocence she had left by forcing her to grow up. I made her have to leave behind her childhood at eight years old and become an adult.

I sit back in the chair, hanging my head.

I was causing her to become me without even realizing it.

Officer Tate clears his throat, "come on."

I stand and place my hands behind my back, allowing him to cuff me. After doing so, he leads me from the room back to the holding cell.

The judge sits high above me in her black robe, reading my crime aloud. Chip and Hope are joined by Charlene and Nathalie in the viewing seats behind me. A small amount of worry melts away as I see Nat's vibrant face sitting in the benches, but my heart grows heavy at the angered look she is directing my way.

I turn back to face the judge as she asks me if I have anything to say. I stand up,

"What I did was wrong, and I know that. I accept the consequences to my actions and I am willing to do whatever it takes to get clean."

The judge nods her head and tells me to take a seat.

I glance back at the four people who mean the most to me and feel lucky to have their support, but as I scan each of their faces I am unable to shake the nagging feeling that someone is missing—the feeling that I wish I could lay eyes on that one person—Lance. Just one look from him and all my nerves would be gone. I would know I would be okay.

The gavel pounds down causing me to jump in my seat. I'm told to stand, so I do.

The judge says, "Since this is your first offense and considering who your father is, I am sentencing you to a two month rehab program."

I let out a deep breath of relief as a smile breaks across my face.

"But," she continues.

I take in a sharp breath, holding it.

"Next time it won't matter who your father is."

I nod, "There won't be a next time ma'am."

"Very well, we are adjourned," she says, slamming her gavel.

I turn around, reaching over the railing, to hug my family and friends.

Char hugs me tightly, while Nat does so limply. Chip squeezes me comfortingly before letting me go so I can wrap Hope up in my arms.

"I'll see you soon, okay?"

Hope nods her head.

I lean in and whisper in her ear, "Make sure to always lock your door. It won't be long, I promise."

Hope looks at me with tears in her eyes.

Wrapping my arms around her, I pull her into another hug.

A court officer reaches my side, "Time to go."

I turn to look at him and nod.

"It'll be okay," I call to Hope as the officer leads me out of the court room, "Dad will take care of you."

CHAPTER FOURTY: LANCE

I sit at the kitchen island and rub my finger against the condensation on the glass. I think back two days when I opened my front door to find Charlene about to knock on the surface.

"Hi," Charlene says as she puts her hand back down at her side.

"Hi," I say, surprised to see her.

Charlene interlocks her hands together in front of her.

"Can I help you with something?" I ask.

"Right, sorry," she says nervously, "God, this is awkward."

"If this has to do about Rizz don't worry about it. I'm headed to go talk to her now."

"You can't," Charlene says quickly as I pass by her.

I stop, "Why not?"

"I mean...gosh this sucks," Charlene pouts.

"What is it?"

"She isn't home."

I shake my head to begin to protest, but Charlene goes on.

"She won't be home for a while."

"A while?"

"Well more like two months or so," she says stepping down from the porch.

"What do you mean?"

"I mean she got arrested."

"What?" I ask in disbelief.

"She got busted for doing drugs. Trust me I'm already pissed at her. I mean I knew she did that stuff, but I didn't think it was serious," Charlene rants, "Anyhow, she's in rehab. I just thought you should know."

I look at the ground trying to understand how she would have gotten caught, "Can I visit her?" I ask looking at Charlene, hopeful.

"Yes, but no," Charlene says slowly, "Uh…she doesn't want you to visit her."

"But I'm her boyfriend."

"Well actually, you're not," Charlene mutters, "Sorry, it's just…I don't know…I don't think she wants you to see her in a place like that."

"That's ridiculous."

"I'm just relaying the message."

"Well is she okay?"

"I don't know. I haven't visited her yet. She just told me to tell you all this at the hearing."

I look at the ground and then back to Charlene, "Are you sure—"

"I'm sure, Lance. Just give her space for now. She'll come around."

I run my finger along the side of the glass tracing little pictures on the glass. The girl I love won't see me, my best friend won't answer my calls and my father is working more now than ever. I haven't even bothered to contact Jack after visiting him at the café. I just couldn't deal with all of it right now.

More than anything I wanted to see Rizz. I wanted to let her know that everything is going to be okay and that she will get past this. I wanted to tell her that I would look out for Hope if she wanted me to. I wanted her to know that I was there for her even if she was in there.

Pop walks hastily into the kitchen slamming a file down on the island. He had been bringing work home lately in order to finish all the paper work that needed to be done.

He rubs his eyelids with his fingertips as he sighs deeply.

"Long day at work?" I ask.

"Unfortunately, yes," Pop replies as he bows his head and walks from the kitchen forgetting his file.

I don't think teachers prepare their students for the emotional toll a job can put on their lives. I feel bad for everything Pop has to see at the hospital in the ER—patients who don't make it, those who are severely injured. It gets to Pop sometimes. He doesn't just see a person. He sees their souls.

I reach for the file that lies on the island. Taking a moment, I listen for Pop and when I am sure he isn't coming back anytime soon I take a peek at the file.

When I read the name of the patient my heart begins to race and I fumble through the papers to find out what happened to this child. As I read on, my heart begins to relax slightly when I read that she is still living. I read the accident report and feel sick to my stomach as I read the all too familiar story.

I push the file away from me and rush out the back door. I knew I needed to talk to someone about this.

I jump the fence between Thom's yard and mine and walk up to the sliding glass doors. I slow at I notice all the lights are off. I know his mom is out of town, but if Thom is home the house shouldn't be as dark at it is.

I open the back door, knowing that the Downey's never lock the door. I walk quietly through the back room making my way through the kitchen.

The further I walk into the house the worse the sick feeling in my stomach gets. Something wasn't right. The silence filled my ears, getting louder and louder with each step I took.

I reach for the light switch in the living room. The lights flicker on and my heart drops to my stomach as I look at Thom in front of me.

"Thom," I yell as I rush toward him. I stand up the chair that fell over and step on it. Wrapping my arms around him I lift him up to relieve the pressure from his neck. I can't unhook him though. The cable cord is tied to the ceiling fan and I am unable to reach up and untie it while holding onto him.

Gently, I set his feet onto the chair in order to keep him held up, but there is no use. His unconscious body dangles off.

I run to the garage and grab one of his dad's sheering scissors from an opened box. I run as quickly as I can to the living room and set the cable between the two blades.

"I'm really sorry, Buddy," I say as tears stream down my face and I cut the rope.

Thom's body thuds to the floor, and I scramble to my knees beside him. I check for a pulse and am unable to find one.

"Come on, Thom," I say through clenched teeth, "Wake up Buddy."

The tears begin to burn as they continue to form in my eyes. I reach for my phone and call the police.

"9-1-1 please report your emergency," a woman's voice speaks clearly over the line.

"My friend…he tried to…he killed himself," I sob into the phone stumbling over the last words.

"Sir, you need to calm down. Can you tell us where you are?"

"26 Wellington Street," I reply.

"Okay, a team is on their way."

I shut my phone as I fight to keep back the sobs making their way out. I hold Thom in my arms.

"You can't die. I need you, Thom," I lay my head against his, rocking him back and forth.

The blur of everyone passing by fades and I'm left with myself standing in a room of bright lights. The silence burns through me and the light penetrates my eyes. That's when I close them and all that is left is the darkness.

CHAPTER FOURTY-ONE: RIZZ

If you closed your eyes and ignored the sounds around you, you'd think your parents sent you on a vacation. That is until someone throws a fit because they are going through withdrawal. Then security comes to keep things under control, which causes the patient to flip their lid.

Some people however, like me, are a little saner.

Janice, a tall lean creature with short jaded black hair got busted when she was only sixteen. She's nineteen now.

"My mom was a crack head. I thought it was okay, because she did it," Janice told me the first day I found myself in this place. This was her second time "passing through" as she put it.

Then there is Katrina. She's about the height of a twelve year old. Her brown hair hung along her shoulders and freckles filled her face.

"I was fourteen when I had my first drink. Thirteen when I popped my first pill," she announced during one of our group therapy sessions.

Kasie is the one who never said anything during group sessions. Janice said it was because she was rebelling the whole rehab thing. Katrina chimed in that she heard Kasie stole her sister's whole life savings to support her drug addiction.

Either way I didn't like Kasie. She had a poor attitude. If she wanted to keep her mouth shut and stay in this hell hole then so be it. I wasn't trying to stay here a day longer than I was sentenced.

Every day is like De ja vu. We wake up at eight, eat breakfast and then break off into our own private therapy session. Then we get to have free time where we can "go play" as if we're a kindergartener. After free time we got the joy of going to more therapy—group therapy. It's like they want to talk the addiction out of you. If we were lucky we got a visitor which turned our days upside down by messing with our routine—at least for those who needed a routine in order to get over their addictions. Bottom line? I hate it here.

Chip and Hope visit me every week, which makes the whole rehab thing feel less like being held in a cage.

The only downfall to visitation is each patient has a reserved time for visitations and mine wasn't until after my personal therapy time, which obviously didn't make the process any easier.

I sit in the pristine leather chair opposite my doctor and inspect my un-manicured nails.

Charlene would kill me if she saw these.

"Laura," a stout little man says as he leans forward in his chair.

I grit my teeth as I bite back the smart remark I desperately wish to say.

This man was Doctor Oliver. I despised his fading black hair that was always parted so perfectly to the side. And his lab coat? Seriously whose lab coat is ever that white every day? It's as if he gets a new one every day. Then there is the fact that he refuses to call me by my name. Let's just say he irks me way too much.

"Rizz," I mumble.

"We've talked about that in therapy, Laura," he says, pushing up his square framed glasses. "Once you accept your real name you'll be one step closer to rehabilitation."

"What does going by my nickname have anything to do with my drug issue?" I snap.

"You mean by your drug name."

I roll my eyes at him—annoyed and ready to jump across his desk and go crazy on his ass. The truth is that Doctor Oliver is just as much of a nut as some the people here. He thinks he has this fancy degree and everything that comes out of his mouth is truth. Oh, please. Like my name change has anything to do with my old friend Mary Jane.

I liked my group doctor better and honestly I wish he could be my personal doctor too. Doctor Taylor understood that my being called "Rizz" had nothing to do with my habit, but it merely had to do with not wanting any similarity to my mother. The best advice Doctor Taylor could give me though was to just go along with it—"cause fewer problems for yourself, Rizz." He had said.

"Right," I say as I grit my teeth.

Doctor Oliver smiles in victory which only makes me want to rip his mouth right off his smug round face.

"I see you have been journaling. How is that process going for you?"

"Pretty well," I respond, "In fact I think I'm in a little need of journaling at the moment."

"Are you craving a fix?" he asks, perking up in his seat.

"Something like that," I mutter.

You see the journal acted as an outlet for when I felt annoyed or when things were out of my reach. Normally in those moments I would turn to a tightly rolled blunt, but in here my only outlet is my journal that Doctor Taylor gave me. But the more I visited with Doctor Oliver I found myself having to write in it almost every day—sometimes even twice a day.

"What makes you want to write in your journal?" he asks knowingly.

I shift in my seat folding my arms across my chest.

"Ah," he says, "You find me irritating, is that it."

I give him a quick nod as I glare at him.

"You are not the first patient to dislike me. Miss. Laura."

I clench my jaw.

"And honestly I will not be the only person that will irritate you. We must work on finding a way for you to be able to deal with 'irritating' people in a healthy manner without going to get a fix and soon without even having to journal. That will be our goal these next two months," he says as he looks down at my file.

"Now today we must cut our session short as it turns out you have two visitors today instead of one."

I perk up and slide to the edge of my seat trying to get a glimpse of what is written in my file.

Doctor Oliver slams the folder shut, "I see that got your attention."

"Who else is here?" I ask as my mind wanders to Lance.

"It says here," Doctor Oliver says looking at the file again, "A Miss Charlene Michaelson."

I fall back into my seat and let out a sigh.

"Expecting someone else?"

I look up at him with tired eyes and shake my head, "No."

"Well, you're free to go. Remember, next session we will work on centering your irritation in order to allow it to subside without any outlet, so be prepared Miss. Murphy."

I give him a small smile and nod, thankful he didn't call me Laura again and walk out his office toward the visitation room.

I walk into the room where a large red couch sits along the back wall. In the center of the room is a table with a few cushioned chairs placed around it. Sitting in one of the chairs with his back to me is my father. I walk up to him and sit in the chair across from him.

I'm shocked to see red rimming his eyes. His face looks as if it hasn't been shaved in three days and his eyes begin to well up as he makes eye contact with me.

I jerk back in my seat as apprehension burns through my body. "What's wrong, Dad? Where's Hope? Is Hope okay?"

My father nods his head and raises his hand in order to get me to calm down. "She's in the hospital. The police are watching her as we speak."

"What do you mean the hospital?" I ask in a level tone as I stand from the chair. "The cops? Dad, what's going on?"

"Your sister has a broken arm. Other than that she is fine. She might have to start seeing a therapist too." My father begins to ramble on and I cut him off.

"Why are the police watching her?"

"You're sister didn't break her arm by accident," he says, meeting my eyes.

My heart starts to race as all my nightmares become true.

"I came home early…to find…" my father bows his head shaking it in disbelief.

"Why didn't you tell me," he asks.

"Tell you what?"

"Tell me how bad it was," he says looking at me angrily, "I knew your mother had problems, but I didn't know they were this bad."

"Don't you dare blame this on me," I snap.

"Sweetie," He coos, "I am not blaming you. I'm just trying to understand why you didn't come to me."

I sit back down in the chair as tears begin to slip down my cheeks.

"I didn't think you cared," I admit, "I didn't think you would believe me. You always stuck up for her."

Tears fall down my father's face as he looks at me with a face that only shows complete failure and shame. He leans over the table and splays his hands out on the table as if he is trying to find his grounding.

"I need you to tell me everything she has done to you. I need to know how serious this all is."

I shake my head at him as tears begin to flow from my eyes, "I can't...I can't relive that."

My father stands and rushes to my side.

"Sweetheart," He coos taking my hand in his as he kneels on the ground, "I know this is going to be hard for you. To have to relive all the pain she has put you through this past year, but it's better for you to tell me than to have the police questioning you."

I shake my head, "Dad," I whisper, "This hasn't been happening for just a year."

My father's eyes widen in horror.

"I've been...abused...since I was six."

May father gasps at my admission.

"She tried to kill me when I was eight, but I got away and that's when I began to fight back."

My father sits up taller and pulls my head into his chest as he wraps his arms around me.

"She burned me with cigarette butts until that night," I choke back a sob, "She choked me until I passed out just a few months ago."

"Shh," my father says rubbing at my back, "You don't have to go on, Sweetheart. That's enough."

"I didn't understand why….you weren't coming to save me," I choke out. "Why… you never stopped her," I say between sobs.

"I promise you, Rizz. I will get her the help she needs. Your mother will never be able to touch you again."

I grab onto the front of my father's disheveled button down shirt and allow myself to cry in the arms of the one person I had always wanted to be there for me. I allow him to hold me—to be my father.

"I'm so sorry, Baby girl."

Elaine, the visitation secretary gives me a moment after my father leaves to pull myself together before she sends in Charlene. I wipe at my eyes with the Kleenex that Elaine gave me. A few moments later she sticks her head in and asks if I am ready to see my friend.

I give her a small smile and nod my head.

Elaine disappears back into the hallway and Charlene appears at the doorway. She looks the same as she has every day I have ever known her. She was never one to walk out of the house without makeup on her face.

She gives me a sad smile as she approaches the table. She stops, but doesn't sit down. Instead she walks to my side and embraces me in a hug.

Surprised, I don't hug her back right away.

"I know you don't like affection too much, but I figured after everything you've been through you needed a hug," Char says as she pulls away from me.

"Thanks," I say as she takes a seat opposite me.

"I'm guessing your dad told you about Hope."

"Yeah," I say quietly.

"It's all over the news you know."

My eyes snap to her.

"Everyone knows that it was your mom who did it."

"How?"

"I guess when your father came home he left the door open and well let's face it after your scene the neighbors have been watching your house pretty intently. I guess a neighbor heard Hope scream and came running in to find your mom…." Char trails off. "Then they saw your father rushing to Hope. He told the neighbor to call the police. I don't think anyone saw that coming."

"Family of the year," I mutter wiping at my nose.

"Nathalie's pretty pissed at you."

"What did I do?"

"Come on, Rizz. We both know that Nat worshipped the ground you walked on. She looked up to you for everything, and then one day she finds out everything was just some façade. You're the one person she thought would never deceive her. How would you have taken it all?"

"Yeah, well…" I trail off.

"I should be pissed off too, but our friendship has always been different." Char says waving her hand aimlessly in the air. "The timing sucks though. She could really use your strength right now."

"Why?"

"Don't you watch the news?" Char asks.

I raise a brow at her, "I've never watched the news in my life. It's always politics. I hate that shit."

Char rolls her eyes, "It's not all politics. Anyhow, you remember Thom right?"

"Obviously, Char. He's Lance's best friend."

"Yeah, well said best friend committed suicide."

I jump up in my seat, "What? Is Nat okay? Is…" I trail off.

"They are both okay…I think. Lance seems to be handling it like anyone would handle finding their best friend hanging from a ceiling fan."

"He found him?" I spit out.

Char tucks a strand of hair behind her ear, "Yeah. I feel sorry for the guy. I mean losing his mom was one thing, and now his best friend. I don't know how he is able to keep it all together."

"Is he really keeping it together?" I ask.

"As far as Nat has told me, yes."

"How would Nat know?"

"I guess she has been hanging out with him. Don't go getting all cave lady on me either. They are just being each other's rock. For some reason Nat and him are able to talk on some level I don't even understand, but it's helping them both cope."

A slight pain stabs at me as I wish I were the one he could talk to like that, but I can't be. I'm no good for him. He deserves better than someone who can't face her own fears.

"I'm glad," I swallow.

"I talked to the secretary lady, what's her name? Elaine? Yeah, that's it. Anyhow, I talked to her and I guess they are going to spring you from this place for the funeral, but they have to put one of those tracker things on your ankle as if you're some criminal," Char rambles.

"I technically am."

"Oh, please," she says waving her hand dismissively in the air.

I chuckle at her.

"What?"

"Thanks for just being you. It's pretty refreshing."

"Well someone has to keep you sane while you are in here with all these lunatic drug addicts."

I let out a small laugh and settle back into my chair.

Char sits up and suddenly grows serious, "I have to ask though. Why didn't you tell us about your mom?"

My eyes go wide.

"The news doesn't say anything about you, but I'm not stupid. I can put two and two together," Char explains.

I take a deep breath and meet Char's stare, "I didn't want you guys to think I was weak—like I couldn't take care of myself...I didn't want your sympathy."

Char shakes her head at me and scoffs, "We're your friends, Rizz. If you can't trust us who can you trust? Our job isn't to pity you. It's to make you feel better."

"I never really knew how to have friends," I admit, "I was always too busy trying to hide what my life was really like. I guess...I guess I was ashamed."

"We all have something we are ashamed of, Rizz. But we also all have people in our lives to share those secrets with in order to find some kind of solace in life." She leans back in her chair, "Jeez, and here I thought you were the smart one. Damn were you stupid."

I crack a smile, "Next time, I'll try not to be."

"Let's just hope there won't be a next time in this sort of situation."

"There won't be," I assure her.

"Good. Now can we please talk about your nail beds? What the hell are you doing?" she asks grabbing my hand and pulling it across the table. "Good thing I always carry my emergency kit."

Charlene takes her kit from her bag and begins working on my nails as she tells me about the latest celebrity news. She begins to put a coating of nail polish on when she tells me which one of my dresses she will bring for me for the funeral on

Monday. I nod and actually laugh when she makes a joke and I begin to wonder why I ever kept her and Nat at arm's length when they could bring real joy to my life.

CHAPTER FOURTY-TWO: LANCE

I stare at the suit hanging on the back of my bedroom door as flashes of me finding Thom filter through my mind. Regret fills me as I hold the crinkled note in my hand. How can four simple words cause so much pain? I look down at the paper and read the only thing Thom left behind. *It's all my fault*.

A knock comes at the door and I ball my hand back up in order to hide the note.

Pop appears around the door, "Are you almost ready, Son?" he asks in a gentle voice.

I nod my head, unable to take my eyes from my balled up fist.

"Okay," Pop says, "We'll wait for you downstairs."

I knew he was talking about him and Nathalie. She has been coming around lately to talk about everything. She's the only one I told about the note that I found later that night after the paramedics came.

Nathalie has been the only person I could talk to about any of this, because she knew what I was feeling. She knew the regret I was holding and the guilt, but she encouraged me to be strong. She would remind me that it wasn't my burden to bare. I wasn't the one to blame. Thom did this because he couldn't deal with it all. His only way out was to just end it all.

It's been a rough few weeks, but I am finally able to not feel guilty, but the regret eats at me at times. If only I would have stopped being so guilty and just talked to him, then maybe he wouldn't have left us too soon.

I pull the suit from the hook on the bedroom door and begin to slip it on. I knew what I had to do today. I had to admit everything to myself and to Thom. I had to let go.

I pull on my suit coat and slide the crinkled note into my pocket as I walk to my desk. Pulling out the top drawer I take a folded piece of paper from it and slide it in next to Thom's note.

The reverend speaks of Thom as if he knew him all his life—spouting crap that Thom was a joyful child and loved to spend his time with his friends. I bite my tongue and let him go on. The last thing

Thom's mom needs is a scene at her son's funeral. When the time comes the reverend asks for me to say a few words.

I stand at the podium that stands behind Thom's casket.

I look out at the crowd to see Thom's father escorted by two police officers standing near the back. His mother stands next to his casket, silently crying into a hanky. Pop and Nathalie stand next to her. Nathalie's hand intertwined with Mrs. Downey's free hand. In the middle of the crowd I spot Charlene politely waiting. My eyes fall to the tear-stained face next to her and our eyes lock—Rizz.

Clearing my throat I look down at the small paper in front of me.

"Thom was my best friend. He was the type of friend any orphan would dream of ever finding. Thom had a lot of redeeming qualities one being that he was loyal to the very end. He never turned his back on you when you needed him—even when he couldn't be angrier with you; he always looked out for your best interest."

I look back up at Rizz as the tears continue to stream down her face.

"Thom was a great friend, but he struggled with himself too. A year ago Thom and I were involved in an accident, and even though it was only an accident Thom took it harder than anyone else involved. Thom felt deeply. Growing up I always thought it was one of his best gifts, but now I realize that the one thing that made him a great human being is the one thing that tore him apart."

I look down at the piece of paper that holds nothing but one small line. Tears begin to prick my eyes,

"Not a day will go by that I won't wish he hadn't taken his own life. Not a day will go by that I won't remember the friend he always was and will continue to be in my heart. Thom was a great individual who couldn't win the battle that was raging inside of him, and if there was one thing I would want him to know today, it's that I don't blame him for what he felt he needed to do in order to be at peace."

I look down at the casket as I let the words printed on the paper fall from my lips.

"I forgive you."

I let the words sink in as I step down from the podium and let the ceremony continue.

For everyone those few words only mean one thing, but for me and for Thom they mean so much more.

They are the only words that Thom ever needed to hear in order to move on, and now he can.

The casket slowly begins to be lowered into the ground as people walk by to pay their respects. Once he is completely lowered I walk by and pull his crinkled note from my pocket, folding it in with my own note. Holding the pieces of paper above the grave I let go and let them float down onto his casket. I screw my eyes shut as I silently forgive him once more.

Feeling someone's gaze on me I turn and find Rizz standing under a tree a few grave heads over.

I place a hand in my pocket as I walk over to where she is standing.

"Hey," she says when I reach her.

"Hi," I muster up.

"I'm sorry, Lance."

I nod in acceptance.

"I'm sorry too."

Rizz lets out a breath, "You shouldn't be."

I nod in understanding.

Rizz sticks her hand out and pokes at the tree.

I look to the ground as I place my free hand in my pocket.

"Nice jewelry," I observe."

"Yeah, Char wanted to spruce it up a bit, but they wouldn't let her," Rizz says as she puts her anklet on display.

"That sounds like her."

Rizz laughs and something warm stirs inside me.

"How've you been?" I ask, kicking at the grass.

"Better," she says, nodding her head as if agreeing with herself.

"Rizz," Char calls out, "We have to go. I don't want them locking me up in that place too for not getting you back at your curfew."

Rizz shakes her head and laughs, "They aren't going to put you in there, Char."

"Hey, you never know. By this time tomorrow you could be looking at your new roomie."

Rizz rolls her eyes as she smiles at Char.

"'Better' looks good on you," I comment.

Rizz meets my eyes and blushes, "Yeah, I think it suits me."

I smile at her and she pulls away from the tree.

Glancing at the grass and then back to me she says, "Look I wanted to talk to you."

"Yeah," I say, "I wanted to talk to you to."

"I know now that Kayla set you up and honestly I probably knew it then too. I just got scared I guess."

I open my mouth to say something, but Rizz cuts me off.

"Let me finish," she says, "I got scared and I realize that you don't deserve someone who is willing to just walk away when things get scary or hard. Especially someone who lies and keeps secrets and pretends to be someone she's not."

"Rizz—"

Rizz places her finger to my lips.

"I need to figure out who I am, Lance. I can't do that right now if you are in the picture."

Rizz brings her hand back to her side and steps beside me so we are shoulder to shoulder.

"You deserve someone who knows who they are, Lance."

Rizz places her hand on my cheek and presses a light kiss on the other.

"You are better off without me," she says and walks off to where Charlene is waiting for her.

I turn and watch her climb into the passenger seat of Charlene's car. Charlene says something to her and Rizz nods her head. After giving Rizz a sympathetic look she puts the car in gear and takes off. I watch as the girl I love drives away from me...again.

Once everyone has left the grave site I walk back to the parking lot with Nathalie and Pop. I take one last look at Thom's grave. Standing in front of his grave is his father accompanied by two officers.

I look back at Pop and Nathalie and raise my finger indicating to give me a moment.

Pop nods his head and Nathalie gives me a small smile both knowing that there is one last thing I must do.

I walk across the grave yard and stop on the opposite side of the grave from Thom's father.

He looks up at me with tear filled eyes, "Lance."

"Mr. Downey," I nod in greeting, "I'm sorry for your loss."

Mr. Downey sniffles and takes a deep breath, "He was a good kid."

"I know, Sir."

Mr. Downey gives a short laugh, "After everything that has happened and you still show me respect."

"What happened was an accident, Sir."

"I just wish Thom would have seen it that way."

I look down at the uncovered grave and see the notes drift down the casket as a small gust of wind blows by.

"You know, he wanted me to blame him—to hate you," I give a short laugh, "I think he just wanted to get me to feel something. To admit I was hurting too."

I look up at Mr. Downey who is staring at me.

"At first I was just pissed off. I wanted to hate you, to blame you. But now? Now, I just want to pity you, because even though I lost my mother and later my best friend you lost everything you ever lived for and that just makes me feel sad for you."

Mr. Downey stays silent.

I turn and take a few steps back toward where Nathalie and Pop are waiting for me. I stop, turning halfway.

"Thom doesn't just need my forgiveness, Sir. He needs yours too."

EPILOUGE: TWO MONTHS LATER

CHAPTER FOURTY-THREE: RIZZ

The multi-colored leaves fall gracefully from the trees as I walk the short pathway to the front door. I stare blankly at the welcome home mat, unsure of how to call this house home. The front door stands open, beckoning me to come in.

This is all part of the process.

I take a deep breath as a warm breeze brushes past me blowing up the loose strands of my hair. A firm hand is placed on the small of my back and I look up at my father's calm face. He nods encouraging me forward. Taking a step over the threshold, I brace myself for the past to come rushing over me; the pain, the hate, but all I feel is emptiness.

I walk into the living room and look at the hanging pictures in awe. Smiling faces of family members I hadn't seen in ages stare back at me. Pictures of Hope and me sit atop the end tables and for the first time I feel welcomed in my own home.

Chip places my bags on the floor next to me as I examine the unfamiliar walls, "I like what you've done with the place."

"The doctors suggested it…something about starting over; eliminating the old environment."

Walking over to the fire place, I look at the family portrait hanging above the mantel.

"Has she made any progress?" I ask, staring at my mother's indifferent face.

"The Doctor says she is getting there."

***

I sit in the leather chair opposite my mother and stare at her doctor in front of us. He scribbles into his notepad as I cross my legs away from my mother. She is staring out the window when the doctor asks her,

"What made you want to abuse your daughter?"

My mother turns and looks at her doctor, "It made me feel powerful."

"Powerful?" he asks.

"Yes," my mother turns to look at me, "See, you're just like me. You thrive for power too. One day, you'll be just like me. It's in our blood."

I look at my mother in disgust, "I'll never be like you."

***

Chip stands beside me and looks at the portrait in silence with me.

"Why are you staying?" I ask, after a moment.

"She's ill, she needs help."

"After everything, you're just going to stand by her?"

"You're mother wasn't always this person, Rizz."

"She hurt me, Dad, and you did nothing," I reply, tears escaping my eyes.

Chip turns, bringing me into his arms, "If I would have known what was happening, I would have gotten her help sooner."

"You act as if she can be saved. As if she could ever change."

"Oh, but she can. Your mother was gentle and caring once. Something in her snapped and she changed for the worse. But, sometimes, people can change for the better."

"People don't change."

Chip holds me tighter, "I beg to differ."

"Why?"

Pulling away from me, Chip looks into my tear stained face, "Because, I've seen a great amount of change in you these last few months. You began to change the minute you allowed yourself to be loved by that boy."

"So, love saves us all, huh?"

"No, but it does help."

"You think she'll come back to you, don't you?" I ask in disbelief.

"I think in time, your mother will get better and she will come to her senses. When she does, she'll be filled with regret and pain, and she will need you to forgive her."

"How do you forgive someone who abused you all your life?"

"She asked me that same question not that long ago."

I look at my father in confusion, before the pieces slowly begin to mend together. My mother and I are sitting back in the therapist's office.

***

The therapist asks, "How did inflicting pain on your daughter make you feel?"

My mother looks him straight in the eye and says, "It made me feel like I was in control, like I couldn't be hurt anymore. I felt powerful."

I look at my mother in disgusted shock. Her eyes meet mine and for a split moment they grow soft as if pleading for me to forgive the words that had fallen from her lips, but as I open my mouth to speak, her eyes grow cold again and she looks away.

***

Suddenly it all made sense to me.

It runs in our blood.

Like I couldn't be hurt anymore.

"She was abused?" I ask, shocked.

Chip nods his head, "Something must have snapped for her. I just—I wish I would have noticed sooner."

He places my cheek in his hand, "You are my baby girl, and I can never be sorrier for what you must have endured."

Tears flow down my cheeks as my father walks closer to me. He wraps me up in his arms and I press my face against his chest saying nothing.

It all made sense now. Why she would hit us. She began when we lost Luke because she felt her life falling apart—like she was losing control. That didn't make everything in the past okay though. It didn't make it okay that my father didn't believe me whenever I told him things were worse. It didn't make it okay that she burned my skin with cigarette butts, choked me until I passed out or even tried to kill me. It didn't make anything better. All it did was give me a reason—a truth. But I was willing to move on—to look to a better future. I'll never have the perfect relationship with my mother or with my father, but it was a start that we were all getting the help that we all needed.

I pull into the café's parking lot and put the car into park. Upon entering the shop there is a loud commotion as Grace comes barreling towards me with opened arms.

"There is my girl."

I welcome Grace into my arms and take in her cookie smell that always made me feel at ease.

"Oh, Cookie, I saw everything on the news. I am just so glad to see you in one piece," she says inspecting me at arm's length. When she is satisfied that I am in fact in one piece she pulls me in for another hug, "How is that sister of yours?"

She pulls away and hooks her arm around my shoulders as she leads me back to the counter.

"It's just so awful what happened."

"She's okay. Healing pretty quickly too," I smile at her.

"And that horrible woman?" she asks bitterly.

"In rehab," I reply, "She'll be there for about two years."

"Oh well, it's good she is getting some help I suppose."

"When did you know?" I ask, cutting off her next question.

Grace eyes me warily.

"It's okay," I say, "I had a feeling before that you knew."

"Cookie, I knew the minute I found you hiding out in my café."

"Why didn't you say anything?" I ask, leaning up against the counter.

"Jackson," Grace calls to one of the new baristas, "Get my Cookie a Mocha iced cap," she says pointing to me.

I give the young barista a smile and he nods in acknowledgment.

Turning her attention back to me she says, "If I would have confronted you, you would have just hid into yourself or worse and run off somewhere else where I wouldn't be able to keep an eye on you."

"I'm sorry I never told you," I say as I take the iced cap from Jackson. "Thanks," I tell him.

"It's just who you were, Cookie."

"I'm glad it was you who found me."

"Me too," she smiles as she pats my hand.

"I better get going," I say. I hold the iced cap up, "Thank you, Grace." I pause and then add, "For everything."

"Anything for my Cookie," she smiles.

I turn on my heels and head for the door when a recognizable red head bursts through the doors.

She stops as her eyes meet mine.

I give her a small smile as I close the gap between her.

She says nothing—just looks at me in shocked surprise.

Unsure of what to say I do the one thing I would have never expected myself to do two months before today.

I open my arms and pull Nathalie into a full on hug as I whisper to her, "I'm so sorry."

A moment passes before she brings her hands up and rests them on my back and begins to hug me in return.

When we pull apart she asks, "When did you get back?"

"Just today."

"I'm sorry I didn't visit you."

I shake my head in protest, "You had your reasons."

"Char would tell me how you were doing. I'm glad you're better."

"Likewise," I say.

"She also told me why…you lied."

I bring my hand with the iced cap to my head and scratch my temple with my finger.

"You don't have to say anything," Nat says sensing my discomfort, "I understand now."

"I never meant to hurt you," I finally say.

"I know," She says. Pointing to the counter she adds, "I was just going to get some coffee. Did you want to join?"

"I would, but I can't. I have to take my car into the shop. It's making some weird noise not being used for a while can mess with it I guess…I don't know. Cars have never been my specialty. I just had to stop and say 'hi' to Grace. You were actually my next stop, but here you are. And now I'm rambling. I guess Char has worn off on me."

Nathalie laughs, "I'm glad to see you healthy, Rizz."

"Yeah, me too."

"And it's okay. Are you going to Ray's Garage?" she asks.

"Yeah, that's the one my dad suggested."

Nathalie nods her head eagerly, "Oh, yeah. Ray's is definitely the best place to get your car fixed."

Nat steps around me, "We'll catch up later. After all, I have your number."

I let out a laugh, "Yeah. Okay. I'll see you later then."

Nat waves and then makes her way to the counter as I head out the front doors to my car and head to Ray's Garage.

CHAPTER FOURTY-FOUR: LANCE

Grease and oil cover my fingers and hands as I tighten down the head gaskets on the engine of the Mercedes. I wipe my hands on my "Ray's Garage" work shirt as I walk over to where Seth is working on the Jaguar.

Things haven't been going as planned for me lately. I should have been on a plane and half way across the states by now, but I couldn't get myself to leave just yet. I knew why too. I couldn't leave knowing Rizz was coming home. I had to try at least once more. I needed to know that the feelings I have for her aren't just one sided.

Nathalie had been keeping me updated about her progress through stories that Charlene told her. It was beginning to sound like Rizz was finally coming into her own, and I couldn't have been any happier for her. I just wish she would have let me be a part of that process.

Seth slides out from under the Jaguar and wipes his nose on the back of his hand.

"Hand me that wrench, will ya?"

I hand the wrench sitting on the work bench to Seth who takes it and slides back under the Jag.

Seth has been working at Ray's since he was nineteen. He moved to Lake Forest for "better job opportunities" or something along those lines. I suspect he was just running away from something. We all tend to want to run away at some point of our lives and some people actually do.

I was able to face everything that happened with Thom. Letting go of the accident helped me deal with his death. There isn't a day where I don't expect him to walk through those doors of Ray's Garage in order to chew my ass out, or to come barging into my house raving about some party. Life has changed without him. I lost my best friend, my right hand man, my partner in crime.

But I moved on, because that's what he would have wanted. He would have wanted me to have peace of mind and to continue to live my life.

"Lance," Ray shouts as he walks through the Garage.

I push off of the Jag and walk toward him.

"What's up, Ray?"

"Quit standing around and get to work. I have a customer out front who says her brakes are making some strange noise."

"Alright," I reply nodding as I take off toward the front of the store.

I love getting cases like these. I find it amusing to hear customers make all these noises that they think their car is making. The truth is, I don't need them to explain the sound to me. Half the time it's usually that the car has something loose or the brake pads need to be changed.

I round the corner of the garage to the front to find the customer standing in front of her Impala.

Her brown hair falls past her shoulders. A few strands blow loose in the light breeze. Her blue eyes glisten in the sun's rays. I stop about five paces in front of her.

Am I dreaming?

"I need my car checked," she stumbles over her words.

This is definitely not a dream.

"It's making these weird noises," she continues when I say nothing.

She reaches up and scratches at her temple with her index finger as she looks anywhere but at me.

"I think it's the brakes," she adds.

I don't say anything. I just continue to stare at her in amazement. I knew she was supposed to get out today, but I never imagined her coming to me. Of course she had no idea I would be here.

Finally she looks straight at me and says, "I thought you would be traveling all over God's creation by now?"

"A change of plans," I finally say.

Rizz nods her head, "It's good to see you." She points my way, "You look good."

"So do you," I reply politely.

Rizz begins to play with her keys in her hand and looks at the car and then back to me.

"Are you going to come look at my car or just stand there?" she asks.

I crack a smile and begin to walk toward her.

"Right, sorry."

When I reach her she hands her keys to me. I take them and walk to the driver's side and slide in leaving the door open.

Rizz walks over to the driver's side and leans her forearms against the open door.

"Listen," she says, "I've had a lot of time to think while I was in that place."

"Rehab does that to you I guess," I reply turning the key in the ignition.

"Yeah. Well, I realized a lot while I was there. Mostly that I was the one making a million and one mistakes."

I look up at her urging her to go on.

"I spent my life looking for someone to save me, but the only person who could really save me was me."

Rizz stands up straighter, putting her hands in her back pockets.

"My life hasn't really been that easy…and now it seems like the whole world knows it, but I think it could be better."

Rizz's gaze meets mine, "I'm glad you haven't left yet, because I want you to know something before you head off."

I nod encouraging her to continue.

"Every day I was in there I thought about you. Well, about us really. I thought about how things should have been. I didn't do all this 'recovering' for you, I did it for me. I did it for me because I realized that I'm deserving of being loved and to love."

Rizz stops and walks around the open door so she is standing in front of me.

"I love you, Lance. I loved you two months ago and I love you now."

I stare at Rizz and say nothing as I get to my feet.

"I just thought you should know," Rizz says her gaze falling to the gravel below us.

I slip my finger under her chin and bring her gaze back to meet mine.

"What do you plan on doing now?" I ask softly, "With your future?"

Rizz takes a deep breath as she crosses her arms over her chest, "I was thinking or reapplying to Princeton for next year."

"And in the mean time?"

"I guess I will work, save up some money."

"Hmm."

"What is it?" she asks.

"How do you feel about spending the autumn in Florence, the winter in Morocco, the spring in Paris and the summer in Germany?"

Rizz's eyes gleam up at me as a smile spreads across her face, "What happened to staying in the States?"

I shrug my shoulder, "Change of plans."

She lets out a giggle as she jumps up and wraps her legs around my waist. I hold her up placing my hands on her bottom.

"I love you too," I say before pressing my lips to hers.

I hear a car horn go off from the garage—no doubt Seth and the guys. I ignore them as I pull Rizz closer to me and deepen the kiss.

Warmth flows through every vein in my body as I devour her in the open.

I let the moment fill the both of us as we make up for lost time knowing it's the beginning of a new chapter of our lives together.

This moment symbolizes a milestone of the lives we broke away from and the memories of the old us. The old screwed up individuals we were.

I guess, when you least expect it…a disaster doesn't stay a disaster forever.

Letter from the author

I first started working on Disaster during my Freshman year of High School. Throughout my High School career I completed a first draft of my story and I was overly excited to start seeking out publishers and get my story on the shelves. However, my eagerness to publish my book quickly diminished once I started my college career. I had put my hopes of becoming an author on the back burner as I dabbled in the joys of being a college student for the first year.

Finally, I went back to my book and started to reread it. The more I read the more I became dissatisfied with the words on the page. I knew I had a great story, but wasn't writing to its full potential.

This is when I decided to take up a Creative Writing Minor and during the second half of my Sophomore year at Canisius College I began to pick apart my book and rewrite each chapter adding in an additional third person's point of view—Thom.

Now, almost eight years later I have the finished piece that I am thrilled about. I wanted to capture the severity of family life and the effects it can have on young adults by encapsulating the lives of modern day teenagers. I feel that too much is being unsaid in the world of teens—we are all know it is happening but it is never truly addressed—so I wanted to create a story to let those who suffer from similar situations know that they aren't the only ones and that there is a light at the end of the tunnel for them.

All I hope is that you, my readers, get the same satisfaction from reading the story of these three teenagers as I did writing it.

Acknowledgments

Thank you to everyone who supported me and my writing. I would like to personally thank the following people:

My parents for helping me succeed through the writer's block and for helping me figure out what I was trying to put down on paper. I would like to especially thank my mom who spent endless hours rereading several copies of my novel and editing it both as a reader and as the punctuation police.

My best friend Sara for being as enthused about my story as I was and for reading it time and time again in order to give great feedback and editing help.

My sister, Rebecca, and my brother, Chris for saying the most random things that would spark an idea I could run with and create a whole new scene that would bring the story together.

My grandmother Cecile Fuerschbach for being as enthused about my writing as I have been and who has always been proud of everything I had put my mind and soul into.

My grandmother Helen Nickles for always being enthused as well about my writing and always being supportive telling me that I will thrive in anything I put my mind to.

Mike Miller for coaching me through the self-publishing process.

All of my friends and family who took the time to read the rough cuts and gave me their feedback in order to make the story you see today.

About The Author

Rachel Fuerschbach grew up in the small town of Lockport where at the age of 12 she began to aspire to become an author. As a young child Rachel always had a voice that tended to be muffled with her shy personality. As she grew older that voice became bolder as did her personality. Today, Rachel hopes to bring light to issues regarding teenagers through her story telling. Her goal in the future is to help teens who are struggling in their home, school and personal lives and help them succeed in the ever changing world.